W9-BII-251

Praise for the Novels of Katharine Davis

A Slender Thread

"In *A Slender Thread*, Katharine Davis illuminates the threads that tie us to family and the ones we loved. She reminds us of both their fragility and their strength. A beautiful book."

—Ann Hood, author of *The Red Thread* and *The Knitting Circle*

"Luminous and deeply affecting. . . . In this novel of the complex bonds of sisters and the pernicious effects of a rare illness, Katharine Davis memorably captures the language of family. I thoroughly enjoyed this novel, and it was a pleasaure to watch it take shape."

—Susan Coll, author of *Beach Week* and *Acceptance*

"With a sure, light touch and a shrewd eye for telling details, Katharine Davis expertly weaves a resonant story about the bonds of family, the tug of geography, and the regenerative power of art. *A Slender Thread* is an emotionally rich and penetrating novel."

—Christina Baker Kline, author of *Bird in Hand* and *The Way Life Should Be*

continued . . .

Written by today's freshest new talents and selected by New American Library, NAL Accent novels touch on subjects close to a woman's heart, from friendship to family to finding our place in the world. The Conversation Guides included in each book are intended to enrich the individual reading experience, as well as encourage us to explore these topics together—because books, and life, are meant for sharing.

Visit us online at www.penguin.com.

"The multiple viewpoints of Katharine Davis's *A Slender Thread* weave in and out of chapters like threads in a tapestry, illustrating the intricate, complicated ties that bind us as family. While this compelling story shows just how fragile—and therefore precious—are our connections to each other, Davis also shows that even the slenderest of threads can have the surprising strength and resilience to hold it (and us) together."

—Katrina Kittle, author of *The Blessings of the Animals*

"With a delicate and loving touch, Katharine Davis explores a deep and often complex relationship—the one between two sisters. Like the tapestry that becomes central to the story itself, *A Slender Thread* is a beautiful and utterly original creation. . . . Emotionally honest, meticulously observed, but also propulsively dramatic and readable, this is a novel that will resonate with women of all ages—and with everyone who loves a good story, well told. If you have sisters, you'll want to share *A Slender Thread* with them. If you don't, it will serve as solace—and a powerful testament—to what you are missing."

—Liza Gyllenhall, author of *Local Knowledge*

East Hope

"Katharine Davis has written an utterly irresistible novel, suffused with the special light and clarity of Maine. A book about second chances and real love, with characters as complicated as we really are. I couldn't put it down." —Lee Smith, *New York Times* bestselling author of *On Agate Hill*

"Katharine Davis has created an elegant and compelling tale about loss, love, and, of course, hope. Her characters are rich, her story is gripping, and her prose beautiful and effortless."

—Joanne Rendell, author of *Crossing Washington Square*

"*East Hope* is a charming love story, delightfully old-fashioned with a very modern twist. Katharine Davis captures Maine not just as a setting but as the character it is." —Lily King, author of *The English Teacher*

"Katharine Davis's captivating novel of loss and recovery follows a forty-four-year-old woman from a long-settled life into one that is anything but certain. The author's clean prose suits the spare setting in which most of this struggle takes place—a small seaside village in Maine. Her keen sensitivity to the people and countryside in that remote place vividly evokes its power to reshape her character's life, slowly but radically, much as the sea reshapes the shoreline."

—Kate Maloy, author of *Every Last Cuckoo*

"Davis's lyrical prose brings authenticity to the journey of two lonely souls trying to reinvent themselves in middle age."   —*Booklist*

Capturing Paris

"The layered experience and sensibilities of Americans in Paris are captured marvelously in this haunting and evocative novel by Katharine Davis. Reminiscent of William Maxwell's *The Château*, *Capturing Paris* is an impressive debut."   —Katharine Weber, author of *True Confections*

"In this graceful and atmospheric first novel, Katharine Davis explores a question that fascinates us all: What if I had chosen differently, when I still had my choices to make? Through Annie's reinvention of herself in a time of flux, we see anew the consequences of deciding to be who we are, and the consequences of questioning all that we have been."

—Carolyn Parkhurst, author of *Lost and Found*

"In *Capturing Paris*, we meet Annie Reed, poet and wife, navigating through a year of upheaval. Through it all, her adopted city of Paris glows, with its abundance of charm, quirks, and moods, all beautifully captured in Katharine Davis's sensitive observations."

—Leslie Pietrzyk, author of *A Year and a Day*

"Dreamy and sentimental, readers with a soft spot for the city of lights will want to give this a look."   —*Publishers Weekly*

OTHER BOOKS BY KATHARINE DAVIS

East Hope
Capturing Paris

A Slender Thread

KATHARINE DAVIS

NAL Accent

Published by New American Library, a division of Penguin Group (USA) Inc., 375 Hudson Street, New York, New York 10014, USA • Penguin Group (Canada), 90 Eglinton Avenue East, Suite 700, Toronto, Ontario M4P 2Y3, Canada (a division of Pearson Penguin Canada Inc.) • Penguin Books Ltd., 80 Strand, London WC2R 0RL, England • Penguin Ireland, 25 St. Stephen's Green, Dublin 2, Ireland (a division of Penguin Books Ltd.) • Penguin Group (Australia), 250 Camberwell Road, Camberwell, Victoria 3124, Australia (a division of Pearson Australia Group Pty. Ltd.) • Penguin Books India Pvt. Ltd., 11 Community Centre, Panchsheel Park, New Delhi - 110 017, India • Penguin Group (NZ), 67 Apollo Drive, Rosedale, North Shore 0632, New Zealand (a division of Pearson New Zealand Ltd.) • Penguin Books (South Africa) (Pty.) Ltd., 24 Sturdee Avenue, Rosebank, Johannesburg 2196, South Africa

Penguin Books Ltd., Registered Offices:
80 Strand, London WC2R 0RL, England

First published by NAL Accent, an imprint of New American Library,
a division of Penguin Group (USA) Inc.

First Printing, August 2010
10 9 8 7 6 5 4 3 2 1

REGISTERED TRADEMARK—MARCA REGISTRADA

LIBRARY OF CONGRESS CATALOGING-IN-PUBLICATION DATA:

Davis, Katharine.
A slender thread/Katharine Davis.
p.   cm.
ISBN 978-0-451-23010-2
1. Sisters—Fiction. 2. Aphasic persons—Fiction. 3. Life change events—Fiction. I. Title.
PS3604.A967S58 2010
813'.6—dc22   2010009830

Set in Garamond Three
Designed by Elke Sigal

Printed in the United States of America

For Anna, who lost her voice, and others like her

Acknowledgments

I would like to thank my writing group—Susan Coll, Ann McLaughlin, Carolyn Parkhurst, Leslie Pietrzyk, and Amy Stolls—for their careful reading and suggestions. Also, many thanks to my sister, Carroll Charlesworth, for her attentive reading and comments.

Thank you to Dr. Richard Restak and Dr. Leslie Williams for answering my questions on neurological disorders and for guiding my research. Any mistakes about the illness are my own.

Stories are often born of other stories, and I would like to thank Jane Freeman for telling me a story about swimming a moon path that she heard from a lovely older friend.

Special thanks to Sarah Haskell, an artist and weaver, who generously invited me to her studio in York, Maine. Her most recent project, *Woven Voices: Messages from the Heart,* was an inspiration to me. Sarah shared her knowledge of weaving and her library, and allowed me to experience the joy of weaving a Tibetan prayer flag on a fall afternoon.

Many thanks to Katherine Fausset. This is our third book together. Thank you also to my editor, Ellen Edwards, who, after working with me on *East Hope*, believed in my next story.

I am especially grateful for the love and support of my family and friends. Most of all, thanks to Bob, husband, editor, champion—the one who makes it all possible.

Who is to blame? The Weaver?
Ah, the bewildering thread!

EMILY DICKINSON,
"A SHADY FRIEND — FOR TORRID DAYS"

A Slender Thread

"*D*on't be scared," my sister, Lacey, calls to me.

Another wave slaps me in the face. I swim harder. My legs won't stay level and drag behind me like an anchor. I turn my head, breathing in at the start of each stroke. The movement feels sloppy, out of sync. My body does not feel whole, but made of separate parts, every limb with a mind of its own.

"You're doing great, Margot." Lacey is rowing Pigtail, our flat-bottomed boat.

The numb feeling in my feet climbs to my knees. My goggles crush my nose. I'm swimming to Junior, the island 411 yards offshore from Grandmother Winkler's camp.

"This way." Lacey's voice from the rowboat carries across the chop. Bow Lake was calm when we started. I swim past the float raft. Alex, the boy next door, stands there, rocking aloft on the lake. He's never far from Lacey.

I'm nine. This is my first solo swim to Junior. Lacey did it five years ago when she was eight. I kick harder. I choke on a mouthful of the mossy-tasting lake. Junior seems farther away than ever. After another burst of kicks, I stop.

"That's okay," Lacey calls out. "Tread water while you catch your breath."

I switch to breaststroke. Lacey has breasts this summer. Sometimes I forget that this grown-up girl is my sister. I cup my hands, pull harder. My arms ache less, but my progress is slower. I keep going. Lacey told me there's nothing to be afraid of. There are two life vests in the boat.

My neck strains forward like a turtle's. I lift my face out of the water. The goggles have fogged. Another wave smacks into my open mouth. I'm choking now, working to catch my breath.

"Turn on your back." Lacey's voice sounds far away.

I do as she says. I won't let her down. Arching my neck, face to the sky, I float. Lacey passed junior lifesaving last summer and has a badge to prove it.

"Do the elementary backstroke," she commands. "That's it. Slow and easy."

I'm blinded by the brightness. My fog-filled goggles blur the clouds. I'm still floating.

"Keep moving." Lacey's voice is clearer now above the lapping of the waves.

"Which way?" Water sloshes over my head. I drink some in. I choke.

"Over here. Just follow my voice."

Slowly, slowly, I relax and let the water support me. I move my arms and legs together, like when we make snow angels in winter.

"You're doing great."

I find my rhythm. The goggles no longer hurt. I don't care about the lake grass clinging to my leg. Lacey's voice guides me.

All of a sudden it's quiet. I turn over, about to thrash. There, twenty feet ahead of me, Lacey is dragging Pigtail onto the beach. My feet touch bottom. The soft grit of sand oozes between my toes. The sun warms my back. I wade to shore.

"I knew you could do it." Lacey reaches out and offers me her pinkie finger. We hook our little fingers together in our secret handshake. "You can do anything, Margot Winkler," she says.

1

Weave: Make cloth by interlacing threads on a loom.

*M*argot heard the news that changed everything just after the bus from the airport reached Portsmouth. It was the Tuesday before Thanksgiving. She scanned the parking lot as the driver slowed and brought the bus to a halt. She saw Lacey and waved from the bus window. Her sister didn't respond; her attention seemed fixed on some distant place, her mind apparently elsewhere. Margot descended the steps and pulled her bag toward the silver Volvo wagon. She called out to Lacey, who smiled abruptly, almost as if she had forgotten why she was there, and then hurriedly came forward to pull Margot into her arms. Margot immediately felt the tension of her New York City life slip away.

"So great to see you," Margot said, barely containing the silly childhood excitement she always experienced when reunited with her sister. Lacey was her only real family.

"You, too." Lacey hugged Margot firmly and then pulled back, studied her briefly, and gently drew her hand across Margot's cheek, a motherly gesture, as if to make sure she was really there. "How's Oliver?" she asked.

"Complaining about his work. He needs this break." Margot shrugged, wondering if she would get the "why don't you guys get married" lecture that Lacey offered periodically. When Margot had bent to kiss him good-bye early that morning, Oliver, still asleep, had put his hand on her neck, the weight of his palm a soundless reminder that he loved her. He was leaving the next day to see his daughter in Atlanta. Margot hoped his trip would take his mind off his worries for a while.

"Let's go," Lacey said in her matter-of-fact big-sister voice, and quickly stowed Margot's suitcase in the back of the car.

They began the ride out to New Castle, a small town on an island near Portsmouth, New Hampshire, where Lacey and her family lived. It was then, in the car, as they left the C&J Bus Terminal and headed toward the city of Portsmouth, that Lacey told Margot about her symptoms, the visits to doctors, and the diagnosis that would eventually change her life. Margot would think later how odd it was that they both remained so calm. Margot didn't cry then. Lacey didn't drive off the road.

"But we all forget words now and then," Margot said, not wanting to believe any of what she was hearing.

"That's how it started. It's been a couple of years . . . like this. I'd be talking"—she paused—"and couldn't come up with a word—something stupid, like I'm going . . . to the post office. I couldn't say 'post office.' Or, Alex . . . Alex would ask me something. I'd open my mouth and nothing would come out. This fall it's gotten worse."

Margot remembered thinking that Lacey had seemed distracted the last time they spoke on the phone. She had pictured her sister stirring something on the stove, glancing at a recipe, all the while listening to Margot's explanation of her travel plans for this Thanksgiving holiday. Perhaps one of Lacey's twin daughters, Wink or Toni, had been hurrying past, mouthing something silently to her mother at the same time.

Yet Margot's sister had always been able to do many things at once, a veritable multitasker before the term was invented. She was organized, unflappable, while Margot was the scattered one—searching through her closet at the last minute for the black skirt to wear to some art opening with Oliver, only to remember that it was still at the cleaners and that the pants that also went with the silk top she wanted to wear had caught on her heel the last time she had worn them and the hem of one leg was still undone. Oliver would fidget in front of CNN looking annoyed while she rummaged in the kitchen for Scotch tape to do a temporary repair job.

"Is it possible it could be menopause?" Margot asked, her thoughts jumping erratically as she sought some explanation for Lacey's illness.

"It's not. And it's getting worse." She puckered her lips and let out a rush of breath.

Lacey stopped at a light. They'd crossed over Route 95, and were driving into Portsmouth. Margot was still foggy from getting up early to make her flight. Lacey's news was impossible to grasp, inconceivable.

"Lack of sleep, some memory loss, sure, that's"—Lacey paused—"normal when you're menopausal. Forgetfulness now and again." She stopped speaking, as if the telling of this string of ideas was exhausting. "Now it happens every day, several times a day. I thought I had Alzheimer's."

"You're too young for that," Margot said quickly, thinking of Alex's elderly mother, lost to all of them in her muffled world.

"Not necessarily. But it's not."

"What's it called again?"

"Primary Progressive Aphasia." Lacey said it like a mantra, as if she had practiced the phrase to be able to say it with ease. These were words she had to know—the words that would come to define her life. She reached into the handbag and handed Margot an index card. "It's hard for me to explain. Read this," she said. "I can give you more information later."

Margot recognized Lacey's handwriting, though her once large and elegant script looked wobbly on the small card. Perhaps Lacey

5

had still been in shock as she copied out the essential facts that the doctors had told her.

Primary Progressive Aphasia, a form of frontotemporal dementia, is caused by brain cell degeneration. "Aphasia" refers to deficits in language functions. The patient slowly loses the ability to use language—first the use of speech, and later the ability to understand, read, or write. The onset of this form of dementia occurs in younger individuals, the symptoms possibly presenting as early as forty-five years of age.

Margot had never heard of this disease. The brutal medical terms were chilling. "Should you be driving?" she asked.

"It's fine. Everything in my brain is fine. I understand. I can do everything." Lacey paused. "Only . . ." Her chin lifted as if in determination. "It's getting more and more difficult to get the words out."

For the next few minutes neither sister spoke while Lacey navigated through downtown Portsmouth and onto Pleasant Street. Margot stared out the window, stunned, barely taking in the passing scenery. Portsmouth was an old city, a Colonial settlement, the home of once-prominent ship captains. The Portsmouth harbor was still a working port. Arriving ships bearing loads of salt for the soon-to-be-snow-covered New England roads would depart heaped with loads of scrap metal, the chopped remains of the rusty vehicles that were victims of the salted highways. Red tugboats were moored along the city wharf, rugged and ready to guide the ships through the mouth of the river and pull them to the docks.

The town was filled with stately eighteenth-century mansions, charming clapboard houses, restaurants, and shops, along with a few worn-out taverns that refused to transform themselves to be like their more fashionable twenty-first-century neighbors. Eventually Lacey turned onto Route 1B, the road that would take them out to Lacey and Alex's home in New Castle.

New Castle, an island reached by bridges and causeways, was a gem of a town, a village really. Since the death of their parents many years before, Margot had been coming to Lacey's house every Thanksgiving. Lacey, her husband, Alex, and their twin daughters had included Margot in many of their family holidays, though since she'd lived with Oliver, she came less frequently. Thanksgiving was the only holiday Oliver spent with his grown daughter and Margot thought he should have some time alone with her, thus the separate trips.

Margot read the card a second time. "Lacey, this can't be true." Margot swallowed and cleared her throat. Her mouth was dry. She didn't know what to say. The irony of being inarticulate made her feel worse.

"We've spent the entire fall going down to Boston to see specialists."

"Why didn't you tell me?"

"I didn't think it was serious. Not at first anyway. We weren't even sure . . . until last week." Lacey was speaking very carefully. "Alex doesn't want to believe them."

"The doctors?"

"He wants to see more . . . more specialists. Like someone else can fix it. Like it's a business problem. And he can find"—she swallowed—"the solution."

They passed the Portsmouth Naval Prison, a huge, gray, decaying monster of a building across the Piscataqua River on their left, abandoned since the 1970s. Since then it had remained empty and silent, but for the rats and seagulls. "He thinks different . . . doctors might come to a different conclusion."

Margot sat very still, almost forgetting to breathe. "Maybe he's right."

"He's not," Lacey said sharply. Her voice pitched higher. "The top neurologists aren't going to lie to me." Her hands gripped the wheel of the car, the beautiful white fingers that loved the feel of yarn, that savored the softness of the fibers she wove into elegant designs. In the near-winter light the skin of her fingers seemed almost translucent, as if the very bones might show through.

"If it's such a rare disease," Margot said, trying to think calmly, "another doctor might have another opinion. Maybe some sort of treatment."

"As usual, I'm the only one in this . . . family to face things."

"I just think Alex may have a point."

"You're as softheaded as he is." Lacey, almost always even-tempered, was nearly shouting.

"Lacey, I only mean . . ." Margot tried to push away the growing fear inside her. Her mind clattered with questions. She felt like she was sinking underwater, being pulled down into darkness where she could no longer see or hear.

"I've seen many doctors. Not just one."

"Still . . ."

"They have . . ." Again she appeared to search for a word. "The pictures. They have pictures of my brain."

"I don't know what to think. This is unimaginable."

"Believe me, it's nothing I ever imagined."

Margot watched her, the strong sister, as she seemed to calm herself, taking slow, even, deep breaths. Lacey's eyes remained fixed on the road ahead and her lips, though pressed together, trembled.

Margot cracked her window. The sharp saltiness of the sea air assaulted her nostrils. The sky was heavy, a pewter tightness, but there was no wind and the temperature was disarmingly mild. This couldn't be happening to her sister, her lovely older sister, who had turned fifty only last summer.

Margot had come for Lacey's birthday in August. Alex had had a small dinner party for Lacey, their twin daughters, and their best friends, Kate and Hugh Martin. That night they'd served steamed lobsters, corn on the cob, and champagne. Kate had brought fresh tomatoes from her garden. It had been a perfect evening and the love of family and friends had been palpable.

Oliver had accompanied her on that trip. He was always charming to her nieces and asked them their opinions on art and music as if they were grown-ups. He enjoyed Lacey's company too, although when he and Margot were alone he complained a bit about the busy schedule she imposed on them—set times for meals, ritual walks, trips to Portsmouth. Though Oliver, an artist, and Alex, a businessman, didn't share many interests, they joked about their very different lives, making money using opposite sides of their brains.

But on that visit Oliver had been a bit impatient. He was caught up in a new painting. Margot recognized the signs. He would appear to be listening to those around him, looking in the direction of a conversation, nodding periodically in agreement, cocking his head with interest, but she knew from the way his eyes grew darker, the pupils almost shrinking in size, that he was seeing something in the far reaches of his mind, an image or an idea that he couldn't let go of. He rarely spoke about a painting in the early stages, like a protective parent not wanting to expose an infant child to germs. She knew that when he seemed to be staring into space he was actually looking at colors, shapes, and shadows. He remained polite and cooperative, but she could tell he was eager to return to New York.

The road from Portsmouth to New Castle curved along the water, with clapboard houses clustered intermittently on either side. Those on the left looked out directly at the river and the ocean beyond, vast and gray. Lacey's mouth was pulled into an angry line. Still, she was beautiful. She had that New England outdoorsy healthiness that makeup or a complicated hairdo would spoil. Today she wore corduroy trousers, a heavy sweater, and a scarf, more like a shawl, pulled around her shoulders. It was a textured fabric, thick and nubby, in colors of turquoise and teal, with flecks of gold, most likely something Lacey had woven herself.

"How's Alex coping?" Margot asked.

"He acts like everything is normal. Like I said, he's convinced he can fix it. Except now. You know how he loves riding his . . ." The tendons in Lacey's neck seemed to tighten, her jaw tensed.

"His bike," Margot said.

"Yes, his bike." She seemed to blink back tears, but went on. "He goes out and disappears for hours. Sometimes I think he's running away. I don't know what he'll do when . . ." She swallowed. "When the roads get icy and he can't ride."

"But there has to be something you can do," Margot said. What was happening? Where was modern science, for God's sake? Hell, they were curing cancer. Her sister was a good person, a wonderful mother, a loving wife. She was an amazing weaver, an artist really. "There's got to be a cure," she said. "I don't know—medicine, surgery."

"There is nothing, absolutely nothing." Lacey slowed the car. They were entering the village of New Castle. "It's extremely rare."

"What causes it?" Margot asked.

"Something wrong with the cells . . . the brain cells. They don't know what until they . . . After you die they do an . . ."

"An autopsy?"

"Stop telling me words. Give me time."

"I'm sorry," Margot said quickly.

"I don't want help."

"I know."

"Do you?"

Margot sat still, now afraid to say anything.

Lacey spoke almost inaudibly. "This is so hard for me."

"Of course," Margot said, feeling an ache in her chest.

"Without an autopsy," Lacey said, emphasizing each syllable of that brutal word, "there's no way to . . ." Again she paused, but quickly added, "To know for sure."

Margot wondered briefly if their mother's alcoholism could have somehow caused Lacey's illness. She shuddered.

Lacey pulled the car off the side of the road just beyond the New Castle post office. She put the car in park and took her hands off the wheel. They were almost to the house. Lacey drew in a breath and let it out. Still, she didn't cry. Margot imagined her at the moment she'd received the news. She could picture Lacey and Alex in the car outside Mass General, the huge hospital in Boston. He would have held his wife. Kind, dear Alex, the best of husbands, would have held Lacey tightly as she cried, maybe as they cried together. What thoughts had gone through his mind? Margot reached across and placed her hand on her sister's arm and waited, knowing that she was about to say something more. She fought back her own urge to weep at the unfairness of it all.

Silence settled between them. The old Colonial houses in the village, painted in dull ocher, faded green, white, and gray, were another world to Margot. It was amazing that only this morning she had taken an elevator down nine floors to the noise and clamor of the Upper West Side. A taxi ride, a shuttle flight, a bus, and now this car, where Lacey had told her the devastating news.

"The girls don't know yet," Lacey said.

"You haven't told them?"

"I can't tell them. Not yet. They're waiting to hear about college. They've got another round of college boards. Exams coming up." Lacey uttered this series of facts in short bursts. As she spoke, she slowly lowered her head, burying her chin in the richly textured shawl. "And Toni's got this boyfriend. He's older. I'm worried about that." She turned to face Margot. "Don't you see? I can't be sick."

"Lacey, this is so awful." Margot felt stupid uttering these words. Words, ridiculous words. For her, they flowed easily from her brain to her mouth.

"I will tell them. Just not now."

"You look so healthy," Margot said. She squeezed Lacey's arm.

"You can't see my brain," she said.

A sudden flash of something gray, amorphous, slowly eroding like the coastline in a storm, swept into Margot's mind. She brought her hands to her eyes, no longer able to hold back tears. How could they celebrate the family holiday with this tragedy looming over them? Shock, sadness, and disbelief overwhelmed her, tangling up inside her chest.

"Don't cry. Please. You mustn't," Lacey pleaded. "They'll know something is wrong if they see you upset."

"I can't help it."

"You can. You must do it for me," Lacey said.

Margot rummaged in her bag for a tissue. Lacey handed her one, conveniently stowed in the pocket of her door; then she put the car in gear and looked over her shoulder before easing back onto the road. "Please," Lacey said. "This time I need you."

Margot nodded. She wiped at her eyes again, drew her hands into fists, and put them in her lap. She looked outside the car window. Beyond the comforting houses where families would gather for the holiday lay the ocean. Fear, a sickening sensation as heavy and menacing as the water, knotted inside Margot's chest. Lacey turned the car onto Wiley Road. They were almost home.

Early in the week it had been unseasonably mild, but the temperature had dropped overnight. Late November, the day before Thanksgiving—it was supposed to be cold. Alex bent forward on his bike, his face in the wind. He wanted to do the eighteen miles out to Sandpiper Point. He should have worn a hat. His eyes teared up in the stinging air.

He pedaled harder, curling his body into a deeper crouch. Thanksgiving, thankfulness, thanks. All that he had to be thankful for—his wife, his family, his home—was going to change. A vast uncertainty lay ahead, as if he were trying to follow a route that was off the map.

He would never forget that afternoon in Boston—Dr. Braithwaite in his starched white coat sitting safely behind the mahogany desk as he explained Lacey's condition. "I'm sure you have questions." His voice was inviting, though probably underneath, the doctor was eager to have them leave so he could get on to his next tragedy, his next neurological disaster. Fury built in Alex's chest.

"What's the prognosis?" His first question. The only question that really mattered. Would Lacey get worse? If so, how soon? What could they do about it?

"Hard to say." The doctor had an annoying habit of rolling a pen on his desktop.

"I mean, when will Lacey no longer be able to talk?" Alex felt Lacey's hand on his arm, as if to quell his anger. She looked pale. Still in shock.

"Mrs. George," the doctor said, as if his patient was not in the room with them, "may have a few more years when she will be able to articulate her thoughts. Long, complex sentences are already challenging. Gradually shorter utterances, fewer words. Maybe even two or three years without dramatic change. Speech goes first, along with small motor skills, eventually the ability to write. Down the road she'll need therapy. You'll both want to develop other strategies for communication. And, of course, eventually she will need total care."

Strategies were for saving businesses, getting companies back on track. It was what Alex did for a living. So now he would need a strategy to talk to his wife? Counselors, support groups, psychobabble crap. He'd find some other doctor.

Now he pedaled hard in one final burst, then let himself coast along a flat stretch of road. His breath was ragged. Thankfully, last week he had found a research doctor at Harvard who had agreed to see them this afternoon. He was also glad that Margot had come and that Lacey had promised she would tell her sister what was going on.

Alex reached a turnout along the road overlooking the ocean. The sun had come out. The burning in his lungs subsided. He got off his bike and leaned it against a stone wall. The hideous events of the last few weeks pounded in his head. He leaned over, clutching his stomach as if he had been hit, then struggled upright once again. He stared out at the cold ocean, a deep navy blue in the November light. He remembered how it was at Bow Lake in the beginning of the summer: the hot sun on your back, taking that first dive of the season, and the momentary smack of oblivion as you plunged into the icy water.

Oliver Levin's long legs jammed up against the seat in front of him. The plane had begun its descent into Atlanta. Shifting his weight, he thought about his day at the studio. It had not gone well again today. He had started a new painting, another large one, a scene in Riverside Park of an old man with his dog staring out at the Hudson River. He wanted to paint that elusive moment just before dark when it was still light but on the verge of night. He wanted to capture the feeling of closing in and the smallness of the man and the dog in the vast, empty park. He hoped that their figures would appear as abstract shapes blending into shadows.

The huge rush of enthusiasm that came when he began something new wasn't there this time. Most mornings when he opened the door to his studio in SoHo he couldn't pull his coat off fast enough. His mind already had paint on the brushes, his hand itching to get the color on the canvas. Today, he had had to force himself to stay in front of the new painting, push himself to keep dipping the brush into the paint. A dealer in San Francisco had expressed interest in his work. What if he had nothing new to show? Maybe it was just the feel of winter coming on? The idea of a possible show in California should have spurred him on. Change might be a good thing. New York was feeling stale to him.

The plane lurched. The woman on the aisle opposite him whimpered. The captain announced that they were less than one hundred miles from Atlanta and that there would be additional turbulence during their descent. A child kicked the back of Oliver's seat. He looked down at his hands. There was still paint under his nails, and a smear of magenta looking like a stain rimmed the back of his knuckles. He hadn't allowed enough time to clean up properly.

His painting was taking on a heaviness, the colors growing

murky. Why couldn't he get that light? Shit. What was the matter with him? His mind's eye had it, but his hands couldn't get the color right. It was as if he could no longer handle his brushes, as if he was painting wearing boxing gloves. Some of his work veered toward abstraction, but something always kept him grounded in nature: a wash of sky, the underlying sparkle of water, the girth of trees. The figures in his pictures created a narrative underpinning, whether he wanted it or not.

The airplane continued to bump its way down through the uneven atmosphere. If Margot had been with him she would have given him one of her pep talks, telling him not to worry, to be patient, that eventually he would accomplish the effect he wanted. Oliver closed his eyes. It was good of Margot to let him have this time with Jenna. His ex-wife, Linda, almost a stranger to him now, had remarried and lived in Phoenix, yet they would always share their child. Hardly a child. Jenna was thirty.

His grown-up child had become his friend. After Linda had remarried and moved to Arizona, it had been difficult to see his daughter. He continued to pay child support, but it had been cumbersome and expensive to fly back and forth across the country. Jenna came to him every July, but by high school she wanted to have a summer job and stay close to her friends. For a while, there was a growing distance between them. Eventually, after dropping out of college, she had moved to Atlanta with a friend to work for a catering company. "Daddy, I don't want to study. I want to do things."

Four years ago, with his help, and his insistence that the money was in lieu of two years' worth of college tuition, she opened Super Soups, a tiny restaurant in midtown Atlanta. Jenna loved the food world, and to Linda's surprise, the business venture was thriving. Jenna's starting the restaurant had brought Oliver into a much closer relationship with his daughter. He liked Atlanta and he liked seeing Jenna there, away from Linda's realm, where the desert landscape reminded him of his failed marriage.

The flight attendant, collecting the final round of trash, bumped his arm. Oliver tightened his seat belt. Jenna. Freckles, that shiny hair, now cut short, nonstop energy, the silly laugh that accompanied a shake of her head, her determination. Always on her feet, always working, always sure the restaurant would be a success. Margot was right. He had only these few days, but it would be good to be with his daughter.

He shut his eyes, imagining Jenna's funky apartment. She had painted the rooms in food colors—aubergine, celery, and cream—and filled them with her treasured "antiques," the kind of furniture dating from his own boyhood. Oliver knew that Jenna's Thanksgiving table would be surrounded by a hip, ragtag group of friends and covered with all the expected dishes, along with some unexpected ones too. She made delicious dishes with tofu and bowls of brownish grains for her vegan guests. Leo, Jenna's boyfriend, would valiantly carve the turkey into strange, uneven lumps, while she smiled indulgently at his ineptitude.

How different from the meal that would take place in New Castle. There, the always competent Alex would carve the bird into thin, elegant slices, and the dining room with its sleek sideboard made by a Maine cabinetmaker would be covered in an array of artfully plated dishes. The silver on the table would be gleaming, the napkins starched and white, a fire crackling in the grate. Lacey, a natural hostess, would bring everyone into the conversation, putting her guests at ease. Everything would be perfect with Margot's sister at the helm. In his present frame of mind, Oliver was glad he didn't have to be there.

The plane hit the tarmac in a final lurch. Oliver was thankful that he and Margot would be apart for only a few days. He missed her already.

2

*Loom: A device to hold warp threads taut so that the weft
threads can be woven under or over them.*

*M*argot tiptoed down to the kitchen on Thanksgiving morning. She wanted to make a cup of tea to bring up to bed. The guest
room, a small space under the eaves, was on the third floor, across
the hall from Lacey's studio. Margot had had a second sleepless
night and her body was sore, as if holding back this news from her
twin nieces was some kind of physical endeavor. She had spent the
day with them yesterday, taking them shopping and out to lunch
in Portsmouth, their annual day-before-Thanksgiving tradition.
Lacey and Alex had gone off somewhere together for the afternoon.
They had not said where.

The stairs creaked in the old house. Margot paused and looked
out the window on the landing. The sky had begun to lighten; the
garden behind the house was cloaked in silvery shadow. All the
leaves had fallen and the flower beds had been heavily mulched,
awaiting the full impact of winter. One lone bench was set in the
curve of the lawn with two empty pots on either side. Lacey called
it her tea place, where she would pause, drink a glass of iced tea,
and decide what she would tackle next.

Lacey had designed and planted this garden by herself. Margot had helped her drag a hose around to determine the curve of the beds the first summer she and Alex had owned the property. Lacey loved her flowers, particularly the richly colored blooms—the deep blues of her delphiniums early in the season, and later the hot pinks of the cosmos and zinnias, and the dahlias, whose jewellike shades didn't fade until frost. She never tired of the relentless daily tasks that a garden required: weeding, deadheading, dividing, pruning, staking a tall top-heavy bloom, or coddling a rare rose more suited to an English cottage garden than the uncertain climate of the New Hampshire seacoast. Margot admired her dedication.

"The best part about gardening is that you always have another chance," Lacey had explained to Margot. "If it's not perfect now, there's always next year." She had wiped a smear of soil off her cheek before picking up the shovel. That was Lacey—positive, always looking ahead, certain that she could make it right. Now she was facing a future she could not fix. What would next year bring?

Margot wasn't used to thinking of her sister as vulnerable. Lacey's life had always been like her garden, well tended, orderly, predictable, the perennial flowers reappearing every year. Always beautiful. Now, with this illness, it was as if Lacey's life had become a garden infested with deadly insects, or an unstoppable blight. Margot shivered. Alex and Lacey kept the house cool at night.

She reached for the railing and continued down the stairs. A light was on in the kitchen. A cupboard door clicked shut. She had lost her opportunity to fix her tea and slip unnoticed back to her room, but she went into the kitchen anyway.

"I hope I didn't wake you," Alex said. "I wanted to get the turkey out of the fridge." The large bird sat in the roasting pan on the counter, its flesh a ghostly white in the dimly lit kitchen.

"No," Margot said, pulling her robe around her and tying the sash. "I was going to make a cup of tea."

"Let me do that for you." He reached for the kettle next to the sink. He wore sweatpants and a shapeless blue sweater. His hair, once a reddish blond, was now flecked with gray. He was a tall man. His face was angular, and with age he had grown into his beaklike nose. He no longer had the freckles she remembered from their childhood summers on Bow Lake. His family had had a cottage just down the lake from Grandmother Winkler's camp. To Margot, he had always been the fabulous older boy in baggy boxer swim trunks diving off the float into the icy blue lake.

"Is Lacey still asleep?"

"The doctor put her on a prescription sleeping pill. She takes it every night now. As you can imagine, we haven't been sleeping too well lately."

"Alex, I'm so sorry." This was the first time they had been alone. Margot knew that the girls would sleep for hours.

"She's going to get better." He opened a cupboard and took out two mugs, then reached in a canister for a tea bag. He shook his head. "There's quite an assortment. You choose." He handed Margot the canister. She took the one on top, country peach, not wanting to search any further.

Alex turned his back to her and began to make coffee in the machine on the far counter. He filled the carafe with water, shoveled out scoops of coffee from a different canister, and pressed a switch. His movements were quick and jerky, as if he were uneasy being alone with her. The teakettle started to whistle.

Margot grabbed it before the noise could wake the rest of the family. She poured water into her mug and stared into the liquid, watching it steep. The amber liquid slowly darkened. "Lacey said the doctors told her the aphasia would grow worse." Margot hesitated. She didn't want to upset Alex, but she wanted to understand everything that was going on. "She said they had taken brain scans."

"Yes, but nothing might happen for years. We saw another doctor yesterday. He said they couldn't say for sure." He crossed his arms over his chest. "Shit, Margot. Why can't these guys give us a straight answer?"

Margot looked away from him. Alex, always so calm, so thoughtful, looked shaken.

He said, his voice pleading, "It doesn't make sense. Lacey's the picture of health. She runs. She does yoga. She's smarter than any of us. So what if she has a little trouble remembering the right word? We all do."

"Can't they give her anything to stop the progression? She seems convinced there's no way out of this. I just wondered."

"They say there's nothing." He rested his elbows on the counter and covered his eyes with his hands. "I'm sure it's because she's overtired. As usual, she's doing too much. She's going to take the sleeping pills, get her rest, and she's not going to get worse. We're going to take it one step at a time."

"Of course," Margot said, trying to conceal her doubt. "Lacey's always been strong." Margot blinked back tears and swirled the tea bag in her mug.

Lacey was the capable one, wise and practical even as a young woman. After their mother died Lacey had been the one to travel home on weekends to check on their father. When his health had deteriorated a few years later, Lacey helped him find doctors, visited him in the hospital, and was with him when he died. She even arranged for the funeral. By then, she was married to Alex and living in New Hampshire. Margot thought of Lacey and Alex as the adults, while she, four years younger, was still floundering and trying to figure out her life.

The kitchen filled with the aroma of coffee. Margot swished her tea bag once more before removing it and putting it on a saucer next to the sink. She sat on a stool at the far side of the counter. She couldn't leave Alex now that they had started to talk.

"Lacey said she'd tell the girls once they had decided about college," she said.

"There's nothing to tell them." He pulled himself up and away from the counter. "Lacey will come through this. I just know it." He had dark circles beneath his eyes.

"But what if she gets worse?"

"You can't say that," he said, his voice sharp. "Okay. She has a problem, a big one—I grant you that, but problems can be solved."

"Lacey said the scans showed deterioration."

"Damn the scans. She's managing fine now." Alex looked down at Margot. She thought he might reach over and shake her, insisting that she listen to him and trust that he was going to find a solution.

"Please, Alex," Margot said. "I want to believe you. You know how I love Lacey. I love both of you. I don't want any of this to be happening."

"I know that," he said more kindly.

Margot wanted to tell him that it would be fine, that maybe he was right. Lacey might not get worse. She wished she could comfort him, but she felt so inadequate. Lacey was always the one who calmed, who soothed, who made the world better for all of them.

Alex's face went slack. He lowered himself onto the stool opposite her. "You can't imagine what we've been through. What she's been through." He spoke more softly. "They've found some deterioration in her left frontal lobe. It could have been there for years." His eyes met hers. "I haven't heard any definitive reason to believe that it might get worse."

Margot took in a big breath and nodded. The final sputtering of the coffee machine ended and Alex got up and busied himself filling his cup and pouring in milk. And why shouldn't she believe him? Alex was smart, good at his work. Years before, he had reorganized and sold his family's manufacturing business. Now he worked as a consultant to other family-run corporations. He fixed things. He was used to grappling with problems—making things turn out right.

"I'm sorry I snapped at you," he said. "We've got a lot going on right now."

"It's okay." Maybe Lacey hadn't really understood what the doctors had said.

Alex put down his coffee and took an orange from a bowl on the counter. "Lacey says that Oliver is working on paintings for a dealer out in California." He tore into the skin of the orange and peeled it off in big chunks.

"He wants to get better known there." Margot could tell that the topic of Lacey's illness was closed. "He's worried that the New York market is fading for him."

"He's still selling for big bucks, according to Toni." He held some of the orange toward her, an offering of sorts. Margot accepted the sections of fruit.

Her niece Toni was curious about Oliver and was always plying him with questions. "His paintings sell for a lot," Margot said, "but the art world is fickle. Oliver is the first to admit that." She didn't want to talk about Oliver's frustration with his work. Any job had its rough periods. Oliver hadn't sold a major painting in over a year, but Alex didn't need to know that. Oliver's problems hardly mattered in light of all that Alex and Lacey were going through.

Alex sat back down. His face had brightened now that they were talking of other things. He had finished the orange and reached for his coffee. He cocked his head and stared at her.

"What?" she said.

"It's funny," he said. "You're looking more and more like Lacey."

"You mean now that I'm older?" Margot said. "You know how to make a woman feel good."

"You know what I mean. You've changed, that's all." He shifted on the stool.

Margot pushed her hair behind her ears. Her hair was longer now, and like Lacey, she often pulled it into a clip at the base of her neck. But her hair was dark, whereas Lacey's was light brown, flecked with gold. Margot apparently took after her great-grandmother Suzanne, who was born in New Orleans, the odd French strain in the family. She was the smaller, darker, more intense version of her older sibling. Margot thought their resemblance had more to do with their outlook, as if the expressions on their faces reflected the way they both saw the world. Friends said they sounded similar too, particularly on the telephone.

Alex stood and started to move about the kitchen, as if he needed to be busy. He opened a cupboard and pulled out a box of salt. "We're going to take the girls on a trip this summer, a graduation celebration for the whole family. Lacey wants to go to Italy, show the girls some art, eat pasta. She talks about wanting to give them as many memories as possible. I think the change of scene would be good for her."

"That's a great idea." Margot noticed the turkey again. "Do you think we should get this in the oven?"

He turned and nodded. "Do we need to put anything on it besides salt and pepper? Lacey said something about rubbing it with olive oil. Or was it butter?" He stared down at the bird.

"Why don't we do both?"

As long as she accepted Alex's optimistic prognosis, he would go back to being her sweet, caring brother-in-law.

Margot went to the refrigerator to look for the butter. Every shelf was packed, but in an orderly fashion. She found the butter in the door next to the sour cream, pints of whipping cream, packets of cream cheese, and other dairy products of a similar size. Margot always marveled at Lacey's organization and thought of the contents of her fridge in New York, a jumbled assortment of takeout containers, aging condiments, and hunks of poorly wrapped cheese that would crack with age. In periodic attempts to avoid wasting food, she would wrap leftovers in foil for the freezer. Oliver called them the UFOs, unidentified frozen objects, and now and then rounded them up for the trash bin.

Margot put a stick of butter in the microwave to soften before spreading some on the turkey. Alex found a short brush for the olive oil and further anointed the bird after Margot's ministrations. They were sprinkling on the salt and pepper when Lacey came into the kitchen.

"You're both up early," she said.

Margot thought she heard a slur in Lacey's speech. Maybe she was imagining it, or maybe it was the effect of the sleeping pill. Sun streamed through the kitchen windows. Margot hadn't noticed that it had become light.

Lacey smiled at Margot and came up behind Alex, wrapping her arms around his waist. "Happy Thanksgiving," she said. She pressed her face into Alex's back and held on as if for dear life.

The Georges' house smelled more and more like Thanksgiving as the day wore on: the roasting turkey, crushed sage, buttery pastry, and the nutmeg and cinnamon for the pumpkin pie. These reassuring scents reminded Margot of the comfort and ease she experienced each time she came to her sister's home. Being with Lacey, sharing in this particular annual ritual, had always made Margot feel secure, part of a family, safe from the troubles of the rest of the world. Even when they were little girls, Lacey had provided that same sense of security. The sound of Lacey's book bag hitting the kitchen table, her footsteps coming up the stairs, or the light seeping from under her bedroom door onto the hall floor made Margot feel more relaxed, almost as if a worry she hadn't known existed had disappeared.

Now, with the knowledge of Lacey's illness, it was as if someone had left a window open and a cold draft was blowing in. That lovely, safe feeling of home had been spoiled.

Kate and Hugh Martin, Alex and Lacey's friends, were coming at four, and Lacey was planning to serve dinner at five. Hugh was running in a 10K race during the day, so they had decided on an early-evening meal. During the academic year, the Martins lived at Warner Academy, a prestigious boarding school where they both worked. They spent summers and school holidays in New Castle, in a white-shingled house a few blocks away from the Georges' home.

In the course of the morning, nothing more had been said

about Lacey's condition. Wink had come into the kitchen around eleven, and she had made the cranberry sauce. Toni appeared an hour later while Wink and Margot sat at the kitchen table sipping tea and enjoying the apple spice muffins that Lacey had made two weeks earlier and frozen to have on hand for the holiday weekend.

"I thought you were never going to get off the phone last night," Wink said, giving her sister a cool glance.

"If you needed the phone you could have said something." Toni glared at her twin. Her long hair, wet from the shower, had darkened the back of her shirt. "Couldn't you have used your cell?"

"Yeah, right." Wink didn't bother to say that cell phone coverage was lousy in their area. They all knew that.

Margot was used to the girls squabbling from time to time. They had the normal adolescent arguments, but now, with the knowledge of Lacey's illness, she was uncomfortable with their behavior. She wanted Lacey's day to be as smooth as possible.

"Why were you on the phone so late?" Lacey asked.

"It wasn't a school night," Toni said. She took a container of yogurt out of the refrigerator. "Ryan is coming to Portsmouth tonight to see some friends. He wants me to go out."

"No," Lacey said. "Kate and Hugh . . . are coming."

"After they leave, Mom. I won't go out till later." She pulled herself up straight; she was not as tall as her mother or Wink.

Lacey shook her head and continued to roll out piecrust. "Aunt Margot's here too."

"I don't mind," Margot blurted out before she had a chance to think.

"See," Toni said.

"But I understand how your mom feels," Margot added, regretting how she'd unwittingly become involved in their discussion.

"I know what this is really about," Toni said. "You don't like Ryan."

"I"—again Lacey paused—"never said that."

"You don't like that he's older."

"That's not it."

"Mom, I'm not running off with him. I just want to go out for coffee. Kate and Hugh will be gone by ten. They're like you and Dad. They never stay late."

Lacey had opened her mouth as if to say something more. Her face was flushed and she shook her head, running her teeth across her lower lip. Margot was saddened to see Lacey upset and wished her daughters knew what their mother was going through.

Toni took a spoon from the silverware drawer and slammed it closed. She walked out of the kitchen, nearly colliding with Alex.

"Hey, what's with you?" he asked.

"Mom is being a jerk," she muttered.

"Toni, watch it."

"Sorry," she said in a perfunctory way, and continued on into the hallway and up the stairs.

"What was that all about, Chief?" Alex asked, calling Lacey by the nickname he had given her soon after the twins were born.

"She wants to go out . . . with Ryan tonight. After dinner."

"Is that a problem?"

"It's Thanksgiving. It's a family holiday."

"Yeah, but if they went out later?"

"You always take her side."

Wink shot Margot a raised-eyebrow glance, as if this argument was nothing new.

Margot knew to keep her thoughts to herself this time. She gathered the dishes on the table and carried them to the sink. Lacey rolled the pastry onto the rolling pin and lowered it into the waiting pie dish. The dough was a perfectly smooth disk, without a tear. After easing it to the center she crimped the edges, her head bent to the task, her mouth resolutely closed. Despite her apparent agitation, her hands moved smoothly and adeptly, capable of creating the perfect crust even though her mind was most likely elsewhere.

Alex took a bottle of water from the refrigerator. "I'm going for a bike ride." He paused and zipped his jacket.

"Now?" Lacey asked.

"Do you need me here?" He glanced at her quickly, moving toward the door.

"Please put me to work," Margot said. She grabbed one of Lacey's aprons off the hook. Alex looked over at Margot as if suddenly remembering she was there.

"You're sure?" he asked, his expression already relieved. Before she could answer, he hurried out.

Not long after, Lacey put the pies in the oven and began to peel the potatoes. She looked furious, peeling fast, the blade glinting in the light as if she wanted to kill them. Margot cut them into quarters, and added them to the pot.

"Are you okay, Mom?" Wink carried her juice glass to the sink. She looked over at her mother, whose lips were still pursed in concentration. "I can help Aunt Margot with that."

"Please, Lacey. Go have a rest," Margot said. "You've been cooking all morning. Wink and I will finish this."

Lacey blinked quickly, an odd mannerism that Margot hadn't noticed before, and let out her breath. "Thanks," she said. "Maybe I am tired." She wiped her hands on a towel, gave them a quick smile, and left the kitchen. Wink shrugged and shook her head.

Margot reached for another potato and began to draw the peeler across the uneven brown skin. Unlike Lacey, who accomplished this task with a masterful competence even when angry, Margot struggled along, some peels coming away long and thin and others falling into the sink in jagged, thick chunks. She couldn't remember Lacey ever admitting to being tired, but everything was different now.

Wink finished cutting up the potatoes, covered them with water, and set them on the stove to cook. They chatted idly about how long to boil them and Margot told Wink she would take over and keep an eye on the stove. Margot was glad to be with her niece and helping Lacey even though preparing mashed potatoes was such an insignificant contribution, ultimately forgettable, merely a side dish at the Thanksgiving feast. Margot took the dishcloth and wiped the counter to clean up the last bits of potato skins, resolving that from now on she would do more.

At the end of the afternoon, when Margot was alone, she reached for the phone in her room, thankful that it was not in use. With everything that had happened she had completely forgotten to call Oliver. First she tried his cell, knowing it was unlikely he had turned it on. Oliver was not a phone person. He claimed he loved a good conversation, but face-to-face, or in the company of good friends. He considered his cell phone a useful tool for small emergencies, such as letting her know if he might be late. At his studio, he checked e-mail but didn't answer the phone, preferring to spend his days in his own silent, uninterrupted world.

Margot tried Jenna's apartment next. The answering machine came on and she left a message wishing them all a happy Thanksgiving and then hurriedly adding that she sent her love to all. There was so much to tell Oliver, but she would wait until they were both home in New York. He needed to have these two days away without such unsettling news.

Margot had looked forward to this visit with her sister and a few days away from the city. Oliver had been in one of his moods. It was as if a shadow had fallen over him, and as much as he wanted to come out from under it at the end of the day, it seemed to follow him home every night from the studio. He had been hoping that the Croft Gallery in San Francisco would give him a one-man show in the spring.

The Van Engen Gallery, where Margot worked, represented Oliver, and he was included in a group show that would remain up throughout the holiday season. Margot and Mario, her assistant, had just hung *Patio at Twilight*, a painting Oliver had finished earlier in the fall. The huge canvas, six by nine feet, depicted a group of people standing around drinking cocktails in a suburban-looking backyard against a yellow sky. A naked man sat slumped in the foreground on the grass. The others in the painting paid him no notice at all.

"You don't like it, do you?" Oliver had said.

He had stopped by the gallery the morning of the opening. Mario was coming in later to help adjust the lighting. Margot needed to unpack the catalogs and oversee the caterers later that afternoon.

"It's a wonderful painting, Oliver."

"What's that supposed to mean?"

"It raises questions. It's haunting."

"You think it's shit." He put his hands on his hips.

"I would never think that."

"I see it in your face."

She looked away from him and back at the painting. "Carl says it's the key piece in this show." Carl Van Engen, the director and owner, always gave Oliver the plum spots.

"He's not showing my triptych."

"It's too big. He has to have enough room for the other artists' work too."

Oliver shifted his weight, sighed, and stepped back. "None of it feels right anymore. I spent months on this, but it's not what I'm after."

"It's a brilliant painting. You know it."

She looked away from the canvas and back at him. His deeply set eyes focused on his own work as if he were trying to see it for the first time. He smoothed his hair back, revealing the worry lines across his high forehead, then looked nervously down at his feet. His paintings were powerful, provocative, and she could understand their attraction. She moved close to him and laced her arms around him under his jacket. "You'll be fine," she said.

He bent and kissed the top of her head. "Forgive me. It never gets easier. I'm being my nasty bastard self."

"I love you," she said. "Why don't you get some air? I'll see you here at seven."

"You're right," he had said abruptly, and moved off toward the door.

Margot opened her eyes. She must have slept. A streak of late-afternoon sun fell across the dresser on the opposite wall. Lacey had set a vase of bittersweet there, and the curving branches and berries made a lovely shadow on the wall. She sat up and reached for the small tablet of paper that Lacey had thoughtfully left on the bed-side table along with a freshly sharpened pencil in case her guests needed to jot down a note in the middle of the night or make a list. Lacey always thought of such details, like the guest bathrobe Margot had worn earlier. She studied the shadow and began to draw.

She remembered her first art teacher at college telling her that an artist must draw every day, and that drawing, like breathing, is something you must never stop. When she was little she had spent rainy summer afternoons drawing at Bow Lake, moving her colored pencils on the paper to the sound of pattering drops on the roof. She did a drawing once of their rowboat, Pigtail, floating at the end of the dock. Even then, she had known not to draw a round yellow sun with straight lines shooting out at the top of the paper. Instead, she had made the sky three bright shades of blue with the fancy pencils that Granny Winkler said came from France. One knew from that sky that it was a beautiful day. Lacey had told Margot how good her picture was and that none of the girls in her class could draw as well as Margot. To Margot, Lacey's praise meant everything. She didn't care what anyone else thought.

Margot looked again at the bittersweet. For the next few minutes her pencil flew across the page. The lines were pale and broken. She examined the result. Her hand had been unsure, as if she was wary of what would end up on the paper. The drawing was all wrong.

Margot's ex-husband, Teddy, had liked the idea of Margot becoming an artist, but he had taken no interest in her actual paintings, particularly after they were married. When she had moved in with Oliver, she had started painting again. Initially, he was encouraging, telling her the work was good, though he never understood why her canvases were so small and he kept insisting that she might try to open them up. He suggested she set up and work in a corner of his studio. When he advised her to try deeper colors, she did. The more she loosened her brushwork, the more uneasy she became, as if she might lose control. His criticism hadn't bothered her at first, but gradually every new technique she tried made her feel more and more uncertain. Her life was stressful enough with trying to placate temperamental artists at her job, as well as coping with some of Oliver's fragile moods. Most of all, she feared that Oliver would see her lack of talent and think her an impostor.

Eventually she put her work aside. And now she saw that she no longer had the confidence to draw.

The sound of voices rose up the stairwell. Kate and Hugh must have arrived. Margot put down her pencil and crumpled up the paper. Thanksgiving dinner was about to begin. Glancing at the clock on the dresser, she hurriedly changed from her turtleneck into a black cashmere sweater, something that Lacey would say was "very New York." Margot's throat constricted. She closed her eyes, not wanting to cry at the unbidden thought that one day, maybe one day soon, her sister would not be able to say anything at all.

3

Castle: The largest upright part of the loom.

The Georges' home was a large shingled house built at the turn of the century. Though it was not as old as the smaller houses surrounding it, Alex and Lacey had chosen it because even on a gray day the rooms were filled with light. Margot and Lacey's grandmother Winkler had left them each a bequest, stipulating that it be used to purchase "Real Estate." This was her way, as it had been explained, of ensuring that her granddaughters would not have to depend on a man for providing them with a place to live, a sort of old-fashioned feminism. Margot and Lacey had called their inheritance "the house money."

Alex hadn't minded selling the small cape in Exeter, New Hampshire, where they had been living and moving to this house in New Castle. He had been running his family's company in Newfields, getting it ready to sell. It had been Lacey's dream to live near the water and this house had room for a studio for her as well as an office for him. As a businessman, he viewed the new house as a good investment.

Margot, then still in her twenties, had used her inheritance to purchase a tiny one-bedroom apartment with a terrace on the Upper East Side of Manhattan. Alex couldn't believe how expensive it was for so little space and thought it a poor choice. Buying it was what Margot's boyfriend—soon-to-be husband—Teddy wanted.

Now, as Alex stood in the dining room in New Castle opening the two bottles of Côte de Beaune to serve with their dinner that evening, he thought of Margot's ex-husband, who had come only once to New Castle for Thanksgiving. Alex remembered how appalled he had been that Margot had fallen for Teddy. He recalled one awful, though expensive, dinner with them in New York, and later, when Margot had brought Teddy home for the four-day holiday, he hadn't liked him any better. That guy was too smooth, too certain of himself, and superficial. In Alex's opinion, Teddy didn't appreciate Margot. Lacey had agreed, and urged Margot not to marry so quickly.

Later, after Margot's marriage fell apart, Alex was sorry that he hadn't intervened in some way, but how do you tell your sister-in-law that her fiancé is bad news? Margot would not have wanted to hear it from him. His mother had used an old-fashioned expression when she spoke of Teddy's effect on Margot, saying that Teddy had "taken the bloom off the rose," when the marriage ended. Still, that was years ago, and Margot looked happier now. Alex assumed Oliver was the reason for it. Funny how he wasn't coming for the holiday this year. Yet lives got complicated with past marriages and grown children added to the mix.

Alex inspected both corks and brought one to his nose. The wine would be good. He surveyed the room. Everything was ready for another Thanksgiving. He liked the brief calm before a party. This room had been the scene of many fine meals: dinner parties with friends, birthday celebrations, and the ritualized holidays that followed one after another. Lacey prided herself on getting everything just right—the combination of guests, the perfect glasses and dishes, flowers, candles, no detail forgotten. On the surface all was well—the gracious room, the table set, the wine open to breathe. But it was not just another Thanksgiving. Their lives had changed. So far, only he and Lacey, and now Margot, knew that.

Alex wondered if Hugh and Kate, longtime friends, would sense that anything was wrong. Hugh had been Alex's roommate in college, a fellow history major, and they had been best friends ever since. Hugh and Kate were the prototypical New England prep-school teachers. Hugh, a slight man, doubtless would show up that evening wearing a tweed sport coat and corduroy pants that bagged at the knees. His prematurely gray hair was usually long and carelessly combed, making him look like a flash-forward photograph of one of his students. He had an endearing earnestness, always giving his full attention to anyone who spoke to him. His former students often returned to visit him years after graduating from Warner Academy, and Alex could see why.

Kate, whom he had married immediately after they graduated from college, also had a sweet, naive quality and the same perennial youthfulness. It was as if living with high school students most of the year kept both of them in a time warp, where normal aging was held at bay. Her shoulder-length brown hair stayed in place with a tortoiseshell headband and she wore no makeup at all on her wide face with its girlish, turned-up nose.

The Martins' lives seemed so easy and uncomplicated to Alex: They had jobs they loved and two happy grown sons already out on their own. Kate and Hugh lived in a small community where they were revered and respected. They had the benefit of free housing at the school and because of this they were able to save for and purchase their home in New Castle, where one day they would retire. Their sons had received full tuition at Warner Academy before going on to college. The school had a world-class athletic center, with swimming pools and a hockey rink, an art museum, a performing arts center, and hiking trails in the adjacent woods. The years seemed to unfold before Kate and Hugh in a predictable progression where little could go wrong.

Alex had loved history like Hugh did, but instead of becoming a teacher, he had decided to get his MBA after college. His family had expected him to work in the family business, George Manufacturing. The company, which made movable window seals for car manufacturers, had grown larger over the years and his father had seemed less and less able to cope in the changing world market. Alex's older brother, Daniel, was already entrenched in his scientific career on the West Coast and uninterested in helping. Fortunately, Alex had been able to sell the company before the threat of foreign competition forced them out of business. He now consulted for other family businesses caught in similar situations. The work could be lucrative, but it was not always steady.

The grandfather clock chimed in the hallway. Time to get changed. Alex took a last look at the sideboard, the wine, and the empty chairs where they would soon gather. He felt weary. He had thought he was used to life's hurdles.

"So, Georgie, how's the company cleanup business going?" Hugh asked. Hugh liked to joke about Alex's name, reversing the order.

Everyone was gathered in the dining room. One of Lacey's colorful handwoven tapestries ran the length of the table and on it she had arranged gourds and pinecones interlaced with bittersweet. Margot had polished the antique silver candelabra that had belonged to Alex's mother. The candlelight illuminated their faces in the growing dark. They had been at the table for over an hour already.

"I haven't had to travel too much lately," he said. As a consultant, Alex often had to accept jobs that took him to far-flung parts of the country. Lacey, always busy and independent, had never minded his trips. But what about now? Margot wondered. Would his time away from home be harder for her to endure? And next fall when the girls left for college?

"I had two projects in the Boston area this fall. I like being close to home."

"I'll agree with that," Lacey said. While Lacey had not spoken at any length that evening, she laughed easily and made plenty of short comments. "Who'd like more?" She started to get up.

"No, let me," Margot said quickly and went to the sideboard. "There's lots more Pot of Gold," she said, referring to the puree of root vegetables, a longtime family favorite. She handed the dish to Kate to pass around the table. "I'll get more turkey." She picked up the serving platter and headed to the kitchen.

Margot was in awe of the way Lacey put on a beautiful meal seemingly without effort. The turkey had emerged from the oven browned to a golden perfection. Lacey had whisked the gravy while the side dishes warmed—mounds of creamy mashed potatoes, bright green beans, and the corn-bread stuffing, its buttery aroma laced with sage. Kate had brought a casserole of creamed onions and a platter of crudités to have as hors d'oeuvres. Just before sitting down for the meal, Lacey had put the pies in the oven to warm. She had timed the meal perfectly. Yet the timing of her words was already less than perfect. Margot could feel the start of tears as she refilled the platter. No. She'd promised Lacey. She wasn't going to fall apart. She squared her shoulders, pushed her face into a pleasant expression, and went back to the dining room.

"I'd love to travel for my job," Kate said. "Dorm duty every other weekend this year is killing me. We're getting too old for this." Kate and Hugh's apartment was in a girls' dormitory at Warner Academy. Kate was in the English department and also the assistant dean, and Hugh was the head of the history department and coached cross-country and track.

"I thought you liked teenagers," Toni said.

"We do," Hugh said. "Only imagine what it's like living with forty-six of the likes of you guys. It can be a little intense at times."

"Besides, you two are perfect, right?" Kate joked.

"Almost," Alex said, giving Toni a quick glance. Toni had been sulkily pushing her turkey around her plate, still annoyed that she was not allowed to go out with Ryan later that night. In the end, Lacey had prevailed, saying it was a time to be with family, implying that Ryan should be home with his family too, and not hanging out in his apartment during the break.

"So how come you didn't run in the Turkey Trot this year?" Hugh asked Lacey.

"Too busy," she said. "This fall more than usual."

"Last year you finished in the top thirty," Hugh said. "Don't tell me you're giving up running. We have to show those forty-somethings how it's done."

"Mom's starting an arts program at the homeless shelter," Wink said. She passed the cranberry sauce to her mother.

"Lacey needs to learn to say no," Alex said. He looked down the length of the table, but she didn't meet his gaze.

"That does sound like a huge project," Margot said.

"It's important," Lacey said, giving Margot an annoyed glance. "Alex, I'm not going to . . . argue with you about this anymore." With a trembling hand she took the dish from her daughter. The serving spoon fell from the dish, spattering the dark red sauce onto the pine table. There was a sudden silence in the room. Lacey moved to rise.

"I'll get it," Margot said. She had been passing the platter of turkey, but set it down and went into the kitchen for a cloth.

When she returned, Lacey was explaining the project to Kate with noticeable care. "The little kids have nothing to do after school. I'm trying to get companies to donate supplies. We also need more . . ."

"The volunteers don't always show up," Toni said. "Then Mom goes flying out the door at the last minute to pitch in."

"Maybe you could recruit more volunteers," Margot suggested.

"I've tried," Lacey said.

"Lacey, that sounds like a wonderful project. You're so generous with your time," Kate said.

"Too generous," Alex said, stabbing at a piece of turkey with his fork.

Margot finished wiping up the spilled cranberry sauce. The rag was sticky in her hand. She wished Alex would back off.

When she returned to the table, Kate was still trying to smooth things out. "We've got a group of students going to the shelter in Manchester," she said. "So far they only read to the kids and help them with their homework. Art projects are a great idea."

"Speaking of art, what's going on in the big city?" Hugh said.

Margot was grateful to him for moving the conversation away from what was obviously a touchy subject between Alex and Lacey. "We have a new show up at the gallery," she said. "Oliver's latest painting is pretty amazing. It takes up the entire west wall."

"A one-man show?" Kate asked.

"Not this time," Margot said, remembering Oliver's distress at not having any solo shows in the offing.

"Who has walls big enough for paintings that big?" Toni asked.

"It's intended for a public space."

"Like a museum?" Hugh asked.

"That, or maybe a corporate space," Margot said. "The drama of a large painting is that the viewer feels like he could become part of the work. It kind of envelops you—sort of like stepping into the scene." She hoped she didn't sound didactic.

Alex had grown quiet. The knowledge of Lacey's illness seemed to be weighing him down as the evening wore on. Margot was almost afraid to look at him.

"How about more turkey?" she said, trying to keep the conversation going. She gestured to the sideboard still laden with food.

"You've got to be kidding," Hugh said. "I've already had seconds, and though I'm seriously tempted, I'd better not get thirds."

"Not if you want to keep showing up the fortysomethings." Kate lifted her eyebrows as if issuing a serious warning.

"How about a walk to the ocean before pie?" Alex asked, as if suddenly aware that his low spirits were apparent.

"Just what I need," said Hugh.

"If I don't get up now, I may not be able to later," said Kate.

"We'll see stars," Wink said. "It's totally clear."

"I don't want to go," Toni said.

"We're all going," Alex said.

"If I stay and do the dishes, can I go out with Ryan later?" Toni asked.

"You're coming with your family," Alex said.

Toni shrugged and gave her father a sour look.

Margot began to rise and reached for one of the empty platters. "A walk's a super idea," she said with what she hoped wasn't false cheer. Over the next few minutes everyone carried their plates and the serving dishes into the kitchen while Lacey and Kate wrapped the leftovers.

Alex, his face closed and impenetrable, extinguished the candles while the rest of the group went off to find their coats. Margot went all the way to the third floor to get her gloves. On the way down she paused on the landing to button her coat. The hall below her was dark. She hadn't bothered to switch on the light. She heard Lacey and Alex speaking in the foyer. The others must have already started down the walk. Their voices carried up the stairs.

"You're not making this easy for me," Lacey said.

Margot held her breath and didn't move.

"I'm sorry," he said.

"One minute you're acting like . . . everything is fine, and the next you're telling me to stop doing the things I love." She paused. "Like I'm some kind of invalid."

"It's not knowing what's ahead that worries me."

"Alex, no one can count on . . . the future. We're going to go on living . . . the way we always have. There's no other choice."

Margot's heart pounded in her ears. She heard Lacey's steps fade and the front door slam. Margot tried to steady her breathing and ran her hand along the wall in search of the switch. The light came on. She continued her descent. Alex stood alone, his back against the door.

"I'm so sorry," she said, not bothering to pretend she hadn't heard their exchange. Alex's shoulders were hunched. He looked at her briefly, then closed his eyes.

"What can I do?"

"Nothing." He sighed. "Nothing for now." His voice was bitter.

"We'd better join the others," she said. What else could they do? Gently, she placed her hand on his arm, as if to help him move forward. "Okay?"

He nodded, turned, and opened the door. They stepped out into the night.

Breathing in the crisp air made Margot feel more alert, better able to cope. She had been deeply shaken at seeing Alex so upset. The night was cold, but with little wind. Everyone had gathered in the road in front of the house. Alex moved away from her and joined Hugh as they began the walk to the beach. Alex, Hugh, and Toni led the way, walking the fastest, and Kate and Lacey followed arm in arm. Kate was bringing Lacey up to date on the doings of her own children. She and Hugh had had their babies early in their marriage. One son was out west helping to run a wilderness program and the other was in a graduate program in London. Neither could get home this year for Thanksgiving.

Margot and Wink gradually fell behind the others. "I want to take astronomy in college," Wink said.

Margot looked up into the darkness. She was weary from her concerted effort to keep smiling. The clean, sharp air felt good. The moon was nearly full, and the sky was filled with stars. They, along with the lights from the houses in the neighborhood, made it easy enough to find the way along the village streets. She glanced over at Wink, who was also gazing upward as if dazzled by the sweep of stars.

Margot loved the twins equally, but she couldn't deny a special feeling of tenderness she kept for Wink. Toni had been the fussier of the two as babies, and when Margot had gone to visit, she had held Wink more often, so that Lacey could tend to Toni. The feeling of that warm little body nestled up against hers, so dear, small, and defenseless, was something she would always treasure.

"Your dad said you wanted to major in math," she said.

"I do, but I like science, too," Wink said. "You need math for all of it. What I love are the patterns in nature. It's amazing that there are all these invisible forces, the moon, the tides, and even when we understand it, there's nothing we can do to control it. We're all swept into the patterns." She looked down and began to kick at some pebbles. Wink was the more serious twin, quiet, often caught up in her own daydreams. She looked like Alex, with the distinguished George nose and soft reddish brown hair. Tall and willowy, she had a less predictable prettiness than her twin sister. Toni, though not as tall, resembled their mother.

Margot remembered once being with Lacey on this very same walk when the twins were little girls. Toni and Wink must have been at least three, as they had trotted along by themselves on either side of their mother, Wink stopping to pick up a random stone and Toni with a wilted dandelion blossom squeezed in her fist. It must have been summer. Margot seemed to recall the girls wearing sundresses and sandals. Their small round feet were tanned from the long days outdoors. There was a strong breeze that afternoon and large puffy clouds tumbled across the sky.

When Toni caught sight of the low wall close to the beach, she started to run ahead, squealing with delight to be reaching their destination. Lacey hurried to catch up and bent over to scoop Toni into her arms, lifting her up toward the sky before hugging her closely to her chest. Toni's shrieks of laughter melted away as she buried her face in her mother's neck.

Margot nearly stopped breathing as she watched the two of them together. She wanted nothing more than to enter into Lacey's loving aura, to be a mother too, to be part of a family; she ached for a piece of that world. The knowledge that her life could never be like Lacey's had crept into her thoughts like a shadow, but her momentary sadness had disappeared when she felt Wink's small, warm hand slip into her own. Margot looked down at the serious eyes gazing up at her and she smiled. "Come on, little Miss Winky, let's catch up with those two. I'm going to draw pictures for you in the sand." They skipped along together toward the beach wall, Margot keeping Wink's hand securely in hers.

Now the chill November night gave Margot a momentary shiver. A wind had come up as they neared the water. Wink stopped for a bit and turned toward her. "Do you think my parents are okay?"

Margot looked quickly at her niece. "What do you mean?" she asked.

"They don't seem very happy right now." She resumed walking. The rest of the group was well ahead, almost to the wall at the end of the road that overlooked the ocean.

Lacey had started the tradition of night walks to the beach when the girls were very young. It had been a special treat for them to walk hand in hand with their parents, winter or summer, toward the sweep of open water at the far end of the village. Walking in the dark was not the same as walking in the daytime. It was more of an adventure, a time to reveal private thoughts, and the shadows dimming one's face made it easier to share special secrets.

"Aunt Margot," Wink said, "don't you see a difference?"

"I haven't been here very long," Margot said, avoiding the question. "It's going to be hard when you guys go off to college. Especially for your mom. She's used to having you around."

"She and Toni aren't getting along now either."

"You mean because of Ryan?"

"Mom thinks it's too serious. She and Dad argue about that. And it's weird."

"What's weird?" Margot asked, feeling her heart quicken.

"Mom isn't like she used to be. She seems out of it sometimes. And when she gets upset it's like she can hardly speak."

"We all do that now and then."

"Yeah, but Dad's not the same either. They don't seem connected anymore."

"Wink, sweetie, they probably just have a lot on their minds. We all have day-to-day worries."

"Maybe. I think something's going on."

"Maybe you should talk to them, share your concerns."

"I'm not sure I can. It's so hard."

"Your parents love each other very much. You never have to worry about that." Margot put her arm around her niece and gave her what she hoped was a reassuring hug. She took her arm and began walking. "Come on. They'll think I'm lagging behind so I won't have to do the dishes." Margot looked straight ahead and, once again remembering the small face gazing up into hers, thought about this lovely, serious young woman and how she would react when she knew what had come between her parents, when she knew the truth.

Margot and Wink reached the others. "Look at that moonlight reflected on the ocean." Hugh gestured grandly at the water before them.

Wink pulled away and went to stand by her sister. They all stood silently and looked out at the ocean, vast and dark, under the roaring sound of the waves. Kate leaned against Hugh, and Alex stood behind Lacey. Her hair blew back against his coat.

Margot stood a little way from the others. She decided to try to reach Oliver as soon as they got back to the house. She wouldn't tell him all she knew yet. She'd wait until she returned to New York. Pushing her hands deeply into her pockets, she hunched her shoulders against the cold. She imagined the feel of Oliver's arms around her, his body shielding her from this wind. Even when he'd had a bad session at the studio or rambled on all evening about the lousy art market, there was always that moment at the end of the day when he would hold her, and even if his mind was elsewhere, the warmth of his body against hers made her feel safe and loved. He couldn't hold her tonight, but right now she just wanted to hear his voice.

. . .

Margot awoke in the dark on Friday morning. It had to be nearly seven, but too early for the sun to rise. In New York, she was less aware of these changes in light. There, it was the noise from the traffic that alerted her that the day was about to start. Giant garbage trucks would roar up the side streets and the clatter of the metal cans was like artillery fire in a war zone. On weekday mornings in New York, Oliver would be up early. He liked to drink coffee and read in the dawn hours. Like Margot, he was not a cook, but he adored strong black coffee and went to great trouble to buy just the right beans. Margot planned to give him the newest coffeemaker this Christmas, an all-in-one machine that even ground the beans.

Margot thought of the small rituals that she and Oliver shared. A little after seven, he would come into the bedroom carrying a pot of tea for her on a tray. She would drink it while he took the first turn in the shower. She would have coffee later after eating breakfast. Oliver would leave the bathroom door open and, across the steam, call out his plans for the day—going straight to the studio, stopping to see a dealer, meeting up with someone for lunch. Oliver put in long hours at his studio, but like a European, he liked to indulge in a leisurely lunch.

Early in their courtship, they had met most frequently for a meal in the middle of the day. Margot would slip out of the gallery, pick up some take-out food, and ride the freight elevator up to the loft where Oliver worked. It was there, in Oliver's studio, amid the crumbs from a baguette and the remnants of some country-style pâté, that they had made love for the first time. After the mess of her marriage to Teddy, Margot couldn't quite believe the simple joy that came from being so desired.

Margot hadn't reached Oliver in Atlanta last night. It didn't matter now. She would see him tomorrow at home.

She must have fallen back asleep, since the next thing she knew, a pale swath of sun was pouring into her room at the top of the house. A few minutes later she heard footsteps on the stairs, but instead of coming to her room the steps continued into Lacey's studio, followed by the door closing. Lacey had told her that she was trying to finish weaving a set of place mats that she was donating to a charity auction.

Margot got up and hurried to the shower. They were all going to Kate and Hugh's house for a chili lunch and an afternoon hike, an annual tradition rain or shine. Margot smiled, thinking how if Oliver were here he would tease her, saying that he didn't appreciate having to go on a forced march.

After getting dressed she went down to the kitchen. Toni sat slumped at the counter eating an English muffin.

"Am I the last up?" Margot asked, trying to be cheerful.

"Wink's out already. Dad's in his office and Mom's up in her studio."

"You don't sound too happy."

"Thanks to me, everyone's in a pissy mood."

Margot took a mug from the cupboard and poured herself the last of the coffee. It was only lukewarm and had simmered down to a dark sludge. "Is it really that bad?"

"I went out with Ryan last night."

"But your parents told you not to," Margot said. It struck her how she sounded like her own father thirty years before, who would admonish her for what he called her "disappointing behavior."

"I was gone for an hour. I was home before midnight. I'm eighteen. God, Aunt Margot. Don't you think they're ridiculous?"

"It's not for me to say, really."

"I know. You have to take their side."

"It's just that your mother told you —"

"She's the one. She's so controlling. It's because Ryan is older and already at UNH. She wants me to go to Columbia. Their journalism program is famous. Blah, blah, blah. She says I shouldn't pick a school to be with a guy."

"Columbia is a great place."

"I probably won't get in. But she keeps throwing it in my face. What's with her these days?"

"Tell me more about Ryan," Margot said. "Is he worth all the parental bad vibes you seem to be getting?"

"Mom's so unreasonable." Toni pushed back her hair, an unruly tangle that made her look both childlike and vampish. "I met him at a play. Over at UNH. And okay, he's a couple of years older. He's twenty-one, a junior. Mom acts like he's thirty or something."

"He's almost through college and you're still in high school."

"But that's what's so great. The guys in my class are such jerks. They never listen. It's all about them. Ryan really pays attention to me. Older guys are so much better."

"I guess your mom wonders why he's interested in someone younger," Margot said.

"What about Oliver? You're ten years younger. So what does he see in you?"

"Toni, that's different."

"How?"

"Well, when you're older, age sort of blurs."

"Exactly. Ryan treats me like a real person, not like some high school girl."

"So it's pretty serious?"

"God, Aunt Margot. He's totally hot. But he's smart, too. He reads poetry."

"I see."

"I can't stop thinking about him. From the minute I wake up, he's sort of with me—it's like I'm different too, just from knowing him."

"That's wonderful." Margot reached over and patted Toni's arm. "It's just that you have so many important things going on right now: your senior year, college applications, lots of decisions ahead. You need to keep your mind on that, too."

"You sound like Mom."

"I understand her concern."

"I thought you'd be on my side." Toni pursed her lips into a little-girl pout and sighed.

"We all want the best for you."

Toni leaned toward her aunt. "Yeah, yeah." Her face softened. "Since I've known Ryan, it's like everything is clearer. I'm more focused on things, not less."

"Well, I'm glad."

"Isn't it like that with Oliver?"

Margot nodded. Life with Oliver was focused. In the last five years with him her life had taken on more meaning. "I need you, Mags," Oliver often said. "Painting uses me up. I couldn't do this without you."

"Please talk to Mom," Toni said.

"Why don't you talk to her?"

"But I do. I talk and talk and all I get is the silent treatment." Toni got up from the table. She lifted the hair off her neck and arched her back. "God, Aunt Margot, don't you remember the first time you fell in love? It's like so impossible. You can't help it."

Margot stood and gave Toni a hug. "I don't know what to tell you." She rocked Toni for a moment in her arms. What could she say to her niece? It didn't seem all that long ago when she was almost the same age, when she had experienced for the first time the very same thing—swamped with feelings, overcome that summer at Bow Lake. Had it been a crush, or had she really been in love with Alex? Margot grew still. What a ridiculous question. She hadn't allowed herself to think of that for years. She stepped away from Toni. "Give it time, sweetie. Things have a way of working out."

4

Warp: Threads running vertically in weaving.

The next day Margot surveyed her bedroom, or what she thought of as her bedroom, across the hall from Lacey's studio. Her suitcase was packed and she had put fresh sheets on the bed. The pillowcases, old linen ones that required ironing, had embroidered sprigs of lavender along the edges. Lacey collected antique linens and textiles, and actually used them. Now the bed was ready for the next guest, or for her, when she returned, whenever that might be. The bittersweet berries had started to fall from the branches on the dresser, so she had carefully carried the arrangement to the kitchen trash.

She was leaving today with a heavy heart. The time with Wink and Toni, the family meals, the hike in the woods—all the makings of a happy family Thanksgiving were now tinged with sadness for Margot. She likened the last few days to a brilliant painting that had been covered over with a thick varnish, rendering the colors dull and joyless. The way she saw the world had changed. As Lacey had asked, she pretended nothing was amiss, yet in her mind the apparently perfect Thanksgiving had been a charade.

It was after two. Lacey had made brunch for the family late that morning, a good-bye meal in honor of Margot on her last day.

Afterward Alex went to his home office to work and Margot helped Wink and Toni with the dishes, telling Lacey to go have some time in her studio to weave. Margot stepped across the hall, knocked lightly, and opened the studio door. "Okay if I come in?"

Lacey nodded while continuing to thrust the shuttle back and forth on her loom. The sound of harp music drifted from a CD player on the shelves along the wall and the airy melody contrasted with the even, mellow thumping noise from her weaving. She sat in the center of the room, her shoulders rounded slightly, her eyes focused on the project before her. Her feet worked the loom's pedals in a steady rhythm as her hands shot the shuttle from side to side, a controlled dance in point/counterpoint. Strands of light wool flew through the open area called the shed, not making contact, like a hovercraft across the water.

"I just want . . . to finish this part," Lacey said.

"No hurry," Margot replied.

This space was nearly twice as large as the guest room across the hall, and with the white walls and wide-planked pine floors it had the spare, open feeling of a dance studio. Margot blinked in the unexpected brightness. Besides the two dormer windows that faced the front of the house, three skylights flooded the room with light. Lacey's brow was furrowed in concentration. Her upper teeth periodically ran across her lower lip, a rhythmic biting that appeared to have gently bruised her mouth.

The loom, dominating the middle of the room, was like an anchor keeping the ethereal space tethered to the earth. On the opposite wall, a lavender-colored hollow-core door resting on bookshelves at each end served as a desk, and a wicker settee painted an apple green was placed next to the front windows. The back wall was covered with shelves. Along with several rows of books, the rest of the space was filled with spools of wool in a rainbow of shades lined up in meticulous order. The colors, all clear and bright, made Margot think of flowers, sun, and blue skies. All was immaculate, and other than a few wisps of dust from the wool that floated across the floor like dandelion heads in spring, nothing seemed out of place.

On the wall above Lacey's desk was a huge bulletin board filled with an inspirational collage of photographs, clippings, and pictures from magazines. There were postcard reproductions of paintings. Margot recognized the work of most of the artists: an impressionist painting of a woman with two children in her lap by Mary Cassatt, an image of clouds on a blue sky by Georgia O'Keeffe, and an abstract work by Helen Frankenthaler that looked like washes of color poured onto the canvas.

Margot leaned closer to study a photograph tucked into the edge of the frame. It was a snapshot of the three of them at Bow Lake: Lacey on the right, about sixteen; Margot, still childlike, on the left, squinting into the sun; and Alex between them, the summer he got tall. Margot thought wistfully of that time—the endless summer days when they were so young and happy, the three of them together all day long. Who had taken the picture? Granny Winkler, or their father on one of his rare visits to the lake? Who had captured the three of them at that fleeting stage of innocence? If only she could jump back in time to the very moment of that photograph.

"I'll be done in a minute," Lacey said.

Margot looked away from the picture and went over to the loom. Different from the colorful assemblage of fibers along the walls, Lacey's current project appeared to be all white. Then she saw that the place mat was actually not pure white; there were shades of cream, and even a bluish white that formed even triangular shapes every few inches. When she looked more closely she noticed slender threads of silver woven in at regular intervals.

"Who are these for again?" Margot asked. "They look too elegant to actually use."

"The . . . scholarship fund at the high school. The auction is next weekend. I hope I can get them done in time. I promised to make six." Unlike the vivid display around her in the studio, Lacey wore faded jeans and a gray T-shirt along with the beige fleece vest that she always kept on the back of her chair.

"Listen, Lacey, I can get one of the girls to drive me to the bus. Or Alex?"

Lacey's hands stopped. "I want to take you. I always do."

"I know that, but . . ."

Lacey looked at her watch and stood up. "Sorry. Forgot the time. I get lost sometimes." She glanced back at the design on her loom. "I don't know if they'll like them."

"You usually use so much color."

"I'm after a . . . different effect now."

"It reminds me of snow. The silver is like sparkling flakes."

"Last winter . . ." Lacey paused and drew her fingers across the upper part of the cloth, as if she were a blind person reading a story in Braille. "Last winter in one storm there were huge drifts. It came so . . . fast. One could easily have been buried in it." She pulled her hand away. "We'd better go."

They went down to the kitchen, where Lacey put on her coat and picked up her handbag and car keys. Margot had already said good-bye to the girls and Alex. No one seemed to be about. The house was quiet.

"You'll be happy to get back to Oliver," Lacey said.

Margot glanced quickly at her sister. Lacey had not always been a fan of Oliver. After Margot's divorce Lacey had fixed her up with a series of "eligible men." She had been particularly unhappy when Margot chose Oliver over Frank, a friend of the Georges' from Boston who had moved to New York. Lacey had thought Frank was perfect for Margot. He was a pediatric surgeon and the widowed father of a little girl the same age as Lacey's twins. Instead, Margot had chosen Oliver.

Margot remembered Lacey asking, "What sort of future does an artist have?" Lacey kept urging Margot to go out again with Frank, who had called several times after their first date. She knew he liked her, and by the end of their dinner together, he was already talking about how he wanted Margot to meet his daughter. Frank was kind, serious, and very much in the market for a wife. After her failed marriage with Teddy, Margot was afraid of making a second mistake. As hard as she tried, she just couldn't get her nerve up to fall into that kind of life, a doctor's wife in a pretty house in Connecticut, and having to make a commitment. Being with Oliver was easier. He had suffered from one bad marriage and a few longer relationships and seemed content to let things roll along in a sort of romantic limbo. And what was wrong with that? Once Margot had moved in with Oliver, Lacey stopped questioning her choice and seemed to accept her decision.

"I miss Oliver," Margot said.

"And things are . . . good with him?" Lacey pushed open the back door and Margot followed her out to the car.

"Everything's fine," she said in what she hoped was a reassuring voice. She loved Oliver. She couldn't imagine her life in New York without him. His recent bouts of insecurity were part of life. Alex and Lacey's marriage couldn't always be perfect either. How would they cope with all they were facing now? Wink was right in sensing that something was wrong. Yet a child had no way of discerning what her parents were like as a couple. That private side of marriage was unknowable. Margot tried to imagine Alex and Lacey alone together. In light of all that had happened, what did they talk about? Were they able to tell each other everything? Perhaps they knew each other so well there was no need to talk. After all, they had been together since childhood. Maybe they shared a tacit understanding, some kind of marital telepathy that went beyond words.

Margot had not told Oliver everything about her own past. Some things—yes. But not all. Was she making a mistake in holding back?

Lacey backed up the car and began the drive to the bus terminal. The sky was blue today and the air cold. "I just wish," she said, "that your . . . life was more . . . stable."

"You don't need to worry about me," Margot said, feeling defiance creeping into her voice. "We're fine."

"I know that." She gave Margot a brief smile and said nothing for a while. After a series of bridges and causeways they wound their way into Portsmouth.

"Have you ever thought of painting again?"

"I could never go back to it now," Margot said, thinking of her awkward attempt to draw the bittersweet. She was glad that Lacey had dropped the topic of Oliver. It was hard to explain to Lacey that she didn't need marriage, children, and hosting family holidays to be happy. "It's been too long," she added. "Besides, I love choosing art and showing it. That's more than enough."

"You were very good." Lacey pulled the car to a stop at a light. The traffic was heavier. Holiday shopping season had officially begun.

"Not really."

"You were. You just let . . ." Lacey closed her mouth.

Margot waited. Lacey seemed to have given up her thought.

Finally Margot spoke. "I don't want to paint now."

The light changed to green. Lacey accelerated. "That's not right," she said emphatically.

"It's fine with me. Having Oliver around is enough artists for one household," she said in a joking way.

"You are better," she said.

"Come on."

"You are."

"Look, it's ridiculous to argue about this."

They had arrived at the bus terminal. Lacey pulled the car into one of the fifteen-minute parking places and turned off the engine. The bus was due to leave on the hour.

Margot stared down at her lap. Why were they even talking about painting or her life with Oliver? How could she have forgotten the real problem, even for a second? "Lacey," she said, "the girls are concerned. They sense something's wrong."

"Did they say something?" Lacey's face was pale in the unflattering light of the car. The fine lines around her eyes seemed deeper.

"Wink is worried that things aren't right between you and Alex." Margot felt guilty about betraying her niece's confidence. She had never been disloyal. Being younger, and not their mother, Margot had found her nieces were inclined to share their feelings with her. "Toni senses something, too."

"Alex and I are going to be fine."

"I think you should tell them."

Lacey slammed her hands against the steering wheel. "Don't tell me that. I know what I'm doing. I'm their mother. Not you."

Margot moved closer to the door, feeling as if she'd been slapped. A few fat clouds blew across the sky, covering the sun. The air in the car grew chilled.

"If I say it," Lacey said, her voice measured and determined, "if I tell them, then it's . . . true."

"I just think it's better to be honest with them. Please, let's go back to the house." Margot tried to keep her voice gentle. She wanted to persuade her sister, not anger her further. "I could change my ticket and stay another day," she said, realizing that taking some kind of action might make a difference. "It might be easier for you if they knew what's going on."

"Absolutely not." Lacey straightened and drew in her breath. "I don't want to upset them. We're going to be fine."

"But you're not fine. I want to help you."

Lacey shook her head and jutted her chin out resolutely. "We'll be okay. I can manage."

"Lacey, you can't manage everything." Some things with her sister never changed. Lacey always had to be in charge, the one in control. Margot had convinced herself that this was a good quality, this strength, this endurance. Alex was usually willing to go along with his wife. Yet during the course of the last few days, his outlook had seemed to alter, as if his determination to carry on was draining out of him, like a tire with a slow leak.

A huge silver bus roared past them toward the bay designated for the route to Logan Airport. Other travelers got out of the waiting cars.

"I don't have to leave," Margot said. "Let's go home and talk to the girls together."

Lacey shook her head and turned to open her car door.

Margot got out of the car and took her bag from the backseat. Lacey came around and hugged her sister. "I don't want to go," Margot said.

"You have to." Lacey inhaled deeply and smiled. "I'm fine. Really."

Margot hesitated and then went to the bus. She was the last to board. After stumbling down the narrow aisle, she took a seat by the window at the rear. A moment later the driver backed out of the bay and circled to the far side of the terminal. Margot looked back at the parking lot. Lacey's car was gone.

Saturday evening Oliver prepared to leave the apartment at five thirty to take the subway downtown. His return flight to New York had been easy. That morning Jenna had served him a bagel, as good as any in New York, and delicious strong coffee. He had been grateful for the time with his daughter. Maybe Margot would come with him on his next visit.

Leonard Witt, a thirty-year-old British artist, was having an opening at the Gearing Gallery in Chelsea. Another young talent on the way up. Carl Van Engen, Oliver's dealer, had told him that some important collectors might be there; he thought it would be politic for Oliver to make an appearance. This whole business of art was wearing him down. He hated parties, schmoozing, talking the talk, trying to act like some kind of personality, the famous artist who'd soared to the top in the nineties.

Oliver particularly hated going to parties alone. Margot's flight arrived at six and he had asked her to join him at the gallery. He wished they could just spend the evening at home, and felt bad that they had to go out. He'd kept missing her calls while in Atlanta, and realized too late that he'd forgotten to charge his cell phone.

Tonight Hector was the doorman on duty. "Hey, Mr. Levin. Evening on the town? Senora Margot still away? Must be—I don't see you smiling."

"Margot's on her way, Hector. After she leaves her things here she's joining me downtown. She may need a taxi."

"Don't you worry. I take good care of her."

Oliver thanked Hector and walked to the subway. Oliver had purchased his apartment, located on Riverside Drive and 109th Street, from an elderly aunt when he first started to make money as an artist. This was not a typical artist's address, not being in one of the edgier neighborhoods downtown or in Brooklyn. Indeed, Oliver was somewhat embarrassed by his upper-middle-class background. He didn't advertise the fact that he lived in this upscale West Side location, though when he had bought the apartment twenty years ago it was a neighborhood in transition, inhabited by Columbia professors and students. Over the years, with the inevitable gentrification, fancier shops and restaurants had taken over the commercial blocks.

The cold night air improved his mood somewhat. He would get back to work tomorrow. He had three canvases in progress now, each one pulling him, begging for his time.

The subway car was bearable at this time of night on a Saturday. It irked him to see young kids, plugged in, legs extended, lounging in the train while an elderly, obviously tired woman held fast to a pole after possibly a day of cleaning hotel rooms or offices. Looking around at the young people in his immediate vicinity tonight, he realized that they would consider him old. How had that happened?

Oliver arrived at the gallery just after six and tried to make his way over to Marie Stone, an artist close to his own age. They had had a joint show together a few years before. She was a large woman, easy to spot in the crowd on the far side of the room. After many years of working as a painter, she had recently switched to sculpture. The humorous clay statues that she had been producing lately made him think of mythic figures on Valium. It was hard to look at her work without smiling. Marie was easy to talk to. It was as if they shared the same artistic vocabulary, yet her work had taken off in an entirely new direction. She saw him and waved.

Oliver nodded and eased past a group of young people dressed in black, presumably other artists. One girl's blond hair stood up in short spiky tufts. A wraithlike redhead beside her was wearing a sleeveless T-shirt. A green and purple snake tattoo slithered down her pale arm. Two men, both in black leather jackets, looked like they needed shaves, and one had the kind of thick black glasses that Oliver's father had worn back in the sixties.

The room was packed and the hot air was filled with the scent of cheap wine and overripe cheese. Margot called it gallery breath, and refused to drink at openings. He paused and looked at one of Witt's paintings. Abstract, intense color, and yet the swirl of paint on the canvas grabbed Oliver, sucking him in and making him wonder where this energy came from. Forget spare minimalism. This guy was a cross between a controlled Renaissance master and the splattering of a Jackson Pollock. The canvas was not large and yet, the painting worked. This young guy had talent.

Oliver took a glass of white wine from a waiter passing with a tray and headed toward Marie. Just then he felt a tug at his arm.

"Oliver, how are you, dear?" Hannah Greene looked up at him.

Oliver dutifully bent and kissed both of Hannah's leathery cheeks. Her silver hair smelled of cigarette smoke. "Good to see you," he said. "How's June?" He looked across the room in search of Hannah's partner, June Wallace, a stringy woman who wrote bad poetry. But she was a rich poet, thanks to her father, who had once owned motel chains in the Midwest. Hannah and June had been a couple for more than twenty years and lived in a brownstone on West Eleventh Street. They owned two of Oliver's paintings.

"She's at a reading, a woman from her poetry group." Hannah was in her sixties, a short, heavy woman who had probably never had a waist. "June is loyal to her friends."

Oliver nodded, trying to think of a reply. Someone behind him jarred his elbow, nearly causing him to spill his wine down the front of Hannah's dress. "Sorry," he said, glancing at her.

She patted the brown velvet that rippled across her bosom. "Not a drop."

Oliver shifted his glass to the other hand and tried to wipe his wet hand on his corduroy trousers.

"That's quite some painting you have at Van Engen's," she said.

"Does that mean you like it?" He forced a smile.

"Ha!" Hannah barked a laugh in reply. "Well, of course it's good. June says she doesn't know where you get those odd figures, the ones who just seem to turn up."

Oliver was momentarily taken aback by June's blunt comment. He didn't know where some of the lone people came from either. He had explained once in an interview for *Art News* that his paintings were stories that came to his mind, and as he worked, the figures often seemed to emerge from the paint itself, as if he had no say at all as to who came onto the canvas. Over the years, he had come to accept his process. Still, the unexpected shapes in his work disturbed him.

"I'm working on something new. You and June should come down to the studio."

"We'll do that. Junie likes to keep an eye on her artists." Hannah looked beyond Oliver to the entrance. "Oh, my," she said. "There's Leonard Witt. Do you know him, dear? June already bought one of his pieces. Come on. I want to introduce you to him." She took Oliver's still moist hand in a decisive grip. Oliver swallowed his annoyance and let himself be led across the room toward the throng of people circling the artist. He glanced back toward Marie, hoping he could excuse himself from Hannah, but she was now lost in the crowd. Hannah bulldozed ahead, and just before reaching Leonard and his admirers Oliver saw Margot come through the front door.

She looked dazed as she entered; then a second later she nodded and moved toward him. Her lovely eyes, the color of the sky after a rain, met his. He pulled his hand out of Hannah's grip, excused himself, and made his way over to Margot. He held her briefly. She smelled of the cool night air, and faintly of lily of the valley, her favorite perfume.

He sensed that something was wrong. "Are you all right?"

She squeezed his arms. "Later," she said.

Oliver handed Margot a glass of wine. She leaned back into the sofa cushions, finally at home, totally exhausted. They had gone to dinner with Carl Van Engen, Marie Stone, and some younger artists from the opening who had studied with Marie at NYU. Margot had never figured out who was with whom, and she had remained on the periphery of the conversation. The restaurant was a Korean barbecue restaurant and her sweater now smelled of kimchi.

Back in the familiar patterns of her life, Margot felt slightly removed from Lacey's terrible news.

"Leonard Witt," Oliver continued with disdain. "They all love him."

"Just because June bought one of his paintings doesn't mean she no longer values yours." Margot was suddenly irritated by Oliver's ill will.

"You're too bloody sweet, Mags."

"I'm not sweet. You're too concerned about what other people are doing."

A dark look fell across Oliver's face. He took a gulp from his glass and propped his legs on the leather ottoman between them. He was a big man, long-legged with a broad chest, but narrow through the hips. He had put on weight in the last few years, but he carried it well. He had a full head of lush, dark hair that grayed at the temples, something a woman would cover up. Margot knew he was vain about his hair, indulging in salon shampoo instead of ordinary products from the drugstore.

"And that pompous British accent. What really gets me," he continued, "is that the guy's only been in the U.S. for two years. He's already got a one-man show lined up with Carl, and Marie said that Stanley Kalvorian's people have been sniffing around."

The Kalvorian Gallery was a sort of mecca in the contemporary art world. Prices started in the six digits and an armed guard stood at the door of the main gallery on Madison Avenue. Oliver loved to rant about the charlatans and phonies who dominated the art markets.

"That's probably all hype," Margot said.

"That girl at dinner said he's got two assistants. Two. What ever happened to painters who put paint onto their own canvases? And he's practically a kid."

Margot could hear the wine talking. "Don't let him get to you."

"I'm feeling more and more like the old man in this town."

"Darling, you're not an old man and you're an amazing painter. Your work will be around when this guy is long gone." Margot took her last sip of wine. "Come on, we've got to go to bed."

She stood and carried their glasses to the kitchen. When she returned to the living room, Oliver was standing by the window in the dark. The lights across the river glimmered in the starless night. Margot took his hand and leaned against him, knowing the sadness she had carried home with her on the plane was not going to go away. He pulled her close, resting his chin on top of her head. His lips brushed her hair.

"You're good for me, baby," he said. "I've been acting like a shit. Sorry."

"I love you," she said. They stared out at the world that never slept, the noise of the city far below.

"What were you going to tell me about? You looked so sad when you got there tonight."

"You're not going to believe this, Oliver." She hesitated, not sure if she had the strength to start. Then, slowly, she told him everything—her arrival, Lacey's horrible news, her wish to keep it from the girls, carrying on as if everything were normal. Oliver took her hand and led her back to the sofa. "Nothing is normal," Margot went on. "Wink thinks her parents' marriage is in trouble, and Toni says her mother gets so upset about her new boyfriend she can hardly speak."

Oliver had been stroking Margot's arm absently during this telling. Now he leaned in closer and touched her face. "My poor Mags," he said. "I'm sorry. You're right. Lacey should tell the girls. They'll be upset, but they need to know. They'll want to help their mom."

"Lacey wants to protect them. As usual, she's thinking of everyone besides herself." Margot's voice grew tight. "Her brain cells are slowly disintegrating. One day she won't be able to speak. Nothing can stop it."

"My God," Oliver said. "Dementia? But she's young. It's not like she's really old and her body is supposed to shut down."

"Not the usual kind of dementia. It's a slow progression. She'll lose speech first. Eventually she'll be unable to communicate in any way. At the end her body will break down too. But she's fine now and will be for a while."

"So she seems okay?"

"You'd hardly notice. Now that she's told me, I see how she pauses when she speaks."

"And Alex?"

"He's terrified. Trying not to show it."

Oliver pulled Margot into his arms. "You need to sleep, baby. We'll talk about it again in the morning."

Margot nodded and allowed him to shepherd her into bed.

She may have needed to sleep, but after telling Oliver about Lacey's illness, she couldn't quiet her thoughts. Describing Lacey's prognosis for him had brought the picture of the future into focus.

Not only would Lacey eventually be incapacitated by this disease, but one day she would die from it. All the time Margot had been with Lacey in New Hampshire, she hadn't dared think about that.

Margot pulled the covers up to her neck. She couldn't imagine her life without Lacey. Her earliest childhood memories were of her sister. When she thought of Lacey, so often it was Lacey's hands that came to mind. Did she remember Lacey reaching out to her, a small hand between the rails of Margot's crib? That couldn't be possible. She did have a vivid recollection of the two of them together under the lilac bushes next to the garage, what they called their secret fort, when they were little. Their parents had been arguing, probably over their mother's drinking. Margot fled the kitchen when their dad threw a vase of peonies to the floor. The crashing sound, the pool of water, and the pale blossoms amid the broken glass terrified her. She ran outside to hide beneath the purple lilacs. A moment later, Lacey found her and took her hand.

"Don't be scared," she said. "I'm here." Lacey's longer fingers encased Margot's in a warm grip.

Margot continued to sob. "No," she cried, sitting on the hard dirt in the shadowed enclosure.

"Come on. It's okay. I'll show you the secret shake."

"What shake?" Margot asked, wiping her face with the back of her free hand, her sobs quieting. One of the lilac branches poked into her back.

"Give me your pinkie," Lacey ordered.

Reluctantly, Margot offered the little finger of her right hand. Lacey linked her longer pinkie finger with Margot's. They locked fingers. Lacey proclaimed this to be their secret shake, a special handshake they could give no one else. "It means we're together forever," Lacey said. Later, Lacey took Margot's hand again and pulled her out from under the bush. It was quiet in the house and Margot knew that as long as she had Lacey everything would be all right.

. . .

Margot awoke once in the night. The apartment was silent except for Oliver's gentle snoring beside her. He made a muffled sound, more like a purring cat. There in the dark, she remembered Lacey slamming her hands onto the steering wheel. She thought again of Alex, Wink, and Toni. How would they manage?

Margot pictured the night sky in New Castle, the large wooden house on the tiny New Hampshire island, a world away from the dense, pulsing island of Manhattan. Wink would be dreaming of tides, bird migrations, the dancing numbers that charted the miracles of nature. Toni, equally innocent of her mother's plight, probably dreamed of the raptures of first love, vulnerable, blissfully ignorant of the possible hurt that could follow on the heels of that fragile, emotional state. And Lacey? Did words come easily in her dreams when they didn't in real life? And Alex? Margot squeezed her eyes shut and pressed her face against Oliver's wide back.

The next morning a heavy rain spattered the city streets. Had it been snow it would have been a blizzard. Oliver poured hot water over Margot's tea, the faintly smoky Lady Grey that he bought for her from an eclectic tea and coffee purveyor on Broadway. He wished he hadn't gone on last night about Leonard Witt. He had no patience for artists who complained endlessly about how the art world was unfair. He didn't want to be one of those snivelers. What mattered was getting back to work. He had awakened with the image of woods, some dark wet trees, and he could feel himself being drawn deeper into the story that was emerging from the paint. Something was about to change.

He carried the tray in to Margot. She looked small on their vast bed, but she had started to stir, instinctively caught in the rhythm of their morning ritual, almost awake. He placed the tray on his side of the bed and opened the curtains. The Hudson River looked cold and nasty in the gloom.

Margot sat up and eased back onto the pillows. "Thanks," she said, accepting the cup. "Have you been up long?"

"Before six. I know it's Sunday, but I wanted to go down to my studio for a few hours. I was dreaming of my painting, the one of the forest. I think I see birches now. Not in the foreground, but deeper. Isn't there a tree called silver birch?"

Margot nodded and sipped her tea. "I have to *do* something."

"Lacey?" he said.

"All those years she was there for me. Now she needs me and I feel powerless."

"You can visit," he said. "You said it might be years before it gets worse."

"She may have already had it for years."

"I can see why she would want to keep things as normal as she can for as long as possible," he said.

"Oliver"—Margot looked at him, her eyes as sad as the river outside—"it's already pretty bad. I'm so afraid for her." She crumpled back onto the pillows.

He reached toward her and gently smoothed the hair away from her face. "Lacey is a strong person," he said. "You know how tough she is."

"Alex isn't."

Oliver drew back. "What do you mean?"

"I can see he's suffering. He's terribly afraid. I can feel it."

Oliver drew in his breath. "Alex is a grown-up. He can deal with it on his own terms. It's the girls you need to worry about." He looked quickly at his watch. "I'll be home in time to take you out for a late lunch. Are you going to be okay?"

"Of course." She set her cup on the tray. "I'll read the paper for a while. And I need to unpack."

Oliver stood in the shower and let the hot water pummel his head. Perhaps he should have gone to New Hampshire. *Poor Margot had had to deal with everything on her own. He closed his eyes. His attention shifted back to his painting. Silver birches, he thought. Maybe a few, mere slivers through the trees.*

5

*Weft: Horizontal threads interlaced
through the warp of a fabric.*

After Oliver left for his studio Margot lingered in bed, not feeling ready to face the world. The newspaper remained on the covers
beside her, untouched. Oliver was right. She should be thinking
about her nieces. They were losing their mother. Margot was close
to the girls, as close as aunts and nieces could be, she thought, but
she could never be Lacey. Lacey always knew what to say to her
daughters; she listened to them when they wanted to talk and she
hugged them not only in spontaneous, joyous moments but also
when they suffered disappointments, when hugs were more important than words. Her way of touching, her lovely arms, and her
hands seemed to know exactly how to move with an instinct that
Margot knew she would never possess.

Yet Margot couldn't think of Lacey and her family without
thinking of Alex too. The girls would not be the only ones to suffer. He was facing a future without his wife. Margot closed her
eyes, picturing them together. Alex had a way of keeping Lacey in
his gaze, as if he could never get enough of her. On the Friday hike,
the day after Thanksgiving, he had shot Lacey a glance that in a
mere second said everything. Just after they had reached the over-

look point at the summit, Lacey had drunk from her water bottle and passed it to Alex. Her cheeks were pink from the climb, and her gesture, so quick and automatic, expressed their tacit understanding. Lacey knew Alex was thirsty, not just for the water but for her attention, to know that she was there. He smiled when he handed the bottle back to her, his breathing now level and calm, his thanks implicit. During that small exchange they had forgotten her illness.

When Margot glanced at them later, after they began the descent, Alex's expression was closed, his mouth tightly drawn. Following closely behind them, Margot saw him look over at Lacey periodically, watching her straight back, her steady gait, her feet avoiding a tree root, deftly stepping across rocks or fallen logs on their path. Had Alex been thinking about what his life would be like without Lacey?

And what about herself? The idyllic summers at Bow Lake were long past.

Once they had grown up, their lives had changed. Lacey had married Alex, and there was no room in a marriage for a full-time sister. Margot had accepted that. Over the years if she thought of Alex at all, it was in terms of Lacey. They were a couple, a unit. With the knowledge of Lacey's illness, everything had altered. Margot considered his life apart from Lacey. How would he cope with the uncertainty ahead?

Once she had finished college, Margot moved to New York, determined to seek a different life. More than anything, she dreamed of becoming an artist. She found a job as an assistant in an advertising agency and took painting classes on weekends. Eventually her college friends had scattered, and her last boyfriend, a sweet guy, tall and awkward in ways that reminded her of a younger Alex, left for law school in Oregon. He asked her to join him there, but she decided there was not enough between them to warrant a move all the way across the country.

Soon enough there had been other men in Margot's life. She

had friends from the office and went off after work to bars and restaurants with different groups. Some guys wanted sex on the first date; others were workaholics. No one seemed right for her. More and more she yearned for the easy, steady, adult kind of happiness that Alex and Lacey seemed to share. At times she wondered if she would ever meet the right person. During her fifth spring in New York she met Teddy at a restaurant not far from her office.

"Mind if I join you?" he asked.

Margot looked up. She was wedged in the corner of a tiny lunch place called Soups and Savories. Since there were only a dozen tables, customers were expected to share with strangers. "Sure," she said, moving her cream of carrot soup closer to her. The man taking the seat opposite her had neatly trimmed brown hair. She glanced at him again while reaching for her roll. He had bright blue eyes and a dimple in his chin. Good-looking, she thought, and what Granny Winkler would have called a "snappy dresser."

Margot took a bite of bread and bent over her paper.

"Real estate section?" he asked, pulling back the lid on his carton of soup.

So much for a peaceful lunch alone. She nodded and began to eat. The cream of carrot tasted too spicy. This was the soup she usually ordered, but the cook must have been experimenting with a new recipe. Now she'd have to find a new favorite. New Yorkers didn't like it when you couldn't make up your mind, holding up the hungry people in line, everyone with little time to spare.

"Are you looking for a new place?"

Margot stared at him directly and tried to be pleasant. This man, probably a few years older than she was, had an engaging smile. Something charismatic about him made it hard to look away. He wore a very crisp blue shirt and a striped red and silver tie. Preppy but cute, Lacey would have said.

"I am." It wasn't easy being polite and nonencouraging at the same time.

"Lost your roommates or just ready to live alone?"

Did she look like the kind of person who preferred to be alone? "I have my own place already," she said. "I'm actually looking to buy."

His eyebrows rose. "I see," he said. He had ordered the oven-roasted tomato. Maybe she should try that soup next.

"Finding an apartment is not easy," she said.

"Most people hope for problems like that."

"I know I'm lucky. Believe me, it's nothing I ever thought I'd be doing. My grandmother died and left me some money." Should she be telling this to a stranger? She could sense his interest, though it didn't feel threatening. "She stipulated that I use the money to buy a place to live. Otherwise, it goes into some charitable trust."

"Ah. An heiress," he said.

"Hardly. What seems like a lot of money to me doesn't go far around here." He ate his soup while she told him about her apartment search. Not a drop fell on his fancy tie. He looked like a guy who would keep his place neat, meticulous even. She glanced down. His shoes, brown leather European loafers, probably Italian, were shined. He must be older, closer to Alex and Lacey's age. "Even if I can afford the price of an apartment, I need to find something where I'll be able to pay the monthly maintenance."

"Where's your place now?"

"Second Avenue. A boring little box."

"You look like a prewar kind of girl." He smiled. Perfectly even white teeth.

He was flirting with her quite blatantly and Margot, who didn't usually fall for the suave types, was surprised that she didn't mind.

"What's that supposed to mean?" she asked.

He put down his spoon and leaned closer to her. "You care about your surroundings. You'd like some charm. An old building, a WBF."

"Wood-burning fireplace," she decoded. "I'm sure that's beyond my means. I do like older places. What really matters to me is light."

"See," he said. "I knew it."

In the next few minutes he told her about himself and his job in the art department of a nationally known advertising agency. She liked his name, Teddy Larkin. He spoke quickly, was lively and energetic. When she told him she wanted to become a painter he seemed impressed and said that the Frick was his favorite museum in New York. He asked her if she'd been to any of the new galleries in Chelsea. He made it easy for her to like him.

Over the next weeks they met for dinner, drinks, hung out at some clubs. Teddy seemed to know people everywhere. He liked going out, trying new places. Margot, who hadn't been dating anyone recently, rarely went out after work. Her favorite friend at the office had moved to Brooklyn to live with her boyfriend and she disappeared right after work. The woman who liked going to movies with Margot had started night courses toward her business degree and no longer had any free time. Margot couldn't paint at night and she was growing tired of lonely evenings. Teddy seemed to make it his job to show her how to have fun.

He also relished the real estate search. Margot had found it daunting to face real estate agents on her own, and together they went all over the city, checking on leads, investigating ads from the *Sunday Times*. Then, through a friend of a friend of his, they had found Margot an apartment—small, but with the charm he insisted on; no WBF, but a terrace. The monthly maintenance fee was manageable. Margot had a small legacy from her grandmother in addition to the money for the apartment that would help. She never told Teddy about that extra income. A month after she moved in, he proposed. Margot still wondered how it had happened so quickly.

Lacey and Alex had come to New York to see Margot's new apartment and meet Teddy. On that weekend visit Teddy, probably hoping to impress them, had reserved a table at Yaeger's, the most sought-after restaurant in New York. The meal was expensive, the dining room noisy, and the entire evening awkward. At first Teddy dominated the conversation with his tales of the art department where he worked. His enthusiasm for his job had sounded more like bragging to Margot that night. Lacey was quieter than usual, and Margot sensed that she wasn't taken in by Teddy's charms. Alex barely said a word, certainly nothing to Teddy. Alex seemed to avoid looking at Margot too, though later in the evening when she asked about their new house in New Castle and their plans for Bow Lake later in the summer, both he and Lacey acted more like themselves. Margot didn't have enough vacation to go to New Hampshire that year. She planned to stay in New York to paint the walls of her new place.

Now thinking back to her marriage, Margot tried to remember if she had ever really loved Teddy. She had felt a flutter of excitement each time she was with him, certainly during that first spring. He had beautiful manners, always opening doors for her, sliding across the seat of a taxi so she wouldn't have to, holding his big black umbrella over her in the rain. He even sent her postcards, sort of old-fashioned love notes of places he wanted to take her in the city—the Empire State Building, the sculpture garden at the Museum of Modern Art, cherry trees in bloom overlooking the reservoir in Central Park.

He paid attention to her at a time when no one else did. While vain about his clothes, he also loved to take her shopping to find the perfect dress in a certain shade of blue that he thought suited her. She remembered him saying, "You deserve the best, Margot. I want you to have beautiful things." And later, "God, how I want you, darling. I want you for my own. I want you all to myself." Eventually, she had learned that for Teddy it was all about wanting, and not about loving. Maybe his wanting the best for her, the little indulgences, his attention, was his way of loving. Maybe it was all he was capable of. Teddy, so handsome, living the fast life with his fast talk, had given her no time to listen, no time to think.

Lacey had come back that September to help Margot plan her wedding. "You've had quite the whirlwind romance," she said.

They were in Paris Blooms, a fancy Upper East Side florist, choosing flowers.

"We've been together for six months," Margot said.

"Together?" Lacey asked.

"Dating. And then together." Margot found herself blushing, as if she were an old-fashioned girl telling her sister she was having sex. Sex with Teddy wasn't quite what she had hoped for. Not yet. They always seemed to make love hurriedly, late at night, after drinking more than they should have. Teddy's drinking had started to bother her. She tried to sip one drink slowly, making it last all evening. Why did every night have to be like a party? Once she and Teddy were married, she assumed, they wouldn't go out as much. She looked forward to settling down.

"Six months isn't all that long," Lacey said.

"Lacey, I'm not rushing into this. You're beginning to sound like Dad used to. You're too young to act like my parent."

"Come on, Margot. It's not like that." Lacey paused, and bent to smell a large container of pink roses. "Perhaps I shouldn't say anything, but Alex has some reservations about Teddy."

"What's that supposed to mean?" Margot felt a forgotten anger rise in her chest.

"Well, I guess we were both surprised when you told us that you were getting married."

"I don't want to hear this. You have no right to judge me. And Alex even less so."

"I know that," Lacey said softly, reminding Margot that her own voice had grown loud. "At least think about waiting until next summer. We could have the wedding for you in New Castle. That way you could take your time."

"I'm not waiting," she said. "And what's Alex got to do with this? He's not my father either."

"Don't get upset," Lacey said. "We're concerned, that's all. All of a sudden you have Granny's money, you buy this apartment, and this guy is moving in and marrying you."

"It's not all of a sudden. I've seen Teddy every day for six months. Besides, he's been wonderful to me."

"There's a lot more to marriage than just being wonderful."

"Meaning?" Margot knew Lacey was right, but she didn't like being grilled or put on the defensive.

"Have you talked about children? Or money? Teddy seems to like fancy restaurants."

"We've talked about our future and that's our business."

Obviously hurt, Lacey looked away. Margot felt like a liar. There was a lot she and Teddy hadn't talked about. She hadn't wanted to spoil their time together. Teddy was the one who wanted to move ahead quickly, and Margot had agreed. There would be plenty of time to figure out their future. After five years alone, she was a little afraid of taking this leap and losing her independence, but like any scary thing, she had convinced herself, she would feel better when it was over with. Wasn't it normal to have doubts before making any big change? Teddy wanted her, she wanted to be married, and at the time it seemed like enough.

"Lacey," she said, trying to make amends, "don't worry about me. It's going to be fine. Teddy and I aren't like you and Alex. We're doing this our way."

"If you're sure," Lacey said, placing her hand on Margot's arm as if to soothe an overtired child. "If this is what you want, then we want it too."

Margot relaxed a little. It was hard to remain angry while surrounded by towering tropical blooms and the wafting sweetness of the giant bouquet of cream-colored lilies at her elbow. "It is what I want," she said, still upset about Alex's view of Teddy.

"Fine," Lacey said, pulling out a pad of paper. "Let's figure out the flowers and then let me take you to lunch."

They studied the vast buckets of blooms in rows at their feet. Margot hardly knew where to start. "What were Mom's favorite flowers?" she asked, calmer now but suddenly determined. Teddy was the right person, she told herself, and she would make this marriage work. She would prove Alex wrong.

"She loved peonies." Lacey smiled. "Pale pink ones. When we were little she had a huge clump of them growing beside the back door. Don't you remember?"

Margot shook her head, though she was glad to have this information about her mother. "Are peonies expensive?" Margot worried about what the wedding was going to cost. She and Teddy had agreed they should host the wedding themselves, and in the end they had decided on a noon service the first Saturday in October, followed by a lunch for forty guests at the Lancaster, an elegant hotel on the Upper East Side.

Neither of them earned much money, and Margot felt Teddy's taste often exceeded his salary. He was still a junior member of the design team at work, but he insisted that one day he'd be at the top, making buckets of money. At first, all Margot and Teddy had agreed upon was the size of the wedding. She wanted a lunch party, knowing it would cost less. He wanted an early-evening service followed by drinks at the Four Seasons. He finally conceded, provided she purchase the flowers at Paris Blooms.

"Peonies would be expensive here," Lacey said. "They're also out of season."

Margot pushed away the anxious feeling that had come more and more often over the last few weeks. No peonies, then. She had also promised Teddy no chrysanthemums, as they reminded him of death and he hated the smell.

"Ladies, may I help you?"

The florist, dressed entirely in black, as if to set herself apart from the flowers and plants, approached them. Margot looked at Lacey, who seemed to know just what to do. Within the next half hour they placed an order for the table arrangements, a bride's bouquet, and a few stems for Lacey to carry as Margot's only attendant.

A wedding was supposed to be a young woman's dream. Now,

in the throes of planning it, Margot was consumed with wedding jitters. Why did it all seem so complicated? Lacey and Alex had been married on a farm in New Hampshire that belonged to one of his mother's friends. Lacey had planned the entire weekend for 150 guests—complete with a square dance in the barn the night before the wedding and an exchange of vows in a hillside field, followed by dinner and dancing in a tent next to the barn. The apple trees had been in bloom and Lacey and Alex had wired sprays of flowering branches to the tent poles.

How had Lacey pulled it off? There hadn't been a drop of rain. The blackflies, usually in their prime in June, seemed to be off duty and the sky remained light for hours. When Lacey stood next to Alex repeating her vows, Margot had wanted to feel only joy for her sister, but instead she felt a profound sense of loss. Alex and Lacey were leaving their childhood behind, a time they had all shared. They were stepping into a grown-up world without her.

All Margot needed to do for her own wedding was to send the invitations and make a few phone calls. She wanted her wedding to be lovely, but she also wanted it to be over.

Margot's marriage ended less than a year after the ceremony. Lacey had stood by Margot on her wedding day and Lacey had been with her at the very end, when Margot needed her most. Even now, Margot didn't know how she would have survived without her sister.

"When is Teddy getting home?" Lacey had asked. It was July, nine months after Margot's wedding.

Margot sat crumpled on the sofa in her apartment, just home from the hospital. The doctors wouldn't discharge her without the company of another adult. Teddy was away on a fishing trip. She had called Lacey.

Margot began to shiver. "Sunday," she said.

Lacey got a blanket from the bedroom and covered her sister. Margot was still in shock. She hadn't felt well when Teddy left for his annual fishing trip with three other designers from the office.

When he didn't offer to give up the trip, she was secretly glad to have time on her own. Finally, when the pain in her abdomen was too severe to bear, she called in sick and went to her doctor.

The examination, the barrage of questions, the hospital stay and massive doses of antibiotics had swelled into one giant hurt. The diagnosis of pelvic inflammatory disease had shocked her. Teddy had given her a sexually transmitted infection.

"But it could have been from sexual activity before you got married," Lacey had suggested.

"Maybe. It hardly matters." Margot began to cry. "I don't think he's been faithful."

"What do you mean?"

"Some nights he just doesn't come home." Margot squeezed her eyes shut, trying not to think about it. "He calls and says he's going out for drinks after finishing a project." She drew in several ragged breaths. "Then he'll say it got too late and he didn't want to wake me, so he stayed the night with a friend."

"You're sure that means an affair?"

"I know. I just know." Teddy hadn't been able to look her in the eye on those strange, tense mornings when he'd come home to change before going to work. His clothes had been rumpled. Once, she'd noticed a rip by the top button of his shirt and she'd wondered if he had been in a fight. That sordid possibility had filled her with alarm. Margot could never tell Lacey that.

"Oh, Magsie, I'm so sorry." Lacey stroked Margot's forehead. Her touch was cool and soothing. Margot tried to shut out the pain by thinking of Bow Lake, the gentle lapping sound on the shore on a perfect July day. It helped to take her mind off this current disaster.

"You're going to be okay." Lacey's voice was soft. "You could try to get counseling. If you could talk to someone . . ."

"Never. It's way too late for that."

Lacey's hand stopped stroking. "What do you mean?"

"I think he's gay," Margot said. "Or maybe bi." All the months of pushing this possibility deep inside of her were over. A month into her marriage she had an odd feeling that something wasn't right. Initially, she had brushed off the small moments that had raised doubts later on. She had noticed one guy looking at Teddy in a bar in a way that seemed too intense, a cloying sort of attention that didn't seem appropriate. Once, a man asked for Teddy on the phone, but refused to leave a message, saying he must have made a mistake.

Telling this to Lacey made Margot feel sick and ashamed, as if Teddy's sexuality was somehow her fault. During one argument when he was furious that she didn't want to go out for a drink after dinner, he had called her a frump. Later, he bought her some sexy underwear as an apology, though he seemed less and less interested in sex. Margot hadn't known what to think.

"Oh, Margot." Lacey reached for Margot's hands and held them in hers.

"I've been tested for HIV," Margot said. "It's negative, but I'll need to be checked for the next few years to be in the clear."

Lacey bit her lip as if to keep from crying herself. "You'll be okay, Margot," she said. "I just know it."

"They told me I'll never be able to have children." Margot started to sob. "He's endangered my life, and now there's that too." She swallowed hard, hoping she would not be sick to her stomach. "What am I going to do when he gets back?"

"I'll be here. I won't leave you." Lacey handed Margot a tissue.

"This is so awful."

"I wish you'd said something sooner."

"I couldn't." She thought of Lacey and Alex, happy and in love, in that clean New England house, while her life with Teddy was so out of whack. Her own marriage reminded her now of looking into a fun house mirror, their reflections elongated and twisted, like something out of an Edvard Munch painting. She had done everything wrong.

"It's okay. We'll figure this out."

"I don't want him here. I want it over."

"You're certain?"

Margot nodded and pulled the blanket up to her chin.

Lacey stayed for the rest of the week. She coddled Margot, bringing her cold soups, cut-up fruit, icy sorbets, glasses of iced tea. She made phone calls: Margot's office to arrange for her sick days and follow-up doctor appointments. And she tracked down a divorce lawyer. Margot, still on high doses of medication, had been ordered to rest. Lacey saw to it that she had everything she needed. Though she had to sleep on the pull-out sofa in the living room and leave Alex behind in New Castle, Lacey never complained, saying it was good to have the one-on-one sister time they hadn't had in ages. Margot realized later that Lacey had been fighting the early weeks of morning sickness, newly pregnant with the twins, and had never said a word.

Lacey was with Margot at the dreaded moment when Teddy returned. The scene was as terrible as she had imagined it would be, Teddy denying everything, saying it was Margot who had probably infected him. His reaction made Margot all the more sure of her decision to end the marriage. Had he married her for the apartment or merely to have a wife at his side, like one of his possessions, just another silk tie or a pair of designer shoes? Had he ever loved her?

Lacey stepped in and fought for Margot when she didn't have the strength. After his initial protests, Teddy packed up his things and made arrangements for moving the rest. He agreed to a divorce. It almost embarrassed Margot how quickly he fled.

Lacey didn't have to teach in the summer, so she took Margot to Bow Lake to recover. Fortunately the cottage was available. The sisters owned the place jointly after their grandmother's death, but kept it rented except for the final few weeks of August, which were reserved for the family. The rental income paid for the maintenance and taxes.

The softness of the air, the shifting light on the water, the deep silence at night helped Margot to regain her physical strength, but something deep inside of her remained broken. At the end of her visit she was able to return to New York, move on to other jobs, and eventually go out with other men, but for a very long time she no longer cared about her art.

After her divorce she felt numb. Painting required her to look within herself, to search deep inside for the creative spark to bring color or line onto a canvas. In a sense, she had to keep her life simple, on the surface, out of range of any troubling emotion. Some days she could barely muster the creative energy to decide what to wear in the morning. Perhaps she was afraid of digging too deeply. Instead of thinking about her own art, she grew into the habit of looking at other people's work, finding solace in galleries and museums.

During those last summer days at the lake, Lacey never once reminded Margot of her prewedding jitters or their conversation in the flower shop. That week in August had been perfect. The sun glittered on the lake. The sky remained a cloudless, vibrant blue. They swam, paddled the canoe, and soaked up the sun on the dock. Alex hadn't come to Bow Lake that time either, because of work or a conscious decision to leave the sisters by themselves. Margot slept in their childhood bedroom—the room they called "up above"—and Lacey stayed in their grandmother's old room on the main floor. The walls were thin. Once, late at night when Lacey heard Margot crying, she climbed the stairs and got into her old bed across from Margot's.

"You can tell me anything," she had said.

Margot nodded, her warm tears spilling down into her ears. She couldn't seem to form words, but she felt better knowing that her sister was there, listening in the dark.

"Go ahead and cry. It will make you feel better."

Lacey didn't say anything else and gradually Margot's tears subsided. She pulled the cotton sheet, worn thin from years of use, around her shoulders, letting her body soften toward sleep. Later, before going back downstairs to bed, Lacey took Margot's hand and whispered, "Pinkie shake?"

They hooked fingers in their silent bond.

Now Margot looked down at her hands. Her pinkie finger was pale against the covers in the New York winter light. Where would she be today if Lacey hadn't been there when her life with Teddy had fallen apart? Now, almost two decades later, Lacey was the one facing a frightening future, an eventual silence closing in on her in this cruel twist of fate. Margot knew that she owed it to Lacey to help her in any way she could. She pushed back the covers and rose to face the day.

6

Tenterhooks: The hooks on a tenter, the framework for
stretching wool to prevent shrinkage after it has been washed.
When one is under tension, one is "on tenterhooks."

*A*lex passed through the automatic sliding doors into the lobby of the Rollinsford Retirement Community. An artificial white Christmas tree covered in pink and purple dangling balls stood on the center table, where a huge bouquet of silk flowers was usually placed. His mother would have hated the fake tree with its false sense of cheer. Edith George loved real things, and as long as she had lived in their family home in Newfields, she had decorated an enormous fir tree each Christmas.

The Rollinsford Retirement Community, nestled in the valley at the foot of Fulham Hill, was once the site of a local ski resort, with a T-bar and a rope tow, but the enterprise had folded in the early seventies. Alex and his older brother, Daniel, had skied there when they were boys. With the aging population and a string of warm winters, ski areas in New England had been suffering. Only the larger resorts with snow-making equipment managed to survive. Alex had been asked to take on one of those struggling businesses a few years ago to help it reorganize, but the family that owned the company lost heart and declared bankruptcy before he could begin the project.

Built twenty or so years ago, Rollinsford was thriving, and the owners were adding another string of cottages for independent living. Alex's mother, now eighty-one, lived in the Maple Tree wing, which was set aside for patients with Alzheimer's disease. Edith had moved to one of the regular apartments at Rollinsford after her husband died, but once she reached her late seventies she declined quickly. In the beginning she forgot appointments, and either went to dinner at the wrong time or missed it entirely. Once, she left a pot of soup on the stove and wandered outside to the community garden plot looking for some fresh herbs to add. Two hours later black smoke poured into the hallway while she dozed on a bench near the garden in the September sun.

It was now December. The community garden at Rollinsford had long been put to bed. Alex approached the receptionist sitting at the "welcome desk," as it was labeled.

"Mr. George, good to see you," Donna Peters said. She had worked at Rollinsford for as long as Edith had been there. While she was not a nurse, she wore a white hospital-style jacket over what appeared to be a pink jogging suit. Alex doubted that Donna, with her reading glasses on a jeweled string around her neck, ever did much jogging, but her kindness as she greeted all the regular visitors by name made him feel grateful to her and the others who worked here, for their steadfast goodwill. It had to be depressing to be among people all day long who were in the last stages of their lives, and most of them in a pretty miserable state.

"These are for you and the rest of the staff," Alex said, handing over a big box of cookies wrapped in holiday paper covered in green holly with red berries. Lacey had tucked a sprig of real holly under the red satin ribbon.

"Lacey is truly an angel," she said. "Her oatmeal raisin?"

He nodded, not bothering to explain that Lacey had made her usual recipe with sweetened cranberries for the holidays. Lacey came to see his mother whenever Alex traveled, and she often brought banana bread or her celebrated cookies, feeling that it was important to keep up the morale of the staff. Alex hoped these periodic gifts of baked goods made them all especially attentive to his mother.

"Your mother is looking real pretty," Donna said. "The hairdresser came in this week, gave her a cut and a perm."

"That's great," he said. "In time for Christmas." He thanked her and headed down the hallway to the wing with his mother's room. He pressed the special code to open the locked doors and felt his heart close down as the doors shut behind him.

A small bulletin board with photographs was placed outside each resident's room as a reminder that the person who lived here had once had a regular life, had been able to recognize friends and family, and had functioned fully in the world beyond the Maple Tree wing.

The largest photograph on Edith's bulletin board was of her and her husband, Spencer, on their fiftieth wedding anniversary. Lacey had hosted a dinner in their honor at the house in New Castle. Alex's dad, trim and erect in a dark suit, his gray hair still thick, had a determined expression, as if some part of his mind was at work fighting the cancer that would kill him the following year. Edith wore a navy wool dress and pearls.

Beside that picture was one of Alex's older brother, Daniel, and his Japanese wife, Noriko. They had not come to the party. Alex frowned, unable to shake a lingering annoyance. Daniel had been in the midst of completing his doctoral degree in bioengineering at the University of Washington when their dad was having trouble with the family company. If Alex hadn't gone to business school and stepped in to pick up the pieces, the company would have gone to ruin, leaving their mother with nothing. Yet his parents had always bragged about Daniel, the brilliant scientist who had the impressive degree and wrote books in his field. Daniel and Noriko rarely came east anymore. It amazed Alex how Daniel had slowly slipped out of his life, almost the way his mother had slipped away, her mind gone from her physical body. Now, in light of Lacey's problems, Alex hardly cared, and rarely thought of his brother.

There was also a photo of Toni and Wink on the dock at Bow Lake, when they were still little enough not to mind wearing matching red tank suits, and a picture of Lacey standing in her garden. Alex bent to look closer and swallowed. The photograph of Lacey must have been taken recently, as the newly planted peach tree in the picture looked much as it did now. Lacey had promised to bring Edith peaches once the tree had matured. Was something eating away at Lacey's brain even when she made the promise?

Alex tapped on the door. "Hey, Mom," he said, pushing it open. His mother sat in her wheelchair next to the window overlooking the woods. At this time of year it was a depressing view. Alex squatted on the floor in front of her. "It's me, Mom, Alex." Edith stared out the window as if he weren't there. "How about a little ride? I'll take you to the sunroom. Maybe we'll see that woodpecker again."

He stood and went behind her chair, releasing the brake and pushing her toward the hallway while keeping up his pointless banter. The woman seated in the wheelchair was his mother and yet she was not his mother. His mother had always worn her hair up on her head in what she had called a French twist. The staff had explained to him that it was easier for them to keep his mother's hair short. Lacey had suggested the permanents to give her some curls. His mother's clothes had changed, too. She now wore elastic-waist pants and loose polyester tops that required no ironing. Ease of care seemed to dictate everything that went on at Rollinsford. The staff didn't have time to wash woolen sweaters by hand or take tweed skirts to the dry cleaner.

More than anything, this woman he wheeled down the carpeted hall was not his mother because this face remained smooth and expressionless, unsmiling and vacant. Unlike his mother, who loved a good conversation and was adept at putting people at ease, this Edith George, the one who was now closed off from the world, never said a word.

"Oh, my, she's so easy," Donna Peters and others often said. "Our Mrs. George is no trouble at all." The staff constantly reminded him that the disease was hardest on the family, that his mother was not suffering. And today, as usual, she appeared content.

This was not the case for all the patients. The last time Wink and Toni had come with Alex to visit their grandmother, the woman across the hall from her had howled nonstop.

"Like a wolf," Wink had said.

"I hate it here," Toni had added, always direct. She spoke the truth.

Alex hated it here too, but here was where his mother had to be. It was the only way they could manage.

Alex steered the chair to the large picture window that overlooked a terrace surrounded by fir trees. The outdoor furniture had been brought inside, but two bird feeders on tall poles were kept filled, and the husks of scattered seed indicated the popularity of this destination for the hungry birds that stayed north in the winter. Did birds ever lose their ability to sing? Were there birds that remained silent? Could birds live with other birds if they lost their normal call? Alex pulled himself away from the bleak, empty patio.

"I think we missed their dinner hour," he said.

It was after four in the afternoon and nearly dark.

"Remember the year Dad took Daniel and me out to the woods to cut the Christmas tree?" Edith George said nothing. Her chin had lowered during the ride to the sunroom. Her eyes were closed. She may have been sleeping; he couldn't be sure.

Alex continued his reminiscence. "Do you remember that Christmas? You accused us of not having an artistic bone in our bodies. We came home with this lopsided specimen that you insisted would be impossible to decorate. That's when Daniel said we should 'trim' the tree, meaning prune it to make a good shape. Dad thought that was really funny. You refused that kind of trimming and made Dad put it outside the kitchen window. A tree for the birds, you said. We covered it with chains of popcorn. Lacey loves that story and she does that every year. One tree for the house, one for the birds. That's thanks to you, Mom."

A faint gong sounded in the hall. Lacey would be starting dinner and sipping tea while she chopped, stirred, and talked with the girls. Here, the residents ate at five. The nurses sounded the gong at four thirty to alert everyone to the coming meal, a pointless exercise in Alex's mind, as there was no one in this part of Rollinsford who had even the remotest idea what the gong meant. Yet how did he know that? Just because they didn't say anything didn't mean they had no thoughts at all in their minds.

"I think the birds have already eaten, Mom. That bell means it's time for you, too." Edith opened her eyes and for just a second she looked around as if mystified as to where she was. She raised a hand, bony and white, her wedding ring loose below the knuckle, and waved once, as if to tell him where he should go. Her lips pursed in displeasure, then slackened. Her face resumed its blank expression.

"Here we go, then," he said, trying to fill the void. With some relief, he guided the wheelchair out of the sunroom and down the dark hall to the dining room. Now he could leave her, walk to the parking lot, and start for home.

Tonight when he left the building tears stung his eyes. He reached his car, fumbled with his keys and swiped at the moisture. For the next few minutes he sat behind the wheel, incapable of moving, thankful for the darkness as tears he could not stop coursed down his face. As sad as his mother's condition was, she was an old woman. Lacey was too young to suffer. His body rocked with sobs. He moaned aloud and leaned back in his seat. There was no business plan for a tragedy. He had done his research—Lacey's illness was a venture that could not be saved. For the first time the loss felt devastating, as if his heart was being torn from his chest.

At fifty, Lacey was all the more beautiful to him. The few wrinkles around her eyes gave proof of the years of laughter they had shared. And talk. The best part of his day was lying close to her in the dark, just before sleep. They might have made love, or not, but they always exchanged a few final words. Sometimes they talked about the girls, his work, hers, something she had read, family. Lacey's voice made him feel like he was warming his hands near a fire or moving into a band of sunlight. He gravitated toward her, toward the soft curves of her body, toward the proximity of her voice. Once at Bow Lake, lying in bed in the early morning listening to the mourning doves, he was reminded of the sound of her words, a mellifluous tune softly entering the whorl of his ear.

Alex jerked his head against the headrest and thrust the key into the ignition. He turned it too far and the engine emitted a high-pitched squeal. *Goddamn*, he thought. *Goddamn. So goddamn unfair*. He turned the key more carefully the second time and put the car into gear.

Every December Margot went to the Metropolitan Museum to buy Lacey the annual spiral-bound desk calendar for Christmas. Each week of the year had two pages devoted to it, one page showing a reproduction of a painting from the museum's collections and the facing page divided into seven blocked spaces, one for each day of the week. Lacey saved these museum diaries from year to year. She marked down all the events that made up her family life—the usual ordinary dates: dentist appointments, car services, school activities for her daughters, dinner parties, family trips, visits from friends, birthdays. She would often add sticky notes to the pages when she needed more space to record the abundance of events. Sometimes she included the weather as if keeping a log: first frost, first snow of the year, rain again. Or other happenings in nature: huge storm, the Thomases' tree down, lilacs blooming, leaves need raking.

Margot was glad to give this book to her sister each year. In her early years in New York it was the only present she could afford.

This morning, while making the purchase, she was haunted by the thought that Lacey's ordinary jottings would not go on forever. How many more years would she be able to live her normal life? It had been three weeks since Thanksgiving. She and Lacey had exchanged phone calls, but fewer than usual. Lacey had sounded almost normal, but she never spoke in long sentences. Then again, most conversations were like that.

One time when Margot had telephoned, Alex had picked up. He had sounded impatient, distant, almost rude, saying that he would have Lacey call her back. This behavior was unlike him, yet Margot knew that he must worry about Lacey even more than she did. He was probably coping as best he could. Margot decided that she, like Alex, would have to go along day by day for now. Sometimes the knowledge of Lacey's illness made her incredibly sad, and she found it difficult to concentrate on her work. Other days, she would be swept into the busyness of her life and forget about her sister completely.

On this annual trip to the museum Margot always went to see the Angel Tree. After leaving the gift shop she wound back behind the medieval collections with the darkly woven tapestries, the jeweled swords, the polished armor standing poised as if the men were still inside ready to fight, and the supine bodies of knights on their cold stone sarcophagi. Eventually, she came upon the large fir tree decorated with hundreds and hundreds of crèche scenes. Carved in Italy, the exquisitely made figures were a powerful reminder of what the Christmas story was all about.

Margot's father had taken her and Lacey to see this tree once when they were little girls. Their mother was away that year—at a special hospital, their dad explained, where Mommy could rest until she was feeling better. No one said the word "alcoholic" back then, at least not to young girls. Margot was six years old, Lacey ten. Surely Lacey must have known what was going on. The trip to New York was a special treat and probably planned so they would not have to endure a Christmas at home without their mother.

They went to see the Rockettes at Radio City Music Hall and visited the Guggenheim Museum. Margot had started to run down the circular ramp and had to be reminded to be a big girl like Lacey. Their father had seemed lively, almost happy, during those few days, so unlike the silent man he was at home in Concord.

Margot stepped closer and studied the face of an angel hanging from a branch. It was a pleasure to have the tree all to herself for a few moments. The museum was quiet. Her father used to tell Margot and Lacey to keep quiet when their mother was having a "hard day." A hard day meant a day when she stayed in her room, the shades drawn, a cool compress on her head.

Margot's father took the train from Concord into Boston each day to his job at an insurance company. They lived in a modest clapboard house near the center of town. Grandmother Winkler, her father's mother, lived in a big old Colonial house five miles away on what had once been a farm. Granny Winkler was a tall, freckled woman who dressed in wraparound skirts and cardigan sweaters, and "ruled the roost," Margot and Lacey's mother used to say. Because of their mother's health, the girls often spent afternoons with their grandmother after school.

Helen Lacey, their mother, for whom Lacey was named, came from Charleston, South Carolina. Their father had met her in Virginia when they were both in college. While the other mothers in Concord volunteered in the historic museums, ran bake sales, carved pumpkins with their children, made costumes for school plays, and carpooled to sporting events, Margot and Lacey's mother rarely did anything, especially not on her bad days. When she was feeling well, she played the grand piano that took up most of the living room. Even now, the sound of piano music carried Margot back to the hours she spent lying on the floor by the piano listening to her mother play. Sadly, those memories of her mother before her "illness" became worse were few. Her other favorite memory was of her mother on the small glassed-in porch in the back of their house watering the geraniums that she tried to keep going through the winter. Margot could still picture her mother in the faded blue bathrobe that she called her wrapper, her lovely honey-colored hair hanging in a braid down her back. "You're my dearest one, Miss Maggie Mouse," she'd say, and her soft hand would sweep across Margot's forehead. Her mother always spoke slowly, her words like clouds floating across the sky on a summer afternoon.

When Lacey was in high school, their grandmother no longer picked the girls up from school. They were old enough now to manage at home, and Lacey wanted to be closer to activities in town: her volunteer job at the hospital, the school yearbook committee, painting sets for the school plays. While Lacey went to friends' houses or remained after school for her special clubs, Margot would stay in her room, knowing that above all she must keep quiet. There were fewer and fewer afternoons for her near the piano.

Gradually, more people found their way to this part of the museum. When Margot went back outside, it seemed as if all of New York and most of the people from the suburbs had spilled out onto the city streets. The sidewalks were teeming. She headed east and then north to Eighty-ninth Street. Since she had moved in with Oliver five years earlier, she rarely came over to the East Side and she decided to take the opportunity to check on her old apartment. She didn't have to be at work yet. Mario, her assistant, was covering at the gallery this morning and Carl had told Margot she could have the morning off.

A few minutes later she stepped into the vestibule of her old building and rummaged for her keys. She took the elevator upstairs and entered the apartment. A thick layer of dust covered everything. The day was overcast, but the light in the living room was good. Margot remembered Teddy telling her this space would be a great place for her to paint. Why was she thinking of him again now?

Margot tossed her coat on a chair and went to the far end of the living room, where French doors led to the tiny terrace. She looked out at the empty flowerpots and beyond at the rooftops punctuated with the ubiquitous water towers that marked the city skyline. Besides the living room there was one tiny bedroom, just big enough for a double bed and a chest of drawers, and next to it, a bathroom with a claw-footed tub. The kitchen was an alcove off the living room.

Oliver had urged Margot to sell this place, saying it didn't make sense to keep an apartment she didn't live in. She could afford the monthly maintenance fees by renting it out now and again. Oliver told her that the stock market would make a better investment, and yet she had put off selling it, partly to honor her grandmother's wishes and partly to have a refuge. She would never have been able to buy this apartment in the current market. More than just an investment, it reassured her to have her own place.

Margot turned her back to the terrace. Teddy had accused her of being messy. Once he was gone, she took great pleasure in surrounding herself with the objects she loved. She began going to the flea markets in the Village and picking up colorful bits and pieces that made her happy: the sage green pottery vase with the crack that faced the wall, the marble bust of a young girl, tortoiseshell boxes, a collection of walking sticks, hatboxes from department stores long out of business. And books—art books, books on botany because of their illustrations, and antique children's books. Some of these had come from Grandmother Winkler's library. Her shelves here were filled to overflowing.

That first year on her own after Teddy had been a struggle. She gave up her job at the advertising agency where she had worked and took a job as a receptionist in a gallery in Chelsea, glad to be in a different part of town from Teddy. That job paid poorly, and after another nonchallenging position, she met Carl Van Engen at a party given by her former painting teacher. Carl needed an assistant in his art gallery. He quickly saw that Margot was capable and eager to learn. To her delight, Carl became a mentor as well as a boss. She slowly became more confident, and she enjoyed getting involved in the art world, though she had never gone back to her own painting.

Margot remembered her failure to draw the bittersweet on the dresser at Lacey's house. She pulled one of her old sketchbooks off the shelf and leafed through until she reached a blank page. Sitting in the club chair by the window with the light at her back, she began to draw the other side of the room: the Victorian love seat, the maple end table, the lamp, its flowered shade, the footstool piled high with books that didn't fit on the shelves. She pretended that the apartment belonged to somebody else and tried to see this interior as an unknown landscape. Her hand was steadier today.

Later, when Margot looked up from her drawing, she found that the morning had slipped away. The zone. She had reached that magic state when the minutes and hours blurred. She looked down at the paper. Not bad, but not interesting either. Certainly nothing she could show Oliver. To him this would be like the scratching of a kindergartener. And yet he was always encouraging her to paint.

Teddy had liked the idea of Margot being an artist. He used to introduce her by saying, "My wife's an artist," never "Margot's an assistant to a nameless vice president in marketing." Yet he was never supportive of her work at home. Once she had been painting on a Sunday afternoon and she had left her tubes of paint out on the table. He had just gotten home from a movie and had lashed out at her: "Do you have to leave your crap out everywhere?"

Margot stood abruptly and tossed her pad on the floor. Why was she thinking again about Teddy? In the bright noon light the dusty apartment looked worse. She really needed to clean it and think about finding another renter. Maybe she should sell it, like Oliver suggested. He was right about so many things. No time to think about that now. She needed to get to work. She leaned over to retrieve the pad, and carried it to the table near the window. On second glance her drawing wasn't that bad. The perspective was accurate, the details convincing. Lacey's recent urging to resume painting sounded in her ears. Maybe she should come back and try again.

"I don't have the answer." Alex reached for the glass of Shipyard Ale on the table in front of him. The city of Portsmouth was the home of several microbreweries, each producing myriad beverages, some with names that didn't sound like beer at all.

Hugh had asked Alex another question about Lacey's diagnosis. They were having lunch together at the Port City Brew Pub the Friday before Christmas. Hugh was on winter break and he had come over to Portsmouth to shop for a present for Kate. When he arrived at the restaurant he told Alex about his triumphant find: a blue pottery vase from the same gallery where Lacey had sometimes shown her work. Once they were seated and Alex had told Hugh about Lacey, Hugh's body almost visibly deflated.

"I can't believe it," he said once more.

"Has Kate talked to Lacey recently?"

"Not that I know of. It's been wild on campus. You know, end-of-semester stuff. The usual. Kate would have said something if she knew about it."

"Lacey doesn't want anyone to know."

"Jesus." Hugh sat still, stunned by the news.

"Neither of you noticed a difference in her speech at Thanksgiving?"

"No. It surprised me when she didn't want to run in the Turkey Trot, but Kate told me Lacey was just busy, with the holidays coming up and trying to make weavings for the auction. She did say she thought Lacey seemed awfully stressed about college. Kind of crazy when your kids are great candidates for any school."

"At first I didn't want to believe the doctors," Alex said. "None of it makes sense. It just can't be happening to Lacey."

The pub was packed. A line of people had gathered at the door, hats pulled off, gloves shoved into pockets, the cold from their jackets dissolving into the heat of the dining crowd.

"You ready to order?" A heavyset waiter in khaki pants and a green polo shirt stood before them. A scrim of sweat across his forehead, he held his pencil poised to write.

Alex ordered a cheeseburger, not wanting to bother with the menu, and Hugh chose the Reuben sandwich, his usual. They had been meeting here for lunch periodically since the restaurant had opened a few years before.

The waiter nodded toward their glasses, now half empty. "Another round?"

"Sure," Hugh said.

Alex wasn't inclined to drink another beer. He planned to spend the rest of the afternoon in his office, catching up. He'd gone to Chicago for a few days to meet with a possible new client and had returned yesterday to a backlog of e-mails and phone messages. Still, with these crowds, lunch might be a while. He ordered a second beer.

It was a relief to talk to Hugh. He had to unload to someone. Lacey had always been the one he turned to, the person he could tell anything to. For the first time he couldn't automatically tell her what was on his mind. What if he upset her more? Could he share his fear without making hers worse? Would talking about her illness exacerbate her symptoms? He felt on tenterhooks every waking moment. Still, how could Hugh truly understand the circumstances they were in?

Alex stared down into his empty glass. "I saw my mom last week," he said.

"The same?" Hugh's forehead wrinkled in concern.

Alex nodded. "Yeah. I hate seeing her like this."

"That's rough."

"It could be like that for Lacey."

"What? You said it could be years."

"There's a difference already. She's talking less, like she's afraid of making mistakes."

The waiter returned with two more beers. Hugh pushed his empty away and took a sip from the new one.

"She doesn't want the girls to know," Alex said. "She'd be furious if she knew I was telling you. I'm also trying to decide about this next job."

"Chicago?"

"It's a fertilizer business. Called Wingate. The usual problems with a family company—the patriarch who's too old, trying to micromanage, and in this case the idiot cousins they can't fire. Some environmental issues, too. I'm going to do a proposal. It's similar to a situation I dealt with in Louisville."

"Keeping busy is good."

"Yeah. I need it. Haven't had a big client lately. College tuitions for the twins. Anyway, with a reorganization this company could be worth a bundle. Some of the family are interested in selling and I'd earn a good cut."

"Sounds like a good deal," Hugh said.

"It would mean being gone a lot. I worry about Lacey."

"Kate and I are around. We'd check on her. We both have lighter loads during the winter trimester."

"She won't want checking on. You don't know about this. Remember?"

Selfishly, Alex wanted the job in Chicago. He longed to put his mind and all his energy into a new project. Work, the pull of it, could distance him from this emotional quagmire. He thought guiltily of a hotel room, where at least some of the time he could escape, like he did on his bike. He hated himself for even thinking that way.

The waiter appeared with their lunch. Hugh's Reuben steamed on the chunky white china plate, cheese oozing out the sides. Alex squeezed a hearty dollop of ketchup onto his hamburger. The cheese on top remained congealed in an orange blob, not having been under the broiler long enough. When he bit into the burger, he felt the juices dripping down his chin. He grabbed his napkin. "So much for well done," he said.

"Send it back," Hugh said.

"It doesn't matter."

"I think you need to take the Chicago job. Move forward."

Alex sighed heavily and bit into the opposite edge of his cheeseburger. It was underdone and tasted off. He poured on more ketchup.

Hugh went on. "I think Wink and Toni need to know. I mean, if anything should happen."

Alex put his burger down and pushed his plate away. "Lacey's adamant. She doesn't want to tell them."

"What if they notice something while you're away?"

"Lacey refuses." Still hungry, he pulled his plate back and grabbed a French fry. "It's so ironic. Lacey has always stressed the importance of telling the truth. She's totally honest with the girls. This is so unlike her."

Hugh nodded and started on the second half of his sandwich. "Maybe . . ." He ate for a moment, then wiped his mouth. "Get Margot involved."

A memory of Margot early that morning in the kitchen at Thanksgiving shot into Alex's mind. For one quick moment she had been so eerily like Lacey; she had caught him off guard. Yet Margot wasn't anything like Lacey. He thought of the many times they had spent together at Bow Lake. He'd thought he knew everything about her then. And then there had been that one summer. He shook his head. That was ancient history. What did he know now? He shifted in his chair. The crowded restaurant had become too warm, steaming over the windows facing the street. The man behind him got up, knocking into Alex's chair.

"See what Margot says," Hugh went on. "She might convince Lacey it would be better to tell the girls. Margot's part of your family, don't forget."

Alex said nothing, thinking deeply of the past.

"Seriously," Hugh said, "she'd do anything for you."

7

Threading hook: Long skinny hook for threading warp.

The digital clock read 2:17. Alex was awake. Lacey slept deeply, her back to him, with barely a rising and falling of breath. Before he could think, a wave of nausea hit him hard. Saliva rushed into his mouth, and not even feeling the sharp cold when his feet hit the floor, he stumbled to the bathroom. He was violently sick. The hideous noise of his body turning on him roared in his ears. Thinking he was finished, he splashed water on his face and clutched the edge of the sink with a shaking hand. The cool porcelain made him shiver. He felt awful.

He vomited a second time, followed by heaving over and over, as if a demon inhabited his body. His stomach felt wrung out, aching. The hard tile floor, icy on his knees, seemed to rise up before him. A moment later he felt a hand softly stroking his shoulder and then another on the back of his head.

"Finished?" Lacey asked softly.

He let out a groan, not knowing if he would be able to stand.

"Wait," she said.

He heard water gush into the sink. Lacey placed a warm face-cloth on his forehead, then handed him a tissue. He released one hand from the toilet bowl and wiped his nose. "Oh, God." His voice came out as a croak. Lacey flushed the toilet.

"Okay to stand?" she asked.

"Yeah, I think." He rose slowly to his feet.

"Lean on me," she said. "Let's get you . . . back to bed."

Alex groaned again. "I'm okay," he said, pulling away from her. The walls of their bedroom seemed tilted. He staggered ahead.

"Come on," she said. "Let me help you."

Feeling his knees jellylike beneath him, he put his arm across her shoulders. The warmth of her body felt solid and safe.

"That's better," she said.

They made their way slowly toward the bed. He was like an old man, feeble and alarmingly helpless. His head was spinning. One day Lacey would need him in this very way, he knew. They reached the bed. Lacey handed him another tissue from the nightstand. His face was wet. He blew his nose.

"My poor love," she said.

"The cheeseburger at lunch . . ." He started to explain. He felt his weight lurch and sank down onto the mattress.

Lacey guided his head onto the pillows. She pressed her warm hand against his lips. "Don't try to talk," she said. "You're going to be okay."

On Christmas morning Margot was surprised to find herself awake before Oliver. The city was quiet. No traffic, no garbage trucks hurtling down the streets below. Perhaps it was the wind that had awakened her, a persistent whistle even though the windows were closed tight. She slipped out from under the covers and crept down the hall. She went to the closet near the front door and removed the large wrapped box she had hidden in back. After struggling to lift it, she placed it on the coffee table and fluffed up the bow. Next to it she placed her other gift for Oliver: a book wrapped by the shopkeeper in an elegant red Florentine paper.

While waiting for water to boil for her tea, she went to the front window and looked out. The wind from the west was heavy and relentless and the Hudson River, studded with whitecaps, looked forbidding. A river view wasn't always agreeable. Today the sight of the water was a reminder of the many cold, bleak days ahead. It would be months before crisp white sails would cut across blue water under a hot summer sun. She wondered how Lacey would be by summer.

A door creaked behind her. She turned. Oliver, his hair wild from sleep, wandered in from the bedroom.

"You're up early, baby," he said.

"I think it's the wind. I never would have made it as a pioneer." She smiled. "The noise of it makes me crazy."

Oliver came over to her and kissed the top of her head. He wore flannel pajama bottoms and a faded navy T-shirt. "Let me get the coffee started," he said, and headed toward the kitchen. "Do you want your tea now?"

"I'll come with you and fix it," she said. "Then let's do presents, okay?"

Margot loved giving presents. She put a lot of thought into finding just the right gift for each person. Gifts for her twin nieces were easy, always something hip to wear or some accessory that was all the rage. A few weeks ago Mario had gone shopping with her during lunch. He suggested a wonderful skinny cashmere sweater in pale blue, with sleeves trimmed in a fuzzy fringe, for Wink. For Toni, he urged her to buy a funky yellow leather handbag with multiple zippered pockets and silver studs. Margot took his advice, knowing he was good at spotting fashionable items and, thanks to his girlfriend, he knew all the hip shops in SoHo. For Lacey she chose a sterling silver letter opener with a green malachite handle. It would be the perfect color against her lavender desktop. For Alex she bought a leather-bound bike log where he could record his trip routes and mileage.

Oliver had had a mostly secular upbringing. His mother was

a lapsed Catholic of Italian origin and his father was Jewish. His family celebrated some of the Jewish holidays, as well as putting up a Christmas tree and exchanging gifts on December 25. Margot and Oliver were driving to Scarsdale later that afternoon for an annual family open house that his sister hosted every year now that their father was dead and their mother too old to give the party.

Margot carried her tea to the living room and suggested they make omelets later. Oliver set his mug of coffee on the end table and went into the bedroom. He emerged a moment later with a mysterious bag of his own.

"You first," she insisted.

"I'll start with the big one," he said. He pulled the bow and ripped off the paper in large handfuls.

"Great," he said, eyeing the printed picture of the coffeemaker. "The old one is about to give out."

"It grinds the beans, too. All in one."

Oliver thanked her and seemed pleased with her purchase.

"This one is the real gift," she said, handing him the costly volume she had found earlier that fall.

This time he took more time unwrapping, first undoing the ribbon and turning the package over to slide his finger under the tape, and then slipping off the paper.

"A book of Greek myths?" Oliver looked puzzled by her choice. He opened the cover and drew in his breath. "God, these are gorgeous." He carefully turned the pages. It was a collection of myths accompanied by hand-tinted engravings. The detail of the illustrations had amazed Margot when she discovered the book on the art table in a bookstore specializing in antique books.

"It's really about the illustrations," Margot said, suddenly worried that this present was not as fine as she had previously thought. "It was published in the 1930s."

Oliver continued to leaf through the book. "Mags, these are extraordinary. Look, here's Pandora before she opens the box. All the troubles on earth locked inside." He pulled her toward him on the sofa and kissed her. "You're a love. This is great."

She looked down at the page he had opened to. Pandora, her head bent, with a graceful hand luring the viewer's eye to the flowers at her feet, was oblivious to the evils inside. Curiosity, her fatal flaw, would entice her to open the box, forever changing the world. Margot couldn't help but think that for her, the box had already been opened. It opened on the day Lacey told her about her illness. As much as Margot wished it, she could never alter the news that was reshaping their lives.

"Now your turn," he said. He reached for the bag and pulled out a gold box tied with an elaborate silver bow. He put the box on the table in front of her.

"That's beautiful, Oliver. Wait. I'll save it for last. I'll open Lacey's present first." Lacey's gift, a white box with a large red bow, had been on the coffee table all week. The sight of it and the red poinsettias Margot had purchased from the Korean deli on Broadway had made the apartment look festive. Oliver had strung tiny gold lights in the ficus tree near the window, the extent of their holiday decorations.

Margot pulled off the ribbon and handed Oliver the paper to fold for the recycling bin. She lifted the lid of the box and discovered a mohair throw that Lacey had woven in warm colors—shades of red, gold, pink—giving it the overall look of a persimmon. A deep purple strand moved through the pattern like a wave. This piece was very different from the quiet set of white place mats that Lacey had been working on at Thanksgiving.

Margot pulled the throw into her arms and began to cry. First for the beauty of it, and then for the item itself, so suitable, so useful. It was as if Lacey had just come into the room, and stood beside her, a silent presence. Margot fingered the soft fibers and pulled it to her face. It smelled of cloves or something not exactly sweet, but homey. Like Lacey, she thought. She spread it over her lap and was immediately warmer.

"Don't cry," Oliver said. "Lacey would want you to be happy. It's beautiful."

Margot nodded and felt the soft woven material again.

"Come on, baby," Oliver said. "Open mine." He handed her the golden package.

Margot unwrapped it carefully, not to save the paper but to gain a moment to compose herself. "Oh," she breathed when she caught sight of the burgundy-colored box. Inside on a bed of white satin was a necklace, a choker of pale turquoise stones. The clasp was shaped like a blossom, the petals made of tiny pearls.

"It's beautiful." She lifted the necklace from the box. "It's too nice. Oliver, it's too much. Really."

"Nothing's too much for you. Let me help you put it on." He reached for the necklace and unfastening the clasp, lowered it around her neck. It felt light, hardly there.

Margot went to the mirror by the dining table. The blue-green stones were the color of her eyes. It would be lovely inside the neck of a blouse or, even better, just the right thing to wear with some of her simple V-neck sweaters. "It's perfect," she said.

"You're perfect," he said, coming up behind her and circling her waist with his hands.

"Hardly." She turned and buried her face in his chest.

He paused for a moment. "I wish you'd let me give you a ring."

She pulled back. "You mean . . ."

"I want you for always, Mags. Let's get married this spring. We've been so happy. Why not make it forever?"

Margot leaned into Oliver again. His chest was warm, his arms felt solid around her. Forever. Why wouldn't she want this kind of happiness forever? Her heart felt light and joyous at the possibility. Oliver loved her. She loved him. They had moved beyond the first years of discovery and delight in getting to know each other. Their relationship, even with its ups and downs, his temper, her own tendency to hold back, had grown richer, in a sense more complete. She looked up at him. "You mean a wedding?"

"I believe that's how it's done."

She remembered Lacey coming to New York to help her plan her wedding with Teddy. Her heart tightened, an involuntary pinch.

"But you always said you never wanted to remarry. We both agreed. Remember?"

"I feel different now."

Margot scanned his face as if trying to see what had changed. Early in their relationship Oliver had told her that his work was everything to him. He stated clearly that art came first. He explained that his marriage to Linda was like having a weight placed on him, dulling his creative drive and sucking all his energy.

Margot had been relieved. Her marriage to Teddy had been such a disaster. More than anything she didn't want to make another mistake. She knew she would never have what Lacey had—safe, predictable, and seemingly perfect. Why even strive for that?

After Teddy was gone Margot savored the sense of freedom, of not having to answer to anyone. The city was a good place to start over. She loved her work, being part of the New York art world, and getting to know other artists, Oliver's friends. No one asked her how many children she had, or if she ever planned to marry. New York was a city where people admired independence, personal choices, creativity. Individuality mattered. No one had to fit into a mold—you could be unique, like a modern painting not requiring a frame.

"What do you mean you feel different?" she asked, wondering what might have brought on this sudden desire to marry.

"I don't know. I guess I'm ready for a change. I've started thinking more about the future. I want you with me, Mags."

"I'm glad." She smiled. "It's just that now . . . well, things aren't the same."

"What do you mean?" His hands slid away.

Margot touched the necklace at her throat. It had warmed to her skin. She went back to the couch.

He followed and asked more forcefully, "What's not the same?" He sat beside her. "You do love me? Has that changed?"

"Of course it hasn't changed." She picked up Lacey's gift, spreading the throw across her lap. Her love for Oliver hadn't changed, but her life had. How she longed to fall into the happiness he offered. She should be crying tears of joy. She should be calling Lacey to tell her the good news. Lacey. Instead, Margot's heart stubbornly refused to lift. It was as if she couldn't make room for happiness now. She tried to explain. "It just doesn't seem to be the time for this." She reached up and smoothed back a lock of Oliver's hair. "I don't know what will happen with Lacey. Everything is so up in the air."

"Getting married isn't about Lacey," he said. "It's about us. We can't predict what will happen to her, but we should be together no matter what."

"We are together," she said.

"That's not what I mean." He shifted away from her and folded his arms across his chest.

"Oliver, please."

"I thought you'd be happy. Is it so terrible to want to spend my life with you—to want to make our relationship permanent?"

"I am happy," she said. Was she? Oliver's intentions were clear and good. What was the matter with her? She couldn't expect him to understand what she couldn't understand herself. Terrible things happened in life. Her mother had been a miserable alcoholic, but Margot had survived. Why did she have to lose Lacey too? This illness was so unfair. She began to cry again. Useless tears, yet she couldn't stop them.

"Come on." Oliver's voice had taken on an edge. "Stop making yourself miserable. We love each other." He reached across and took her hand. His expression softened. "I'm really sorry that Lacey's sick, but it doesn't have to ruin our future together."

"I just don't know," she said.

"Know what?"

The phone rang. Margot looked up at the clock. It was just after nine. Oliver went to the phone and checked the caller ID. "Lacey," he said.

Margot shook her head, indicating she was unable to talk. Oliver let the rings continue, loud and intrusive until the machine clicked on and Lacey's voice filled the room.

"Merry Christmas." Her voice was bright, pitched with excitement. "Wonderful presents. Love the letter opener." An uneasy laugh. "I'll call . . . tonight?" There was a pause. Other voices in the background filled the void. "Love you," she said. The line clicked dead.

Oliver didn't come back to the couch but went across the room and stared out at the river. "I'm sorry about Lacey," he said softly. "You know that."

"Let's just get through the winter," Margot said, pushing the throw aside and going to stand next to him. "I'm sure we'll all get more used to the situation. We'll find ways to cope. Maybe Lacey won't get any worse." She leaned against him. "I love you, Oliver." She felt better saying this. "In the spring let's talk about getting married." She kissed him lightly on the mouth.

"Does that mean yes?"

Margot kissed him again. "For now let's just keep loving each other." She had no idea what the spring would bring.

Oliver turned his collar up against the wind. He was walking to the garage where he kept his car, a nameless business on 108th Street between Columbus and Amsterdam avenues. He had yet to figure out what language the garage attendants spoke. The monthly fee was a bargain, but they only took cash. When he returned with the car, Margot would meet him in front of their building and they would drive out to Scarsdale for the open house. His mother had sold the house he grew up in, and his sister, Nancy, and her family lived a few streets away, but returning to the town always reminded him of going home. Even after all these years, it was never easy.

He crossed Broadway. Hunks of paper, plastic, small bits of unrecognizable debris soared along in the brisk wind. Anything near the top of the wire mesh trash containers on the streets lifted off in the gusts of cold air. Useless. He imagined the taste of grit in his mouth.

Oliver had come home from college one winter break to tell his parents that he had won the Walter Newman Arts Award, given to a student showing exceptional promise in painting. The award came with a stipend to study at the Castello Brunelli, an arts colony in the hills outside of Rome, for three months of the summer.

He had arrived in Scarsdale the day of his parents' holiday open house, having stayed on at college for a few days into the break to finish a painting for a class on perspective. His pursuing a degree in fine arts had greatly disappointed his father. Sam Levin had wanted Oliver to follow in his footsteps and attend the Wharton School for his MBA after getting his undergraduate degree at the University of Pennsylvania. Oliver had been a strong student, and though he was accepted at Penn, he chose to go to the Rhode Island School of Design.

Oliver's concession to his father was to promise to work summers for his uncle's investment company in New York. The summer job involved doing all the boring work that the secretaries hated, but after work and during his lunch hour Oliver visited galleries and museums, soaking up art whenever he could.

He had come home excited about telling his parents the good news. The house was full of people. It was early evening. He threw his duffel into the back hall off the kitchen and went in search of his parents. He had gone to the trouble to wear a sport coat, knowing that his long hair, which he wore in a ponytail, was already a source of controversy. He found his dad in the den talking to a neighbor.

As soon as they were alone Oliver told his dad about the award.

"What about your job with Uncle Stu?"

"He doesn't need me. Besides, another summer filing documents is a total waste."

"A waste? That's what you think? And you think hanging out with a bunch of would-be artists in Rome all summer isn't a waste?"

"It's not just the experience of working with the artists there, Dad. This is something that really matters for my future." Oliver stared at his dad. His father was a lawyer in New York who dealt with enormous financial transactions. He was a responsible man. Work was about providing for your family. His father accepted the daily grind of riding the train to the city, hauling yourself up into an office tower, and working at a desk until it was well past dark, only to repeat the process in reverse—the steady pattern that meant a mortgage paid on time, a nice home for your wife, a good education for your children.

"So you think you're going to be an artist?" Sam Levin's shoulders dropped. "Where's the security in that?" Oliver knew that in his father's mind the four years at RISD were for getting the art enthusiasm out of his system, as if Oliver's passion were an adolescent phase that he had to work through before turning to business. His dad leaned against the edge of his desk as if he needed support.

"This prize is an honor, Dad. I thought you'd be pleased."

His father pressed his lips together. Art didn't matter to him. There were no real paintings in their house, only a few reproductions his mother had bought, and those were chosen to match the furniture, like the ship painting that hung above the blue sofa in the living room. All tasteful and unremarkable. Oliver shifted his weight from foot to foot, waiting for his father to speak.

"Let's drop it for now," his father said at last.

"Dad, I'm an artist. Nothing will change that." Oliver had to paint. It was that simple. It wasn't like working for a bank or an insurance agency. It wasn't a job. It was more than a career. Art had chosen him and not the other way around. He knew he faced a life fraught with instability.

His father shook his head. "I need to get back to our guests." He walked out of the room, leaving Oliver behind. If only his dad had argued with him and given him the chance to fight back. Once alone in the den, Oliver sank down onto the sofa and buried his face in his hands. His father's distance made him strangely furious as well as sad. Nothing Oliver did in the years following—stellar reviews, one-man shows, a plum job teaching at Columbia—nothing seemed to please his dad or change his opinion of his son.

Now Oliver stopped at the corner, waiting for the light to change. Would his father finally consider him a success if he were alive today? A bus with a few lone passengers whipped by. Hannah Greene and June Wallace had come to his studio a couple of days ago. He'd shown them the two canvases he'd finished. They had been cordial and admiring, but they seemed pressed for time, making the excuse of the holiday rush. Oliver hadn't sold a major painting in almost a year.

He walked the final blocks to the garage. He mustn't let his mood spoil the entire day. And Margot. He needed to remember what she was going through with Lacey. A single piece of newspaper blew across his path, lifting in the wind.

"You're looking glum," Margot said as she got into the car. She waved briefly at Hector, the doorman. "Your mom will be glad to see you," she said. "And I promise, no more tears today." She reached across the seat and touched his arm.

Looking reluctant, Oliver turned onto the West Side Highway heading north. The Hudson River was almost black in the waning light. It was four in the afternoon. Margot was looking forward to seeing Oliver's sister. She had three of Oliver's paintings in her house and she loved to dote on her brother, "the famous artist."

Oliver's marriage proposal had caught Margot off guard. Like the beautiful necklace she had put carefully away in the velvet box, she tucked his proposal away in some part of her heart, to bring out later at an easier time. Lacey's illness and her family were what mattered now.

Margot's happiest Christmas memories were of times she'd spent with Lacey's family in New Castle. Lacey saw to every detail, making sure no annual ritual was forgotten, that everyone around her was looked after and loved. Lacey had had to learn how to do this early in her life.

One Christmas in Concord when they were still girls, their mother had become increasingly despondent as the holiday grew closer. There were no signs of festivities ahead. No decorations, no apparent shopping trips for surprises, no writing of cards. Margot, about ten at the time, remembered thinking it odd how the unread mail piled up on the hall table. Her father carried the mail to his desk on the weekend and must have read the cards and paid the bills and dealt with whatever was necessary. That Christmas Eve Margot's mother said she must be getting the flu and went up to bed shortly after lunch. A roast beef, frozen solid on the kitchen counter, needed somehow to be thawed and cooked. Grandmother Winkler was coming to dinner.

Lacey, then fourteen, had told their dad not to worry. With Girl Scout–like practicality and good cheer, she took *The Joy of Cooking* from the shelf and busied herself with the preparation of Christmas Eve dinner. Margot set the table and went up to her room to make elaborate place cards from construction paper, ribbon, and glitter.

All afternoon their mother's bedroom door remained shut. At five their father went to pick up his mother. Granny Winkler arrived with presents for her granddaughters and somehow they all muddled along, no one speaking of Helen, who remained behind closed doors. The roast beef was stringy and tough, the mashed potatoes lumpy, and the peas almost mush. Still, everyone praised Lacey for the wonderful meal. Fortunately, their grandmother had brought along her favorite dessert, sticky toffee pudding, the signature dish that her own mother used to make.

Much later that evening, after their dad had taken Granny Winkler home, he returned to find both daughters doing the dishes. Margot stood at the sink while Lacey dried. Hot, soapy water trickled down Margot's arms. She reached into the water to remove one of the crystal water goblets and blew at the puff of bubbles on the rim of the glass. The bubbles did not lift off into the air as she had hoped. Instead, as she raised the glass higher to blow again, it slipped from her hand and crashed onto the stone kitchen floor.

"For God's sake!" her father yelled. "This isn't helping." He pulled a terrified Margot away from the sink and sent her upstairs to bed.

Margot lay in bed sobbing at the injustice of her father's rebuke. Her father was angry, her mother was sick, and there was no Christmas tree that year. She cried from being scolded, from being sent to bed, from knowing that there might not even be presents in the morning. Then, hopeless and alone in the dark, she heard the door of her room open. Lacey appeared and tiptoed over to her bed. She stroked her little sister's back and said, "There, there, it's okay, Magsie. I love you. You'll always have me."

Margot understood now the stress her father must have endured. His lovely Helen Lacey, the soft-spoken girl from South Carolina, suffered from alcoholism, maybe depression as well, and there seemed to be nothing he could do to help her. During those years Phil Winkler must have been angry at his wife, at his predicament, at the entire world.

Many years later, when Margot and Lacey talked about their mother and some of the difficult times, Lacey made light of it, saying that it hadn't been as bad as all that. Lacey claimed she had no recollection of that particular Christmas Eve meal.

Oliver pulled the car into the driveway of his sister's house, a large stone Tudor, undoubtedly worth a lot with its big lawn, stately trees, and proximity to the city. Nancy and her husband, Ken, had bought their home when their two children were small and they had watched their kids grow up here. Their sons, one still in college, the other in business school, would have made Oliver's father, their grandfather, proud. They were nice young men, too. As Oliver and Margot walked up to the door, Oliver thought about what it might be like to have sons, throwing a ball around on the lawn and going to sporting events.

Coming here, to the town where he had grown up, always filled him with doubts. Would he be any happier now if he'd gone into business, lived in Scarsdale, had a secure life? He missed Jenna today. His daughter was in Phoenix for a few days with her mother, the annual reminder of a painful divorce.

Margot pressed the bell. A moment later, Nancy was pulling her into her arms.

"Welcome, you two." Nancy smiled and kissed Oliver on the cheek. Her dark hair was thick and springy, cut in short curls and graying slightly, like her brother's.

Margot greeted Nancy warmly and handed her the bag of fancy foods that they brought every year as a gift, including a box of Nancy's favorite chocolates. "Not a painting for me this year?" she joked, looking beyond them as if they might have carried a big wrapped present with them. "College tuitions are draining us. We can't afford any more of your masterpieces."

"Hang in there," Oliver said. "My prices may plummet any day."

Margot gave him a quick look, more like a warning. They took off their coats and Nancy signaled for one of the helpers hired for the party to come and take their belongings upstairs.

"Mom's in the living room," Nancy said. "Stuck on the sofa next to Mrs. Keller. Let me warn you, she's gotten a bit dotty. No, not Mom," she added, as if sensing her brother's alarm. "Ken and the boys are in the family room. They're taking turns tending bar, if you want something. The servers are passing wine and eggnog."

Margot thanked Nancy and took Oliver's hand. They wove through the group of neighbors and friends, making their way across the living room toward Oliver's mother. Margot accepted a glass of wine from one of the servers on their way, but Oliver decided to wait.

"I was wondering where you were," Janet Levin said. She smiled up at her son as he bent and kissed her cheek. Her hair, brushed and sprayed into an immaculate bubble, tickled his face as he drew back.

"You look great, Mom."

"That's what everyone tells old ladies." Janet laughed and reached for Margot's hand. "I'm so glad you're here," she said. "I hope my boy is behaving."

"So good to see you," Margot said. "Happy holidays."

"You remember my neighbor Mrs. Keller? You may have met her here last year."

They both turned toward to the small old lady seated next to his mother. She had wispy, unruly hair and she wore a misbuttoned cashmere sweater with a scattering of stains across the front.

"Why, I remember your son, Janet. The artist, the famous one."

"Good to see you, Mrs. Keller." Oliver reached for her hand but saw she was twisting a tissue in her lap. He pulled back.

"This must be your wife." Mrs. Keller smiled up at Margot.

Oliver glanced at his mother. Margot reached down and took the old lady's hand.

"Mrs. Keller, I'm Margot Winkler. Oliver and I live in the city."

"Do you have boys? Nancy has these two handsome boys."

Oliver wanted to say yes, they had six illegitimate kids stashed in their apartment, but he didn't think she would get the joke. Unlike him, his mother seemed to find her neighbor's inquiries mildly entertaining.

"Mom," he said, "would you like me to bring you a drink or some food?"

"No, darling. I've already had plenty. I want to hear about

what you're showing next." She turned to her neighbor. "Oliver shows in the best galleries in New York."

Margot handed Oliver her wine. "I'm going to go say hello to Ken and the boys." She gave him an indulgent smile and slipped away before he could stop her.

Oliver looked once again at his mother. She seemed to be studying him carefully, as if looking for signs that something was wrong. Janet Levin was a woman who didn't miss much.

Alex had thought they were going to make it through Christmas Day without a glitch until Wink pulled him aside as he was turning out the lights before going up to bed.

"Dad, can we talk a minute?"

He stepped into the hall. "Sure, Winky, what's up?"

"I think something's wrong with Mom."

"What do you mean?" They both listened as Toni's footsteps clattered up the stairs. Lacey had gone up to bed a few minutes before.

"She seems so scattered these days."

"Wink, it's the holidays. Mom's been busy. You know that."

"They say women get forgetful because of menopause." Wink looked away on saying that word. "But she doesn't really forget stuff. It's more like her mind gets jumbled when she's trying to talk."

Alex felt his chest tighten. "Mom's exhausted," he said. He turned and switched off the downstairs hall light, leaving them in near dark. "We're all tired. Let's get to bed."

"But, Dad—" She leaned against the banister.

"Not now, sweetie. I'm beat too." He kissed her on the cheek, a dismissal.

Wink shrugged and went on up to her room.

When Alex went upstairs Lacey was in bed reading. The book, a history of textiles that Kate had given her for Christmas, was propped against her knees. He pulled the curtains at the window.

The night was black. Not a star in the sky. He quickly got ready for bed.

"We need to talk," he said, getting into bed. He put his hand gently on the curve of Lacey's hip.

"Not tonight," she said. She closed the book and placed it on the nightstand.

"Please," he said.

Lacey said nothing and clicked off the light on her side of the bed.

"Come on, Chief." He arranged the covers and moved beside her. Her hair smelled of cooking and a woodsy botanical shampoo. "We haven't had a moment alone all day."

She turned toward him and kissed him once and rested her hand on his face. "I'm tired. Okay?"

He nodded. He knew it was late. What would they accomplish raising these tough issues now? Lacey must have picked up on Wink's concern, and even Toni had seemed more watchful of her mother while they were preparing their contributions to that night's meal. They had all gone to Kate and Hugh's for Christmas dinner, taking with them a roasted beet salad, a sweet potato casserole, and Lacey's signature Christmas log cake. Wink had spent the afternoon making tiny mushrooms out of meringue to decorate it. With the Martins' extended family, they had been sixteen around the table. The meal had been festive, everyone talking and laughing at once, making their own household seem especially quiet when they returned to it.

"I love you, Chief," he said, taking Lacey's hand and kissing her fingers. She squeezed his hand, a wordless reply, then turned away from him, drawing her knees toward her chest. Alex reached for the switch of his own light and pulled the covers up to his neck.

He found it impossible to let go of the day. His brain began to unleash a litany of worries he had kept coiled inside him like a snake under a rock. Hugh had asked him if he had contacted Margot to enlist her help in convincing Lacey to tell the girls about her illness. They had been alone in the kitchen, opening the wine before dinner. Alex confessed that he hadn't spoken to Margot or told Lacey about the consulting job in Chicago either. How could he go so far from home when so much was at stake? He hadn't even found the right moment to bring it up.

Now, lying in the dark bedroom beside his wife, he felt all the pleasures of the day—the fun of exchanging presents, the solace of food and friendship, the joys of a celebration—evaporate. A painful new feeling swelled inside his chest. Suddenly Lacey, a few inches from him across the bed, seemed oceans away. He moved closer to her, her warm body so familiar and sweet. Gently, he pushed her nightgown aside and brought his mouth to her shoulder. He rested his hand on her arm. He knew the feeling of her, every inch—the softness of her breasts, the length of her thigh, the curve of her waist—yet he never grew tired of her. Lacey's breathing had deepened. Alex wanted her, but he would let her sleep. He was possessed with an unfamiliar longing. Would he ever again be able to think of her the way they were before her illness? He withdrew his hand and rolled away.

8

Thread: Fine cord of two or more filaments twisted together.

*A*lex stood by the window staring out at the whiteness. It was a week after Christmas. New Castle was covered with snow. There had been no wind in the night and the change in weather had crept up on the town unexpectedly, silently, more like a snowfall in a dream, making one wonder at daybreak if the newly white world was truly real. The morning was still. The bird feeder dangling on a wire between two trees was empty. He was sipping his first coffee of the day when Lacey came into the kitchen. She reached for a mug on the open shelves near the stove.

"Let me get your coffee, Chief," Alex said.

"I'll do it."

He pulled the pot from the heating base and took the mug from her. "You go sit. I'll get you some milk."

"Fine," she said.

"Did you sleep okay?"

She nodded, took a seat by the window, and stared into the garden. Alex placed her coffee in front of her and sat beside her. He liked the early morning when they could be alone together.

"I thought I'd make pancakes after the girls wake up," he said.

"That could be hours."

"I'll fix you something now." He moved to get up. "Do you want eggs or an English muffin?"

She reached for his arm and pressed it. "Nothing."

"You're sure?" he asked, hoping for a smile.

"I'm fine." She looked away.

Alex thought Lacey looked pale this morning. The sun wasn't out, but the sky was opalescent, like the interior of a shell. He squinted in the brightness near the window and glanced at his wife. She was thinner.

He was trying hard to keep things going as normally as possible. At night when they retreated to their bedroom, Lacey still barely spoke at all, claiming exhaustion. Alex was afraid to say anything, not wanting to upset her. He didn't want to increase her worries by sharing his own. It was as if the calm they were trying to hold on to was extremely fragile, a brittle icicle that could suddenly snap and crash to the ground.

"Are you feeling okay?" he asked.

"Because I want to eat later you think . . . I'm sick?" She gave him a quick glance.

"I'm only worried you might be coming down with something. Toni's been complaining of a sore throat. There's a lot going around. You need to take care not to get overtired—"

"Stop," she interrupted. "You've got to stop this. I feel your eyes . . . b-boring into me . . . watching me . . . like I might . . ." Lacey leaned back in her chair and closed her eyes.

"I just worry. . . . Sorry. I can't help it." Alex lifted his coffee. It was now cold. He carried it to the sink and poured it down the drain. He refilled his cup, emptying the pot. He would make more later.

"You haven't been . . . working much," Lacey said.

Alex stood very still, as if he'd been caught doing something wrong. He took a breath and went back to the table, pulled out his chair. "I've been talking with a potential client," he said. He sat and told Lacey about the new client in Chicago.

"When?" she asked.

"When do I have to tell them?"

"When would you start . . . start the job?"

"I'm not going to take it."

"What do you mean?"

"This assignment is huge. I'd be gone a lot. It might take months, maybe half a year."

"Take it," she said, shoving her coffee away. The light brown liquid sloshed out onto the table.

"Let me get a paper towel," he said.

Lacey reached for a cloth napkin in the center of the table and began to blot the mess with quick, impatient gestures. Alex went to the counter and ripped off a stream of paper towels. He balled them up and shoved them in Lacey's direction. She shook her head and pushed the napkin over the coffee, leaving the towels to slowly unfurl. The cloth in her hand was stained brown.

"I don't want to be away that much," Alex continued.

"I don't mind."

"Well, I mind."

"Alex. I'm not sick. Not now." She let go of the napkin and grabbed his wrist, squeezing tight. "Yes. One day it might get worse." She gripped harder. "Now, we need to live our regular lives." She withdrew her hand and brought both hands to her face. "If you want to help me," she continued, "you have to treat me . . . like you used to."

"Come on, Chief," he said softly and patiently, as if he were speaking to a child. "I can't leave you to cope alone. The girls don't know what's going on. They can't help."

"You've got to . . . take that job."

"You've got to be honest with the girls," he said. "You're keeping everything in. I know it's hard for you to talk. I mean . . ."

"It's the way I want it."

"Well, it's not the way I want it." He pushed back his chair and stood. "We've always been open with the kids. We need to share this with them. This has to do with our family and you won't let me say anything."

"Alex, this is my problem. I will decide."

He felt pressure building in his chest and tried to speak calmly. "Why do you think you have the right to decide everything?"

"I don't."

"Oh, come on, Lacey." He started to walk back and forth, punctuating each statement with a wave of his arm. "You said that Cornell has the best science program, so of course Wink should go to Cornell. In your opinion Columbia is best for journalism, so Toni should go there. So what if Wink might want a smaller college? So what if Toni wants to stay near her boyfriend? Can't I decide to pass on a job so I can be near my family? You won't let me do what I think is best for you."

"Shhh. Not so loud." Lacey pressed her hands to her temples.

Alex felt as if he might explode. He sat down again and crossed his arms on his chest.

Months ago, in the car while listening to a Schubert symphony, he had thought of how that experience was like being with Lacey. The pleasure of familiarity mixing with desire, like the harmonies themselves, was a gift. Knowing that the warmth, the richness of all this beauty was his, like a light shining inside of him, had made him swell with gratitude. What had changed since then?

Lacey rested her hands on the table and spoke calmly. "You've got to take that job." That one sentence flowed easily off her tongue.

He looked over at his wife. "There you go again—always telling us what to do. You're always calling the shots." Alex couldn't calm down. He felt pushed to the edge.

"That's not true," she said tersely.

The sound of a toilet flushing came from upstairs. Lacey reached over and rested her hand on his shoulder. "Okay. I know I can be hardheaded." She tilted her head and her mouth softened. "A little stubborn?"

He nodded and said nothing. Sometimes stubborn was good. In his second semester of business school he'd had a terrible time with a statistics course. He had wanted to drop out of school, thinking he might actually flunk. Instead, Lacey had tracked down a tutor for him and sat beside him while he worked the problems over and over until they made sense.

She'd been vigilant with the girls about homework, too, but she made it fun—making games of spelling lists and creating imaginary quiz shows when they had social studies tests. She soothed them by making hot chocolate and whipped cream, or fixing bowls of popcorn when they had an extra-hard day at school. No one was more encouraging or loving and willing to celebrate each success.

"You know we need the money." Her voice became placating.

"We'll manage. I've got some local proposals in the works."

"Nothing right away?"

"No."

"Then go ahead . . . with Chicago. More than anything I want our lives . . ." She paused. Her lips trembled and she pressed them closed. She sighed deeply. "As long as we can, I want our lives to be normal."

"Okay," he said. "Fine." He felt his anger ease a bit.

Footsteps on the stairs echoed from the hall. Alex stood and shoved back his chair. "Anybody for pancakes?" he called into the void.

January. A tight, wet cold had settled into the city. Margot wished for snow, thinking the weather would improve after a storm, as if some precipitation would offer a release from winter's nasty grip. The gallery was closed for the first two weeks of the month. Tomorrow, Monday, she would go in to help hang the next show, the work of a printmaker from Germany. She was not looking forward to it. The works on paper were dark and turgid and had to be handled with great care due to the handmade paper and organic inks.

Oliver had spent all of Saturday with her, but today he had awakened with that distant expression that meant he was thinking about his paintings. He had spent hours studying the illustrations from the book of Greek myths and a few days before he had picked up a copy of Edith Hamilton's *Mythology*, a book he said he hadn't looked at since high school.

Besides the beautiful illustrations in the book Margot had given him, Oliver seemed taken with the stories themselves. He talked about the ancient gods and goddesses and told her a myth about two sisters, Procne and Philomena. Procne's husband, Tereus, was happy with her for a while, but when her sister, Philomena, came to visit, Tereus raped his sister-in-law. To keep her from telling what had happened, he cut out her tongue and threw her in a dungeon. While she was imprisoned she wove a robe for her sister telling of her ordeal. As if suddenly realizing how this story of a mute sister weaving was too close to home, Oliver had quickly launched into the tale of the young Phaeton driving the chariot too close to the sun.

Once Oliver had gone to his studio on Sunday afternoon, Margot went back to her old apartment. After sharpening her pencils she set up a still-life arrangement and spent the afternoon drawing it from multiple angles. Margot was still dragging her heels about putting the apartment back on the rental market. She'd told Oliver she was going to give it a good cleaning and then decide if she needed to repaint.

Today her pencil had felt good in her hand, as if she was regaining her old dexterity for putting line on paper. When the light dwindled and she had to turn on a lamp, she realized that when she was immersed in her drawing she thought of nothing else. While working she forgot about Lacey's illness entirely. She even forgot about Oliver.

Now at home, she decided to surprise Oliver with a nice dinner. His marriage proposal rose up in her mind from time to time, along with a sense of guilt about putting him off. She was relieved he hadn't pushed her further. Feeling suddenly industrious, she chopped green peppers and onions for turkey chili. While not a natural cook, Margot had half a dozen dishes in her repertoire, most of which Lacey had taught her. Oliver jokingly called them her sloppy suppers: a beef stew that cooked for five hours and dirtied only one pot, a vegetable soup with pasta, a spaghetti sauce, a shrimp gumbo she'd copied out of an airline magazine, and her grandmother Winkler's recipe for corn chowder. Winter was her cooking season, as none of these dishes was well suited for hot weather. Oliver was good at assembling salads from odds and ends at the deli, and with that, and the infinite variety of take-out options, they managed.

Margot and Oliver had eased into their living arrangement gradually. There was no one day when she had decided to move in with him, no specific discussions: "Let's give it a try. Maybe this is a good first step?" In the early days of their relationship they had gone back and forth between their two apartments, but as Oliver's place was far more spacious, she ended up staying more and more often with him. Her belongings, her clothes, her favorite books, the jade plant she had tended since college, had slowly crossed the park and taken up residence on Riverside Drive, a migration that seemed to work for both of them. The few times that Oliver had broached the topic of their future, Margot had said there was no need for talk. What would happen would happen.

When she had been with Oliver for almost a year, Carl, her boss, had asked if she'd be willing to sublet her furnished place to a friend of his for a few months. After that, through word of mouth, she had kept her apartment rented most of the time. Technically subletting was against the co-op rules, but if you kept the arrangements quiet and the renters didn't cause problems, the other tenants turned a blind eye.

Since Margot had returned from Thanksgiving, she'd crossed the park frequently, making her way to her old address. She had never forgotten when Lacey stayed with her there after Teddy had left. Lacey had taken charge of everything: changing the locks, hanging curtains to make the place cozier, stocking the fridge, buying flowers, making Margot feel once again safe and secure, creating a sense of home. Now, as then, Margot was grateful to Grandmother Winkler for ensuring that she had a place to live. In some ways, going to her old apartment was like going to her own studio where she could forget everything and work. She was considering buying some new paints now that her drawing was going better.

Margot added the ground turkey to the sizzling onions and peppers. The smell of the browning meat filled the kitchen. The exhaust fan roared above, doing little to draw out the smoke. She used a wooden spoon to move the ingredients around the pan. Granny Winkler's kitchen had always smelled of good cooking— roasting meats, baking bread, Margot's favorite ginger cookies just out of the oven and cooling on the counter. Margot wished now that she had paid more attention and really learned how to cook. When the meat was nearly browned she added the chili powder and cumin. Oliver liked his food with a bit of heat.

A second later he grabbed her from behind. "You scared me to death," she said, dropping the spoon and turning to him with delight. "I was literally just thinking of you."

He kissed her neck and seemed to breathe her in along with the scent of the food. His mouth was warm, his coat still cold from the night air. "Great news, Mags." He kissed her mouth this time.

"Well, tell me. Stop grinning like you've just won the lottery."

"I've been on the phone with the Croft Gallery. They're sounding serious now. Jack Wallace, the owner, and his partner, the guy who actually runs it, want me to come and see the space."

"They want to represent you?"

"It's not definite yet." He stepped away and took off his coat, then got a beer from the fridge. "It sounded like it, though. He kept saying that my work would show well there. They've got my digital images and they're really enthusiastic. Jack saw the work I sent out to the guy in LA last year."

Margot turned down the burner. It was time to add the canned tomatoes. "That does sound promising," she said.

"How about a long weekend in San Francisco at the end of the month?"

"Both of us?" A small part of her wondered if this was too good to be true. Oliver had pretty much given up on showing at that gallery. Maybe the busy holiday period had kept the curators from getting in touch before now.

"Of course. Come on, Margot. We need a vacation. Just you and me. Away from everything."

She didn't disagree. Oliver had been upset when Carl Van Engen hadn't sold his large painting by the end of the last show. The art market was slow, and she knew his sales were down to nothing. Margot hadn't seen Oliver so happy in a long time. She was pleased for him. And yet . . .

She thought about calling Lacey later to share the news. That morning Lacey had phoned to tell Margot about the storm in New Castle. Margot hadn't noticed any further problems with her sister's speech. She had almost seemed like her old self.

"I'd love a trip to San Francisco," Margot said. "What's the weather like in January?"

"Nothing worse than this," he said.

Two days later, a second snowstorm followed the first. Alex sat at his desk in his home office, leaned back in his chair, and stared out the window. The sky had turned a hard, dull gray. Alex had never minded winter. He liked rising to the challenge of the weather. On stormy mornings he enjoyed being the first out, clearing the walk, shoveling from the garage door to the street. Others might complain of being stuck inside on the rare days when the weather made it impossible to travel or when school was canceled, but he thought there was something rare and old-fashioned about gathering around the fire on a late afternoon after an unexpected day of being at home. After sledding or building snow forts, his daughters would have pink cheeks from the cold. When the sky grew dark and Lacey closed the curtains to the rest of the world, an intense feeling of privacy seemed to cloak their family, inside and safe from the cruel weather. Often on cold nights, while he was falling asleep, his mind would drift to memories of summer. After long New England winters, summer came each year like a gift.

It was impossible to think about summer without thinking of Bow Lake. Alex, Lacey, and Margot had gone there year after year since childhood. Summer was what brought them together. The New Hampshire lake was home to the cottages, known as "camps," which remained in the same families for generations, though once Alex's father had died, the George family had decided to let their place go. During their growing-up years Lacey and Margot stayed with their grandmother Winkler, and Alex's mother spent the entire summer at their camp next door with Alex and his brother. His dad came up to be with the family on weekends.

Alex had few memories of Lacey when they were small, though certainly they had played together. He could conjure up vague images of a bigger girl in pigtails running with a group of children. Lacey was always the pied piper, leading the younger ones on hikes through the woods, organizing a puppet theater or putting on actual plays, setting up relay races in a neighbor's field. Eventually, she left Bow Lake for six weeks at a time to attend sleepaway camp in Maine, where her grandmother had gone as a girl.

He remembered more clearly the summers when they grew older. One particular day with Lacey was still vivid. He was fifteen and had finally started to grow. It seemed as if overnight he had reached nearly six feet. At last Lacey, a year older, was shorter than he was.

That late August afternoon they swam out to the raft together. Her arms, smooth and tanned, cut through the water in what appeared to be an effortless crawl. His own body, long, skinny, and awkward, thrashed alongside her, working hard to keep up. She climbed the ladder and the water streamed off her as she stood. Her hair was slicked to her head and down the length of her back like the pelt of a seal.

Alex clambered up next to her, grinning foolishly, trying to keep his focus on her face. Her skin sparkled with wetness. His eyes wanted all of her. They both smelled of the lake, mossy and clean. The sun sparkled on the water, and he remembered thinking it was as if he were seeing her for the first time.

On that one perfect afternoon they stood bobbing on the raft out in the lake with the breeze cooling their skin for what might have been only a few minutes. Alex had no memory of what they might have said. What he would never forget was the sun, the feeling of goose bumps forming on his skin, the blue lake, the sky without a cloud, the sweetness of Lacey's laugh, her eyes looking into his. Had he ever been alone with her before? He remembered wishing that instead of rocking and swaying on the raft, they were on a desert island, or better yet, set adrift in a small boat headed out to sea.

Lacey may have challenged him to race back to the dock. He may have said, "Sure, but you'll win." She may have answered, "Don't worry. You'll win when it matters." Or had he invented that?

All these years later, Lacey and Alex were still together and on an island, New Castle, set adrift in the snow on a January afternoon. Alex had decided to accept the contract with the company in Chicago. Lacey was right. They should try to keep their lives normal. He had made the call. That was the easy part.

Still, the thought of spending so much time far from home made him uneasy. How many years would they have together living like a regular family? The girls would be leaving for college in the fall. Alex felt he was cheating his daughters by not letting them in on the knowledge that their lives would change dramatically over the next few years. He remembered Hugh's urging him to talk to Margot about convincing Lacey to tell the girls about her illness. Would Margot think it was right to accept Lacey's wish to keep her illness a secret?

From upstairs he heard the distant sound of Lacey's loom clanging and thumping, periodically filling the silent house. He got up from his chair. The winter day suddenly felt confining, bearing down on him like a low-pressure weather system. He wanted to talk to someone. He'd given up on Lacey. Her mind was made up and any further discussion would only lead to another argument. Hugh had a point. Why not call Margot? She, too, was threatened by the eventual loss of her sister. Surely she would understand what he was going through, how hard it was to keep withholding the truth. He would ask her what she thought. Just thinking about confiding in Margot made him feel less alone.

Oliver closed the door to his studio. His work this week was going well. Margot was meeting him at Nice Matin, a French-style bistro, for dinner. She had sounded exhausted when he called to make this plan. Mario had been helping her hang the new show and the artist was being difficult—insisting that the pieces be presented in a certain order that didn't work in the space. Besides that, she reported that Carl wasn't happy with the catalog copy and it was already overdue at the printer. He and Margot were leaving for San Francisco that weekend. He had found inexpensive last-minute tickets from an online travel site.

When he reached the restaurant there was a line where the hostess stood, but he spotted Margot at a table for two in the back near the window. She wore the gray sweater he liked with the scooped neck, and the necklace he had given her glimmered at her throat. Oliver loved the curve of her neck and the vulnerable whiteness of her skin. He made his way to her table, knowing just how she would lift her head, a scant tilt to the left, and exactly how her lips would part in a combination of pleasure and wonder to see him suddenly there. Margot sometimes had a way of appearing lost in thought. He found this vaguely secretive look appealing.

The tables in the restaurant were spaced close together. Twice he excused himself after hitting the back of a chair with his backpack or bumping the edge of a table as he crossed the room toward her.

"Hey, Mags," he said. "Sorry I'm late."

She wasn't smiling, but did not appear to be annoyed. He bent to kiss her and tried to ease into the fragile-looking café-style chair opposite her. The chair, the tile floor, and the floor-to-ceiling windows that opened to the street in summer were not well suited to this cold January night. Most people's coats, draped over the backs of the chairs, made the close seating even tighter.

He picked up the menu that rested at his place. "Red wine okay?"

Margot nodded and Oliver signaled the server, a young woman with short dark hair who looked as if she could be French. He ordered a bottle of Côtes du Rhône and the server, sounding like she'd grown up in Brooklyn, reported that they were out of the braised beef. Oliver and Margot came often to this restaurant and they were familiar with the menu. Without hesitating, she chose lamb chops and he asked for the steak.

"You look like you had a good day," she said when they were alone.

"It was hard to stop tonight."

"We didn't have to meet for dinner. I would have been okay on my own."

"I could have painted all night, but this old body can't take any more. I needed a break."

"Stop saying you're old," she said with a touch of a smile.

"Too old to stay on my feet all night with a brush in my hand."

The server appeared with their wine. Margot leaned away from the table to allow the uncorking, the ritual tasting and nodding of acceptance. They lifted their glasses and sipped.

"Sorry you've had a rough day," he said.

"I think I've fixed the catalog. The artist is finally happy, so Carl's relieved."

"I'm glad," he said. "Won't it be great to get away?"

Margot swirled the wine in her glass, then set it down. "Oliver, Alex called me."

"Is everything okay?" He reached for Margot's hand.

Oliver tended to forget about Lacey, but he knew Margot worried all the time about her sister. Ever since Thanksgiving, Margot had seemed more preoccupied. He would catch her standing by the window, but her gaze would be inward, oblivious to the view of the river, and her mouth pinched shut. It was as if a part of her was back in New Castle, trying to figure out what she could do for Lacey or how to find some way to help. Her concern was understandable, but Oliver couldn't help feeling uneasy. Lacey was bound to get worse. It was only a matter of time.

He was working again on the painting of the man and the dog in Riverside Park. The colors in the sky itself were still a challenge, but the canvas was beginning to take on a feeling of foreboding. The water in the background had become more abstract. While he worked he kept thinking about Pandora's box, how until opened, the box kept all the trouble inside. The illustration of that myth in the book that Lacey had given him for Christmas continued to haunt him. It struck him how the energy, the forces that were about to be unleashed in the myth, was emerging in the movement of the water in his painting.

"Oliver, where are you?" Margot asked.

"Sorry. Why did Alex call?"

"He's going to Chicago next Monday. He's starting a new job that will keep him there most of the winter. He wants me to come to New Castle to persuade Lacey to talk to the girls about her condition."

"Why tell them now? You told me Lacey felt strongly about keeping it from them until later."

"Alex is having a hard time with that. He's really torn up about it. By not letting them know, he feels like he's cheating them. He hates lying." Margot's eyes were sad, but Oliver could tell she was making an effort to stay in control.

"Can't you just call her?"

"The phone is hard for her. He thinks having me there is really important."

"Can't Alex work this out with his wife? It's their problem."

"Oliver, once the girls know, they're going to be devastated. Toni had another fight about Ryan. Toni told Alex that her mom was so furious she couldn't even talk, as if she were cracking up. Alex feels as if he's living a lie. And it's my problem too."

"Fine," Oliver said, reaching for his glass.

"He wants me to come this weekend."

"Margot, we're going to San Francisco."

"Couldn't we go the following weekend?"

"All the arrangements have been made. The tickets are non-refundable. I can't change them now. More than that, I've set it all up. These are businesspeople. I don't want to blow this chance. If I put them off, who knows what might happen."

"I'm sorry," Margot said. "Really, I am. If you can't get credit for my ticket, I'll reimburse you."

"It's not the money. Why can't you go to New Hampshire when we get back?"

"Alex has to be in Chicago this Monday. The opening meetings with the board have been set. I have to go this weekend when the girls are out of school."

"So you're not coming with me?"

"You know there's so little I can do. This is one time when maybe I can be of some help." Margot looked away from him as if embarrassed. "I'm sorry. Really, I am."

Oliver was speechless. What could he say? How could he argue?

"I know the trip to San Francisco is important to you," she said. "I feel torn. I've been agonizing over this all day."

"I guess I can't change your mind."

"Please, understand just this once I need to be with my family." She reached for her water and took a sip.

The people at the table behind him stood to leave, pushing at the back of his chair.

"Sorry about that," a jovial blonde said.

Oliver nodded. The server arrived with their dinners. "So, that's it, I guess." Oliver cut into his steak. The knife hit the bone, causing the meat to slide across his plate, smearing the neatly piped mound of root vegetables.

Margot's hands remained in her lap. "Oliver, I'm sorry."

"Aren't you going to eat?"

She let out a breath and picked up her fork. "This is a hard time for me. For my family."

"Let's not talk about it. Okay?" Oliver resumed eating. Her family. He wished she'd stop saying that. How did he fit in? He was her lover, but clearly not part of her family. He swallowed, nearly choking on the steak, and reached for the wine bottle.

Margot savored the silence in the gallery. She and Mario had finished hanging the new show yesterday and she had come in this morning to proof the labels and double-check the accuracy of the price list. Mario was in the back office sending out a second round of electronic reminders to their clients. He was much better at the computer tasks than she was. At twenty-eight, he was completely tuned in to the Internet world, keeping up with multiple blogs, tweets, and the social networks of the art world. Together, they made a good team.

Carl had been pleased with Margot's placement of the pieces, and she had to admit that this show had come out better than she'd expected. Carl, as owner and director of the Van Engen Gallery, decided which artists he would show, but increasingly he took Margot with him to the artists' studios to help choose the actual paintings to exhibit. He valued her judgment in selecting what would look best on the gallery walls.

When she had first taken the job at the Van Engen Gallery, she had been a typical "gallery girl"—answering the phone, sitting at the front desk, responding to inquiries. She had no real authority. After the first few months, Carl had noticed her ability when she innocently suggested that a particular painting would have more of an impact if it were placed on the far wall, giving the viewer more distance. A client purchased the canvas that very afternoon. From then on, she had taken a greater role in setting up the exhibitions. Carl also turned over the catalog work to her, and her salary increased along with her responsibilities.

Mario, now the young assistant, had taken on Margot's former duties. Margot was leaving at noon today. She was going to take a cab to Oliver's studio so they could travel together to the airport. She kept telling herself that going to New Hampshire was the right thing to do. In fact, Lacey had been pleased when Margot called asking to come for this quick visit before life got too hectic in the spring. That night Mario would be there for the opening of the exhibit, and Margot knew she could count on him to oversee the caterer and manage the event. He had taken over for her several times before. Mario's position was part-time, and he was glad to have any additional hours at the gallery to earn extra money. He was a painter, too, with a studio in Brooklyn. Sometimes Margot wondered if every other person in New York was an artist.

"Lookin' good, I'd say." Mario emerged from the office and smiled. "Boss seems pleased."

"Yeah, Carl really likes it." She stepped away from one of the smaller paintings. She hadn't immediately taken to the dark smudgelike images, but when placed on the white walls with a suitable distance between them, they began to take on an almost ghostlike presence. She had placed the calmer, more spare works early in the progression, slowly building to the last three paintings on the rear wall of the gallery.

Mario came up beside her. He was small and slight, not much taller than she was. "So do they speak to you?" He was wearing his daily uniform of black jeans and a white shirt. At gallery openings he dressed completely in black. When she first met him, he had explained he never wore color; color was for his own art. He painted huge geometric canvases in brilliant hues, the shades of jelly beans.

She laughed. "Not exactly. But a few of these manage to take me away."

"Meaning?" He put his hands on his hips and appeared to study the picture in front of them.

Margot read the label. It was called *The Deep*. The dusky, complex swirls, darkest at the center, reminded her of the surface of the water at Bow Lake during a storm. "When I look at it long enough," she said, "it's like my mind goes somewhere else."

"Somewhere good?" He was looking at her now.

"Sometimes," she said, then frowned. "Sometimes not."

"I think all art is telling us a kind of story." He turned to the next painting. "With the abstract pieces, it's just harder to read."

"I think I'd agree with that." She remembered Lacey telling her how women were among the earliest storytellers, weaving their narratives into cloth long before the invention of paper or books.

Mario looked at his watch. "You'd better take off. You never know what traffic will be like."

"Gosh, it's later than I thought." Her stomach tightened. "I lose track of time in here." She glanced out the front window. The sky was gray. Had they predicted snow?

Oliver had been moody and temperamental all week and she didn't blame him. She knew it wasn't fair to have canceled her trip at the last minute. She remembered his excitement about California and his delight in planning their vacation.

She felt awful. She didn't want to disappoint Oliver, but Alex had asked for her help. She felt pulled in both directions—yet this was for her family. The girls needed to know what was going on with Lacey. Unfortunately, the timing was terrible. She couldn't be in two places at once.

"You okay?" Mario asked.

"Sure," she said, going in search of her coat and overnight bag. Her stomach churned, making her think again of the murky water during storms at Bow Lake.

"Don't worry about a thing," Mario called after her.

Margot stepped into the street, more anxious than ever. There wasn't a taxi in sight.

9

Web: Woven cloth, but also the cloth remaining on the loom.

"*I* told Lacey I had an errand nearby," Alex said, giving Margot a quick hug. He opened the passenger door for her before returning to the driver's side. Margot had been surprised to see him in the parking lot when her bus pulled into the Portsmouth station.

Alex jerked the seat belt across his body. "She's always reminding the girls not to waste gas." He gave her a quick smile and put the car in reverse. "I wanted a chance to talk to you alone."

Margot felt ill at ease, uncertain about what might happen during the next few days. Alex said nothing, but appeared to concentrate more than necessary on backing up, as if he too was uncomfortable with the situation. He turned out of the parking lot and headed toward New Castle.

Margot recalled only one other time when she had met Alex by himself since his marriage to Lacey. He had come to New York to talk to her about buying out her half of the cottage at Bow Lake. Lakefront land had skyrocketed in value over the years. Alex and Lacey could afford to carry the expenses by themselves, and Margot could then invest the money from selling her half to provide her with additional income. Lacey had known Margot was having a difficult time making ends meet in New York. Alex had explained that Margot could still use the cottage whenever she wanted in August, sharing it with them. The solution had been Lacey's idea.

Margot remembered Alex's hand shaking slightly when he handed her the papers requiring her signature. Margot had signed quickly, feeling uncomfortable. Had it been the topic of money or the fact that Alex had known about her finances that made her uncomfortable? Or was it due to being alone with him?

Margot stared out at the grimy snowbanks along the highway. How different this was from the late fall weather during her last visit. Today on the bus, she had envied the other passengers on their way to New Hampshire. For them it might have been just an ordinary winter afternoon as the bus rolled northward. One woman had brought out her knitting, and worked on what looked to be a baby's sweater, perhaps for a grandchild. Several people read newspapers, others fat paperback novels. An older man dozed peacefully behind her, awakened now and again by his own snores. Yet they too might be arriving to their own troubles, their own particular sorrows, hidden behind their complacent expressions.

Margot swallowed. She loosened the scarf at her neck. "How are things going?" she asked. The car was warm.

"There's no real change. We had another meeting with her neurologist in Boston. He said she might consider some speech therapy in the spring."

"Would that help?" Margot asked, relieved to finally be talking about the problem.

"There are ways of making it easier for her to link words. Different coping mechanisms to ease fluency. At least for now."

For now. How grim he sounded. "What about learning sign language?"

"Too difficult. If this progresses further . . ." He paused. They had come to a red light. "If it gets worse, all language deteriorates. Sign language is its own language. She wouldn't be capable of that."

"Oh, my God," Margot said. The enormity of Lacey's illness

hit her once again. Eventually, Lacey would have no way of communicating her thoughts, her needs. She would become out of reach to them, shut inside herself. Margot's stomach flipped over in fear. Alex had said "if," but the terrifying question was when.

Alex sighed. The light changed to green. He moved his foot to the gas pedal. His thigh was still long and thin. She remembered his skinny boy body, the way he looked wet from a swim long ago at Bow Lake—Alex out on the raft, his eyes following Lacey as she dove in to swim back to the dock, Lacey emerging from the blue water and calling back to him, urging him to race her to shore.

They reached the streets of downtown Portsmouth. Pedestrians hunched forward, buffeted by the wind. It was nearly evening. The decorative holiday wreaths that dangled from the light posts looked tattered. Margot wondered when the city would take the decorations down. They couldn't last long in the harsh winter storms.

"On the plus side," he said, "she's weaving a lot. She spends hours in her studio."

"Good," Margot said, struck by the fact that she too had started to spend more time drawing this winter and, just recently, painting. Initially the brush in her hand had felt awkward. It was like being a first grader coping with a newly sharpened pencil and trying to keep the letters between the rigid lines of that funny school paper. Art was an escape for her. Maybe it was for Lacey, too.

"She also joined a gym," he said. "Now with the snow she can't run outside. She seems to crave exercise."

Margot pictured Alex on his bike. At Thanksgiving he had gone out every day, even after the weather turned cold. "What about your biking?"

"Not happening these days," he said. "When the snow's gone, there's ice and of course the dark. I'm okay."

Alex didn't look okay. He looked pale, somewhat gaunt, as if his skin had been stretched across his face. His Adam's apple protruded. Sitting in the car so close to him, Margot thought she detected tension in his jaw. He looked both angry and vulnerable in the waning light. It was obvious that Lacey was not the only one suffering.

"How are the girls?" she asked.

"Wink was home sick. Maybe the flu. She's better now. Still, it was a lousy way to start the new year. She missed the first few days of school and she hates falling behind. She takes after me. Worrying is her best subject."

"And Toni?"

"Out with Ryan all the time. Lacey's annoyed because she hasn't finished her essays for the college applications." He glanced quickly at Margot. "Toni will get them done. She works better closer to a deadline. She didn't catch Wink's flu, but she's been unusually withdrawn lately. It's like she knows something's up. That's why we have to tell them what's wrong."

"Lacey must know that."

"She won't talk about it." Alex drew his mouth into a tight line. They crossed the first causeway leading to the island. "I thought couples grew closer in difficult situations," he said. "Every time we talk about it we start to argue. We never used to fight."

"I'm so sorry," Margot said, remembering how she and Oliver had argued when she decided to cancel her trip to California. They had returned to the apartment after their dinner at Nice Matin and gone to bed without speaking. That had never happened before. The next morning when she started to explain how she felt, he had snapped at her, "You've made up your mind. I don't want to talk about it."

Since the Christmas holidays Oliver no longer lingered at home in the morning while she sipped her tea. He left the apartment for his studio with no indication of when he might return. More books on mythology had appeared on the living room coffee table, and after dinner each evening, he would bury himself in the ancient stories. Margot didn't mind too much. She had learned to recognize when he was in one of his intensely creative spells. She also went more often to her old apartment in the early mornings before going to the gallery to work. Her drawing was improving and it helped to keep her mind off Lacey's situation.

But after their argument at Nice Matin, Oliver and Margot had spoken only briefly, and then only when absolutely necessary: she asking him if he had anything for the dry cleaner, he letting her know that he would be late on Thursday and to eat without him, she telling him that the plumber was coming back again to try to fix the drip in the bathtub. Once, she had tried to initiate a conversation by asking his opinion on a controversial article in *Art News*. He told her he hadn't had time to think about it. Another evening she set out a large wedge of his favorite cheese, Saint André. He helped himself without remarking on it. It had been a miserable week.

Oliver's silence had upset her. The atmosphere in their apartment was unfamiliar. Margot knew she had brought about this change. She felt exposed and raw, as if she'd lost a protective layer of skin. Oliver's withdrawal made her feel fragile, almost like she was going to get sick. Yet part of her was annoyed at Oliver. She had made a choice, maybe the wrong one, but he didn't have to be in such a snit. Why couldn't he just get over it? Rather than argue further, Margot said nothing.

He had been quiet in the taxi to the airport. Soon the entire breadth of the country would be between them. Then, while the cab hurtled over the Triboro Bridge, Oliver reached for her hand. "You okay?" His familiar grip reassured her. She nodded and stared out the window as the city skyline grew distant. When the driver reached her terminal, Oliver spoke again. "I love you, Mags." She kissed him, fumbled briefly with the door handle, and hurried inside to catch her flight.

Now, in Alex's car, Margot stared at the passing scenery. The Piscataqua River looked turbulent and uninviting. There were few boats at this time of year. She knew the area so well, but on this visit she had the strong feeling that this was not where she belonged. Alex passed the New Castle post office and the white Congregational church at the center of the village. They were five minutes from the house. "I'm so relieved you're here," he said, breaking the silence.

Margot pulled at a loose thread in her scarf. It was a pale blue one that Lacey had woven for her several winters ago. "I'm not sure what I can do," she said. The image of her sister arguing with Alex was unpleasant. She was uneasy about entering this controversy. Margot had always agreed with Lacey. She couldn't recall ever having to take opposing sides, not in anything that really mattered.

"I hope you can get through to her. Now that she's sick it's harder to talk to her. I don't want to upset her. I don't want to leave for Chicago without letting the girls know what's wrong. Maybe if Lacey hears it from you, Margot, she'll agree." He lifted his shoulders and released them, as if trying to shake off a burden. "After all, when is it wrong to speak the truth?" His voice had taken on an angry edge.

"I'll do what I can."

"Please, do it for me."

If he only knew what it was costing her. Oliver's parting words at the airport had comforted her, but this was the first time they had gone through a rough patch. Sure, they had had small disagreements—her annoyance when he was in a bad mood, his impatience with her when she had misplaced her keys or forgotten to buy coffee on the way home from work. Those arguments had been superficial, like a minor cut that would heal overnight. Her decision to give up the trip had caused a rift between them, a deep wound that would take time to mend.

Alex slowed the car. His body, so close to hers, smelled of the outdoors and of a wool sweater, clean and reassuring. His lips, grown-up lips now, were pale and chapped.

"I know telling them is for the best." He reached over and put his hand on her arm, clutching her wrist. He held her firmly, as if trying to squeeze his message right into her bones. His awkward gesture was connecting them, bringing them together in this un-expected alliance. She considered placing her other hand on top of his, touching his skin, making a pact. "I'll try to convince Lacey," she said without moving.

"Thank you," he said softly. He released his hand and Margot felt adrift once again. Her task wasn't going to be easy. Alex's reasoning made sense to her; making Lacey see his point was another matter. But as Alex pulled the car into the driveway, Margot became less sure of his argument. What was wrong with letting Lacey try to keep their lives just the way they were? Would it do the twins any good to know their mother was ill?

Margot stepped out of the car into the cold New Hampshire air. What was she doing here and not with Oliver on a plane to California? The gray clapboard house loomed large in front of her. Alex grabbed her bag and slammed the car door shut. Where did she belong?

Alex stood up from tending the fire and took a seat beside Lacey on the sofa. He, Margot, and Lacey had just finished dinner. Wink and Toni had gone off to get pizza with an old friend, a girl who was still home on winter break from her freshman year at college. The twins probably wouldn't be back for a while.

Alex was fairly certain that Margot hadn't said anything yet to Lacey about telling the twins about her diagnosis. He had left Margot alone with Lacey in the kitchen while she made the butternut squash lasagna for their meal. At the table Margot hadn't avoided his questioning looks, but she had seemed to be making an effort to keep Lacey in good humor. As much as he wanted to get the tough conversation over with, it was probably wise to have Lacey in a good frame of mind. He hoped she would be more understanding of his point of view with Margot there. All during the meal Margot had been great, keeping the conversation going and never speaking of Lacey's illness. Alex thought Margot was giving him secret signals now and again, with a glance or a nod, as if telling him that it was important to make everything seem normal and to be patient until the time was right. Or was he imagining that?

The house still smelled of cooking and of the pot of herbal tea Lacey liked to serve after dinner. Alex would have liked a brandy, but decided against it. With repeated prodding, the fire seemed to take hold and amazingly it didn't smoke. After all these years he still didn't understood how the flue would somehow draw without a problem, and then the next day fill the house with smoke. Margot sat in the wing chair opposite them. Lacey, tall and athletic, glowed with health, while Margot, the smaller, darker version, had deep circles beneath her eyes. He marveled at the bond that held these two women together.

The house was quiet without the girls moving about upstairs. Margot had been telling Lacey about Oliver's trip and the possible show in San Francisco. Alex noticed how Margot's hands shook slightly as she lifted her cup from the saucer to take a sip of tea.

"Why does he care so much about . . . California?" Lacey asked.

"Partly for a change," Margot said. "New York's a bit dreary at this time of year. Also, his career. You have to keep putting your work out there. It's part of the job of being an artist."

"So you think it's likely?"

"I hope so," Margot said.

"Maybe we could go?" Lacey said, turning to Alex.

"What?" He had stopped paying attention. He thought again about fixing a brandy.

"To San Francisco, to Oliver's art show."

He nodded. "Yeah, sure, depending on when it is." Since he had agreed to take on the consulting job away from home, Lacey had seemed a little less tense around him. She had actually laughed the other night at dinner when he told her about the cast of characters who ran the fertilizer business in Chicago—the uncle who refused to sign a paycheck for his nephew who came to the office at forty seconds past nine, and the elderly grandfather and founder who had his sons so terrified they wouldn't speak up at board meetings. He had described how one son, the only one who really knew the business, had to contact Alex by cell phone from out of the building, as his two younger brothers were threatening lawsuits. Lacey had suggested that Alex show up wearing a Superman costume when he arrived to save the day.

"If all goes well they'll give Oliver a show later this spring," Margot said. "We're keeping our fingers crossed."

Alex cleared his throat. "I was telling Margot," he said slowly, thinking this might be a good time to bring up the topic, "how I was going to be away so much this winter."

Lacey shrugged. "If we knew the date for the opening"—her voice seemed to catch on something in her throat—"you could arrange your schedule . . . around it."

Alex ignored this. "I told Margot that I was worried about leaving you so much."

Lacey gave him a sharp look, and then appeared to force her face back into a pleasant expression. "It's not a problem. You know that."

"The girls need to know what's going on," he blurted out. He looked across at Margot.

"I agree with Alex," Margot said, as if on cue. "I think maybe it's time that Wink and Toni know about your illness. You're okay now, but what if things were to change? I mean, with Alex so far away . . ." Her voice trailed off. She appeared to be watching him for the next signal.

"No," Lacey said.

"We just think—" Margot said.

"We?" Lacey interrupted, her voice high-pitched. "What do you mean, *we?*" She set her cup down abruptly. She turned to Alex, her eyes intently focused. "This is about us." Her eyes opened wider, as if she suddenly understood. "What? You wanted Margot to—"

"Wait," Alex said.

"You wait," Lacey said.

Margot stared at the floor, looking as if she wanted to disappear.

"Lacey, listen," Alex said. "The girls have applied to college. This is their last year at home. They need time to get used to the situation."

"I don't want to."

"But why not?" Margot asked. "I think they're old enough to handle it."

Lacey looked at Margot. "You don't remember." Her voice was accusing. "I was in high school when . . ." She seemed to search not only for one word but for words strong enough to remind Margot of something she had forgotten. "When Mother was really sick. You were still little." Lacey groaned. "If you had any idea—" She stopped and drew in a breath. "I don't want that for my girls. I want their last year to be . . ."

"Lacey, they already suspect," Alex said. "I've given them excuses—you're tired, you're stressed. They're not little kids. They know something's not right."

"Wink was worried about you at Thanksgiving," Margot said. "Alex is concerned that—"

Lacey turned to Margot. "So he asked you to get involved?"

Margot seemed to shrink into her chair. "I came because we thought—"

"Stop!" Lacey covered her ears. "This is about my family. Not you." Her face was flushed. Margot moved to the edge of her chair. Lacey pointed at Margot as if reprimanding a child. "You listen to me." Her chin thrust forward. "I will tell my girls. When I'm ready."

"Tell us what?" Toni stood at the door to the living room. Wink lingered in the shadow of the hall.

Alex stared at his daughters. He froze, incapable of saying a thing. All the breath had been knocked out of him. He and Lacey had lived with the diagnosis for several months. Primary progressive aphasia, frontotemporal dementia, cell disintegration—a tragic vocabulary that had entered his lexicon. Not an hour went by when some part of him didn't pause and cower, fearful of what was to come. He had become used to the knowledge. He didn't know how their lives would change, how they would cope, but the hard reality had settled into his consciousness, had become part of how he saw his life. It blurred his expectations.

"You started this, Alex," Lacey said, backing away from Margot. "You tell them." She pointed her finger in his face. Her entire arm shook. A horrible sound rose in her throat. She turned, sank down on the sofa and buried her face in her hands. "You, you . . . how could you?" When she looked up, her face was wet with tears. He had never seen such anguish on her face before.

He took a deep breath and launched into the sequence of events and the doctor's final evaluation. Toni leaned against the doorframe and Lacey remained on the sofa, saying nothing. Wink sat beside her mother and took her hand. When Alex finished speaking, Toni stepped over and faced him squarely, and began firing questions, her anger clear. "I can't believe this. You've known since before Thanksgiving and you didn't tell us? Why? God, you treat us like babies. That's called lying."

"Daddy, have you talked to other doctors?" Wink, on the verge of tears, turned to her mother. "Your speech isn't that different. It could be years before you get worse, couldn't it?"

Lacey stroked Wink's face. "It's not that bad, sweetie. I'm going to be fine for a long, long time."

"And you believe that?" Toni asked. "It's not like we're getting the truth around here." She walked away from Alex and stood before her mother. "So you were giving me all this 'must be menopause' shit when you have some weird brain sickness?" Toni's face crumpled like a child's before crying. "You lied too, Mom. You're just as bad."

"Please . . . don't think . . . that," Lacey said.

"What should I think? I'm supposed to take it calmly when my parents have done nothing but lie to me?"

"It's not like that," Wink said, hope in her voice, though she had quietly started to cry.

"So it's like—" Toni made a choking sound, then continued. "You won't be able to talk one day, and eventually not understand, and then one day . . ." She couldn't go on. She too began to weep.

Margot remained silent, clearly distressed. Alex could see that the damage had been done. What could Margot do now anyway? "I'm going to set up a meeting with Mom's neurologist," he said. "So we can go in as a family and talk to him. You can ask him all your questions."

"Like that's going to do any good," Toni said.

Wink, her face now stained with tears, appeared to force a smile. "I'm sure he can tell us what we can do for Mom," she said.

"You're right," he said, relieved that one of his daughters was looking on the positive side. "Further deterioration might be years away. We need to help your mother, be supportive, care for each other." As he said these words an overwhelming dread came over him.

Toni lashed out a final time. "I can't believe you didn't tell us, Mom. That's just so shitty." Her voice broke.

"Your mom was only trying to protect you," Margot said. "She didn't want to worry you."

Toni paid no attention to Margot and headed back to the hall. "I'm out of here," she said.

Alex was surprised by the bitterness in her voice. He called after her, "No one's going anywhere tonight."

"And why the hell not?" she shouted back at them.

"Don't raise your voice," he said.

"Raise my voice," she said, coming back into the room. "Pretty soon Mommy won't have a voice."

Alex watched her stomp up the stairs to her bedroom. He leaned against the banister, feeling sick and unsteady. Toni hadn't called Lacey "Mommy" in years. In the meantime Lacey had taken Wink in her arms and was swaying gently, almost cooing. "It's okay, sweetie, it's okay." Alex continued to stand away from them, as if he were the monster that had brought this tragedy on everyone. Margot, looking forlorn, gathered the cups to take to the kitchen.

He drew in a breath and straightened before going back to Lacey and Wink. "It's hard, Winky, but your mom and I are adjusting." He searched Lacey's face as he put his arm around his daughter. Lacey turned her head, avoiding his gaze. "We're going to manage. We're going to find ways." He couldn't think of what else to say. The fire had gone out, but he didn't get up to put on another log. Lacey pulled away, drawing herself into the corner of the sofa. He stroked his daughter's back, feeling each fragile vertebra.

Margot rinsed the cups and put them in the dishwasher. She wrapped the leftover lasagna in foil. The casserole dish was riddled with hardened bits of cheese and charred cream sauce stuck to the rim. After scraping it as best she could, Margot set it to soak and slumped down at the kitchen table. Sorrow, nothing but sorrow, overwhelmed her. She felt like a fool. What had made her think she could do any good here? This was Lacey's illness. She and Alex would have to find a way to help their daughters live with it. Lacey's piercing stare when she learned that Alex had called on Margot to help him had gone straight to Margot's heart. Alex was wrong to have brought her into this decision. They had hurt Lacey deeply.

Margot thought again of the terrible week with Oliver. She longed for him now. What a mess. She kept turning the awful days over in her mind. If only this gallery in San Francisco would take his paintings and give him a show. That would be some solace. But then what? Lacey's illness wasn't going to go away. Now, by taking Alex's side, Margot had become involved more deeply than ever. And she had thought she could help. What a joke.

Alex came into the kitchen.

"Where's . . ." She started to ask about Lacey.

"Upstairs with Wink. Trying to calm her down."

"Shouldn't you be with Toni?"

"Toni won't even look at me. And Lacey's furious."

"I'm sorry, Alex."

"Shit. This wasn't what I wanted." He sat down across from her.

"You wanted the girls to know. Did you really expect it to be any different?" Margot pushed her chair back, wishing to be anywhere but here. "You knew the girls would be upset. Remember, we agreed they should know." Margot was struck again that agreeing with Alex and ignoring her sister's wishes was a breach of loyalty—like switching sides, going over to join an enemy army. But she had chosen, and part of her still thought they had been right.

Alex stared blankly out into the dark garden. There was no moon. He closed his eyes for a moment.

"Alex, they had to know sometime," she said, raising her voice. "Leaving for Chicago just pushed the issue."

"Lacey wanted me to take the job."

"I know that."

"It's just so hard."

"You have the rest of the weekend. Keep talking to the girls. Do something fun. Something normal—maybe go to the movies together or out to eat. Just live the way you usually do. That's what Lacey wants."

"You're right."

"Not totally. I shouldn't have come here."

"Don't say that."

"Alex, this is about you and Lacey. How you get on with your lives is between the two of you."

He rubbed his forehead. "I just don't understand her these days. Everything has changed. It's like she's closing herself off from me."

"Of course things seem different. But even though she's sick, she's still the same person."

"I don't know, Margot."

"Alex, you can do this." She stood. "I'm going up to bed. If Toni's willing, I'll talk to her for a bit. Why don't you check on Wink?"

"Margot." He looked up at her as if not quite sure of what he intended to say.

"I'm leaving in the morning. I need to get home."

"I'm glad you were here. Even if . . ."

"I shouldn't have come."

Margot pulled the blankets around her. The guest room on the third floor was not well insulated and cold air from the outdoors leaked in around the window frame. The sheets felt like ice. She shivered and longed to cuddle up against Oliver's warm body. After leaving Alex in the kitchen she had come upstairs to bed. From Lacey's room had come the sound of muffled voices. Lacey was with her daughters. Margot had slipped by unnoticed. Now, curled up in the dark, she knew sleep would be a long time coming.

January, she thought. Look how the new year was starting out. Margot clenched her teeth to keep them from chattering. She pictured the unheated cottage on Bow Lake. Sometimes in late August the temperature dipped into the forties at night. She and Lacey would huddle under the moth-eaten blankets that Granny Winkler took out of the trunk at the foot of her bed.

The August when Margot was eight and Lacey twelve had been incredibly hot. The temperature reached record heights in New Hampshire and one July day it peaked at 104. There, at Bow Lake, Granny Winkler gave each granddaughter a Japanese hand fan, and they sat on the shaded porch in the late afternoon playing Crazy Eights, one hand clutching the limp cards, the other fanning gently at the wisps of hair clinging to their sweating foreheads. Margot had particularly loved that game, being eight herself.

The old cottage had no air-conditioning and the hardest time of the day came at bedtime when the girls tried to fall asleep in the creaky old cots upstairs under the eaves. Margot remembered that night when the temperature hardly dropped, there was no breeze, and the sticky air weighed them down like an unwelcome wool blanket that they couldn't kick off. Margot tried to lie still and Lacey was telling her about the locker she would have for the first time when she went to junior high in the fall. Margot was already worried about what it would be like to be at the grammar school without her sister. The junior high started an hour earlier in the morning. They wouldn't even leave the house at the same time.

"Girlies," their granny called up to them, "are you still awake?"

"Yes, Gran," Lacey called down.

Margot thought their grandmother was going to scold them for talking so late at night.

"Moon's full," their grandmother said. "Put on your suits. I think we could all use a swim."

Lacey flipped on the light. Margot stared across at her sister, amazed. This had never happened before. Grandmother Winkler was warm and loving, but she ran an ordered household. Going to bed early was a virtue in her book. Swimming at night was not part of her routine.

The sisters hurriedly pulled off their nightgowns and reached for their bathing suits, which hung drying on hooks on the open stud walls. Margot had to yank at her wet suit to pull up the stretchy fabric. The cool, damp cloth felt good on her skin. When they reached the foot of the stairs, Granny Winkler met them with towels and flashlights. The path under the trees was dark, but the air was still as hot as daytime. The dry pine-covered ground seemed to crackle under their flip-flops. Once they reached the lake they turned off their flashlights. The full moon shone brilliantly on the water. Margot gasped in awe. "It's so bright," she said.

"It's nighttime and we have to swim together," Grandmother Winkler said. She announced they would each take an inner tube and float together in the lake. The black inner tubes were heaped in a pile next to the dock.

Granny Winkler wore a billowy cotton bathing suit with wide straps and a skirt. Tonight she didn't put on her bathing cap with the unpleasant rubber smell, but her hair was pulled high in a topknot on her head. Margot never understood the bathing cap, as her grandmother swam a ladylike breaststroke, her head and neck always well out of the water.

The lake felt delicious. Neither girl shivered or squealed as the water touched her skin. The surface was smooth, broken only by the gentle wake made by their bodies as they glided along. The event of swimming at night alone with their grandmother felt ceremonial, and in keeping with the occasion they followed her, nearly silent. Grandmother Winkler rested her fleshy arms on her tube and moved her legs in a scissors kick. She glided slowly and evenly through the water. Margot followed, her own legs moving faster and froglike while she clutched the black rubber ring. Lacey brought up the rear of their little procession. The water felt like silk. Their progress out into the lake was almost effortless.

Lacey spoke. Her voice rang out clear in the night. "Granny," she said, "the moon is making a path for us." Her laughter carried across the water. "We're swimming the moon path."

That night was perfect. Margot and her sister were happy. What could ever be better? Lacey had found just the right words. They were swimming the moon path on Bow Lake.

Margot shivered in the cold room. She rolled over to face the wall. How much longer would Lacey be able to find the right words, or any words at all?

The wind was howling the next morning as Margot packed her bag. Despite the costly penalty, she had changed her flight to return to New York a day early. A steady thumping and clanging came from Lacey's loom across the hall. When Margot went down to the kitchen for breakfast she was relieved to be alone. She made tea and put a slice of bread in the toaster. A large flock of birds had gathered around the feeder outside the kitchen window. They dove and circled, all trying to grab what they could. Smaller birds scurried beneath, taking with relish the seeds that had fallen to the ground. In the garden the last of the perennial flowers were nothing but raggedy brown stalks against the snow.

Margot was sitting at the table eating her breakfast when Lacey came into the kitchen. Her hair was pulled tightly into the barrette at her neck. She didn't smile, but there was color in her cheeks. She wore jeans and a teal-colored sweater and had taken the time to put on dangling silver earrings. She took a bowl from the cupboard and filled it with granola.

"Well, now everybody knows," Lacey said. Her voice was level and resigned.

"Lacey, I . . . " Margot began, her words coming out in a jumble. "It wasn't easy for any of us. It's terrible, terrible. But it was time they knew and better for them to hear it from Alex and you together."

"That's what you . . . and Alex took from me." Lacey spoke very slowly.

"What do you mean?" Margot asked.

"Time," Lacey said.

"I'm not sure I understand."

"I tried to tell Alex. I wanted a few months. A few more months for everything." Lacey stopped and took in a large breath. "I wanted my girls to live with me like it . . . always was. I wanted to give them normal days. It's over now."

"Oh, Lacey," Margot murmured.

"What I wanted was so little." Lacey spoke very softly, then whispered, "A little more time. That's all."

10

Shed: Open space between upper and lower warp threads.

It was already March. Margot felt that the winter had slipped by much like the clouds now bolting across the sky, one moment casting a shadow, the next disappearing altogether. There had been no major winter storms, despite intermittent dire predictions. The weather was still cool, but the days were lengthening, that inevitable sign of hope, and now and again when walking in the park she could smell the change in the seasons: the earthiness of damp ground, the pungent wet of the Hudson, and the sweet spiciness wafting from pots of narcissus perched outside flower shops on sunny afternoons.

After the disastrous weekend with Lacey in January, Wink had been Margot's principle source of communication with the family. Lacey rarely answered the phone. Wink seemed to enjoy talking to Margot and she reported that the first few weeks after Margot's visit had been hard, but after the family conference with Lacey's neurologist they had all calmed down a little. The doctor had urged them to carry on as usual. Wink assured Margot that her mom wasn't getting any worse.

Eventually, Lacey spoke to Margot when she called and her tone grew gradually warmer week after week, almost in keeping with the weather. When they had spoken earlier this month, Lacey had sounded much like her old self, getting stuck on a word only now and then. Margot tried to keep her calls cheerful, not wanting to reenter any unsettling territory. Oliver accused her of avoiding difficult situations. Sometimes he was right, but in this case doing otherwise was just too painful.

Last week Wink had been accepted at Cornell and Toni had gotten into Columbia as well as the University of New Hampshire. Lacey called to say that she and Toni were coming to New York to visit the school again. She explained that Ryan was still in the picture—all the more reason to get Toni away from New Hampshire and out into a wider world. Lacey spoke slowly. She seemed to be making an effort to be understanding of her daughter's wishes, and yet, she told Margot, she thought if only Toni could hear more about New York from Margot, and how it could open up so many possibilities, she might feel more enthusiastic about the school. Margot agreed to talk to her niece about the advantages of attending college in New York.

Here was a chance to do something for Lacey. If Toni was in New York, Margot could be more of a hands-on aunt. She imagined taking Toni to gallery openings and introducing her to the art world, or simply meeting for coffee to have a chance to really connect and know her niece better.

Toni and Lacey arrived at Margot's apartment for their visit to New York at the end of March. Margot felt hopeful. They were looking at colleges, living a normal life, not hiding at home mired in unhappiness because of Lacey's illness. This trip had to be a good sign.

Oliver's visit to San Francisco had paid off. The Croft Gallery was giving him a one-man show in early June. His dark mood had lifted and he was now in a working frenzy. Gradually, they had settled back into their usual routine. Their argument over her trip to New Hampshire to help Alex had shaken her. Those few anxious days when he was away had made her feel wobbly and unsure. It was a relief when he returned, and their lives seemed much the same, except for a few changes.

All winter Margot had gone to her old apartment early in the morning before going down to her job at the gallery. Oliver encouraged her return to art, though when he got home in the evening, he was usually caught up in his own work and didn't always ask about her progress. They ate their "sloppy suppers" at nine or later, as he often forgot the time. Soon it would be salad season, and Oliver's turn to cook. They didn't talk about Lacey's illness and they didn't talk about Oliver's marriage proposal, almost as if they had an unspoken pact.

The Saturday afternoon of their visit Margot found Toni alone at her apartment. The night before Oliver had taken them all to a Brazilian restaurant for dinner. The food was good, but he had chosen the place thinking that Toni would like the music as well as the hip young waiters, many of them students at Columbia.

"Where's your mom?" Margot asked when she let herself in.

"Taking a run," Toni said. Toni and Lacey had toured the university that morning and met with an admissions officer.

"It's almost warm out today," Margot said, putting her shoulder bag on the chair near the door.

"Mom's more of a fitness freak than ever." Toni was sitting on the love seat with a large Columbia catalog open in her lap. She pushed it aside and looked up at her aunt. Toni's hair was messily clipped up high on her head. She wore a long, slouchy sweater over tight jeans that flared at the bottom. Her resemblance to Lacey was stronger than ever, though the trace of worry in her gaze reminded Margot of Alex. Toni had the beginning of a fine line between her brows like her father, perhaps undetectable to someone outside the family.

"So how'd you like Columbia?"

"Pretty amazing," she said. She poked at the catalog of the course listings. "They have everything."

"You don't sound enthused."

"I'm sure Mom's filled you in." Toni wrinkled her lips into a pout.

"I'd love to have you here in the city."

"Thanks." She offered Margot a slight smile and sighed. "You don't have to worry. Mom wins," she said, her voice tinged with sarcasm.

"So you'll come to Columbia?"

"Do you think I have the guts to disappoint her? My poor mother with this tragic disease?" Toni's face crumpled, becoming more childlike, her eyes filling with tears.

"Oh, sweetie." Margot came and sat next to her niece. "It must be so hard."

"You have no idea. Wink has become little miss research girl. She prints out all this junk that she says we need to read. Her latest thing is brain food. Like Mom hasn't spent her whole life as some sort of health Nazi." Toni was crying harder now. "Dad tiptoes around us like he's some kind of mass murderer who doesn't want to be found out and then he disappears to Chicago. I kept hoping if we just kept going nothing would happen. Like maybe it was some big mistake after all."

Margot put her arms around her niece. Behind her flip, savvy exterior was a girl deeply worried about her mom's illness. Like Alex, she held everything inside. "It's okay," Margot said. "You can tell me about it."

"Mom's so hard on Ryan, so totally unfair. She always thinks she knows best."

"She did know best in my case."

"Meaning?" Toni wiped her wet face with her hands. She was young and pretty. Her face showed no traces of having made irreparable mistakes.

"When I was engaged to Teddy, your mom told me not to get married so quickly. She tried to warn me."

"Dad said that guy was a jerk."

Toni's words stung her. So Alex had also thought she was a fool.

"I was young then, just a couple of years older than you are. I was lonely and desperate to find the kind of happiness your parents had."

" 'Had' is the operative word."

"You mustn't think that way. Toni, your parents are doing their best. They're adjusting to all this, too." Margot hugged her niece. Lacey would have known how to comfort her daughter. She had spent years putting Band-Aids on skinned knees, calming her frightened girls after nightmares, and later soothing them when they were let down by a friend or didn't get invited to a party. "Just take things slowly," she said, thinking how inept her own words sounded.

Toni sighed and lowered her head. Margot stroked her hair.

They both looked up at the sound of a key in the door. Lacey came in, her face flushed and happy, then appeared concerned when she saw Margot with her arm around Toni. "You okay?" she asked.

Toni stood up. "I'm going to Columbia, Mom."

Lacey came and pulled her daughter into a hug. She smiled down at Margot. An expression of delight mixed with relief fell across her face. Over her daughter's shoulder she mouthed the words "Thank you" to her sister. But Margot knew she'd had nothing at all to do with Toni's decision.

Oliver watched Hannah Greene walk slowly from painting to painting in his studio. He was working on a series of oils based on the twelve Olympian gods. Each piece was meant to stand alone, with the figure painted in a somewhat abstracted modern rendition, merely hinting at the actual Greek character. Hannah paused in front of Artemis, goddess of the hunt. Oliver had portrayed her as a figure of strength, her muscles shimmering but her head cast down toward the carcass of an animal. Her tears were shot with raylike lines radiating throughout the canvas. The figure wore modern dress, a twenty-first-century Diana.

"This is different for you," Hannah said.

Oliver said nothing. He remained at the far end of the huge space, allowing Hannah to explore the work on her own. The walls of his studio were a dirty white and marred from the canvases he had hung at various stages of completion. The wooden floors were spattered with paint. A bookshelf near the door formed an alcove where he kept his desk, a computer, and files of images. A notebook on the desk was open to a page of pencil drawings and daubs of paint, colors he intended to use in his next composition.

"Powerful stuff," Hannah said, then moved to the next painting. She had kept her coat on, since Oliver left the temperature in the studio low. Heat was expensive. He preferred to dress warmly, and as he painted, actively moving in and away from the work, he often grew hot and shed a few layers of clothing. Today he was down to a white V-neck T-shirt and his old jeans that sagged at the knees. Hannah, appearing very much the affluent collector with her expensive leather boots and matching handbag, was deeply tanned. She and June had just returned to New York after having spent the winter months at June's house in Antigua.

He decided not to comment on or explain what she was looking at. His work had been evolving this winter in unexpected ways. While he was thrilled to have the commitment from the Croft, he was nervous about completing all the work in time. Still, he was oddly confident. He hadn't felt this inspired in many years. He remembered when he first drove a motorcycle. He was scared shitless, but he never wanted to get off. Preparing for a show felt like that.

"So all of this is for California?"

"I took a few studies out there. They liked what they saw." He shrugged.

"I'd like June to see these," she said.

"None of them is finished."

Hannah moved to another painting. The subject was Hermes. Oliver had created rays of what seemed like cable wires with a series of dots and dashes. On top he had painted an overlay, sheer like a piece of lace, of a large spread of bird wings, recognizable only from a distance. Hannah turned to Oliver. "This work's amazing."

"It's coming." He appreciated her approval. It had been a dizzying spring and he still had more to do to be ready for the show.

"By the way, how's Margot?" Hannah asked.

"Busy right now," he said, thinking of her mornings when she hurried away to paint. He was glad she was going back to it, but he missed having her in the apartment first thing in the day, watching him, listening to him, sharing her thoughts. Margot hadn't shown him anything yet, saying that none of her paintings were ready. "She's coming to San Francisco with me for the show. We may stay a while." Oliver had no specific plan yet, but he hoped this trip to California might be a kind of turning point—not only for his work, but for Margot and him. He wanted her permanently in his life. Together. He thought it was time to consider the future.

"Be careful."

He gave Hannah a questioning look.

"California can be addictive."

Not long after Lacey's trip to New York with Toni, Margot invited her sister back to see a special exhibit. A gallery in SoHo was exhibiting a group of weavers in a show called Woven Voices: Women Connecting the World. Surprisingly, the invitation had been Oliver's idea. He had thought Lacey would enjoy another chance to get away and had told Margot that if she wanted to do something for her sister, this might be one way to help. Margot was touched by his thoughtfulness. Lacey had accepted gladly and taken the train from Boston to New York.

They stood now in front of a huge tapestry woven in the Japanese ikat style by an artist from Vermont. This piece was at least four feet high and ran the length of one wall. Sweeps of black and gray were interspersed with patterns of vivid blue that reminded Margot of Asian calligraphy with a visual strength all its own.

"Do you think it says anything?" she asked Lacey.

"There's always a . . ." Lacey stepped closer to the weaving. "A message," she said finally. "There's always a story."

Margot thought back to the introductory panels of the exhibit explaining how weaving was one of the most ancient art forms. The loom itself had changed very little over the ages. The creation of cloth to cover the body was only the beginning, and soon cultural identities emerged through fabrics. Oliver loved the story of Penelope weaving a burial shroud while waiting for her long-departed Odysseus, unraveling a little each night to show her belief that he would return, hoping all the while to keep her suitors at bay.

Oliver was often in Margot's thoughts. He continued to be in a good mood and the long hours in his studio never seemed to tire him now.

Margot and Lacey paused in front of another large piece.

"This looks like the ocean," Margot said.

"Reminds me of waves. Sound waves." Lacey's speech seemed fluent first thing in the morning, though she kept her sentences short.

"You always chose weaving as an art form. I can't believe I've never asked you why."

"It's useful. I like making things. And I like the feel of it." Lacey looked down at her hands, spreading her fingers wide, then turning her hands over to study her palms.

"You do beautiful work," Margot said, thinking how her sister's hands were not only lovely but expressive.

Lacey said nothing. They had come to a weaving in which dried grasses and pieces of twigs were incorporated into the design. Lacey stood close to the work, then backed up to get a better sense of the whole. There was a bench in the center of the room and a few moments later she sat. Margot joined her.

"Are you tired?" she asked.

"No. I just want to slow down. There's so much here."

Lacey's skin was glowing from her run in Central Park first

thing that morning. She pressed her lips together and then opened her mouth as if to speak and closed it.

Margot placed her hand on Lacey's arm. "Is something bothering you? Is it the girls?"

"No. Wink is so excited about Cornell. She still can't believe she got in." Lacey swallowed and took in a breath. "I wish Toni was happier."

"She will be. She loves New York." Margot hoped she sounded encouraging.

"It's something else."

"Finding words?"

"Not only that." Lacey shook her head. "It's Alex."

Margot's shoulders tensed. "Alex?"

"He's gone so much."

"That must be hard."

Lacey raised her hand to stop Margot from speaking. "It's not that. I wanted him gone. Less strain. I hate the way . . . he . . . watches me."

"I see," Margot said.

"When he's home . . . he's so distant. It's like there's a wall between us."

"What do you mean?" Margot shifted forward on the bench.

Lacey looked at Margot. "I know I'm at fault. We don't talk much and when we make love . . ." Color came to her face. "It's like he's afraid of me. I still need that . . . part of marriage."

Margot swallowed and withdrew her hand. "Oh," she said. How could she talk about this with her sister? Years before, they had talked about "cute boys" or joked about TCBYB, their secret code for "This could be your boyfriend," referring to some terrible guy they had seen. Margot had never asked Lacey about what it was like to love Alex, certainly not about their sex life. Margot felt a blush rising from her chest.

"Do you think there's someone? Another woman?" Lacey asked.

"Oh, no." Margot spoke quickly. A visitor looking at the tapestry with twigs turned and stared at them. Margot lowered her voice. "Lacey, he loves you. He's worried, that's all. Maybe that's made him seem a little distant."

"When he's home, he av . . . avoi . . ."

"Avoids?"

"Don't tell me words." She pursed her lips. "Yes. He avoids me." Lacey's normally smooth brow had furrowed. Her mouth trembled.

"You must be imagining that," Margot said abruptly. She didn't want to think about Alex that way either. She had stashed away her confusing memories of him years ago.

"Listen, I'm starving." Margot glanced around nervously. "Let's finish looking. Then I want to take you to lunch. You must be hungry, too."

Lacey stood up slowly and followed Margot into the final room of the exhibition.

Alex boarded the shuttle to New York. It was the end of April and the green shoots of bulbs had begun to emerge in Lacey's garden. Usually on Mondays after a weekend with his family in New Hampshire, he went to Chicago to meet with his new clients. After months of intense effort he had gotten the Wingate Company back on track. His work was far from over, but he had set up meetings in New York with an interested buyer. He had finally convinced the family board of the advantages of a reorganization and sale. Fred Wingate and his cousin Mark had wanted to enlarge the business and go public, selling the family shares in hopes of making a few quick millions. Alex had advised against that plan, however, explaining that selling the entire company sooner rather than later was less risky. Given the dismal track record of the two men, he envisioned only further pitfalls if they took the helm.

Alex found his seat. All that was available this morning was a middle seat toward the rear of the aircraft. He didn't care. It was a relief to escape New Castle. Toni's accusing gaze followed him everywhere, as if she was still angry that he had kept Lacey's illness a secret from her. Wink was solicitous of Lacey, hanging out at home more, seeing her friends less often. He didn't want to offend Wink by telling her to lighten up.

After Margot's visit in January, Lacey had been cold and unreachable for a while. She had made it clear that she wasn't "in the mood" the first few times he had reached for her in bed. Gradually she let go of her anger, but their lovemaking became awkward and hurried. When she turned away from him afterward, he was left with a hollow sense that the woman he'd been holding and caressing hadn't been there at all. He was afraid to say anything for fear of upsetting her again.

Often when they were alone, Lacey remained silent. Alex had never minded silence before. He liked the comfortable silences that settle in between two married people, the kind full of implicit understanding, making it unnecessary to talk. He savored those moments when all they exchanged was a look: her glance at a party if a boorish guest was dominating the conversation, a look of pleasure after one of the girls said something endearing, the expression on her face that made him feel as if he was the only one that mattered and that she could hardly wait to be alone with him. Now the silences between them were anguished and empty. Was he losing her already?

After Lacey's last trip to New York to see Margot, he had hoped they'd gotten through the worst. He yearned for the comfortable way their lives used to be. He hoped it was still possible to return to that. Yet something was always getting in the way. One weekend he had been preoccupied with his mother, who had fallen out of her wheelchair. Fortunately, nothing was broken, but leaving the retirement home for the hospital had upset her. This past weekend Wink had insisted that she didn't want to go away to college and leave her mother alone. Lacey had talked to her daughter for hours, trying to convince her that she didn't want her to stay at home, that it would be years before she needed help.

For Alex, the terrible thing about spending time away from Lacey was that when he returned, he could see the progression of her disease more clearly. He was convinced that her speech had grown more choppy over the winter. Every few sentences she would stumble over a word. She had an odd habit now of shaking her head no, a slightly jerky movement, like a nervous tick. This occurred when something slowed her down. Her lips would tighten and tremble for just a moment before she would sigh and shrug, as if she were merely inconvenienced.

The flight crew made the announcements for landing, interrupting his reverie. The plane circled and dipped as it approached New York. Alex unclenched his fists and tried to relax. He had to put these thoughts aside, if only for a while.

Alex's day in the city went well. His first round of meetings was amazingly successful. It felt great to explain a complicated financial situation, to cast it in a positive light, to have the answers ready, to speak with knowledge and conviction. He was thankful that he hadn't lost his touch, and, indeed, he finished the agenda ahead of schedule.

He took the elevator down to the lobby and stepped outside. The air was mild, the trees bursting with new leaves. The late-afternoon light softened the sharp, angular buildings, making the city seem less intense, more manageable. He walked over to Fifth Avenue and headed north, toward the Metropolitan Museum of Art. He had several hours to kill before dinner with his clients and their accountants. Thinking over his successful day, he felt almost cocky.

Pedestrians with shopping bags hurried along looking as if they had places to go, people to see. He tried to distinguish between the visitors, like him, and those who lived here. Why hadn't he thought of calling Margot? She lived here. He reached for his cell phone. She answered immediately, explaining that Monday was her regular day off. She usually spent it at her apartment—her "secret studio," she joked—and asked him to stop by. He arrived within minutes.

She opened the shiny black door on the landing when he stepped out of the elevator, and he followed her inside. The apartment was like a doll's house, the one main room not as big as his dining room in New Castle. Lacey kept their home in New Hampshire spare and neat. This room was the opposite. The dish on the little table by the front door overflowed with keys, pens, paper clips. Next to it was a vase of drooping tulips, a telephone, a tattered spiral notebook, and one lone glove.

"You haven't been here in ages," she said, giving him a quick hug.

He stepped away from her. "Lacey loves this place," he said. "So this is where you paint." He glanced over at the round table near the windows, cluttered with paint tubes, paper, notebooks, and a scattering of photographs. A few had been tacked up on an easel just above the canvas she had presumably been working on.

She nodded. "Most every morning. On Mondays I'm here all day. Right now I'm glad it's not rented."

"It's a great place," he said.

She gestured around her. "Oliver says he can hardly fit in here."

Alex thought of Oliver, tall and bulky, the kind of guy who would be a large presence in any room. Margot's apartment looked girlish, not the kind of place where a man would feel comfortable, yet her ex-husband, Teddy, had once lived here.

"Please sit down," she said.

He lowered himself onto the sofa, pushing aside a ruffled pillow. "I can't stay long," he said, suddenly uncomfortable in what seemed such a personal setting. He had a strange sensation, as if he were seeing the inside of Margot's handbag or peering into her closet.

"You mustn't rush off," she said. She glanced at her watch. "Why don't we have a glass of wine? I have a bottle of white in the fridge from when Lacey was here." Margot's hands fluttered above him, as if now that she wasn't painting she didn't know quite what to do with them. She wore as a sort of smock, a large man's shirt—Oliver's, he presumed—over jeans. Her hair was clipped up on her head, reminding him of the way his daughters sometimes looked. It made her seem young.

He shifted on the sofa. It was low. He had a hard time fitting his knees behind the coffee table. "Sure. That'd be great."

She disappeared through the doorway into what he imagined was the kitchen. "The wine's nothing fancy," she called to him. "I don't have a thing to offer you. I don't keep food here."

He assured her he wasn't hungry.

She reappeared with the wine and two glasses on a bamboo tray. The tray teetered briefly as Margot balanced it on the stack of magazines in the middle of the coffee table. She poured the wine and smiled, handing him the first glass.

"Lacey had a wonderful time at that exhibit. I should have thanked you sooner."

"No need to thank me. There's so little I seem to be able to do." She poured herself a glass of the wine.

"Just knowing I can talk to you makes a difference." He lifted his glass.

Margot lifted hers and reached over to click his. "Cheers." Color rose to her cheeks.

"It's nice to be in New York. Away for a bit." He felt guilty saying this.

"Getting away is good for all of us sometimes." She sipped her wine. Then, setting her glass down, she fiddled with the hem of her shirt. "Sorry. I must look awful." She stood and took off the big shirt and placed it on the chair next to the easel. She wore a pale blue sweater underneath, the color of her eyes. "Painting is a messy sport." She smiled again.

"Lacey is happy you've gone back to it." Saying this made it sound like they'd discussed it at length, when in fact they spoke so little.

"It was her idea."

He cleared his throat. "Does it come back to you easily?"

"Hardly. I feel like a beginner again. Mostly I'm working on small studies. I like painting objects close up and then far away."

"Is Oliver helping you?"

"God, no. He'd find this laughable. He's the real artist. I'm the wannabe."

Alex remembered Lacey explaining how Margot's marriage to Teddy had in some way ruined her sister's desire to paint. Alex wondered if Oliver's larger-than-life creativity might put a damper on her, too. He looked around him. "This is a great little place."

"Little is right, but I'm glad I've kept it all these years."

"I remember thinking it seemed like a lot of money. I gather it's been a good investment."

"I guess it's worth a lot more than I paid for it. Oliver thinks I should sell it. But I like having my own place to work."

Alex shifted, hitting his knee on the coffee table. The last time he had been alone with Margot was during her visit to New Castle in January. She seemed different in New York. "Did you notice any change in Lacey's speech when she was here?" he asked.

"Not really." She paused. "Well, maybe a little." She looked away from him.

"I'm sorry to bring it up. Some days I just want to forget. I know that sounds selfish."

"None of us can forget."

"I want things to get back to normal, if that's even possible. I know it's my fault. Every time I go home I think we'll be okay again. I feel like I'm walking on a frozen lake, only the ice isn't solid and I'm just waiting to fall through."

"Maybe take Lacey away for a weekend. I'd come stay with the twins."

He shook his head. "I've got too much work now." That was true, but would Lacey even want to be away with him?

"You need to keep trying, Alex. Lacey needs you."

"You're right. I will," he said, suddenly weary. His gaze fell on a pile of photographs next to the magazines. The top one was a picture of a lake.

"Some old photos of Bow Lake," Margot said, noticing his interest. She put down her glass, picked up the stack, and came to sit beside him. "I wanted to try some landscapes. I found these in a box of mementos. Here's the cottage." She handed him a picture and continued to sort through the others.

"The old place never changes." He caught a whiff of her perfume, a flowery scent.

"Here's a sunset." She handed him another picture. "Remember the path to the beach?"

Alex held the images in his hands. He was aware of Margot close beside him—her leg not an inch from his. He focused on the picture. He could imagine the smell of the woods just from looking at the lush green leaves, the mossy forest floor, the gentle bend of the ferns. A photo of the sun glinting on the lake brought back all the old memories of summer. He remembered their grandmother. What an incredible gift she had left to Lacey and Margot. It was more than a fine piece of real estate. It was a piece of history that made them who they were. Summer after summer they returned to Bow Lake, and now Wink and Toni were contributing to their own bank of memories.

"Here's one of Lacey." Her arm grazed his. "It could be Toni. See?"

He took the picture. Lacey stood holding a paddle next to the green Old Town canoe. Her tanned legs and arms were lean and strong. They used to race the canoes out to the island. She wore a winner's smile.

Margot was staring at another photograph and about to shuffle it to the bottom of the pile. "Come on," he said. "Is that one of you?" He took it from her.

"It makes me feel so old to look at these," she said.

In the picture Margot looked just the way she had the summer before he went to business school. He stared at her shy smile, her secretive gaze. "You were beautiful," he said. "I mean, you still are." Alex felt color rising to his face, remembering the one summer he had pushed to the far reaches of his brain.

"Don't be silly," she said, getting up, nearly toppling the bottle of wine. She sat again in the chair across from him and forced the pictures back into a neat pile. "We were all much younger then."

Alex stared at his hands, opening and closing his fists. What had come over him? "I need to go," he said. He rose, trying to avoid hitting the table with his knees.

"Already?" she asked.

"It's getting late," he said. He stood and picked up his jacket, thinking he shouldn't have come. A small painting rested on the easel. It was a picture of the tiny island they called Junior, a short swim from her grandmother's dock. "This is really good," he said. Maybe he shouldn't have looked. Artists could be funny about showing their work.

"You recognize it?" Her brows lifted.

"Junior. I'd know it anywhere."

"I'm working on other things, but I keep going back to Bow Lake."

He nodded, suddenly overwhelmed. Bow Lake. A generation ago. A jumble of memories rose up in his throat as if they might choke him. His life might have taken a completely different path. Abruptly, he put one hand into his jacket and reached around for the other sleeve. Margot guided the jacket up and around him. "Thanks," he said, and turned to face her. He hugged her briefly. It was only for a moment, but the warmth of her, the softness of her hair against his cheek, caught him off guard.

"I'll call you." He went to the door and let himself out.

Yarn: A continuous strand of twisted thread.

After Alex left, Margot quickly washed out their glasses and put the wine bottle back in the fridge. She reached for the photographs on the coffee table, but rather than tuck them back in the box, she sat down again and shuffled through the stack. She placed the best one of Lacey on top. In the photo she stood with her back to the dark woods, smiling out at the world, young, strong, and seemingly perfect. Margot closed her eyes and leaned back into the cushions.

She remembered the first time she was jealous of Lacey. It was at the end of one summer at Bow Lake. Lacey, twenty, was halfway through college, and Alex had finished his freshman year. Margot, still in high school, had been only sixteen. The unexpected emotion had made her feel physically sick, as if she were coming down with the flu. The clichéd expression "green with envy" was accurate, though not the soft green like the leaves that fluttered in the trees, or the green of the ferns waving on the woodland floor, but the nasty green of overcooked asparagus, or the canned peas her mother slopped onto her dinner plate, too careless to drain them properly.

Both Alex and Lacey had lives away from Bow Lake, lives she

could not yet imagine. Margot had been living that summer with Granny Winkler until this final week in August. She had a job at the Girl Scout camp down the lake, assisting the arts and crafts counselor. Her fingers were blistered from hours spent helping cranky little girls make lanyards, bracelets, and key chains that would end up at the back of a kitchen junk drawer by October.

Lacey was tanned and looked gorgeous, having taught sailing at a sleepaway camp in Maine. Alex had spent the summer working in the shipping department of his father's manufacturing company. He didn't see Lacey at all during the school year, since he went to a small college in western Massachusetts and Lacey went to school in Vermont. The only time they spent together was at Bow Lake. Granny Winkler joked that Alex was making up for lost time, following Lacey everywhere. "Here comes the cocker spaniel," she would whisper to Margot, referring to Alex's worshipful eyes.

Lacey had always treated Alex like a buddy, one of the gang who came to the lake year after year, but that year Margot had noticed a difference. She was with them almost the entire final week, and they did everything together the way they always had—racing canoes out to Junior, or rowing to the island in Pigtail, the wooden skiff that had been in the water every summer since 1935, according to their grandmother. Sometimes they took a picnic lunch and stayed for most of the afternoon, swimming off the tiny beach. Alex's family had a motorboat, and now and again he took Lacey and Margot to Cedar Point, where a marina snack bar sold sodas and ice cream.

Sometimes they biked over to the public tennis courts, a three-mile trip to the end of the lake, and played Canadian doubles. Lacey was the strongest player, so Alex usually paired up with Margot. Alex had a long stride and ran everything down. Margot would yell "yours" from the net, knowing he was there at the back ready to bail her out of trouble. No longer awkward, Alex was more talkative now, and he and Lacey spoke of things Margot had no part of: courses at college, professors, foreign films, concerts they had attended during the school year. Margot had not crossed over into that independent world. They wouldn't be interested in her long hours spent reading art books in the public library, trying to put off the moment when she would have to go home and listen to her mother knocking around in the kitchen, if she came down at all.

Alex and Lacey had seemed to include Margot gladly in all that they did, yet it was as if there was some invisible thread that had begun to connect them that year. They listened to each other with real attention. There was no casual or flip repartee. Even at sixteen Margot could see the way they communicated with their eyes, a lingering glance, or with their hands as they pulled a boat out of the water, fingers touching longer than necessary.

One afternoon the three of them swam out to the raft in front of Granny Winkler's camp. It was a hot day. Stacks of clouds were building in the west. Earlier, Lacey had brought the laundry in from the clothesline, as their grandmother warned of a storm. Margot had helped her fold the cotton sheets bleached white from the sun and the towels that would feel scratchy and rough on their skin when they dried off later after a swim.

Lacey reached the raft first, followed by Alex. When Margot pulled herself up the ladder, they were already lying beside each other, on their stomachs in the sun. Margot shook herself and squeezed the water out of her ponytail before lying next to Lacey. Her arms were covered with goose bumps. The breeze was picking up and the waves rocked the raft in a gentle motion. The lake water evaporated quickly on her skin, causing her to shiver momentarily. Gradually, the heat of the sun warmed her back. She already dreaded the day next week when she and her father would drive Lacey back to school. She pushed that thought away and dozed beside them.

The night before, Alex had driven them to the movies two towns away. They had returned late. Margot had tiptoed upstairs so as not to wake her grandmother, eager to have first turn in the bathroom. Lacey and Alex had remained on the porch. Margot wondered how late Lacey had stayed up, though today Lacey had been at breakfast earlier than usual. Margot wondered if they had made out there in the dark. Were they now boyfriend and girl-friend? She didn't want to ask Lacey, for fear that if they were a couple it would mean she would have to leave them alone.

Now that Margot was awake, her hip bones felt sore against the hard surface of the raft. She came to her elbows. Alex and Lacey were still beside her, but Alex seemed to have moved closer to Lacey, his left foot touching hers. Lacey's head faced away from him, but his arm lay across her back, his forearm against her bare skin. He had light blond hairs on his muscled arm. His hand curled around Lacey's hip, as if he owned her. Margot wondered what it would be like to have his arm around her own waist, the weight of it pressing onto her warm skin. At that moment, she wanted to be Lacey, to have Alex's attention, not as a tennis partner, a playmate, or a friend, but as something more.

Saliva rose in her mouth as she watched them sleep beside her, unaware of her scrutiny. She felt an uneasy loosening between her legs when she imagined what it would be like to have Alex so close to her. Suddenly, she wished she could disappear; she felt like an interloper, the one on the outside looking in.

Carefully, she got up on her hands and knees, then pushed to her feet and rose. She stared down at Alex and Lacey. Saying noth-ing, she stepped to the edge of the raft and dove into the lake.

Margot glanced at the photographs once again, this time pull-ing one of Alex out of the pile. She instantly recalled that light fluttery feeling when you first liked a boy, that lovely sexual aware-ness that seemed to come out of nowhere. She rose from the sofa looking down at the place where Alex had been sitting. It had got-ten late. She stashed the photographs back in the box and went to get her coat.

"Mags, where've you been?"

Oliver heard the clatter of Margot's keys being tossed onto the tray in the hall. He had set the table for dinner in the living room.

Four white cardboard containers from Mai Thai cooled on the kitchen counter. It was almost eight. He had come home earlier than usual, expecting Margot to be there, and after watching the news for a while, he ordered from the Thai place, imagining her imminent arrival.

"Sorry," she said, coming into the kitchen. Her face was flushed, as if she'd walked quickly. "You already ordered?" She leaned into him and kissed his cheek. Her skin felt cool and moist against his.

"I thought you'd be here earlier." He opened a container of rice, a solid gummy mass. "We'll have to nuke it."

Margot reached for the set of glass bowls they used to reheat takeout. She poured out the gelatinous-looking shrimp pad thai. "Didn't you get the tofu one?"

"The other carton."

She nodded, and while the first dish revolved in the microwave she emptied the second carton into the other bowl. Oliver opened the fridge and pulled out a beer.

"Beer or wine?" he asked.

"Wine," she said.

"So what made you so late?"

"Oliver, you're the one who's usually late."

He shot her a glance, but she didn't appear annoyed.

"I had a visitor," she said. The microwave dinged and she removed the pad thai, set the steaming dish on the counter, and added the tofu. "Alex stopped by." Her back was to him. She mashed up the boxes of rice.

"What's he doing in New York?" Oliver pictured the gaunt New Englander in a heavy sweater and corduroy pants on the streets of the city.

"He's selling some company. The buyers are based here. We didn't talk much about that."

"He came to your apartment?"

"He had some free time late this afternoon. He was walking up to the Met and got me on my cell." She stopped talking to put the rice in the microwave after covering it with a sheet of wax paper. "He wanted to talk about Lacey."

Of course, Lacey. Margot carried both dishes of food to the table. He followed with the rice. It smelled nutty and damp, making him suddenly hungry. He returned to the kitchen for his beer and to pour a glass of wine for Margot. The cork in the Chardonnay was wedged tightly in the bottle and didn't yield to his tugging. He grabbed a dish towel and yanked harder, finally opening it with a dull pop. He was annoyed to think of Alex calling Margot and going to see her at her apartment. Why hadn't he called ahead and arranged to meet them both for dinner the way he had on a few previous trips to the city? Lacey's illness was altering the way they all operated.

He filled Margot's glass and carried it to the table. She was sitting still, not having served herself from the dishes of food.

"You okay?" he asked.

She nodded and spooned some rice onto her plate. "Thanks. This is nice."

"So what did he say about Lacey?"

"She's not great. He can see it more than the girls can. Each time he comes home from a trip she seems a little worse." Margot sighed, allowing her shoulders to droop.

They ate quietly for a few minutes.

"You came home early," she said. "Good day?"

"Not bad. I needed to stretch another canvas. I'd rather tackle that in the morning." He'd left his studio on another high. The images were coming with a kind of urgency. Most nights it was hard to stop working. "So, were you painting when Alex dropped in?" he asked.

"I was cleaning up. About to come home."

"Did you show him your work?"

"I didn't show him, but he saw it." She put down her fork and looked across the room at the window overlooking the river.

"You won't let me see anything." Oliver realized he sounded petulant.

Margot frowned and turned to meet his gaze. "He literally popped in. I wasn't planning on his visit. I couldn't exactly run around and hide things."

"So why are you so secretive with me?"

"I'm not ready to show you, that's all." She resumed eating.

"You come to my studio whenever you want to," he said, taking a large mouthful of shrimp and noodles. Small pieces of peanuts fell off his fork and scattered onto the table.

"That's different. I don't want you to see my work until it's better."

He leaned back in his chair and took a swallow of beer. "How long will Alex be here?"

"He's leaving tomorrow. He'll probably be back a few more times before he closes this deal." She shrugged as if she hadn't given it any thought. "Let's walk tonight. We should take advantage of the full moon on the river."

Usually, Oliver liked after-dinner walks with Margot. They both agreed it was one of the pleasures of New York to stroll along Broadway after a good meal, looking in windows, maybe going as far as the big chain bookstore to browse. It was open until ten. There was a gritty Italian coffee place where they sometimes stopped for an espresso and to watch people hurrying along the crowded sidewalks. New Yorkers were out on the street until all hours. But tonight he wanted to stay in. He felt the urge to hibernate, to keep Margot to himself. He was working as hard as he had in years and at the end of the day he was exhausted.

"I don't know," he said.

"Oh, please. I want to be out. It's a beautiful night." Margot looked unusually energized. Tonight he felt the ten years older that he was. She started to clear the table. He rose and followed her, his legs heavy and stiff.

The May evening was cool, but the knife-edged sharpness of the New England spring had eased. Lacey had spent part of the afternoon working in her garden. Alex had observed her from the distance of his office window. It was too soon to plant, but she had told him earlier that she wanted to clean up the perennial bed. She looked happy out in the fresh air, bending and moving with the same easy grace she had had when they first moved to New Castle.

Age was an odd thing. On some days he awoke feeling no different from when he was a young man; on others his tiredness at the end of the day amazed him. It was as if his body was betraying him. What could be so hard about his white-collar job? He thought of the fishing boats going out to sea before dawn, the men facing hours of grueling work. He knew he had nothing to complain about.

At seven it was still light. Lacey was in the kitchen starting dinner. He decided to make a fire in the living room. After carrying in some logs from the shed off the garage, he knelt before the grate. His mother had loved having a fire on a spring evening. She used to exclaim over the smell of wood smoke in the spring, especially in June when it mingled with the scent of roses.

Alex had meant to get over to see his mother in the afternoon, but work had kept him in his office. The sale of the fertilizer company to the New York investors seemed to be unraveling all of a sudden, and after a series of conference calls he had booked a flight to New York for the following day. So much for thinking he had accomplished his goal. He felt the hard brick of the hearth beneath his knees. After crumpling the newspaper that Lacey kept in a basket by the fireplace, he arranged the logs toward the back of the hearth. He waited for the flames to build.

Soon enough, puffs of gray smoke wafted back in his face. He grabbed a clump of newspaper and fanned the flames. He thought of the huge stone fireplace at Lacey's grandmother's camp at Bow Lake and remembered one summer just before he and Lacey were about to leave for college. Was he in love with her then, or simply an eighteen-year-old in lust? He had never considered Lacey his girlfriend. She was a year older; he would be a lowly freshman in a school hours away from hers. Lacey had seemed like a dream come to life, but in reality she had remained out of reach.

They used to make out on the sagging sofa in front of the dying embers while Grandmother Winkler snored in a room at the end of the hall. Margot, still a kid, slept upstairs. He rarely saw Lacey the summers after that except for the few days at the end of August before returning to their separate lives on different campuses. Their earlier flirtation became a distant memory. It seemed to him that Margot changed overnight in those years, going from a sprite of a girl following Lacey around like her shadow to a young woman who was very much her own person.

Margot. He really shouldn't have gone to see her last week. Yet it had felt good to talk to her about Lacey. He didn't want to burden his daughters, and outside his family no one loved Lacey more or understood her better than Margot.

"Mom always cracks the window to make it draw."

Alex, startled by the sound of Wink's voice, staggered to his feet. "The chimney's a little damp." He leaned in again and fanned the flames. The logs were starting to burn. "Where's Toni?" He looked at Wink, who had slumped down on the sofa.

"Do you need to ask?" she said.

"Mom okay with that?" Lacey had complained less about all the time Toni spent with Ryan, having decided that once Toni went off to college the romance would probably peter out.

"She'll be home for dinner."

Alex looked at his watch, then back at the fire. "Let's hope so." The smoke didn't seem as bad to him. He reached for the poker and pushed the logs farther to the rear, then took a seat in the chair opposite his daughter. Part of him wished she had a boyfriend too. Wink, always so studious, seemed almost brooding these days. Even now her head rested against the back of the sofa as if she were too burdened with worries to raise it. "What's going on with you, Mouse?" he asked, using his special pet name for her.

"Have you paid my fall tuition yet?" She appeared to be studying her fingernails and then pushed at her cuticles.

"We sent the amount to hold your place," he said, watching her face carefully. Her initial excitement after being accepted at Cornell had waned. "The first-semester tuition is due in August. Don't worry. Your old man is working hard." He smiled, wanting her to think this was a joke. Although he and Lacey had saved for years, knowing they would have two in college at once, he couldn't afford to let his business slack off. He was well aware of when the tuition payments were due.

"I don't know, Dad."

"Know what?"

"If I want to go. That's all."

"Wink, Cornell was your first choice. Going to that university is a dream come true."

"Mom's dream."

"Not just Mom's dream. You told me you loved the place. They've got that awesome observatory."

"It's not the school. I'm kind of thinking I'd rather be home."

"Winky, everybody leaves home sometime."

"But Mom needs me. I can help her when it gets harder for her to speak."

Alex got up and went to Wink on the sofa. He put his arm around her. "Mouse, you already help her so much. Mom's going to be fine without you. She's strong. She's going to figure out how to deal with this. I'm going to help her. The last thing she wants is for you to put your life on hold."

"I'm afraid, Dad. I think it's worse." Wink curled forward.

Alex rubbed her back. What could he tell her? Lacey *was* worse. "You'll make Mom proud and happy by going to college. She wants you to move on." He kissed the top of Wink's head. Her heavy golden hair fell across her face. "There's a whole world out there just waiting for you," he said.

"Alex, this room is filled . . . with smoke." Neither had heard

Lacey come in. Wink sat up. Alex withdrew his hand. Lacey went to the front window and struggled to lift the sash.

"Wait," he said. He got to his feet and crossed the room. "Let me help you. I think it's drawing now," he said, raising the window. "Still, if you want to air it a bit . . ." Before he could complete his sentence Lacey went over to Wink.

"What's the"—she coughed and flapped one hand up and down as if the smoke was making her cough—"the matter?"

"Wink and I were just talking about college. She's concerned about going away."

"She's going." The words flew off Lacey's tongue.

"Mom," Wink said, her voice imploring.

"You'll be fine." Lacey spoke carefully, her words measured.

"Mom, can't we just talk about it?"

"Not now," Lacey said. She gave Wink a hug and squeezed her shoulders. "The chicken." She gave Alex a dark look, as if she assumed he had been the one who'd raised the question of college in the fall for Wink. Her lips were pursed and trembling. "Is ready."

Before Alex had a chance to explain his discussion with Wink, a door slammed in the distance and Toni called out, "I'm home. Where is everybody?"

Lacey turned away and headed to the kitchen. Her back was rigid, her step determined.

"Dad," Wink said, "I just want to be able to talk about it. I tried to tell Mom the other day and she had a meltdown."

"Not now, Mouse," he said. "We better get in to dinner." He poked once more at the fire and moved the screen to the front of the hearth. He could hear Toni and Lacey in the kitchen and wanted to get in there to keep the peace. He pulled Wink to her feet. "It'll be okay," he said. "I promise."

Margot was surprised to hear from Alex the following Monday. She had been at her apartment all day painting and had to dig wildly through her handbag to retrieve her cell phone, thinking it might be Oliver wanting to make plans for dinner.

"I'm on the last shuttle tonight," Alex said.

"Oh," she said faintly, disoriented that it was him.

"Any chance you could meet me for a drink?"

"You're in the city again?" Hearing his voice so unexpectedly made her feel as if she'd been swimming underwater and had just broken through the surface, her ears still clogged and her eyes blurry.

"Yeah. I've had a lousy day. I just wanted to talk. I mean, well, you must be busy. You and Oliver probably have plans." His voice faded.

"No. It's fine." She looked over at the canvas she'd been working on. A wet brush filled with a leafy shade of green lay on the table. "I need a few minutes here to clean up."

His voice brightened momentarily and he asked her to join him at the bar in the Michelangelo Hotel, where he usually stayed when in the city. He paused and added, "If it's not a good time . . ."

"It's okay. Sure. Tell me where again."

Alex gave her the street address, in midtown.

Margot didn't need to hurry home. Oliver had been working late all week. His paintings had to be shipped soon for his show's opening at the end of May. The night before, he had arrived home after eleven, smelling of turpentine, his hands speckled with paint. He'd brought his supper on a tray and a glass of wine for each of them into their bedroom. Margot had been reading, trying to stay awake. Drinking the wine dulled her earlier annoyance, but later, when sleep eluded her, she thought back to Oliver's marriage proposal at Christmas. That intense discussion of their future together seemed to have been forgotten in his all-consuming painting. Lately, when they talked at all, it was about California, the show, Oliver. She might as well have vanished. Why not go out for a drink with Alex? Didn't she deserve a little fun?

When Margot emerged from the subway, the early-evening air was gentle. The people on the street seemed to have spring fever. Two young women passing by her had bare legs and tropical-colored scarves knotted around their throats, as if in anticipation of summer. One man clutched a bouquet of daffodils and took a moment to straighten his tie while waiting at the light. Margot felt a brief twitter of excitement at the idea of going into a bar to meet Alex. She couldn't remember the last time she'd even been in a bar by herself.

But as she approached the hotel, thinking of Alex again made her slightly uneasy. She remembered the way he had stared at her painting of Bow Lake. His expression had grown distant, as if he'd forgotten she was there. While he'd fumbled with his jacket on his way out, she had wondered what memories he still kept from those long-ago summers. All week her mind had wandered back to his visit. Why had he come in the first place? After leaving so awkwardly, why did he want to see her again?

Before stepping through the revolving door into the hotel, she smoothed her T-shirt over her pants and buttoned her linen blazer. She tucked a loose strand of hair behind her ear. The hotel was an expensive one, filled with businessmen during the week and offering theater package deals on weekends. The lobby had a hushed seriousness that promised comfort and anonymity. Margot didn't spend much time in midtown. She felt out of place and quickly scanned the room.

The bar was to the right of the reception desk, between two ornately carved doors. She stepped into the darkness and waited for someone to seat her, her eyes adjusting to the dimness. A hostess in a slim skirt and four-inch heels asked her name and then led her across the room to a banquette along the wall, where Alex sat. He wore a dark suit and white shirt. His angular nose gave him an elegant profile. It would have been an austere face if not for his mouth, which was wide and softened when he smiled. He stood and kissed her lightly on the cheek while the hostess moved the table out so that she could join him on the bench. The chairs and the walls were covered in brown velvet, giving the room an expensive intimacy.

"You look like spring," he said.

Margot felt underdressed in the swishy bar. She slid in next to him. Her legs seemed to stick on the velvet banquette like one piece of Velcro to another.

"So, you had a bad day?" she asked, wishing he wouldn't look at her so intently. She noticed he was already sipping a glass of wine.

"The whole deal is starting to unravel." He lifted his glass. "I hope you don't mind I started without you." He smiled and asked her what she'd like.

"Whatever you're having," she said.

He signaled the server and pointed to his glass. The waiter returned in no time with a glass of wine for her. Alex looked serious and important to her tonight, more at ease than when he had come to her apartment. He raised his glass and she clicked hers against his. She was startled to see their reflection when she glanced in the mirror across the room. Here, in this unexpected environment, they looked like two strangers.

"It's a long way from New Hampshire. I hope this place is okay." He put his glass down after taking a sip.

"Is this about the company you're helping in Chicago?"

"It's tough when you're dealing with a family business. For the people involved, everything is personal." He told Margot about the complexity of family-run businesses and how family-owned companies rarely lasted beyond the second generation. She listened, sipped her wine, and began to relax.

"I came to talk to the potential buyers in person. They're getting nervous about some environmental issues."

"Because it's fertilizer?" she asked.

"Anytime you deal with chemicals." He stopped abruptly. "Gosh, Margot. I've gone on too long. Please forgive me."

"No, not at all. You make it interesting."

"You're great to listen. Tell me about your painting."

"I seem to be hooked again. Carl lets me start at the gallery at eleven and I've cut back my hours. I'll put in extra hours when we hang the next show."

"Lacey's always said you have real talent."

Margot straightened, realizing that they hadn't spoken yet of her sister. "How is she?" she asked.

"The same." He motioned to the waiter. "Would you like another?"

Margot hesitated, but Alex raised his hand to indicate two more glasses of wine.

"She sounded pretty good earlier this week," Margot said quickly. "She gave me the date for the girls' graduation in June to be sure I had it on my calendar."

"Always planning ahead." Alex leaned against the bench as if weary. "I'm trying to get her excited about Italy. I'm hoping this trip will be good for all of us."

Margot remembered what Lacey had said about Alex, the way he acted almost afraid of her. She shifted her position and looked around the crowded bar. The wine tasted good and slipped down easily. "Where will you be going?"

"A few days in Rome. Then we're driving up through Tuscany. Two weeks in all."

"It sounds dreamy."

"The girls are at least pretending to look forward to it."

"You know they'll have fun." Margot hoped Toni wasn't making a fuss about leaving Ryan for so long.

"We haven't been to Europe since our honeymoon." He swirled the wine in his glass and seemed to study it.

"I'm sure it will make her happy."

"I don't know, Margot. Things are strained." He turned to face her.

She swallowed and met his gaze briefly.

"I probably shouldn't have called you again, but I wanted to talk. You're the only one who understands."

"I'm not sure what I can say." She wished they weren't sitting side by side. The velvet bench held her trapped.

"Lacey's shutting me out. No matter what I do or say, it's never the right time. We used to tell each other everything. Now, she tells me nothing. It's not just the speech." He interlaced his fingers and pressed his hands together, then drew them apart.

"She's working through so much," Margot said. "I mean, the girls are graduating, going away in the fall. That's got to be hard for her too."

"Wink's getting nervous about going away from home. Lacey's trying to convince her it's for the best."

"At least they're talking about it," Margot said, knowing she didn't want to get involved.

"It's not just that. There's the homeless shelter. She's trying to get a grant for the arts project for the kids. Now she's formed a committee for that."

"She's always liked being busy."

"Busy all right. I'm the last person on her list. If I'm even on it."

"Alex, you mustn't say that." Margot eased slightly away from him.

"I know I sound like a selfish bastard. Is it wrong to want time with her? She won't let me in." He picked up his napkin and tossed it onto the table.

"Talk to her," Margot blurted out, feeling annoyed. "She needs to know how you feel." She longed to be outside again, drinking in the warm air and not this wine that was making her head fuzzy.

I've tried," he said. "This disease is turning us into different people." He pushed his glass away from him and slumped back in his seat.

Margot drew in her breath and tried to remain patient. "You've got to give her time. Lacey is trying to find a way to live with this

too. And you'll have those weeks in Italy. Getting away will help."
Just then Margot longed to get away herself. She wanted to help
Alex, but this conversation was going nowhere. She'd given up her
precious painting time for him, and was thinking now about the
shade of green she wanted to layer into the woods on a canvas she
had begun that day.

"I'm sorry to unload on you."

"There's also Bow Lake. Lacey loves it there. She's never missed
a summer. Time up there in August will do her good."

For the next few moments neither of them spoke. The bar was
growing busier. The hostess seated two couples next to them and
Margot had to shift closer to Alex to make room for the woman's
oversized handbag on the banquette between them.

He turned to face her. "I've been thinking about your paintings."

"They're not very good." She smoothed her hand across the table. The surface was cool and polished. "I should try something
else."

"That one of Junior is amazing. You got that light—the way it
spills across the water in the late afternoon."

"Life was so simple then, so uncomplicated." She brought her
hand to her mouth. She considered the group of paintings she'd
been working on over the last weeks. Was that why she kept trying
to paint the scenes from her childhood summers? Real artists challenged themselves, pushing themselves into uncomfortable zones,
reaching for the edge, whereas she kept hungering for the simple
beauty of something long ago. She was making pretty pictures.
That was all. Oliver wouldn't call it art.

"I've been thinking of all our summers there." Alex paused.
"There was that time. . . ."

Margot was afraid of what he might say. She put her hands in
her lap and felt for her napkin. She twisted it in her fingers. Her
stomach churned and she regretted having had a second glass of
wine.

"I still feel bad that I didn't talk to you after I left that last summer."

"There's no need to say anything." She threw her napkin onto the table, suddenly knowing that he hadn't forgotten that last summer either.

"I shouldn't have . . ." He reached for her hand, and held it briefly.

"Alex, all that was a long time ago." Margot pushed the table out an inch or two. "Please."

"Your paintings make it real again."

"You mustn't talk about that. Not ever." She had to get out.

"I'm sorry. I don't know what's come over me. Please forgive me."

"I need to go." She motioned to their waiter, who pulled out the table, releasing her.

"Please, Margot." He stood as if to embrace her. The waiter stepped away.

"We mustn't look back," she said, aware of the people around them who must be wondering what was going on, the table ajar, Alex looking distraught. "Really. I'd better leave." She hurried to the door.

Once outside, Margot breathed in the fresh air. The evening had cooled. Her legs felt wobbly and her balance unsteady. She looked down at the hand Alex had held, half expecting some kind of mark to remain on her skin. Ridiculous. All that remained was what was inside her head.

12

Draft: Map of the pattern to be woven.

$\mathcal{M}$argot hailed a cab, gave the driver her address, and collapsed onto the backseat. Her heart pounded as the taxi bumped and lurched out of midtown. When the driver reached West Seventy-Second Street she asked him to let her out at the edge of Riverside Park, hoping that walking the rest of the way home would help to clear her head. Neither the soft, freshly green leaf canopy of the trees nor the gentle evening light mangaged to soothe her. She navigated her way north, dodging baby strollers pushed by nannies, dogs pulling ahead of their owners, clots of teenagers plugged into electronic devices. The sounds of children echoed up from the playground below.

The ringing of her cell phone startled her. For a second she feared it was Alex, calling to apologize. Or worse, to say more.

It was Oliver. "You have to come here right now."

"What?"

"The shipper is coming tomorrow morning."

"To take your paintings?"

"I need you to help me decide."

Margot caught her heel on the cobbled path and lunged forward, but managed to regain her balance without falling. At first confused, she felt her anger grow. "Decide? What are you talking about?"

"Mags, the Croft chose twelve paintings and they told me they'd pay the shipping for an additional three. I want you to help me choose. You've got the eye."

"Right now?"

"Grab a cab. We'll get dinner after."

Margot was furious. Oliver had been working full tilt for the past month, barely home at all, and now she was supposed to come at his beck and call.

"I really need you, Mags," he said. "And I want you to see the work."

Need, she thought. *Now* he *needs me.* Alex had needed to talk because only she could understand. And now Oliver. What *she* needed right now was to be left alone. She slowed her steps. Alone. Did she truly want that? She pushed aside the image of Alex's anguished face and saw Oliver—energized, driven, wanting to capture in art what no one else ever had. Some days Oliver stayed lost inside himself, unable to surface into the real world. Once, she had awakened in the night and he had held her close, whispering reassurances that only she could get him through, that without her, nothing would matter. She looked once more at her hand, the hand Alex had taken in his. "I'm on my way," she said.

Margot found a taxi on West End Avenue. The driver began the slow, lurching journey downtown. Thanks to Alex, the memories she'd stowed carefully away like the old photographs in her box of mementos had surfaced in sharp focus.

She and Alex had both gone to Bow Lake by themselves the summer before her sophomore year in college. Margot had volunteered to close the cottage for her grandmother. It was after Labor Day. Alex had come to do some final chores for his parents before leaving for his first year of business school.

The lake was quiet. Most summer residents had departed. The hum of motorboat engines no longer filled the air, voices ceased to echo across the lake, and gone were the creaking and banging of porch doors with the revolving arrival and departure of visiting family and friends. That night only the sound of a loon carried across the water, breaking the silence like a lament.

"Anybody home?" Alex had called through the trees.

"On the porch," Margot replied, immediately recognizing his voice. She listened to the soft approach of his footsteps on the pine-covered path that connected the two camps through the woods. She had arrived that afternoon but had not yet mustered the energy to tackle the chores on her grandmother's checklist: emptying the flowerpots into the compost heap, draining the hoses, bringing the porch furniture into the living room, dragging the canoe under the porch, stripping the beds, doing the final wash, and stowing the linens and pillows in the cedar chests, out of the way of the hungry critters that somehow always found a way to make themselves a home in the cottage for the winter. Margot knew the routine. She had helped her grandmother do it for years.

Alex opened the screen door and stepped onto the porch. "No electricity?" he asked, as though he had seen Margot only the other day. As they had grown older, Margot, Lacey, and Alex had spent less time at Bow Lake, but the old cottages in New Hampshire always remained part of their lives—a special place to which they returned periodically, like migratory birds.

"Too lazy to get up and turn on the lights," she said. "I kind of like sitting in the dark." She stood and they hugged briefly, the way they usually did, though being alone with Alex at the lake seemed strange to her, as if they were both playing hooky or had been caught somewhere they weren't supposed to be. Lacey and all their other friends were already at their jobs or back in school.

"How've you been?" he asked, joining her on the wicker settee.

"Wishing I'd spent more time here. I worked at a frame shop in Concord this summer."

"Lacey told me."

"She said she saw you in Boston earlier in the summer." Margot knew that Alex was starting at Harvard Business School in the fall and that he had spent his summer working at his father's company in New Hampshire.

"Yeah. I went into the city to look for an apartment." He shifted his position. The wicker creaked. "She showed me around her neighborhood. I ended up getting a place with two other guys closer to school."

Margot couldn't see his face, but his body seemed to give off a kind of energy. Summer after summer they had swum to the raft, raced the canoes, hiked the trails in the woods. Though still tall and lanky, he seemed more solid now, more like a man. Over the summer she'd gone out with a few of the guys she'd known in high school. Compared to Alex, they seemed like boys.

She smoothed her hair back, relieved that it was dark. "Well, you'll probably get to see more of Lacey," she said, wondering if there was anything between Alex and Lacey now, or if their summer flirtations were a thing of the past.

"Sure. Maybe. I'm going to be pretty busy with business school. They say the first semester is brutal. Is she coming up this weekend?"

Margot realized Alex couldn't have talked to Lacey recently. "She's on a retreat with some of the faculty from her school. She starts teaching next week."

"Too bad. This is my favorite time here," he said, turning toward her as if to share something more.

"Mine, too. I've missed this place." Margot leaned forward and rested her arms on her legs. "Bow Lake feels like an escape. Now more than ever."

"Margot, I know you've had a rough spring. Lacey told me how sick your mom was at the end."

Margot could picture her sister, strong even when their mother went into the hospital with her liver barely functioning, and after her death, remaining kind and generous, being a help to their father. Lacey would have had the composure to tell Alex what they had been through, recounting the events in the calm voice of a real grown-up. Margot had either raged at the injustice of barely ever having had a mother or remained curled up on her bed during the final quarter of her freshman year, eventually flunking two of her four classes. It had been Lacey who called the dean and arranged for Margot to take incompletes, allowing her the summer to make up the work.

Alex had come to their mother's funeral. He'd worn a navy blazer, and a recent haircut had made him look boyish and vulnerable. At the end of the service, he hugged Lacey outside the church, and he hugged Margot, too. It was a windy day. His blazer had felt cool to her touch.

There was a reception at their house in Concord after the service. The living room was filled with neighbors, some of her father's friends from work, and a few of the cousins from South Carolina, one of whom monopolized Margot in the dining room. Lacey passed trays of sandwiches while her father remained by the door greeting their guests. Margot kept watching for Alex, thinking how seeing him made her feel better.

Now at the lake, sitting on the porch with him months later, she found it easy to talk. "I wasn't that sad when Mom died. Part of me was relieved. How shitty is that? Now I don't know if it's guilt or what, but some days I just start crying for no reason."

"I'm really sorry." Alex reached over and placed his hand on her back. "It's going to get better. You've got college ahead, your friends, and . . ."

"It's like I can't move," she said. "I got here this afternoon, and all I've done is look out at the lake, like maybe I can just stop time if I stay totally still."

Alex shifted closer to her and took her hand. His hair was thicker now and coarser than she remembered, curling slightly where it met his collar. Being in the near dark gave her courage, and without a second thought she sat back and leaned against him. The sleeve of his flannel shirt was soft on her cheek. "I'm kind of a mess these days," she said.

"Hey, it's okay," he said, putting his arm around her. "Really."

Margot felt the warmth of his breath in her hair. They sat quietly for a while. Never-forgotten images of past summers rose in her mind: his tanned legs, the length of his back as he climbed onto the raft, the fine blond hairs on his hands.

"I'm glad you're here," she said, turning her face toward him.

Alex brought his hand to her face. His fingers traveled across her forehead, down the length of her nose, touching her lips and chin, pausing at her neck. She imagined he was feeling her profile as if to compare it with Lacey's. She and Lacey had the same nose, the same chin, and in the dark he might think she was Lacey, maybe the Lacey she had seen him flirting with over the years.

She sat very still. Yes. In the dark, she could be Lacey. She could be the Lacey who teased the skinny boy next door, who joked with him, who coaxed him onto the sailboat in a stiff breeze, who hiked ahead of him on the trail to Boulder Mountain. Lacey, the capable one, the leader, the girl who made Alex laugh, the girl who made him come alive. Had he ever made love with her sister?

The wicker settee squeaked again. Margot raised her face to his. She wasn't so different from Lacey. They shared the same history and the same love of this place. She put her arms around him and kissed him first.

He returned the kiss, then pulled back.

"Is this okay?" She touched his lips.

"I didn't expect . . ." He covered her hand with his. "We've hardly seen each other this year."

"Does that matter?"

"I'm surprised, that's all."

"I want to be with you." A voice she didn't know she had poured into the dark. "I've thought of you so much." She kissed him deeply this time. He said nothing, but kissed her back, bringing his hand to her waist.

"You've been through a lot this year." He touched her face.

"Let's not talk." Margot kissed him again. Suddenly nothing mattered anymore to her except to be held and loved by Alex. Whether her need rose from loneliness, simple longing, or something more, she wanted him.

The wind brushed through the trees high above them. He smelled like the pine woods around the lake. His body felt warm and familiar to her, as if she had always known it.

"We'll always be friends?" she asked.

"You know that," he said.

"It's my first time," she said, standing up and pulling him with her.

He hesitated. "You're sure?"

"Please." She kissed him. "I want it to be you." She led him inside to her old room.

The following morning Margot awoke with the light. Alex had left her asleep sometime during the night. He had covered her with a blanket, though it hadn't been cold.

Throughout the morning, as Margot went about her chores, she heard from his cottage the sounds of a ladder being moved, a car engine starting, a screen door slamming. Maybe he was cleaning gutters or putting on a coat of paint to touch up the camp before winter.

Margot went down to the water for a swim before lunch. Alex didn't appear. She closed her eyes and dozed on the dock, replaying the feeling of his hands, the scent of his skin, and the warmth of his body. No matter what happened, she was glad they had been together.

She spent the afternoon packing the staples in the kitchen into boxes to bring home and then started on the laundry. Eventually the memory of the previous night began to fill her with doubts. Why hadn't he come over to visit and acknowledge what had happened? Did he regret their night together? She had come on to him. Maybe he was wishing she had been Lacey.

Before losing her courage entirely, she took the path to the Georges' cottage. Alex was seated on the porch sipping a beer. "Margot," he said, coming awkwardly to his feet.

"Are you sorry about what happened?" she blurted out.

"No. God. I should have come over sooner." He looked away from her, out at the water.

"You can't just walk away."

"Sorry. I've been thinking and . . ."

"Alex?" She said his name as a question, afraid of what exactly to ask.

"I don't know, Margot."

"What don't you know?"

"I didn't come over because I didn't know what to say. I know that's no excuse."

"Just be with me. That's all I want."

"I'm just not sure if this is what you need right now."

"I can be the judge of that," she said, studying his expression carefully. "Unless maybe you just felt sorry for me."

"That's not it at all." He stood, moved toward her, then stopped. "I was only thinking that this is kind of sudden."

"We've known each other forever."

He set his beer down and shook his head. "We'll be going off in separate directions."

"I don't care." Margot laughed uncertainly. The tightness in her neck released a bit. She shrugged. "Let's not think about that." She walked toward him. "Come on. This is Bow Lake. The last days of summer."

He smiled at her. "You said it." He put his arm around her.

He reached for his beer. "Want one?"

She nodded, filled with relief.

He handed her a beer and asked if she wanted to go down to the dock. They walked side by side on the worn path, their arms brushing. The bottle of beer was cool and wet in Margot's hand. She sipped from it when they reached the water. The sun was about to set and the trees on the opposite shore formed a purple silhouette against a pink sky. She remembered Lacey telling her to keep her eyes off the setting sun when they were little girls, saying she would go blind if she stared too long. The memory of Lacey at Bow Lake on an afternoon like this felt like a bubble caught in Margot's throat. She took another swallow of beer, telling herself there couldn't really be anything between Lacey and Alex.

"I was thinking about what you said last night," Alex said, breaking the silence that had settled between them. "You're right. It's like time stops at Bow Lake. I'm here and I'm almost twenty-three, but it's like I'm still ten. Nothing changes." He sat down on the dock, cross-legged, facing the water. Margot joined him, allowing her knees to touch his.

"The air smells the same. The lake too." He paused and appeared to be lost in thought. "You know how when you're swimming and the water is icy cold, and then you hit a warm pocket, maybe a spring-fed place, or an area heated by the sun?"

Margot nodded. Alex understood everything about the lake.

He had been looking across the water, his gaze set on Junior, the island now a dark mound in the distance. He turned to Margot and spoke softly. "This is one of those times."

She reached over to take his hand.

He picked up his beer and drank, arching his neck to swallow the last of it. He set the bottle down. "Still, even when it's like that, one of those amazing warm places, there's all this cold water you've got to swim through to get back."

"Don't say that," she said.

"I'm not sure if this is right."

"Please. For now let's just pretend that time's stopped." Margot got to her feet and pulled him up beside her, leading him up the path to her grandmother's porch. They made love again that night.

During the three days that followed, they did their chores at their separate places, but at the end of each afternoon Margot went to Alex's cottage, or he to hers.

On Margot's last day at Bow Lake, Alex met her on the dock to help her carry the green canoe up to the cottage to stow under the porch. There, she would cover it in the heavy gray tarp that smelled like the old raincoats pushed to the back of the hall closet.

"How about a final paddle to Junior?" she asked.

Alex glanced at his watch. "I don't know," he said, shifting his weight from one foot to the other. "I need to get on the road."

"We don't have to stay long." She put her hand on his arm. "Just one last quick trip?"

He let out his breath. "Sure, one more paddle."

When they reached Junior, Margot, who had rolled up the legs of her jeans, swung her leg over the canoe and waded toward shore. Alex followed, towing the canoe by the rope. After pulling the boat onto the beach, he sat beside Margot on the shale-covered shore, digging his heels into the stones. The water lapped at their feet.

A steady breeze was coming from the west, though the sun was warm. The surface of the lake was broken by a light chop. Margot's arms were tired. She followed Alex's gaze as he shaded his eyes with his hands and looked across the lake. The two old camps were barely visible in the distance. Neither said a word. She closed her eyes, happy for the beautiful day, comfortable that there was no need to talk.

After a few minutes Alex got to his feet. "We really need to go." His voice had taken on a cool edge.

There was a clearing on the wooded shore of Junior where they used to take picnic lunches when they were children. Margot pointed to it now. "Let's stay just a while longer," she said, pulling him toward the shelter in the trees. "Please, just once more." She imagined making love with him there under the branches with the sun peeking through the leaves.

"I've got to get back." His brow had furrowed and he went over to the canoe, shoving it into the lake. Resigned, Margot yanked up her pant legs, waded into the cold water, and helped push the canoe off the shore. They paddled back. The wind picked up. Goose bumps emerged on her arms. Their easy banter had trickled down to a few words.

"That's it, then," she said as the canoe reached the shore.

"Leave the paddles for now," Alex said. "I'll get them on a second trip."

They each carried an end. Water dripped off the edges when they flipped the boat over, hoisting it above their heads. The canoe wasn't heavy as much as ungainly as they made their way up the path.

"I'll take it from here," he said, pulling and then pushing the awkward green form up under the porch decking. Like a fish, she thought, the canoe looked more graceful in the water.

"I'll take care of the paddles," she said.

"You're sure?"

She nodded. She knew he had to leave. His mother had asked him to be back in Newfields for a family dinner that evening. "Thanks for everything," she said.

"You're sure you're okay?"

"I'll miss you." She felt her heart tighten in her chest.

"Yeah. Maybe once I get settled you could come for a weekend."

"That would be great."

"Yeah. It's going to be busy for me this fall."

"Sure." Margot bit at her lower lip. "I understand."

"We'll just have to see," he said.

Margot wanted to say more, but couldn't think what. He bent and kissed her lips lightly, then turned and walked back to his cottage to finish loading his car.

Margot went to the screened porch to bring in one final chair. Her father expected her home as well. Tomorrow the caretaker and his helpers would take in the dock and drain the pipes in the cottage. Soon, she and Alex would be hours away from each other.

Who knew what might happen? And there would always be next summer at Bow Lake. She remembered Granny Winkler's words— if you don't go home, you can't come back. They didn't make her feel any better.

Margot paid the driver and took the rattling freight elevator to Oliver's studio. She had to pull herself together.

"Don't say anything right away," Oliver said. He looked a mess. His hair needed washing, as did his jeans, which sagged at the knees. He pushed the sleeves of his sweater up to the elbows and rubbed his hands together in a nervous gesture. "Just walk around and take it in."

She forgot her irritation at being summoned after her unsettling meeting with Alex. She couldn't have spoken if she had wanted to. Oliver had hung the walls of his studio with half a year's work. He had created a new world, and she was immediately drawn in. The paintings appeared abstract on an initial glance, but after looking more carefully, Margot could see distant figures and objects. She saw layers of color, some nearly transparent. The paintings seemed to have a kind of energy, almost a pulse that moved her from one to the next.

Within minutes the turmoil of the afternoon dissolved. She let herself sink into the work, completely forgetting Lacey and her family. Oliver's paintings were so utterly compelling that without even thinking, she was caught up in the language of art. Where had this vision come from? How was it that a single individual could close himself off with nothing but blank canvas, tubes of paint, and brushes, and make this? She faced his view of the world, the results of his creative drive, and she was speechless. From a few materials came this extraordinary beauty. The pictures were all different from anything he had painted before.

"Astonishing," she said softly.

Oliver looked relieved and delighted. "You really think so?"

She nodded. The work came across almost like a new language

to Margot, yet all of it was Oliver's voice, Oliver's take on the world.

"How did you do this? So many and each one is right."

"Help me choose three more. They're taking these already." He gestured to the two long walls.

"They're all perfect. Any three would work."

"You can see how they relate. You choose."

She was touched that he had such confidence in her eye. Walking back and forth and studying the last wall, she paused before a tall, narrow canvas that looked like sheets of ice breaking up. "That one, for sure," she said. "And this one would be a good counterpoint."

He moved the two paintings to the other side of the room, near the ones designated for the shipper.

"What's that one about?" She stopped in front of one of the smaller paintings.

"What do you see?"

Margot studied the gray and brown markings that looked like spring branches. Tiny dots resembling buds seemed about to burst. The background was a pale blue, barely a color at all. "It makes me think of lying on my back under a tree and looking up through the branches to the sky. I did that when I was a kid at Bow Lake."

"Ah, the famous Bow Lake," he said, stepping away from her. He looked like he was going to say more, then shrugged. "Let's not talk about that now. I want to go home, Mags."

13

Spin: Twist fibers into thread.

The warm days came more frequently in New York, while in San Francisco the weather was cool. It was the end of May. Margot and Oliver had arrived there two days before.

"Romantic, isn't it?" Oliver said, drawing Margot out of her reverie. The city felt completely foreign to her. The hills, the charming tumble of Victorian houses in sight of a cluster of tall buildings, the colors themselves were all different from the shades in New York. The light was gentle and from a distance the city looked pale and soft, as if it were painted in watercolors instead of oils. The brisk chop in the bay appeared dramatic, if not a little frightening, and the air itself held a sense of anticipation.

He lifted his glass. Piano music tinkled in the background, familiar, watery tunes with elusive titles. They were at the Top of the Mark, a restaurant on the highest floor of the Mark Hotel, perfect for special occasions. The vast view spread below them in every direction. Oliver's opening had taken place the night before at the Croft Gallery. He had brought Margot here to celebrate with a glass of champagne.

"It's lovely," Margot said. Oliver had given her the seat closest to the window. The sunset sky was pink. In the distance pockets of fog hovered at the edge of the bay. Earlier that day she had remarked on the temperature. Though San Francisco had that otherworldly light that made everything look fresh, the air at night was damp and cold. She wore a cornflower blue shawl that Lacey had woven for her birthday the year before. When Margot had put it on before leaving their hotel room, she'd had to swallow back an uncomfortable lump that welled in her throat when she thought of her sister.

"You're beautiful," Oliver said, picking up his glass.

"To your success." She clinked her glass to his, remembering how recently she had raised her glass in a hotel bar with Alex.

"To us." Oliver took gave her hand a gentle squeeze. "To our California adventure." He swiveled his chair to take in the view.

"It's going to be a great week," she said. She hoped she sounded eager. It was unfair to Oliver to brood.

Oliver had had an amazing few days. Three of his paintings had sold during the opening, and the dealer had called this morning to say he had sold two more. To top that, a favorable review had appeared in the arts section of the *San Francisco Chronicle*.

Today, he had spent the day with her, walking through Golden Gate Park, stopping for lunch at a restaurant that offered healthy wraps and salads, sitting at an outdoor café in a patch of sun at the end of the afternoon. Oliver's face had a ruddy glow. The tight lines around his mouth had vanished. He finally looked relaxed.

Margot wished she could stop thinking about Lacey. What could she do for her now? Certainly nothing from here. At some level she was getting used to being concerned about her sister. Perhaps being so far away was making her unduly anxious. She had hoped that the distance between them would make it easier to focus on other things. This was Oliver's big moment and she wanted to make him happy.

"Are you with me, Mags?" Oliver asked.

"Sorry," she said. "Maybe we could visit Carmel?" The photos she had seen in the guidebook showed streets of charming houses with flowers tumbling over fences, reminding her of English cottage gardens. "Carl said there are lots of galleries there. We could check out the local talent." She lifted her glass and smiled.

"Sure, but tomorrow I have a surprise for you." Oliver leaned back and gave her a sexy look, his lips not quite breaking a smile, his eyebrows lifted.

"What?"

He shrugged, looking like a large, secretive lion. His hair was long at the moment, falling below his collar.

"Come on," she said. "Tell me. You know I hate surprises."

"I'm taking you somewhere. I've rented a car for the rest of the week. I'll tell you one part of it. We're going to start with lunch at the Petite Auberge in Sonoma." He took her hand again and cradled it in his larger one. "It's a country inn, sort of French style."

"Sounds delightful," she said, grateful to Oliver, who was doing his best to make up for his preoccupied behavior in the spring.

"It's one of Grant's favorite spots." Grant Redfern was an old friend from Oliver's art school days who lived in Sonoma. Oliver had called him when planning the trip for suggestions on what to see. Grant had left recently for Italy to run a summer painting program in Umbria and would not be there during their visit.

Oliver leaned closer and whispered in her ear, "The real surprise comes after that." He kissed her neck. "You'll never guess." He kissed her once more.

The following day Oliver drove Margot to Sonoma. After the promised lunch, which was lovely, he took a secondary road and headed deeper into the countryside. They wound through fields and acres of leafy green vineyards for some time before turning down a narrow dirt driveway. Oliver pulled to a stop in front of a simple modern house. When they got out of the car the breeze smelled earthy and sweet. Margot followed him along the path around to the far side of the house. She felt as if she'd come into an oasis of calm.

"It's perfect," she said, resting her hands on the stone wall that looked out over acres and acres of vineyards. "This is amazing."

"Grant's place."

She had expected he might bring her to a hotel for the night, though they had left their clothes in San Francisco. She turned and looked at the house. "I had no idea your friend had a place like this."

"I wanted you to see it," he said.

She pointed to the fruit trees that lined the driveway. "Are those plums?" The delicate branches were covered in the palest pink blossoms. Lacey would have known the answer to her question.

"You like it?"

"It's as if we're a million miles from New York."

"Exactly," he said. "Grant said I could show you around."

Oliver took a key from its hiding place under a pot of rosemary by the back door. He walked Margot through the house, a one-story stucco building that turned out to be larger than expected once they were inside. The house had a central living area with an open kitchen separated from the living room by a long counter. There were two bedrooms and a bath off to the left, and a small book-lined room with a television and plump chairs off the living room to the right. The other room was an office with a built-in desk and file drawers. The furnishings were modern: sleek wood tables and chairs, a couch in cream-colored linen with a few pale green pillows. The effect was clean and spare but welcoming.

The entire house was oriented toward the view of the valley below. They went back out to the terrace. It was as if a gravitational pull was making Margot want to be outside savoring the view. She thought of the din and commotion that was New York.

"I'm sure Umbria or wherever Grant's working must be nice, but I can't imagine wanting to leave this." Margot enjoyed the sensation of the sun's heat on her shoulders, so different from the cool San Francisco weather.

"Do you see the building down there? The one with the sky-lights?"

She nodded.

"That's his studio."

Margot thought of the drafty loft where Oliver worked, with the rattling elevator that made her sure each ride would be her last. Grant's studio couldn't be more different, nestled in a grove of trees below the house.

She followed Oliver inside. This time she noticed that there was no artwork anywhere. Light poured in from windows high above, and as the sun sank, shadows formed patterns on the walls, a kind of art all its own.

"Here's the surprise," Oliver said, capturing her attention. "When I was here in January, I came out to see this place. Grant had just accepted the gig in Italy."

"You never told me you visited him."

"You were so preoccupied with Lacey then. Plus you'd have to see this to believe it." He stopped speaking, raised his hands, and let them fall to his side. "Mags, this place is so powerful. The light, the landscape. All winter I tried to forget about it."

"I can see why you'd like it," she said. She sat down on the sofa. "It's so quiet, too. I'm not sure I could get used to such silence."

Oliver took a seat beside her. "When I e-mailed Grant last month to get suggestions for restaurants, he asked me if I'd like to rent his place for the summer. A nominal rent, just to cover maintenance and utilities. You can see he doesn't need the money." Oliver traced his hand along her neck and jawbone. "I'd like to paint you sitting outside on the wall."

Margot blushed, remembering the way Oliver used to look at her when they first met. When he had taken her to his studio for the first time he had stared at her intently and with a kind of longing that it made it difficult for her to breathe.

"You don't do portraits," she said jokingly.

"I want to do you now." He caressed her cheek. His touch was always gentle, as if he saw the world with his hands, too. "What do you think? How about we live here for the summer?"

"You mean leave New York?"

"Spend the summer away."

"But my job?"

"Mario's there. I'm sure you and Carl could work something out."

Oliver was right. Carl closed the gallery for part of July and almost no one came in August. Summer was the slow time of year. As much as she enjoyed working at the gallery, her own painting had started to matter more. She pictured her apartment, the easel, and her notebooks with the drawings she had worked on this winter. She could sublet her place to cover her expenses. But Lacey? She would be across the country from her sister. "It is beautiful here," she said. Her voice sounded tentative in her ears.

"We could both have the summer for painting," he said.

Still, something weighed on her. "It might work. It's just that Lacey . . . and the girls' graduation. I can't miss that."

"You don't have to. You can fly back for that weekend. The summer's on me. Five paintings sold in two days. It's like it was fifteen years ago."

Margot got up and walked out again to the terrace. Rosebushes lined the path to the studio. The buds were white. She could imagine their smell on a June evening. Oliver came behind her and drew his hands around her waist. He rocked her gently from side to side. "I can see us here," he said. His lips rested above her ear. "I love you, Mags."

Suddenly, Margot thought Oliver's idea might work. She didn't like the way they'd seemed to drift apart this winter and spring. She was as much at fault as he was. She could feel tears coming to her eyes. The grapevines across the valley blurred together below the darkening sky, looking like a vast lake. Margot turned, wrapped her arms around Oliver, and held him tightly.

.   .   .

As Oliver drove back to San Francisco, he felt that comfortable ease and happiness settle back between them again. He thought over their day together. What a relief to be able to make Margot happy. They talked easily about possible plans. He explained that they could return to New York and come back to rent Grant's place starting the first of June. Margot suggested shipping some of their things ahead of time. She was going to get in touch with Mario and Carl to see if they could work something out. With any luck, in a matter of weeks they could be ready for this interlude in California.

By the time they reached their hotel in the city it was dark. Oliver left the car with the valet service. They planned to drive south of the city the next day and possibly go as far as Carmel. Neither of them was hungry, so they agreed to go out to dinner later at a Japanese restaurant near the hotel. He tilted his head to each side, trying to release the crick in his neck, and followed Margot into the lobby.

Oliver knew that Margot didn't like change. She had her half dozen favorite restaurants in their neighborhood, and the three upscale places they saved for special occasions. She stuck to her limited repertoire of recipes, always went to the same Duane Reade drugstore, despite the fact that there were almost identical others every few blocks, ordered the same coffee drink at her preferred Starbucks, and used only one particular cash machine. She even had a favorite bench in the park.

He found this single-mindedness endearing and frequently teased her, saying she acted like a little old lady, set in her ways, not daring to try something new. Surely she would agree that some changes could be a good thing—his recent success, this trip, their plans for the summer.

He also wanted to talk about marriage again. Soon he would be fifty-seven. As old-fashioned as it seemed, he wanted to grow old with someone he loved. Like his parents had done. Maybe he had a traditional streak. Somehow growing old with a girlfriend, a lover, was not the same as being married.

When they returned to their room, Oliver told Margot he wanted to shower before going out. While he undressed she rummaged in her purse and pulled out her cell phone.

"I forgot to turn it on," she said, pushing the requisite buttons. "I've got a message." Her lips pulled together as she listened. He paused at the bathroom door. "It's from Alex," she said.

"Alex?" he said, feeling the warmth of the afternoon slip away. "What could he want?" This could only have to do with Lacey, he thought. Oliver's lower back hurt. The car they'd rented was a compact, the cheapest available. It had been impossible to adjust the seat to a comfortable position. Or was he just getting old? Margot glanced at her watch. He calculated the time difference. "It's not too late," he said.

In the shower Oliver made the water as hot as he could stand, letting it pummel his back. A call from Alex couldn't be good. Oliver was sorry about what Lacey and her family were going through, but selfishly he didn't want Margot to be so tied up in their affairs. He wished she could simply live with it and move on.

One of the abilities that came with age, he thought, was getting used to unhappiness. You had to accept a backlog of disappointments, hurts that could never be healed, sadness for which there was no cure. You got better at putting some of the tough things aside.

Oliver lived with the knowledge that he wished he had told his father many things before he had died. Regrets cluttered his mind—the way he'd reacted to past criticism, the way he'd let it get him down. He knew he'd been difficult to live with this spring—preoccupied, jumpy, not as attentive to Margot as he should have been. Art was hard. That was his excuse, at least.

Early in their courtship Margot had told him how she had once planned to become an artist. She had wanted to go to graduate school in painting after college, but it had seemed impossible then to come up with the time or the money. Her sister, who also loved art, was the practical one who had majored in education to be able to teach it. Margot had taken classes in art history, thinking it might be useful for getting a job, but eventually she couldn't resist the lure of the art studio at college, that huge, bright space that smelled of paint. Naked in his arms, she had told him all that as if it had been a confession. Later, when he asked what made her stop painting, she blamed it on a bad marriage. He knew what that could be like and didn't press her for more.

Oliver reached for the shampoo. This summer would be a reprieve for both of them. He stayed in the shower longer than usual, then turned off the water and grabbed a towel. He put on the thick hotel robe and gave his hair a quick comb. When he emerged from the bathroom Margot was seated on the edge of the bed still holding her phone.

"What's up?" he asked, trying to recapture the upbeat mood of the afternoon.

"I spoke to Alex."

"Yeah?"

"His mother died. He sounded terrible."

"I'm sorry," he said, recalling the angular, vigorous woman whose eyes were blankly clouded and remote. He had met her one summer, a number of years ago. It must have been when the family had gathered for a family birthday in New Castle, when she was still well enough to leave the nursing home.

"Massive stroke," Margot said before he had a chance to ask. "At least she didn't suffer."

"Will there be a service?" He sat on the bed beside her.

"Alex said he didn't know when. Lacey's started to plan the funeral."

"It's Alex's mother. Why isn't he planning the funeral?"

"He's stuck in Chicago. He can't get home until the end of the week. There's some environmental issue with the company he's selling and he's in crucial meetings with a mediator. They're trying to avoid a lawsuit." Margot put her hand in his. "That's not the real problem."

"What do you mean?" he asked, wondering what could be wrong on top of this.

"Wink called him, saying that Toni's been acting really strange and that she's been sneaking out at night. Wink is terrified of getting Lacey upset. Wink thinks something weird is going on. She hated telling on Toni and said she never would have called her dad if something wasn't really wrong."

"I'm sorry, Mags." Oliver felt bad for Alex. The death of a parent was always hard, and a troubled teenage daughter was not what Alex needed right now. He remembered that volatile stage with Jenna.

"I need to book a flight."

"You want to fly back?"

"Alex is dealing with this work crisis."

"He expects you to fly across the country?" Oliver was furious.

"He didn't know I was out here. He wants me to see what's going on with Toni and to be there for Wink until he can get home."

"Why doesn't he tell Lacey?"

"I guess he's afraid of upsetting her."

"She's his wife, for God's sake."

"But she's not well."

"So he's telling you?"

Margot said nothing, as if trying to make sense of his argument.

"I hope you explained you were in California," he went on.

"I told him I'd come."

"What?"

"I didn't think."

"I'll say you didn't think."

"Oliver, I want to be able to help the girls. I really should go home."

"Home?" The pain in his back was stronger. "So Lacey's house is home."

"That's not what I mean."

"Mags, this is our vacation. We have plans."

"Alex was really upset. He's worried about Lacey. Stress only makes her worse."

"Alex calls and you jump?" He slapped his hand down on the bed. His breath was coming faster.

"How can you think that?" She stood and moved away from him.

"Come on, Mags. I'm sorry about his mom," he said, trying to regain his calm. "Toni's having some kind of boyfriend trouble. She'll get over it. Besides, it's their family. They'll be able to manage. You can go up for the service. I'm sure it won't be until after we get home."

"You don't understand."

"I know you want to help. I just don't think you need to be involved right now."

"I'm already involved. This is my family."

"It's Alex's family. His mother. His daughters. Remember?" Oliver recalled his fights with his ex-wife, Linda. Was he out of line? Was he acting like a shit?

"I came out here for your show," she said. "I was here for you. But I think Toni might need me. You told me when Lacey got sick, I should think about her children and what I could do for them." She hugged her arms to her body. "Oliver, I really think I should go." She looked suddenly small to him and unhappy. "We'll have the rest of the summer."

Oliver reached for his clothes and started to dress. "So you think you can fly in and fix everything?" He yanked on his pants, then his shirt.

"I think I have to try."

"I don't want you to go." His fingers fumbled with the buttons. "We were off to such a great start. We need to think about us for a change."

Margot's voice grew louder. "I am. You know that. I'm willing to rearrange my whole summer for us."

He continued to dress. "I'm worried."

"About what?"

He didn't know exactly. He just knew the entire day seemed to be fizzling before his eyes. "Go ahead and get ready for dinner. I'm going out for a walk." He grabbed his coat and left the room.

The fog had come up and the city was covered in a fine, damp mist. He started down the hill toward the marina. His stomach had tightened into a knot. Was he asking too much of Margot? Linda had accused him of putting art before his family. He would fire back, "You've got to understand. I'm an artist. First and foremost." Selfish. He had been selfish saying that.

Was he being selfish in wanting Margot to himself? Did some part of her always have to be caught up with Lacey? Or with Alex? He strode on through the night. Seagulls screamed and soared above his head as he drew closer to the water.

Big mistake. Not a mistake. Yes, a mistake. Not a mistake. A mistake. Margot watched the luggage on the conveyor belt at Logan Airport, designating each item the way she used to pull off daisy petals—he loves me, he loves me not. She glanced at her watch. The bus for Portsmouth came in ten minutes. If she missed it she would have to wait another hour for the next one. A lumpy brown duffel went by. Not a mistake. A red plaid suitcase, three black suitcases.

Oliver had stayed in San Francisco to complete the week. He had changed her ticket, sending her to Boston to see Lacey and her family. The luggage continued past her feet. Wink was going to meet her bus in Portsmouth. She had told her mom that Margot was coming to help with the funeral. Lacey was still unaware of anything going on with Toni. Wink had said that Toni hadn't come home at all last night and that it was getting harder to cover for her sister.

"I know I'm a traitor for ratting on her," Wink had said, "but if Mom were to find out, she'd have a breakdown or something."

Oliver felt it was wrong to keep Toni's troubles from Lacey. When he put Margot in the cab to go to the airport in San Francisco, he'd told her again he thought she was making a mistake.

At this point Margot felt physically sick. She took a swig of water from the bottle in her tote bag. Her mouth was sour from the diet soft drink and a bag of chips, all she had eaten on the nearly six-hour flight. The movie on board had been some goofy comedy and she had been unable to concentrate on her book. Mostly she had closed her eyes and thought of Oliver. The sight of him walking into the hotel without her as her taxi pulled away, his shoulders slumped and the back of his head with clumps of hair still messed from a fitful sleep, tore at her heart. What was she doing? Yet Wink's voice had been so relieved when Margot told her she was coming and that she would agree to talk to Toni and figure out what was going on. More suitcases passed by. A large brown bag, another black one. A mistake, not a mistake. The carousel was temporarily empty. Another round of luggage passed down the chute. Her gray duffel bag appeared next.

14

Spinster: A woman employed at spinning.

$\mathcal{M}$argot blinked. The book she had been reading had slipped to the living room floor. She must have dozed off. Someone was in the kitchen. Had she heard voices? She pushed her feet into her shoes and stood. The room was chilly. Now fully awake, she was aware of a muffled sound. She started toward the kitchen. Her clothes were rumpled and her mouth felt dry. Beyond the dark dining room, she saw a dim light coming from under the kitchen door. Finally, Toni was home.

Lacey had gone up to bed not long after dinner. She had been busy all day making plans for Alex's mother's funeral. Edith George had treated Lacey like a daughter and Margot could see that Lacey was affected deeply by her death. Lacey's speech seemed more fragmented than Margot remembered, and maybe in an effort to compensate, she spoke less. Margot could understand Wink's concern. Lacey, always so strong, seemed to have become more fragile since the last time they were together.

That afternoon, when Wink had met Margot at the bus, she filled Margot in on her sister's unusual behavior, explaining that Toni had been sneaking out to see Ryan almost every night for the past few weeks. What worried Wink was that Toni had become so secretive. She no longer told her what they did or where they went; instead she came home with an odd, closed smile, saying that things were good, really good, promising that she'd be able to say more soon. A few days ago, though, she had started acting touchy and strange. She was going to meet Ryan that evening, having told their mother she was going to be with friends to plan a camping trip following graduation. She had pulled Wink aside to assure her that she wouldn't be very late.

"You don't think they're planning to run away, do you?" Wink asked Margot as she drove toward New Castle. "Nobody does that anymore, do they? I mean, she can sleep with him if she wants. That's their business. I don't care about that. I just don't want Toni to do anything that would upset Mom."

"Your mom must know something's up," Margot said.

"Are you kidding? Toni's an incredible actress when she needs to be."

Wink crossed the bridge into New Castle. Spring was not a generous season in New England. Though it was the end of May, a gray drizzle, not quite rain, hung in the air. This kind of dank weather could linger for weeks, Margot knew. Wink wore a jean jacket and a dark green scarf knotted at her neck. Her hands, holding the wheel tightly, looked chapped from no longer wearing winter gloves. "Mom's so sad about Gram," she added softly. "You'd think it was her own mother who died."

"I'll try to find out what's going on with Toni," Margot said, though her greatest concern was always Lacey. Edith George's death could only remind Lacey of her own mortality—one form of brain disease could not be much different from another.

"I feel better just knowing you're here, Aunt Margot. I mean, in case Mom gets upset or something."

Well, now was her chance to help. Margot walked quietly to the kitchen. As she expected, it was Toni. She sat slumped at the kitchen table, her head in her hands, a glass in front of her. It was two thirty in the morning.

"Toni?" Margot said.

"Aunt Margot, you're here." Her face was pale and drawn, with deep circles beneath her eyes. "Gram's funeral isn't until this weekend."

"I came to help your mom." She glanced at Toni's drink.

"It's just O.J. I thought about getting wasted, but what good would that do?"

"What's wrong, honey? Wink's been worried about you."

"She doesn't have to worry any longer." She let out a deep sob.

"What do you mean?" Margot asked, taking in Toni's swollen eyes and blotched skin. "She said you've been spending a lot of time with Ryan."

"Oh, God." She covered her eyes with her hands.

Margot moved closer to Toni and put her arm around her. "What is it, sweetie? You can tell me." She was suddenly aware that these were not mere childhood tears, but something more troubling.

"Ryan's going to Africa this summer. Ghana." Her back shook with sobs.

"And that makes you sad?" Margot asked, trying to inquire gently, not wanting to upset her niece further.

"I was supposed to go with him. Then a few days ago everything changed. We had been making plans."

"To do what?"

"He's going to work for some peace group. A volunteer job. He wants to help people."

"And you wanted to go too?"

Toni sat up and pulled away. She nodded and wiped away the tears on her face. "But now he doesn't want me to come. I don't get it. We've been together for weeks, figuring it out."

"A summer goes by quickly, Toni. You'd be surprised. He'll be back in the fall, won't he?"

"He's changed his mind. He's decided he wants to go for six months, maybe a year."

"I see," Margo said.

"Tonight he said it would be better for us to stop seeing each other. He thinks we're too serious. He gave me all this crap—like I'm too young, we'll be too far apart, he's not sure of the future. It's just so cheesy."

"Well, at least he's being honest with you."

Toni shot Margot a traitorous look. "How can you say that? I love him. Don't you understand?" She lowered her head and continued to cry.

"I know it's hard, sweetie." Margot sighed. "Believe me, I know." She thought back to her own ancient hurts, but was at a loss when it came to easing Toni's pain.

Toni straightened. Her voice took on an angry edge. "He wants to take the whole year off and come back and finish his degree later. He said we should go our separate ways."

Margot thought Ryan's plans sounded reasonable. Toni would be in New York in the fall. He couldn't be expected to wait around for her, to carry on their relationship at such a distance. But Toni would not want to hear that.

Tears covered her niece's cheeks. She wiped them with the back of her hand.

"Do you want me to make you some tea?" Margot asked, knowing the minute she said it how useless a gesture it was.

Toni shook her head.

"He isn't leaving right away, is he?" Margot asked, trying to offer a bit of hope.

"Another month. But he says it would be easier if we end it now. Do you believe that? I find out my mother's sick, my grandmother dies, and now this. I wanted him to come to graduation. We had this trip all planned." She began to weep once again, heaving anguished sobs that she couldn't seem to control.

"Don't forget the trip to Italy that your dad's planned." Margot placed her hand tentatively on Toni's shoulder.

"I don't care about that."

"Maybe not now. You have to give it time." Margot moved her hand across Toni's back, saying over and over how sorry she was. She couldn't think of what more to do. She knew too well the misery of being left, how it felt to be rejected, to no longer matter to the person you cared about.

The overhead light came on. Lacey stood in the doorway. Without hesitating, Toni went to her mother, who took her into her arms. Lacey seemed to know instinctively what had happened. "Lamb, lamb," she crooned, her arms tight around her daughter. In the next few minutes Toni's sobs faded to a quiet keening, her body clinging to her mother, as if Lacey were the only one who could make it all right.

"Mommy," Toni said through her tears. "It hurts. Mommy, it hurts."

"I know, lamb. I know." Lacey looked over at Margot and gave a sad smile before ushering Toni into the hall and leading her slowly up the stairs.

Margot remained at the window, not seeing her reflection in the black glass. She folded her arms across her chest. When Lacey came into the room it was as if Margot had disappeared. After she had come all this way, her presence barely mattered. The urgency of her departure from San Francisco seemed ridiculous now. With a niggling sense of shame, she remembered Alex's voice on the phone. Oliver was right—why had Alex called her and not Lacey? Margot stood, turned off the kitchen light, and made her way upstairs in the dark.

She found it impossible to sleep that night. Her worries loomed large in the silent house. The future seemed to be spinning ahead of her as she grew more and more powerless to control it. Lacey's speech faltered with greater frequency and Margot thought she saw a difference in other ways, too. Lacey was more withdrawn, perhaps because of Edith's death, and the tension in the house was palpable. Wink, the worrier in the family, was nervous about leaving for college; Toni continued to be distraught over Ryan; and Alex, if not absent because of work, seemed distracted and remote. Margot's own history had taught her the difficult complexity of family life. Yet Lacey's family had always been so happy, as if immune from trouble. Now they all seemed fragile.

Margot lifted her head and turned her pillow over, resting her cheek on the cool side of the pillowcase. Closing her eyes, she tried to picture her time with Oliver in Sonoma, distant and dreamlike to her now. She pictured Lacey's loom across the hall with the threads taut, pulled equally in two directions.

Alex let his bike coast down Waldoboro Hill. He had pedaled twenty miles inland, a long distance this early in the season. After a winter without riding, it took him several weeks to rebuild his endurance, going farther and farther with each ride. His travel schedule this spring had allowed him little time for his bike. His muscles spoke to him, but today the exertion made him feel alive. He closed his eyes and let himself drift, euphoric in a brief moment of oblivion, thankful to be out of the house. The tires bumped along the gravel shoulder. His lids flew open. Fuck. He couldn't go and get himself killed.

The road leveled and rolled gently for the next few miles. A fine drizzle kept his face cool. It was a typical spring day. Summer was a ways off in New England. The temperature was in the low sixties. By July, he'd be sweating doing that hill.

His mother's service was tomorrow and Margot had put off her return to New York. Apparently, Oliver was still in California and she didn't need to go back to work until Monday.

Fortunately, nothing major had gone wrong in his absence. As Wink had suspected, Toni's troubles had been boyfriend-related, and not as dire as she had originally thought. Toni would get over Ryan. She had the resilience of youth on her side and her whole future ahead of her. What worried him more was Lacey's sadness. Margot had assisted her with the funeral arrangements and kept her company on her rounds of errands, as if sensing that Lacey shouldn't be alone. Thankfully, the lawsuit threatening his business deal had been averted. He had arrived home exhausted and tense, but at least he wouldn't have to travel again for a while.

"I think you need to get out and get some air," Margot had said earlier that morning when Lacey had gone upstairs to have some time in her studio. He and Lacey had been going over the program for the funeral service and Margot was taking it to the printer later. She was taking Toni with her. The two of them had been on lots of long walks and Toni seemed to be gradually coming out of her funk. "I'll be okay, Dad," she had told him when he stopped by her room last night on the way up to bed.

Alex had tried to tread lightly since he'd been home, as his household felt like a minefield of emotion. Lacey was keeping her grief locked inside. When he had hugged her on his return and thanked her for taking over for him, her eyes had brimmed with tears. "I loved her, Alex," was all she had said.

He had loved his mother too, but weeks of arguing with lawyers and negotiating with hard-nosed business types had momentarily cordoned him off from any deep feeling, as if he couldn't rid himself of a tough outer shell. His mother had been gone from him for years already, it seemed. For now, he remained numb.

He was sorry to have pulled Margot away from her trip, but he was grateful for her quiet presence, which seemed to have a calming effect on all of them. Their awkward conversation in New York seemed remote to him after all that had happened. He needed to remember that the Margot who was with them now was a different person from the one he had known long ago.

He reached the trailhead that led to the lookout tower, a rickety platform with a view of the entire valley. He and Lacey had hiked here one summer when they still lived in Boston. He had brought her to New Hampshire to see his parents. Shortly after that visit he had proposed.

Had it been a day like this one, misty and gray? Lacey was teaching art at the Barnhill School in Brookline. He had finished his first year of business school and they had been living together for several months.

Alex leaned his bike against a tree, out of sight of the road. He walked the few hundred yards to the tower. The climb up was not as high as he remembered. The steps creaked under his weight. The sound of the wind grew louder when he reached the platform at the top of the stairs. He stood alone above the trees and looked at the valley below. Rolling fields, humble farmhouses, weathered barns, clusters of fruit trees in flower, and the spiky tops of pines edging the woods were all slightly blurred in the damp haze.

The dilapidated state of the tower made him wonder if the county or state looked after it at all anymore. When he and Lacey had hiked here it had been like new. He recalled how it was Lacey who had initiated the kiss when they had reached the platform those many years ago.

"Alex, Alex, my sweetest sweet," she had said, laughing and putting her hands in his hair. Her hands had roamed over him. "Let me feel you," she whispered. Her hands, those beautiful hands, were at first like feathers and then firmer, sure of what they wanted as they explored his skin. The two of them slid to the floor of the tower and began to make love.

He liked that Lacey was often the initiator. She had been the one to suggest he move in with her and he had jokingly said, "Whatever you say, Chief." That day he had taken her shirt off and was kissing her breasts when they heard voices and had to scramble, readjusting their clothes and coming to their feet.

Now, remembering that long-ago afternoon, he yearned for Lacey, for the way they used to be then, for the urgency, the simple lust, that came over them so suddenly. Alex sat on the floor of the lookout. It was a weekday. No one would come out here now, if they did at all anymore. He still wanted Lacey. He wanted her hands in his hair. He wanted to make love. Since she had been sick, it was as if they no longer knew how to start. The few times they had come together, their lovemaking had been hurried and unfamiliar. He rubbed his eyes with the heels of his hands.

And Margot—why had he started thinking about that brief time when they were together that summer at Bow Lake? Their short relationship was ancient history. He shouldn't have said anything to her in New York; he should have left the past behind them, where it belonged. Yet he had felt something, a strange unsteadiness, when Margot walked into that bar. When she sat down beside him, smelling faintly of flowers and the spring evening, it was as if he had been on a boat too long, and once he was on the shore again he'd lost his sense of balance. He thought that all he'd wanted was a chance to talk.

New Hampshire was a long way from New York. Alex wiped his face and stood up, stretching his legs one at a time. His muscles had grown cold. He worked his hamstrings and descended the stairs. He needed to get home.

It was an ordinary Tuesday evening at the start of June and the city pulsed. The first blast of warm summer air made New York come alive. No one wanted to be inside. At seven thirty it was still light. Oliver and Margot walked side by side in Central Park, his arm draped loosely around her shoulders. He had arrived an hour earlier from the airport and Margot, just home from the gallery, had agreed to join him for a walk. They reached the Great Lawn. The path encircling the grand sweep of green thronged with people—couples arm in arm, babies and children being pushed in all sorts of conveyances by their dreamy parents, and of course dogs, large and small, the rare and the pedigreed, along with the mixed breeds, a canine cornucopia.

Oliver said nothing about their disagreement in San Francisco, but kept up a lively account of the rest of his trip. The day after Margot had left, he had sold two more paintings. One, his largest and most expensive piece, had sold to a wealthy collector who had asked Oliver to visit his house in Napa so he could see the rest of his art collection. Oliver had gone there over the weekend with his dealer. He described the house to her—an incredible estate on acres of vineyards, complete with formal gardens, allées of trees, fountains, and peacocks on the lawn. Imitating the birds' piercing cries, Oliver made Margot laugh.

"Shall we sit for a while?" he asked her.

Margot agreed and followed him to a bench. The trees in front of them had low, sweeping branches flush with new leaves, and even as the sun lowered, the day's warmth lingered. She wanted to enjoy the sweetness of this lovely evening, but somehow she couldn't shake off the chill New England spring she'd recently left behind. "You haven't asked me about New Hampshire," she said.

"I told you I was sorry about Alex's mother." His tone hardened. "You made the decision to go."

"Oliver."

"I hardly knew Edith. You didn't expect me to come for the funeral, did you?"

"Of course not."

"Did you fix the boyfriend crisis?"

"You don't have to say it that way." Margot tried to ignore her growing irritation.

"Look, Mags, you know how I feel about this. I don't want to argue again."

"I spent a lot of time with Toni. Listening seemed to help. But you were right. Toni wasn't about to do anything drastic. Wink overdramatized the whole thing."

"I'm glad." He rested his elbows on his knees. "I know those girls are going through a lot. I don't want you to think I'm hard-hearted."

"I don't think that," she said, touching his arm.

"Did you talk to Carl?" Oliver stretched his legs out and moved closer to her.

Margot drew in her breath. "Oliver, Lacey is worse." Saying this brought back the painful memories of her last visit.

"You noticed a difference."

She nodded. "She's terribly sad about Edith. That may be part of it."

"But she's managing okay?"

"Sort of. You know how in the winter she was almost angry? Well, now it's as if she's lost her spunk." Margot felt sadness rise in her throat.

"Maybe that's only temporary."

"I'm afraid it's not. For so long she refused to give up any of her activities. Alex begged her to do less and she ignored him. All of a sudden that's changed. Wink told me that Lacey's given up most of her volunteer work. She spends almost all her time in her studio weaving."

"You told me she loves to weave."

"Not for endless hours. She's not the same."

Oliver turned to Margot. "I'm sorry to hear that, Mags." He smoothed her hair back. "What did Carl say about our plans?"

"He didn't say anything. I didn't discuss it with him."

"What?"

"I can't go this summer." Her chest tightened. It was hard to breathe.

"Margot, come on. You told me you wanted to do this. Here's this chance for us. We can both paint. A sabbatical, remember?"

She shook her head. Her resolve began to waver. "It would be hard to get all the vacation time."

"Mario can fill in for you. You've told me he'd like the extra hours. Carl wouldn't have a problem with that."

"I'm just not sure." Margot couldn't get rid of the gut feeling that she needed to be near Lacey in case . . . in case what? Another crisis with Toni? Wink falling apart? Alex needing her? This had never been true before. Everything had changed with Lacey's illness. It was as if they had all become vulnerable.

"I spoke to Grant. We have the house from the middle of June until the middle of September."

"It's not just my job." Margot spoke more resolutely. "I want to have some time with Lacey at the lake. There's that and the girls' graduation. I can't afford to fly back and forth."

"You said you'd come."

"This might be my last summer at the lake with Lacey."

"You don't know that for sure."

"No, but . . ." How could she explain the way she felt about Lacey? Her sister was the last thread connecting her to her family, to her past. How much longer would Lacey still be able to talk? "Maybe we could go this winter?"

"Mags, I want to go now. I've got the house. I'm meeting new people through the gallery. This move is important for my career."

"Does it always have to be your career?" She felt that forgotten pinch of anger. "Having time with Lacey is important to me. I told Alex I'd be there for her."

"So it's Alex again?"

"What's that supposed to mean?"

"He's already summoned you several times."

"I need to be with my sister. That's what's important right now. And the girls will need me one day, too."

"What about us, Mags? You and me?" He took her hand.

She looked into his eyes. Why couldn't he understand? "I want to be with you, but I need this summer with Lacey."

Oliver pulled away and stood. "I'm not going to let you make this mistake again. Mags, we're meant to be together."

"I'm not making a mistake," Margot said. "I just need this summer."

"And then what? The fall? The winter? The years are flying by."

"But Lacey's worse."

He stood. "So you're willing to be apart all summer?"

"You're the one who's leaving."

"That's how you think of it?"

"Okay, I know the work out there's important. Go ahead. It's only one summer."

"A lot can happen in a few months," he warned.

"What are you saying?"

"I think you're making a mistake."

She shook her head.

"You won't change your mind?"

"No, Oliver. This time I'm right." She remembered how Teddy had pushed her to do things. She wasn't going to let Oliver do it too. She'd had enough.

Alex tapped on the door of Lacey's studio and stepped in. It had been a week since his mother's funeral. She was bent over her loom, a basket of fabric pieces on the floor by her feet. She reached down and picked up a strip, not seeming to pay attention to the color, and placed it inside the shed before moving her feet to activate the loom.

"Can we talk a minute?" he asked.

She continued to work, this time sliding the shuttle across, pedaling her feet, and moving the shuttle back in the opposite direction.

"Please, Lacey."

She stopped, resting her hands in her lap. "What is it?" She didn't meet his gaze.

Alex tried to quell his growing anger. Lately, Lacey seemed to make it her mission not to talk to him when they were alone. That morning, just as it was growing light, he had reached for her. She had rolled onto her back closer to him. Her breathing softened. The moment her eyes opened he touched her cheek, then kissed her ear. Then without pausing, she threw back the covers, and went to the bathroom to shower.

"I feel like you're avoiding me."

"I don't . . . mean to." She leaned back in her chair. "I'm sad. I miss Edith."

"I do too. But we have to go on. Mom was already gone from us."

"Like I'll . . . be."

"Lacey, stop. You can't think like that."

She pursed her lips and stroked the tapestry in the loom.

"Did you have trouble sleeping again?" he asked.

"I was up. In the night. Toni." She picked up the shuttle and resumed her work. It was as if she had to constantly be doing something, her body always in motion.

"Is she okay?"

"Ryan called her." She took a big breath of air. "To say goodbye. He's leaving for Africa."

"I see," he said.

"He shouldn't have called." Lacey reached for another rope of fabric. Her hands threw the shuttle from side to side. "He made her upset . . . all over again."

"Can't you stop for a minute?"

Lacey sighed and hugged her hands to her waist.

Alex continued now that he had her attention. "I wish we weren't having this graduation party. The cooking is too much for you. You'll wear yourself out, Chief."

She shook her head. "I want it to be . . . normal for the girls. Besides, Margot will be back. She'll help."

"We can't expect Margot to be here all the time." He looked away, knowing the difference his sister-in-law made to the household. Those few days before his mother's funeral, Margot had helped with everything—running errands with Lacey, doing laundry, cleaning up the kitchen, even taking Wink to an interview for her summer internship at the science center. Mostly, it had been a relief to have her with them at meals, easing the conversation along, gently trying to cheer them all during that sad time.

Lacey sighed. "You don't . . . ."

"What don't I?" he said.

She met his gaze, and for just a moment her expression softened, as if giving him a brief glimpse of all that was churning inside her mind. "When I stay busy." She reached for the fabric scraps at her feet. "I forget. I forget the bad things."

"Italy will be good for you," he said. "A real rest."

"You think that . . . that going . . . away will change anything?" Her lips quivered.

"Lacey, we've got to try." He brought the desk chair closer to her loom and sat beside her. "Mom's death has been hard for you."

"Don't forget Toni."

"She'll get over Ryan."

Lacey looked up at the ceiling and shook her head. "If you only knew."

"What's that supposed to mean?"

"Last night. Crying again." She paused.

He reached for Lacey's hand. "Lace, you're the one holding us all together. I haven't thanked you enough, especially for planning Mom's service."

"Margot helped."

"With your direction."

Lacey took a piece of fabric larger than the other scraps from the basket. She made a small tear in the cloth and then pulled the two halves apart.

Alex glanced downward. "What are you doing with those?" He touched the edge of her basket with his foot.

"Do you . . ." She paused. He could see her struggle—the pursed lips, the tremble of her head. "Recognize," she said forcefully, adding, "Do you recognize them?" She lifted a handful of the scraps from the basket.

The long strips of cotton dangled from her hands. He shook his head.

"The girls' dresses. When they were kids." She grabbed another wide strip and ripped it in two, tearing this one faster.

He took a piece of the cloth, studying the tiny white flowers on a green background. He remembered the matching sundresses

Lacey had sewn for the twins when they were little. "Why have you ripped them up?" Lacey had saved many of the girls' special outfits over the years. They were stored in neatly labeled boxes in the crawl space off their bedroom. She had said she was keeping her favorites. Now the little green dresses had been torn into strips and knotted together to form one long strand. It was just cloth, but seeing them in tatters seemed so cruel.

"But you were saving them for—" He closed his mouth. She had been saving them for the grandchildren she would probably never see, for babies she would never hold. Lacey looked into his eyes as if she were reading his thoughts.

"I'm making . . . a tapestry." She drew her hand across the emerging piece in the loom. The weaving was unlike her usual work, work that was smooth, even, and ordered. The ripped scraps of fabrics from the girls' dresses all but disappeared into the chaotic mix of line and textures.

Alex couldn't think what to say. The quiet but intense destruction going on in the studio sickened him.

"I'm calling it . . ." She paused and swallowed. "Commencement," she said. "I'll look at it. And I'll remember."

15

*Woolgatherer: A person who wandered through
the fields gathering tufts of wool left on low branches from
the sheep that had been grazing there. To woolgather
is to indulge in fanciful daydreams.*

*M*argot shifted on the folding chair. They had taken their places in the vast rows of seats set aside for family and guests at the twins' graduation ceremony. It was a humid afternoon, unusual for June. Margot's skirt was already sticking to the backs of her legs. Her mother, born in South Carolina, would have called it swampy weather. She imagined a June afternoon in the South feeling exactly like this, the warm air syrupy and thick.

Her mother had come to her own high school graduation in Concord. Margot remembered how her mother had stayed close to her father's side and smiled vaguely, looking fragile in a blue linen dress. Lacey had been home from college for the summer and had taken their mother shopping for the new outfit. Lacey saw to it that her mother was there for the occasion. Margot had not appreciated then what it must have taken for her father and Lacey to get Helen out and ready: keeping a vigilant watch, seeing to it that she never had the car available to restock her secret stash of alcohol, making her eat, getting her to a hair appointment, and on the day itself, gently coaxing her along, allowing sufficient time for her to fix her makeup and dress.

Margot pushed her dark glasses up onto her head. Her eyes themselves felt hot and in need of air. She breathed in deeply, pushing aside the long-forgotten day of her graduation, a day when her one desire was for the ceremony to be over so she could go home and get ready for the summer at Bow Lake.

"I remember Wink and Toni as babies," Kate said, turning to Margot. She and Hugh were sitting on Margot's right, and beyond them Alex and Lacey. So much had happened since Kate and Hugh had sat at the Georges' Thanksgiving table the previous November.

"Where has the time gone?" she added with a wistful sigh. Kate and Hugh had known the girls all their lives. Margot knew Lacey considered them part of the family.

Margot nodded, as if she had been pondering the same question. Hugh's head was bent toward Alex. They were talking softly together. Lacey sat at the end of the row, closest to the aisle where the students would walk toward the podium and their seats in front. She appeared to be watching the crowd, taking stock of the arriving families, all families she had come to know well over the years at soccer games, bake sales, theatrical productions.

"Exciting to see them so grown-up," Margot said, feeling the need to say something. She liked Kate, but never knew quite how to relate to her. Being a dean at the academy as well as a teacher, Kate made Margot feel like an adolescent again, in some way not measuring up.

"It's too bad Oliver couldn't be here," Kate said.

"He's working in California for the summer."

"Where in California?"

"The Wine Country. Sonoma."

"That's so gorgeous," she said. "Hugh and I went for a long weekend for our anniversary. Our twenty-fifth. Have you ever been?"

"We were there last month. You're right. It's beautiful." Margot shifted in her seat. She could feel perspiration behind her knees.

"Will you be going too?"

"I'm afraid not." Her stomach growled. "I didn't want to miss this. I wanted to be able to have time with Lacey at Bow Lake in August, too."

"I see," Kate said, looking mildly surprised by this explanation; then she turned her attention back to Hugh. Margot fanned herself with the program in her hand. The slight movement of humid air offered little relief. She wanted to savor this important day in Wink's and Toni's lives, but her thoughts kept going back to Oliver.

Why couldn't he understand? Her sister was ill, for God's sake. How long would Lacey have? Margot had tried to block out the eventual end of her sister's life. Once communication went, what would be left? The body itself would slowly degenerate. The hideous thought of caregivers, nursing homes, the realm of the aged would come all too soon. Five more years? Possibly ten?

The last several days in New York with Oliver had been awful—one argument after another. He had insisted that Margot couldn't cure her sister, that she needed to live her own life too. How could she turn her back on him? He wanted a future with her. Didn't she care about that? On and on it went. Nothing had been resolved except that Oliver had gone to San Francisco without her. Was this the beginning of the end of their relationship?

Now, under the hot sun, the prescribed commencement music wafted over the crowd gathered on the football field. Was it "Pomp and Circumstance"? Margot wasn't sure. She turned and watched the young people gathering to make their final walk as high school students. They wore sky blue robes instead of the standard black, yet signs of each one's uniqueness abounded. Earrings, tattoos on necks and ankles, sandals, boots, bare legs, the pant legs of jeans, flowing skirts peeking below hems, each graduate imagining he or she was different now, ready to spring into freedom, official adulthood, leaving childhood behind. The sun was bright. Margot put on her sunglasses again.

Lacey craned her neck, seeming to watch for her own two girls in the clumps of seniors assembling in the distance. She was running now for an hour every morning. Her skin held the beginning of a summer tan. Margot marveled at Lacey's energy. Her physical body was becoming stronger and stronger, despite the failing in her brain. Since she had given up her volunteer work she now spent more time in the garden, a place where she never had to speak. An enormous pile of composted cow manure had been delivered from the garden center and Lacey had been transferring it by wheelbarrow to the flower beds before shoveling it around the base of each plant. Margot had offered to spread it, but Lacey had adamantly refused.

Margot had arrived yesterday in time to help with the cooking for the picnic supper they were hosting that night for the girls and their friends. With Lacey's guidance she made four dozen brownies and a pound cake. After that was done she boiled the potatoes for potato salad and made the barbecue sauce for the chicken that Alex would cook on the grill. The party would start at six that evening.

In many ways the household had regained its regular rhythm, yet it was as if an unseen hum vibrated among them like an undercurrent. It had no definable sound but was more like a worrisome subliminal rumble that alerted you to something, that kept you on guard.

The groups of students began to shift into formation. The music changed and the crowd stood. Margot pulled her skirt away from her legs.

"Here they come," Kate said. Two by two, the students made their way forward to the designated seats in front of the podium. With grinning faces, hurried waves toward parents, attempts at solemnity, they marched by. Margot tried to see her nieces beyond Kate and the others. Hugh's broad back kept blocking her view. A moment later she caught a glimpse of Wink and Toni passing their row. Wink's mortarboard tipped precariously. Margot had watched earlier that morning as she struggled to secure it with bobby pins.

From her vantage point, Margot couldn't see Wink's new sandals or her freshly painted toes. She had given the girls manicures and pedicures as a treat. Wink had chosen a subtle pale pink and Toni a deep burgundy that looked almost black.

Toni walked next to her sister. She tossed them a glance, tilting her head in recognition, her walk so like her mother's. She looked happier than she had in a while. Margot wondered if her niece would look back at her graduation one day and associate it with the end of her first love. What would she remember of Ryan? Would her memory of him fade when she fell in love again, leaving only a vague recollection of this momentous time? Memories were elusive. Margot imagined that both girls would always equate their last year of high school with the final healthy days of their mother.

She looked down the row of chairs to check on Lacey. A glaze of tears appeared to well in her eyes. Alex, beside her, smiled, a wash of amazement across his face, as if he could hardly believe they had reached this point in their daughters' lives. The lines around his mouth looked deeper. Kate and Hugh waved as the twins walked past.

When the sea of blue gowns had finally assembled in front of the audience, the school principal began his opening remarks. Margot's thoughts wandered and the sound of applause roused her at the moment he introduced the featured speaker, a state congresswoman who had graduated from the high school thirty years before. "The future," she began, and launched into memories of what she had thought her own future would be when she had sat in this very same place.

The idea of the future had become frightening to Margot. It kept her awake at night. In spite of everything, Toni and Wink faced a future full of possibilities. But it was only a matter of time before Lacey would no longer have her voice, no longer be able to tell her daughters how proud she was, how she loved them, how they were her life.

Oliver would return to New York in September. He was caught up in his own commencement—enthralled with a new place, painting in a new way, wanting to take Margot with him on his new adventure. Why shouldn't she let herself be part of that?

Margot reached down for her handbag. With a shaking hand she undid the clasp and took out a tissue. She dabbed under her sunglasses.

Kate touched her arm. "You okay?" she mouthed.

She nodded and closed her mouth tightly. She swallowed and quietly blew her nose. Kate patted her arm once more and turned her attention back to the speaker.

Hugh's expression was intent, as if he didn't want to miss a word of the speech. Beyond him, Alex had lowered his head and drawn his arms across his chest, his back curving slightly, looking like a man trying to hold himself together. Lacey's eyes, still damp, seemed to be focused on the tops of the trees beyond the podium. A breeze had begun to stir the leaves. Her hands rested in her lap, her fingers curled upward and empty. The voice of the commencement speaker floated out above the students' heads, echoing slightly to those listening on the periphery.

"I want all of you, both graduating seniors and your guests, to think about this day, about where you are now, about the people you are with and all who care about you, and to ask yourself these questions: What have I learned so far? What do I hope for? What are my dreams? But don't ask these questions only today, on this day of new beginnings, on this day of celebration. These are questions we all need to carry with us, questions we need to keep asking ourselves, day after day, year in and year out." The speaker finished with a final "Congratulations to all," which seemed to rise in the air like the sea of blue and white balloons that were released on cue. With roaring applause, the crowd stood.

A cloud momentarily blocked the sun. As Margot bent to pick

up her bag, she saw Alex uncross his arms and reach over to Lacey. He took her hand, placing it firmly in his own, and intertwined her fingers with his. Seeing that moment of tenderness made Margot's heart expand in her chest, almost like a pain. She didn't dare breathe.

She thought again of Oliver. The first few months after meeting him had been dizzying with change. No more quiet evenings, no more evenly shaped days. Suddenly she was fitting in hurried phone calls, rushing to meet him at his studio for lunch, sharing dinners in tiny restaurants she had never known existed. Once, Mario had called her down from a ladder where she was adjusting the lights for a new exhibition, saying Oliver was double-parked outside and had a quick question. She had gone out to the car and gotten in beside him. Before she could say a word his lips were on hers. "Are you for real, Margot?" He had kissed her again before saying, "I had to be sure. I couldn't wait until tonight."

After making love, they would talk for hours, each wanting to know everything about the other. One night, months into the relationship, Oliver had asked Margot to tell him what had gone wrong with her marriage. Until then she had only alluded to her troubles with Teddy, but knowing Oliver better, she felt she could trust him with the whole story. Still, it had been difficult to explain how she'd been taken in by Teddy's attention—his looks, his charm, his sense of fun. She joked that he had been like some kind of elaborate, overly sweet dessert that left her sick and empty inside. When she told Oliver about Teddy's affairs, and the eventual illness that left her unable to have children, he took her hand and held it without saying a word. The warmth of his skin, the firmness of his grasp, felt like forgiveness. That night, Oliver had made Margot feel like she could begin again. It was as if she had been swimming underwater all those years after Teddy, and Oliver had brought her back to the surface.

Margot rose and followed Kate and Hugh into the throng of happy families. Everywhere she looked, people were laughing, hugging, and calling out to friends. A heavy older man in a seersucker jacket jostled her arm and excused himself. When Margot turned away, Lacey was at her side. She grasped Margot's arm. "I'm glad . . ." she said softly. "I'm glad you're here." She smiled and then glanced up. The scattering of balloons had become tiny specks in the open sky.

"You okay?" Alex, holding two glasses of white wine, looked down at Margot. It was a soft evening in Lacey's garden, the day after the twins' graduation.

She closed her sketchbook. She had been drawing a peony. The pink blossom, lush and ruffled, was hard to capture. Odd, how easy it was to draw a gnarled branch, or a mottled leaf, each imperfection interesting and alive, yet something as perfect as this flower eluded her. She set her drawing down.

"I saw you from the kitchen," he said. "Wine time. May I join you?"

"Of course," she said, reaching for the glass. "Thanks."

"Glad we're not cooking for a mob again tonight," he said.

Yesterday's graduation party had been a huge success. Margot had loved seeing her nieces so happy, and preferring to be on the sidelines, she had kept herself busy passing food, refilling platters, and carrying away empty plates. Lacey had mingled with the guests, accepting the compliments for her well-loved barbecue sauce. Only a few of her closest friends were aware of her illness and Margot knew she wanted to keep it that way.

"Any leftovers?" she asked.

"Lacey put aside enough food for tonight," he said. "Always thinking ahead. Cheers." He lifted his glass.

She raised her glass to Alex, suddenly aware of being alone with him on Lacey's tea bench. A golden light fell across the lawn, like the color of the wine.

"I'm afraid we're taking advantage of you," he said.

"Absolutely not. It was a pleasure to help with the party." She looked away from him. A climbing hydrangea with fresh new leaves clung to a trellis on the back of the house. Lacey was training it to cover the cable box and some of the unsightly wires running up the clapboards.

Margot was leaving the next day. What more could she do for them now? The girls would be starting their summer jobs, Lacey had her garden and her weaving, and Alex would be back at work. Thankfully, she would have plenty to do in New York. Carl wanted her to hang the summer show as soon as she returned. Even if she had decided to go to California with Oliver, it would have been difficult to leave before August, and August had always been her time to be with Lacey at Bow Lake.

"Where did Wink and Toni go?" she asked quickly, feeling suddenly awkward alone with Alex.

"Some concert in Prescott Park. There's a series this summer."

"Toni seems a bit happier."

"Boyfriends are hard on a father."

"What do you mean?"

"I guess that part of me hopes I'll always be the most important man in my daughters' lives. Maybe that sounds sick. I don't mean it that way. Right now I'd like to clobber that guy for making Toni so miserable."

"I'm not sure you ever get over your first love," Margot said, and instantly wished she could take back her words. The memory of that uncomfortable night with Alex in the bar had upset her. Knowing that he still remembered what had happened at Bow Lake made her uneasy. Why had he even wanted to speak of their time together after all these years? He was a responsible adult, he had a family and, of course, Lacey. She glanced back at the house, thinking of Lacey up in her studio weaving during her every spare moment.

For a while Alex said nothing.

"Do you miss Oliver?"

His question surprised her. It was usually Lacey who asked about Oliver, ever hopeful that Margot would finally marry him.

"I don't mean to pry," Alex went on. "Lacey said he was staying in California for the summer."

"He is." Margot sipped her wine. She remembered drinking wine like this with Oliver on Grant's terrace in Sonoma. She could still choose to go to California. The white roses would be in full bloom by now. She sighed. California seemed like the other side of the moon. "He wants me to join him, but I don't want to be so far away right now."

"You mean far from here?"

"I want to help Lacey and be around for the girls."

"Margot, you've already done a lot. I—I mean, we—don't want you to put your own life on hold. I already ruined your last trip. I wouldn't have called if I'd known you were out there."

"It's okay. Lacey took your mom's death so hard. It's been a rough time."

"You've been great with Toni, too."

"Alex, I wondered—" She paused. "Why didn't you just call Lacey when you were worried about Toni?"

"Maybe I should have, but I feel like I've dumped so much on her. She's the one who has to deal with everything day to day, and she's the one who's sick. I feel like a louse."

"But she wanted you to take the job in Chicago."

He lowered his head. "Shit, Margot. She's getting worse. "

"Maybe your vacation will help." She stared at her glass, not daring to look at his face.

"She's cut back on her activities. I thought that would improve things, but it hasn't." He gulped his wine. "Since Mom died it's as if Lacey has closed another door. I can't seem to reach her anymore."

"It's the illness," Margot said. "You know that." She started to reach over to offer a reassuring touch, but stopped herself. "I'm sorry," she said. "Along with everything else, you must miss your mother."

"At her age and with her illness, it had to be expected. Losing your mom must have been much worse. Lacey's never said much about it."

"She had to be the strong one. I have so many regrets in that department. I was young and selfish." Didn't Alex remember? Their summer love affair had happened just after her mother's death. She sipped her wine, thinking she should go inside and see to setting the table for dinner. She certainly didn't want their conversation to go in the direction of that last summer at Bow Lake.

"You're too hard on yourself," he said.

"I almost killed my mother." Margot set her wine on the armrest of the bench.

Alex turned and stared at her. "What are you talking about?"

"There was this party when I was in high school," she began. "I must have been fifteen because I still didn't have my driver's license. Dad was away at some annual insurance conference—one of the few times he was away on a weekend. Of course Lacey was at college. I had always depended on her to drive me places."

Margot shifted. The bench was growing hard and the air had started to cool. "I made dinner for us. Mom had been drinking, as usual. I could tell by the way she pushed her food around. Dad said I was to be sure she ate and be sure she got up to bed. My friend Janice was going to take me to the party after dinner. I don't remember why it was so important to get to this party except that it was at Greg Summers' house. He was one of the cool kids. I couldn't believe I'd been invited. While we were eating Janice called and said she'd been grounded for having flunked her biology test. There went my ride."

"No one else could take you?"

"I kept calling. My friends had already left for the party. I was so furious that Dad and Lacey were away. Mom said she wasn't sure she could drive, but I persuaded myself that she sounded pretty clearheaded, and I talked her into taking me. She used to drive to the grocery store first thing in the morning when Dad was at work. Early in the day she was usually fine. I convinced myself that Greg's house wasn't that far. It wasn't totally dark either. So it must have been spring. I pretty much begged her to drive me."

"You're sure your mom was drinking?" Alex asked.

"Mom was always drinking. Some times more than others. We got in the car. I saw immediately I was making a mistake. I had to tell her to stay on the right side of the road, to slow down, and to stop at the intersections. Somehow we got there. I was totally furious. I was angry at her for drinking, for being a stinking alcoholic and ruining my life as well as hers. I was miserable at the party. I vacillated between hating myself for putting my mother at risk and wishing she were dead."

"What happened?"

"Some miracle. She made it home without killing herself or anyone else. Eventually, I got a ride home. Our car was parked halfway off the driveway. I found her keys and backed it up and pulled it in straight. Lacey had shown me how to do that. We were used to covering for Mom."

Margot took a last sip of wine. For years she'd worried that alcohol would be a problem for her. Now and again she wouldn't drink—just testing, she'd think, wanting to be sure she wasn't like her mother. "The really horrible part was that my mother had no memory of any of it in the morning. Thank God. If Dad had found out, he would have killed me."

"You were acting like a normal teenager," Alex said.

Margot shook her head. She had never told anyone this before. "I abandoned my mother. It was a terrible risk."

"You've got it all wrong. Don't you see? Your mother was the one putting you in danger. She was the one drinking and driving. She was the adult."

"But I was the one forcing her to take me. I never should have done that."

"You were a kid. Margot, you're too hard on yourself," he repeated.

"I won't abandon Lacey," she said. Tears welled in her eyes.

"I know that," he said. They sat together for a few minutes more.

"I'd better go inside," she finally said, getting to her feet. "Thanks for listening," she added.

"It helps to talk. I'm the one who should thank you." His gaze seemed to linger on her face.

Margot turned away from him and walked toward the house. She looked again at the trellis, and from the window above it she saw Lacey looking down, her eyes fixed on the garden bench where Alex now sat alone.

During their childhood, Alex had thought of Lacey and Margot almost interchangeably. His memories of long-ago summers were a mixture of the two sisters. Was it Lacey who ordered coffee ice cream every time, or Margot? Had Margot called for help when bailing out Pigtail, the old rowboat riddled with cracks during its final summer before Granny Winkler declared it beyond repair? Was it Lacey who found the fossil when they were skipping stones on the beach at Junior?

Later, when Lacey entered puberty, the confusion ended. The sight of her long legs, her breasts, her nipples pointed and showing clearly through her bathing suit after a swim were riveting. Margot remained the kid sister then, tagging along, following them everywhere. He had always liked Margot. She was quiet, and game for most anything, willing to carry oars, fetch life jackets, bring lemonade down to the dock. She never whined like some little kids, though more and more, he found himself wishing she wasn't always with them.

Alex had been so focused on Lacey by the end of his teens that he had failed to notice that Margot had grown up too. Her face was like Lacey's, but her skin was paler, her hair darker, and she had those light blue eyes that seemed to soak in the world around her. Though the curves came eventually, Margot never grew as tall as Lacey and there was a vulnerability, a tentativeness in her demeanor that belied her abilities in the water or on the tennis court.

Now, sitting in the garden at dusk, Alex tried to sort out what had happened between him and Margot. Okay, he'd been only twenty-two. Had it just been college boy lust? It still troubled him that he had slept with Margot when he had been attracted to Lacey first.

At the beginning of that summer, he had visited Lacey for a night when he was in Boston looking for an apartment. She seemed years older, having already taught for a year, and despite the summers of flirting, he had felt a bit awkward around her far from their familiar surroundings of Bow Lake. He had known things might begin to happen between them. He felt she sensed it too.

Then after an entire summer thinking about Lacey, he had gone to Bow Lake for that final week. And there was Margot and that inexplicable pull. Once he returned to Boston, he managed to persuade himself that their time together hadn't really mattered, was more like something he might have dreamed. He hardly knew the grown-up Margot and yet there seemed to be something between them—more than the chemistry, more than the sex.

When he'd called her a few weeks later from Boston, she had sounded distant, shy. The conversation between them had been strained. His workload the first semester was overwhelming. Their second conversation had been shorter. Maybe he should have invited her for a weekend, but he was pressed for time, and even if she had traveled all that way, they might have had nothing to say to each other. Weeks went by, and when Margot left a message later in the fall, Alex, swept up in midterms, never called her back. Also, by then he had started seeing Lacey. How could he have explained that?

He hadn't planned on falling in love with Lacey. They had a few dates, took long walks by the Charles River, talked for hours over dinner at a tiny Lebanese restaurant that ended up becoming their favorite. She made him feel confident that not only could he finish business school but success would certainly follow. In no time at all, he couldn't imagine a day without her—if not seeing her, then at least hearing her voice.

When Lacey had asked him if he had seen Margot at the end of the summer he told her that they had overlapped a few days at Bow Lake, and despite his guilt-laden feelings, he had said nothing else. He had felt bad as he uttered those words—they were not exactly a lie, but they weren't the truth either. He should have told Margot something too, found some way to put the interlude behind them. As the months went by, he convinced himself that it couldn't have mattered to Margot either. She didn't call him again. She, too, was probably busy with schoolwork and maybe involved with someone else by now.

Alex rose from the bench. The tall hedges around him, along with the house, made an intimate enclosure. A lone seagull called out in the darkening sky. He walked toward the house, trying to quiet his mind. What if he had made an effort to see Margot that fall? What if she had been more outgoing? Would he ever have been able to love Margot the way he loved Lacey? He thought of the old expression "Still waters run deep." Had his mother said that about Margot? Or was it Lacey?

Margot climbed the stairs to the guest room at the top of the house. The door to Lacey's studio was closed. Hesitant to disturb her, she went across the hall to her room. Her suitcase was open at the foot of the bed and she began layering in her clothes. She hadn't brought much and in no time she had packed her things. She closed the lid and stretched out on the bed. Downstairs, the table was set and she had arranged the leftovers on platters. Across the hall, Lacey's loom rumbled and clanked in a relentless rhythm.

Margot closed her eyes. If only Oliver could see how Lacey had weakened he might understand. More than ever Margot wanted one more summer with her sister—one more summer to hear things that only Lacey could tell her.

When they were girls, just before going to sleep on summer nights Margot would ask Lacey to tell her stories about their mother before she got sick. Lacey was maybe ten or eleven by then, Margot four years younger.

Margot knew their mother had been pretty. There were photographs around their house in Concord. In one, she wore a white wedding dress, her dark hair pulled back under a band of real daisies, her eyes a pale blue like Margot's. She clutched their father's arm. Their father looked sunny and confident, one foot extended as he strode out of the church with his delicate Southern bride.

"Did Mom play the piano every day when you were my age?" Margot asked.

Lacey's voice carried across their room in the dark. "She never missed a day. She used to give lessons. Daddy said she stopped after you were born. Her students were grown-ups. Granny said Mom could have been a concert pianist. If it was your birthday she would play whatever you wanted," Lacey continued. "She played 'Farmer in the Dell' for me when I was really little."

"Did she make you a cake?"

"Strawberry shortcake. She said she loved having summer babies because strawberries were in season. She claimed that nothing was better than strawberry shortcake."

Margot regretted that she had no memory of those early happy days. As hard as she tried she couldn't recall her mother reaching into the oven, removing the biscuitlike cakes, and spooning on the sweet red berries and large dollops of cream. Her mother still managed to fix dinner for them, but it was always a hasty event. She fried pork chops in a black skillet until they smoked, or broiled chicken in the oven, sometimes not cooking it long enough, so the inside was still raw. She would forget the canned vegetables until they boiled over, but the frozen potatoes that came in a bag—Tater Tots or shoestring—usually turned out okay. If there was dessert, it might be the cherry gelatin that Lacey had made herself. Her mother made a few other things, but her repertoire was slim.

"Tell me about the songs," Margot said.

"It's getting late," Lacey would say. "Granny will scold us if she hears."

"Oh, please," Margot would beg.

Lacey would resume her story in a whisper. "Mom loved old songs. One guy was Stephen Foster. She loved his music. He wrote songs in the olden days. She'd sing, sitting on the edge of my bed. My favorite was 'Beautiful Dreamer.' She loved 'Oh! Susanna.'"

"I know that one." And Margot would sing the refrain.

"There was this really sad one," Lacey continued, "called 'The Voices That Are Gone.' When she sang that, tears would roll down her cheeks."

"Mom really cried?"

Lacey nodded. "Mom used to lie down right next to me and hum that one just before I went to sleep. She used to say the world would be a better place if people just hummed more often. She said that humming made your heart feel better if it hurt."

"Can you do it for me?"

Lacey would sigh heavily, and then in a clear melodic hum one of their mother's old favorites would drift across their small room. Margot thought there was no better way to fall asleep. She would close her eyes and pretend that Lacey's voice was her mom's voice, there in the dark room.

Lacey's loom was quiet. Margot knew she should go down for dinner. Tomorrow she would return to New York. She dreaded the silent apartment awaiting her. It would be a long summer without Oliver. Swinging her legs to the floor, she promised herself she would stay busy. When she wasn't working she would get back to painting. And in August she would have her time with Lacey at the lake.

16

*Texere: Latin for "to weave," from which
the English word "text" is derived.*

"*Lei e una bella regazza,*" Alex said, "or maybe it's *belle regazzae?*"
He glanced up at the blue Italian sky as if searching for an answer.
"I think that's the plural, at least in Latin." He and his family were
finally taking the long-planned-for trip.

"Dad, quit trying to talk Italian. You sound totally weird."
Toni rolled her eyes.

Alex flipped through the small dictionary and phrase book.
Lacey sipped San Pellegrino water and leaned back in her chair,
closing her eyes, allowing the sun to warm her face. They were
gathered around a table at an outdoor café in Orvieto across the
square from the cathedral. After they'd wound through the narrow, cobbled streets, seemingly a ghost town at midafternoon
with closed shutters and no signs of life, it had been like a mi-
rage to emerge in this open piazza dominated by the immense
black-and-white marble church. The city was still closed for the
siesta, with only a few cafés and shops remaining open for the
tourists.

Wink plopped a cube of sugar into her coffee, a tiny cup of
dark liquid, a fraction of the size of an American coffee.

"*Babbo* is *pazzo*. *Pazzo* is crazy," he said, lifting his eyebrows up and down, a further attempt to amuse his daughters.

"Dad." Wink joined her sister in protest.

Alex shrugged and smiled, knowing they tolerated his occasional silliness. He was glad they had stopped to rest. He sipped his beer, yeasty and cool, the right choice for a hot afternoon. They had driven to Orvieto from Todi, an Umbrian hill town where they had spent the night. He was still getting used to driving the rented Fiat on the curvy Italian roads. In spite of his careful planning and numerous maps, they had already gotten lost several times, once having to return to the auto route and exit in the opposite direction.

He stretched his arms back and yawned. The warmth of Italy felt great. After the hot spell during the girls' graduation, the weather in New Hampshire had remained cold and drizzly all month. The Italian sun felt amazing. He imagined the bodies of his entire family filling up with this Italian light like a magic cure, one of those alternative healing therapies that people sought when regular medicine failed. And why not? They were breathing different air, eating Italian food, drinking wine—all infusing them with the possibility for change.

"I think the waiter likes you," Wink said to Toni.

"Come on."

"Seriously, he keeps looking this way."

Toni gave Wink a sarcastic grin. Besides a Diet Coke, which had come with a piece of lime but no ice, she had ordered an ice cream, a block of chocolate and strawberry, and was passing the dish around the table so they could all take bites.

"Dad, can we go back to that shoe store we saw on the way?" Toni asked. The girls and Lacey had paused in front of several shops as they meandered up the street. "Everything should open again soon. It's nearly four."

"*I scarpi*, shoes," he said.

"Dad, most of the shop people speak English," Wink said. She took another bite of Toni's ice cream and gave her sister a conspiratorial glance.

"Go ahead," he said. "Mom and I will come find you after I pay the bill." He looked around for the only waiter, who when not sizing up his daughters had been busily shuttling drinks back and forth to the other tourists gathered on the terrace.

"I want to go . . ." Lacey paused, then added emphatically, "too." She sipped the last of her water and reached for her handbag. Alex noticed that jet lag had not made Lacey's speech worse. He had worried that the fatigue that usually affected her fluency would be a problem after the long flight and time change, but in the three days they'd been there she was showing no ill effects.

"Where will I meet you?" Alex asked.

"How about by the car?" Toni said. "There's that park there, remember?"

He agreed, recalling the benches across the street from where they had left the Fiat. The location was high above the valley. He might have time to take some pictures of the views he had only glimpsed while maneuvering the car up the steep hill to Orvieto. The dreamy landscape punctuated with dark green cypress trees looked like the backgrounds he had seen in the Renaissance paintings in the Borghese Gallery and Museum in Rome. Everything in Italy connected to the past. Rome itself had looked like a theater set from the sixteenth century.

"An hour or so?" he asked.

Wink told him that would be fine and he watched as his family gathered their bags, sunglasses, assorted maps and guide books, leaving him to wait for the bill. Lacey smiled down at him. She wore a straw sun hat with a wide, floppy brim that shaded her face. Just before turning out of sight, she glanced back at him once more. Yes, maybe the sun was doing its work.

Now by himself, Alex studied the people around him. Two large groups of Japanese tourists and several handfuls of Germans sat clustered in pockets. Closer to Alex were some hikers sharing tall pitchers of beer—Swedish or Norwegian, he guessed from their coloring and stature, and from the few words he overheard. They had piled their backpacks in a dusty mound behind their table. They looked flushed and weary from the steep climb up to the town.

Those gathered on the terrace in Orvieto had no idea that Lacey was suffering in any way. No one even gave her a second glance when she left the restaurant with her daughters. She seemed like any mother, happy to be out on a beautiful afternoon, looking in store windows, shopping for shoes. Being in Italy was like starting over, he thought again.

The three women at the table on Alex's other side were Italian. He picked up snippets of their discussions, mostly the easily identifiable words he'd been studying—words for "please," "thank you," "you're welcome." Now that he was alone, he concentrated on their conversation. The stream of Italian that poured out amid laughter and emphatic hand gestures was all but unintelligible to him. It had been easy to copy and repeat the few phrases from the CDs he'd been playing in his car back home, but it was a totally different experience to try to decode the entire sentences that poured out of their mouths with such alarming rapidity. No sooner would he puzzle out a word and try to look it up in his dictionary than the ladies would be paragraphs ahead, and seemingly on to another topic.

The waiter appeared and Alex handed him his credit card. The older woman at the next table said something to Alex. She had gray hair and fine wrinkles set into her well-tanned face. She pointed to the chairs recently vacated by his daughters and seemed to be asking him something. Suddenly Alex guessed that she was asking if his daughters were twins. He responded with *"Si, si,"* and tried to say "My daughters, my wife." He pointed to his shoes, and then said *"tre"* for "three," and lifted his right hand, rubbing his thumb and forefinger together to indicate the expense of three women shopping for shoes. The Italian ladies seemed to acknowledge his message with more lyrical utterances before breaking into laughter.

Alex kept smiling and moved his head up and down, as if he could follow every word they said. When the waiter brought him his check and credit card, he told the ladies good-bye in Italian, and felt pleased for making himself understood.

He decided to visit the cathedral before taking the street down through the town to the park where they had left the car. He crossed the square as more people spilled into the streets, and walked through the swinging leather door at the side of the church. The central doors were probably opened only for important occasions. The air inside the old building felt cool and calming; it smelled of age-old stone. After the heat and chatter of the café, he appreciated the silence in the dim interior. He tried to imagine the peasants, farmers who worked the fields in the surrounding countryside, making the pilgrimage to this place when it was first built, hearing prayers in a language they did not understand. Staring up into the Gothic vaults, he thought how trivial language really was. In the café he had been able to read faces and gestures, a simple form of communication. Even without the right words, he had understood what was going on. Would Lacey still be the same person when she lost her ability to speak? The very thought of her words locked inside, no longer accessible to him, was frightening.

Prayers, another form of communication, were more than words, he thought. Prayers were about seeking answers, trusting in faith. Did he have that in him? He continued to walk around this sacred space. His footsteps echoed. This church had no seats, no pews. Aged frescoes covered the walls, and a triptych was displayed in the nave. It was more of a museum now than a church. He shivered and, once again hungry for the sun, decided to go outside and walk to the car.

Alex and his family settled into the country inn outside Montepulciano, where they would spend the week exploring the hill towns in Tuscany. The innkeeper served a multicourse dinner on the terrace that evening: a platter of cured meats, olives, and roasted peppers, followed by pasta with vegetables in a lemon cream sauce, then roasted pork. They all turned down dessert, but indulged in glasses of Vin Santo, a dessert wine, in which they dipped hazelnut biscotti. After this sumptuous meal they stumbled up to bed.

The girls were sharing a room off the terrace close to the pool and Alex and Lacey had an upstairs room with a balcony. Before collapsing into bed, Alex threw the French doors wide open. The tile floor under his bare feet was still warm from the day, but the air was growing cooler. Lacey was already asleep. He slipped under the linen sheets and brought the blanket to his chin.

The wine had made him sleepy. He heard the lonely bark of a dog on the hillside in the distance. The air smelled of mown hay— dry and sweet. *Like summer should be*, he thought as he drifted into unconsciousness.

During the night Alex dreamed of Bow Lake many years before. The call of the loon cut through the air and water lapped at the shore. Leaves rustled high in the trees. Unseen nocturnal creatures scurried through the pine-scented woods. Even though the surroundings were familiar, in this dream he was lost in an overpowering darkness. Was he floating? No. His back was pressed into the earth. The ground was hard. He felt the prick of pine needles. The dark was intense, and no matter how hard he tried, his eyes wouldn't open. Then he felt a flutter of kisses on his chest, the sweep of hair across his face. He lifted his arms to reach out. An inner voice told him to stop. A command. He must not. He was unable to speak, to call out. Helpless. Suddenly, he knew. Margot. Margot was with him. Margot's mouth was about to touch his own. He gasped and began to choke.

He opened his eyes to a swath of moonlight across the bed. There was no scent of pine. The Italian night had grown warm. Had he called out? Lacey's hair spilled out across his chest and her hands touched him, stroking his arm, his neck, his face. Her breath warmed his ear and she kissed his cheek, his forehead, the hollows of his eyes. Her lips were light, barely there, until she met his mouth. In the middle of a moonlit night in Italy she had come back to him.

"Lace," he whispered.

"Shhh." She brought her fingers to his lips.

They made love. After he felt the initial surprise of holding her close once again, his uncertainty disappeared. She loved him fully, and he loved her. After so many months complicated by doubts and fears, he was finally able to forget for a short while the burden they both carried. It was as if Lacey's diagnosis, the sense of doom they wore like a second skin, had slipped away into the night air.

Moonlight flooded the room. He could see clearly. He pushed himself onto his elbow and touched Lacey's face. Her cheeks were wet with tears. He started to speak, then silently took the hem of the sheet and patted her face dry. Her fingers briefly touched his hand and then she drifted into sleep. There was so much he didn't want to think about, so much he wished he could forget. The unpleasant taste of his dream lingered in his mind. He watched for the dawn and eventually dozed.

When he woke the next morning Lacey was not in bed. He wondered briefly if their lovemaking had even happened. He pulled on the hotel robe and walked to the balcony doors. Lacey and the twins sat at a table eating breakfast on the terrace near the pool, their faces shaded by a large green umbrella. He remembered dreaming about Margot, and swallowed, feeling suddenly unwell. He tried to convince himself it was the wine from the night before, the rich food, his exhaustion from the long drive. Italy would cure him, he thought, and headed to the shower.

"A hair to the left," Margot said.

Mario stood at the top of a stepladder, adjusting the spotlights for the summer exhibition at the Van Engen Gallery. "Can you angle it down just a bit? That spot needs to flood the whole picture."

"Let me move this one over." He reached out for the next light, teetering precariously as he leaned to the left.

"Careful," Margot said. He didn't seem to mind her maternal cautioning. Technically, she was old enough to be his mother. Now and again, he had even come to Margot for advice about girlfriends. For the last year he had been seeing Julie, four inches taller than he, with a wide smile, and an intelligent face, who worked in the education department of the Museum of Natural History. Margot, who liked to think of Mario as a younger brother, had encouraged the relationship.

"Yes. That's it. Just right." She stepped away and walked back and forth, checking the lighting on the entire wall.

"So we're done?" he asked, descending the stepladder.

"It looks great. Carl will be pleased. I'll finish the price list in the morning. You won't need to come in until late afternoon."

The summer show, titled Waterworks, was the work of a group of five watercolor artists who painted scenes from the Adirondacks. She gazed at the quiet views, horizontal compositions of woodland streams, leafy valleys, undulating hills. The opening reception was the next evening. Carl liked having less controversial art up for the summer, pieces that he called easy on the eye. Margot thought of the studies she was doing of Bow Lake. She wanted her pictures to be beautiful like these on view, but she hoped to convey something more—the peace, the ephemeral quality of an unspoiled place, nostalgia for what might no longer exist. That was the difficult part.

"Do you have plans for the weekend?" Mario asked, kicking the two sides of the stepladder into place and carrying it toward the storage area behind the office. He knew that Oliver was away for the summer.

"Nothing much," she said, forcing a smile. She sat behind her desk and quickly checked her home e-mail account. Seeing nothing from Oliver, she clicked the computer switch off. She worried again that they were growing dangerously apart. "I may go to the chamber music concert in the park on Saturday. Our downstairs neighbor has put a group together. They're organizing a potluck picnic supper. How about you?"

"Apartment hunting with Julie. We've decided to get a place together."

Margot looked up at Mario, who had perched at the edge of the desk. "It must be getting serious."

He smiled with almost childlike delight. "Yep. Moving in together makes it real. Now that we'll be sharing the rent, I'm hoping I can afford some more studio space." He cocked his head. "Carl said you've been painting a lot."

Margot nodded. "I'm using my old apartment as a studio. With Oliver away I have plenty of time." *Too much time*, she thought. The hours she spent painting helped, but she was often lonely. Oliver called intermittently. He insisted he was having an excellent summer. If he missed her, he wouldn't admit it. Margot could still become angry thinking about the way he had tried to set the agenda for their lives. She had only wanted one summer. Oliver had grudgingly agreed in the end.

"Have you checked out the real estate market lately?"

"What?" she asked, not sure what he was talking about.

"Man, Margot, you could sell your little place for a ton. You wouldn't have to work here if you had that kind of dough."

"You're probably right." She lifted her shoulders and released them with a sigh. She thought of the painting she had started just a few days before, a picture of the moon path on Bow Lake. She was trying to capture the cool water, the gentle lapping sound along the shore, the delicious feel of lowering your body into the lake on a summer night. It was proving to be the most challenging piece she had ever attempted. She remembered the way Oliver had rendered the night sky in Riverside Park with just the right shades.

"Say," Mario continued, interrupting her thoughts, "do you

want to join me and Julie for a drink? I'm meeting her downtown. I'm not sure what we're planning for dinner."

"Thanks, but I have a few errands to run on the way home." Margot smiled, touched that he would think of including her. She hoped she hadn't been looking too down these last weeks. "Another time, maybe?"

"Sure thing." Mario picked up his backpack and set out to meet Julie, telling Margot he'd be at the gallery tomorrow in plenty of time to set up the wine for the opening.

After he left, Margot cleared her desk and took one final walk around the gallery. The show looked lovely, the pictures restful, dense in the blues and greens of mountains and lakes. These paintings would certainly appeal to New Yorkers stuck in the hot city for the summer. She'd done a good job of hanging the show, but oddly, she wasn't feeling her usual sense of satisfaction now that she'd finished.

She turned off the last lights, armed the security system, and locked the door behind her. As she walked home, she pictured Mario heading in the opposite direction, on his way to meet Julie. She imagined his happy anticipation, that effervescent, floaty feeling of being in love, and knowing that someone else felt the same way about you. And now they were moving in together, possibly taking the first step toward beginning a lifetime as a couple.

Margot would never forget what had happened when she had gone to Boston at the end of her sophomore year in college to visit Lacey. The last of the winter grittiness had washed away in heavy rains early in the month, and the city seemed to be on the cusp of summer weather. She hadn't seen Lacey since Christmas and this was the first time she had gone to Lacey's apartment.

She got out of the cab in front of the gray clapboard building on a quiet residential street. Most of the houses seemed to be broken up into apartments, judging from the multiple mailboxes in front of the doorways. The neighborhood had an old-timey feel about it, as if one might expect mild-looking men in felt hats and belted overcoats to amble home along the sidewalks, clutching the evening paper.

Lacey's apartment was on the second floor. The staircase was steep and narrow, but the stairs were carpeted in a tough-looking material in an appealing shade of green. Margot's heavy bag bumped periodically against the wall. She caught her breath and rang the bell.

Lacey hugged Margot at the door and pulled her into the living room. The white room sparkled with color. Two bright green butterfly chairs were separated by a low table painted a vivid yellow. The sofa was upholstered in a nubby beige fabric, but Lacey had covered it with boldly printed pillows in fresh Scandinavian colors: blue, hot pink, and the same shade of yellow as the table. The kitchen beyond was the same brilliant blue found in the cushions. Nothing appeared fancy or expensive, but the effect was dazzling.

"What do you think?" Lacey asked, obviously delighted with what she had accomplished. "We just finished painting in the kitchen."

"It's beautiful," Margot said. "Beautiful" wasn't really the right word. Fresh, bright, zinging with life. "It's so happy," she added, wondering who was included in the "we."

"Look at this." Lacey pulled out a huge poster board covered in a collage of children's artwork. "I asked the kids in my class to make spring flowers that I could hang on my wall. Some are painted, others just crayons."

"All the colors in the room."

"I'm going to dry-mount it and hang it above the couch. First, I'll take it in to school so the kids can admire it. These children are so talented."

Margot was about to ask more about Lacey's students when she heard something behind her. A door opened and she turned in the direction of the sound.

"Hey, Margot." Alex stepped out from the bedroom, rolling up the sleeve of his shirt. Instantly, she understood everything. Momentarily speechless, she stepped quickly into his arms for a hug—the rote, expected gesture of an old friend. "Good to see you," he said, clearing his throat and stepping away from her. "The paint fumes are pretty bad. Lacey insisted we get it done in time for you." He looked down and fumbled with his other sleeve. He had obviously just stepped out of the shower and put on fresh clothes.

"Here's my big surprise," Lacey said. She came to Alex's side and put her arm around his waist. He drew his arm around Lacey in an uncertain manner, as if he was unsure where to actually place his hand: whether to rest it on her upper arm or lower it to her hip, a more proprietary, intimate gesture. Instead, his hand dangled oddly in midair, as if the hand itself had been caught doing something wrong.

In the space of a moment a door had slammed shut for Margot and the deafening noise continued to reverberate inside her head. She hadn't seen Alex since their time together at Bow Lake nine months earlier. The few awkward phone calls they'd had afterward had left her feeling empty and strange. Did he ever miss her the way she sometimes missed him? She had known Alex since childhood, he'd always been her friend, but now that he had been her first lover, nothing seemed the same.

Fortunately Lacey began to speak, turning and looking up at him: Alex, her childhood friend; Alex, her helper; Alex, her lover. "I told you I'd seen Alex a bit this fall." She leaned into him, pulling him slightly closer. "He was such a drone then. Always making excuses about work." Lacey squeezed him in a playful gesture. "This winter," she laughed lightly, "things just started to happen."

Alex stood very still during this explanation, his pale hand still hanging loosely in the air. He offered a tentative smile, almost a question as his lips parted, then quickly bent down to take Margot's duffel bag. "I'll put this in your room." He clutched her bag and disappeared beyond the kitchen.

"You're not surprised, are you?" Lacey asked softly. "After all those summers?"

"Uh. I guess not," Margot said, somehow finding her voice. "So you're living together?"

"Alex moved in a few weeks ago. I kept putting off telling you. I know you really care about him. I remember how disappointed you were when he didn't come back to the house after Mom's funeral. And we had all those years at the lake." Lacey spoke quickly now as if she sensed some awkwardness.

Margot's throat pinched as she spoke. "No. I'm glad for you."

"You're sure?"

Margot nodded and forced her unwilling lips into a smile.

"One thing kind of led to another. You know how that is," Lacey continued. "I've wanted to tell you, but then I thought it would be easier in person."

"It's okay, really." But it wasn't okay. Margot wasn't going to let Lacey see how she felt. She would have thought Lacey might have told her something, anything. She remembered Lacey saying that she had seen Alex, but dating, getting serious—how could she have kept this from her?

Alex came back into the room and went to Lacey's side. Margot looked away. Her mouth felt dry. Her brain was muddled. She didn't know where to begin. "You sure you have room for me? I can go home to Concord." Margot suddenly began to speak in a torrent, her words rushing out all at once. "Dad wants me at home before I go to the lake. He seems kind of down. I don't like the sound of his cough." Margot directed this to Lacey, not daring to look at Alex. She told them she'd be happy to take a bus to Concord that evening if they could get her to the station, or she'd even get there on her own.

"No way. You're staying with us," Lacey said. "We've got a futon set up on the porch off the kitchen. It's comfortable, too. Alex can attest to that." She put her arm around him.

A look passed between them. Had Alex spent nights on that

sun porch before he moved into Lacey's bedroom? When had it started? Had Alex already started dating Lacey that summer before he entered business school? The summer when he had slept with Margot?

"We have the weekend all planned," Lacey went on. "It will be the three of us again. Just like at the lake."

"Let me show you where you'll be," Alex said, stepping away from Lacey.

"It used to be a sleeping porch," Lacey explained, "but it's all closed in now. I left a clean towel on the bed."

"Thanks," Margot said. Her jaw was trembling. Could Lacey tell something was wrong?

"Follow me," Alex said, and started through the kitchen.

"If you don't mind, I'll grab a quick shower," Lacey said. "Alex is taking us to this fun Italian restaurant in the North End tonight. Special treat in your honor."

Margot nodded and followed Alex, trying to remain composed. The smell of the paint was stronger in the kitchen.

"The walls in here are still wet," he said. "Good reason to go out." He spoke softly.

Margot heard a door close, and a moment later, the sound of water running. She followed Alex to her room, the enclosed porch in the rear of the apartment. It also was painted white. She sat down on the bed and leaned forward, resting her elbows on her knees.

"Margot," he said, "I should have explained. I'm sorry." He shifted his weight from foot to foot. "Like Lacey said, it just sort of happened. I mean . . ." He turned and looked out the window into the trees below. He thrust his hands deep into his pockets. "We started seeing each other."

"Last fall? Right after you left Bow Lake?"

"Not immediately," he said hesitantly. "School was impossible at first. I was swamped, in over my head with the quantitative stuff. Lacey was always there, backing me up. Later, we saw more of each other. It was fast, I guess, but . . ."

"Shut up," Margot said, her voice strangled, barely a whisper.

He lifted one arm toward her, then let it fall to his side. "Try to understand."

"Enough. I understand. You've made it pretty clear." Margot couldn't decide if she was more hurt or angry at him. She lowered her head.

"Wait, Margot. I care about you. I do. It's just that this is different."

"Don't say anything else." She wiped at her tears. "Don't ever tell her."

He nodded and paused by the door, and seemed to hesitate as if genuinely sorrowful, clearly worried about the damage he had done.

"You must promise," Margot whispered. The sound of the water in the bathroom had stopped.

"I promise," he had said.

Margot continued to walk toward home, astonished at how painful her memories still were. She paused in front of an art gallery she had never noticed before. She stared into the vast plate-glass window. The walls were covered with paintings of vividly colored still lifes with backgrounds that appeared to float off into the distance like landscapes. Rich purple eggplants, ripe tomatoes, red and green peppers, plates of sardines, crusty loaves of bread, and bottles of wine filled the canvases. The food looked Italian, as did the countryside beyond. She thought of Lacey and Alex in Italy at this very moment with their daughters. She imagined the artist with his own family and friends painting these pleasurable scenes. By now, Mario and Julie would be enjoying glasses of wine, talking about finding a new apartment, a place to share. And here she was, going home alone.

Her last argument with Oliver loomed once again. She wasn't completely at fault. Oliver had been so insistent. He had wanted her to rearrange her work schedule, maybe even putting her job in jeopardy, so that she could fit in with his plans. He couldn't seem to understand that she truly needed this time with Lacey at the lake. But was it so important? Needled with doubt, she told herself that a summer wasn't really that long. She and Oliver would be together in the fall. She had planned to stay busy painting and she had, though recently the summer was seeming endless.

Margot came to a light. Exhausted, she couldn't walk any farther. She stepped to the curb, and waved her arm for a taxi. She suddenly had to get home.

17

Shuttle: Tool that carries the weft threads through the shed.

Oliver breathed in the deeply satisfying scent of coffee. He had been studying the paintings in the San Francisco Museum of Modern Art and decided to stop at the museum café for an espresso before heading back to Sonoma. He had driven into the city early that morning to deliver two more paintings to the Croft Gallery. A longtime client from Santa Barbara was coming up specifically to see more of his work.

He knew the caffeine would probably keep him awake tonight, but he had become accustomed to sleepless nights. He'd gotten into the habit of sipping a glass of red wine before bed, the one time of day when he allowed himself to think about Margot. Sometimes the alcohol would help him drift off and forget her for a while. But in the morning his memories of her would be as sharp as ever. Now, at the beginning of August, he had been away from her for more than a month.

Margot would be joining Lacey soon at Bow Lake. Maybe Lacey was worse, and maybe this was the last summer that she would still be able to talk to Margot, but the more he thought about it, the more his irritation grew. He knew he was being selfish, but he hated the way Margot was putting their life on hold. Why did the time with her sister seem to matter so much?

Bow Lake was something Margot had never shared with him in the five years they had been together. There always seemed to be logical reasons for him not to join her there. The family had the use of the place only during the month of August and that was when his sister invited him to share their beach house on Block Island. Oliver had gone there instead and sometimes Margot came there after her visit to Bow Lake The last two summers he'd been too caught up in his work and hadn't left the city at all, so Margot had gone to Bow Lake by herself. It wasn't so much not ever having gone to New Hampshire with her that bothered him; it was as if Bow Lake represented a piece of her that she kept hidden from him, inaccessible, much like the way she wouldn't let him look at her paintings.

Since his arrival in Sonoma, Oliver had tried not to let Margot's absence bother him. During the daylight hours he kept to a rigorous schedule. After his morning coffee, he would walk up the hill behind the house. The exercise and fresh air seemed to clear his head, renew his creative energy. Usually by ten, he would walk down the path and begin work in Grant's studio. He found it energizing to paint in a new space and didn't miss his New York studio at all. Around lunchtime he would snack on some cheese and an apple, and in the late afternoon he'd return to the house.

He could imagine Margot filling vases with flowers, draping a scarf over a chair, arranging pears on a plate. Among the many things that he missed about her were the small ways she made a place feel like home. Her nightgown on the hook behind the bathroom door, her hairbrush and other mysterious feminine accoutrements that lay cluttered on her dresser, around the sink, on the night table—all the small, personal things were missing in this house. One night as he sat reading on the sofa, he half expected her to wander in, sit at the opposite end, and tuck her feet under his legs, the way she used to in New York on winter nights. But it was summer, and he was alone.

In the early evening he drove into Santa Louisa, the nearest town, to do his errands and eat a quick dinner. By now he was a regular at Marconi's, a Sicilian restaurant in the center of town. Some nights he met up with a few other artists, colleagues of Grant's, and he had become friendly with the couple who owned the vineyard next to his house. They were in their late sixties and had bought the winery after retiring from jobs in the city.

He liked living in Sonoma. The country felt a bit more rustic than the adjacent Napa Valley, but there were pockets of sophistication. He could buy good coffee, the restaurants were terrific, and on Sundays he could find a copy of the *New York Times*.

Oliver took a last sip of coffee and looked around. He liked this museum. The light in the modern building made the artwork seem energetic and fresh. While he gravitated to his longtime favorite painter, Richard Diebenkorn, he enjoyed the visiting exhibitions. Most days he loved locking himself away from the world, but he needed a periodic dose of other artists' inspirations, much the way he sometimes hungered for a hamburger after too many vegetarian meals.

"Would you like another?" the waiter asked, eyeing Oliver's cup. The café was almost empty. An older woman sat writing postcards a few seats away from him, a pot of tea and a half-eaten cupcake beside her. Two younger women were nibbling at salads, a late lunch after a morning spent looking at art.

"Just the bill. Thanks." He watched as the server nodded and reached in his apron for his pad. He was a young man with green and purple stains on his hands—probably an artist too, working this job to cover the rent.

"Pay the cashier up front," the waiter said, placing the bill on the table next to the envelope that held the one postcard Oliver had purchased from the shop.

Before reaching for his billfold Oliver removed the postcard and stared at the picture, his favorite Diebenkorn: *Woman in Profile, 1968.* The colors weren't quite true to the original, but the brushwork was powerful even in this reduced size. The woman in the painting sat in profile in front of a window. Light fell across her face and lap. Her right hand rested on the table, but her left hand was lifted, making her seem about to speak. The view from the window was abstracted, vast planes moving into the distance that created a tension with the window frame itself. Something in the reflective nature of the figure, the slope of her shoulders, the level gaze, reminded him of Margot—one of those Margot moments when she would appear lost inside herself. He slipped the postcard back inside the bag.

Not now, he thought, coming to his feet. He headed to the exit to pay his bill and drive home to Sonoma. Could this place, this countryside that kept him engaged in his work, ever be truly home? He had begun thinking about moving here permanently and bringing Margot. What was holding them in New York? They could get married and start over. He imagined her all the way across the country, some part of her mind on Lacey, as if perennially attached by an unbreakable slender thread.

Oliver walked toward the door, then remembered the skinny server with paint on his hands. He returned to his table to leave a hefty tip.

Alex stood at the kitchen sink with the faucet running, waiting for the water to cool. He had returned from his business trip to Texas an hour earlier. His meetings had not gone well. He had made a presentation to a potential new client, but he sensed that he had not connected. He turned his head from side to side, trying to release a crick in his neck. He'd slept briefly on the plane with his head bent at an awkward tilt. The vent above his seat was stuck and had shot icy air directly onto his head.

It was rare for him to be alone in the house and he was unaccustomed to the stillness. After dropping his bags in the hall, he had gone from room to room, opening the windows to let in fresh air. Without the familiar sounds of female voices, footsteps on the stairs, the periodic opening and closing of doors or the echoing noise of movement from other rooms, the afternoon itself seemed to have paused.

He filled his glass, carried it to the kitchen table and stared out into the backyard. Lacey had been away for a week and the garden had already become overgrown. The view from the window no longer resembled a well-tended garden, but a chaotic jumble of plants. An overgrown climbing rose was pulling the trellis away from the wall. Maybe there had been a storm. He would go out later to see if he could fix it.

No sooner had he imagined his family elsewhere—Lacey off with Toni and a few of Toni's friends at the Bow Lake cottage and Wink with a group of her pals hiking in the White Mountains—than he heard a car in the driveway. A moment later a key turned in the back door and a heavy bag hit the floor with a thud.

Wink came into the kitchen. "Dad, what are you doing here?"

"Hey, Miss Winky." Alex stood and gave his daughter a hug. "I live here too, remember?" He smoothed her hair away from her forehead. There were dark circles under her eyes. "I just got home. Believe me, Houston's not the place to be in August." He stepped away. Her tired-looking T-shirt hung loosely from her shoulders, making her look too thin. "I thought you were off with your friends until next week."

She slipped out of his arms and sat down at the table. "I got a ride home early. Kristen had to be back for field hockey, so I came with her."

"How come?" he asked, taking the seat opposite his daughter.

"I haven't been sleeping. Try hiking when you're totally shot."

"So what's keeping you awake?" Alex knew that Wink was the worrier of the twins. He hated seeing someone so young seemingly so burdened. Both girls were upset by their mother's illness, but Toni was better at setting her worry aside and living in the moment. Once they had returned from Italy, she had resumed seeing friends and went out frequently in the evenings after work. Wink received her share of calls and invitations, but it was hard for her to join in and act as if her life was still the same.

"I can't do it, Dad."

"Do what, honey?"

"I don't want to go away. Maybe next year. Right now I want to be with Mom." Wink began to cry.

It always came back to Lacey, the mother, the wife, the one person on whom everyone's happiness seemed to hinge.

Alex reached across the table and took her hand. "Mom won't let you give up college. She's so proud that you got into Cornell. And the scholarship from the astronomy department—that's pretty amazing."

"I know the money's important."

"It's not just the money. It's the opportunity to be part of their program."

"Dad, you're not listening. It's making me crazy."

"I am listening, but we talked about it earlier," he said. "Mom thinks you'll feel different when it's time to leave for college."

"I don't feel any different. I don't want to go."

"Didn't you talk to Mom before you left?"

"She doesn't understand."

"Did you try to explain? If she knew how unhappy you were about this . . ."

"How can I argue with her? She starts stumbling over words. Then her speech gets worse. Shit, Dad. It's awful." Wink drew her arms across her chest and continued to cry. She had an angry red mark on her arm, a bug bite she had scratched. His sweet daughter, the one the mosquitoes loved to attack.

Alex got up and came behind her chair and placed his hands on her shoulders. "Winky, I don't know what to tell you."

"Can't you just talk to Mom? Tell her I'll have a breakdown or something. Anything. Please."

Alex massaged Wink's shoulders gently, trying to think. He had no trouble talking to clients. Even when his projects weren't going well, the problems were concrete, definable. He could illustrate his reasoning with detailed spreadsheets, projected sales figures, product research, demographics. He had answers ready before the expected questions were posed. At work no one burst into tears.

With his family, his decisions came from his gut. He knew that Wink's delaying school might be a good solution, and that in the long run it would hardly matter. But how could he explain that to Lacey?

Suddenly Wink jerked away from his touch and got up. "No one can say anything in this family anymore." She wiped at her face with her hand, grabbed for a tissue on the counter, and blew her nose. "It's hard for Mom to talk. You won't talk. You're either away or leaning on Aunt Margot to bail you out."

"Wait a minute," Alex said, suddenly defensive. "Aunt Margot is worried about your mom. She loves our family and only wants to help."

"Come on, Dad, I love Aunt Margot. You know that. It's just that when she's around it's not the same. It's like we're not our real selves."

"What's that supposed to mean?"

"Face it. Whenever things get bad you bring her in—like to get yourself out of a bad situation. Don't you remember? You couldn't even tell us about Mom's illness until Margot got here. Then you have her talk Toni into Columbia. Gram dies. What happens? In a nanosecond she's here."

"That's because you were worried about Toni and I couldn't get home."

"I know, but then she stuck around."

"She helped Mom with the funeral. Remember?"

"I know. I guess what really makes me crazy is that you and Mom aren't the same. You never talk like you used to."

"You seem to be forgetting your mom has a problem." Alex regretted his words as soon as they shot out.

Wink winced, then shook her head. "Dad, what you call 'the problem' isn't only that. Think about it. It's about communication. Don't you see? It's not only the not talking. It's like you guys have totally disconnected." Wink turned her back to him and stared out the window at the abandoned garden. Her shoulders drooped.

"But if you stay home, what will you do? Mom doesn't need taking care of now." Alex felt his throat constrict. He knew that Lacey would need care someday. In three years, five, maybe ten if they were lucky. The doctors could give them no definite answers. He pushed these thoughts aside.

"I just want another year at home." Wink bent her head and blew her nose again. "College will be there. Mom won't."

"Don't say that." Alex felt tears burning his eyes. He took a deep breath and tried to speak calmly. "Sorry. Would you get a job?"

Wink turned to face him. "I want to go see the admissions person at UNH. I know I turned them down, but if I lived at home, maybe I could take some classes and defer going to Cornell. I want to see what my options are."

"I don't know," he said.

"Please, Dad."

"You're serious about this?"

She nodded. Wink had always been a thoughtful child.

"Will you talk to Mom?" Wink twirled a strand of her hair.

One evening at dinner in Italy, Wink had worn her hair swept up on her head. Toni had put eye makeup on her sister before they left the hotel and Wink had worn a new sundress that flattered her shoulders and long neck. There, in the candlelight, she had looked as if she could have been thirty. This afternoon, with her tearstained face, his daughter looked like a tired twelve-year-old.

"Please, Dad."

Alex sighed. "I'll talk to her."

"When?" She eyed him dubiously.

"Soon. I've got to go to New York for a few days."

"How come?"

"I'm hoping to finally close the fertilizer deal."

"Dad . . ." she said.

"Look, Wink." He heard annoyance creeping into his voice. He swallowed and went on. "I need to think about this. Don't worry. I'm going to talk to your mother."

"You think you can make her understand?"

"I'm going to try."

Wink sighed. "I'm telling you, Dad, I need to be home. Please help me."

Alex came over and hugged his daughter. Despite her height, her shoulders and spine had a fragility that made her still seem like a little girl. He kissed the top of her head.

She pulled away. "I'll go unpack my stuff."

Alex dropped his arms to his sides. It used to be so easy to solve his daughters' problems: wiring the head back onto a broken doll, running beside a two-wheeler, helping to solve a math problem for homework. He carried his water glass to the sink. Convincing Lacey to let Wink stay home in the fall would be difficult. Lacey had been adamant. She wanted everyone to go on as if nothing had changed.

New York was a different city in August. All those who could afford to had escaped. Tourists still clogged the streets and the large buses with open upper decks continued their rounds with their loudspeakers belting out a litany of facts about the Big Apple. Margot pulled her nightgown on over her head. She had been painting in her apartment all day. It was nearly ten, and rather than make her way back to Oliver's apartment, she'd decided to stay at her place for the night. She put the kettle on to make tea.

The Van Engen Gallery had shorter hours in summer. Carl decamped to the Cape for all of August, and Margot and Mario were covering the few administrative duties between them. After a few hours in the morning working in the office, she returned to her apartment to paint. With Oliver gone, she had started spending several nights a week at her old place. Their apartment on the West Side had begun to feel huge without him.

They called each other less frequently now. Why would he want to tell her about people she didn't know? They were living in separate worlds. If they were meant to be together, surely they could survive a summer apart. Besides, the time alone wasn't all bad. Margot remembered the relief she had felt after Teddy was gone. That solitude was like drinking a glass of clear water after months of acute thirst. Her days were finally hers to fill—no one telling her what to do and what mattered. She never wanted to be under that kind of pressure again. Fighting off loneliness now and then was nothing compared to that.

Some days she practiced drawing, and did exercises from a workbook she had used in an art class she took when she first moved to New York. Her paints continued to lure her, and she could feel her breath quicken when she'd been able to mix just the right shade of green. She had set up different still-life arrangements. Perhaps it was the summer heat, and her recollections of childhood that kept pushing to the surface, but she found herself more and more attempting to capture scenes of Bow Lake. A combination of memory and old photographs served as her muse.

She had gone back to working on the picture of the moon path at the lake. Painting the water itself was extremely difficult, all the more so because the view was at night. The hardest part was getting the color, or the noncolor, of the lake. Water was so elemental, so basic, and at times totally impossible to paint. The moonlight on the lake was an entirely different problem. How to achieve that silvery glow, brilliant, completely mesmerizing as if drifted into the distance?

She took the canvas off her easel and propped it up at the table. Stepping back, she considered the composition. Maybe the image was too stark, too bold. What if she was farther away from the lake and viewed the moon path through the trees? She had no photos of that view to work from. Seeing the moon on the lake once again in real life might be her only hope.

The kettle whistled just as Margot's cell phone rang. Whisking the kettle off the burner, she flipped open her phone, thinking it must be Oliver calling from the West Coast. Instead, it was Alex.

"My Chicago deal went through."

"That's great," she said, hearing the excitement in his voice. "Are you here in town?"

"Yeah. I know it's late. I've been meeting with auditors and got the final approval. I was hoping if you were free we could meet for a drink. I'm flying home in the morning."

Margot hesitated. She'd caught up with a few old friends since Oliver had been away, but she hadn't been out at all recently. Suddenly, taking a break seemed like a good idea. "I'm at my old apartment," she said. "I've been painting."

"Is there someplace near you?"

"There's a little French bistro, Chez Antoinette on Lexington. This late, I'm sure it wouldn't be busy."

"Maybe some dessert, too? We had sandwiches in the office hours ago. I'm starved."

"Okay," she said. "Half hour from now?" She gave Alex the address and went into the bedroom to dress. The gray linen pants she'd had on earlier were a wrinkled mess. She slipped them on anyway. This was Alex, her brother-in-law. It was dark out and he wouldn't care what she wore. She turned up the collar of her white shirt, making it look marginally more sophisticated,

Somber thoughts began to darken her mood. She remembered the awkwardness of meeting Alex at the bar last spring. Would that happen again? Suddenly she doubted what she was doing. Her hands trembled as she rolled the cuffs of her shirt. Seeing him alone didn't seem like a good idea at all.

She glanced around her living room—paint, canvases, brushes everywhere. She drew in her breath and realized all that she had accomplished here. Somehow reassured, she pushed aside her ridiculous thoughts. Meeting Alex would be fine. His deal had been successful. He and Lacey had had their trip to Italy. Why not take a moment to celebrate? Margot picked up her keys and headed out into the night.

Alex was seated at a tiny table by the front window when she arrived. "I ordered a bottle of Prosecco," he said a little nervously, half standing to greet her, but pulling back, as if he too remembered the awkward ending of their previous encounter in the bar, when Margot had gotten up from the table and fled. "Hope that's okay. They're bringing a dessert menu too."

"Sure." She smiled and sat. "Congratulations. So you sold the company?"

"Finally. It's been a real roller-coaster ride." His hair was windblown. There had been a thunderstorm in the afternoon, but warm, humid air was still blowing in from the south. The evening was tropical. He wore a blazer over a pale blue shirt, and no tie. "I wanted to celebrate. I'm glad you were free."

His eyes were fixed upon her. Maybe this had been a mistake. She felt color rise to her face. "So how was Italy?"

The waiter arrived with the sparkling wine. Alex tasted his and nodded. The waiter filled her glass and returned to top off Alex's.

"I guess I shouldn't have ordered Italian wine at a French place." He shrugged. "Italy was great. We had some really good days. At times Lacey was almost her old self."

Margot sipped her wine, imagining the family exploring sun-drenched villages a world away. "So the trip helped."

"For a while." The lines in his forehead deepened. "On our last night in Rome, it totally fell apart. Lacey sort of closed up and became angry all over again." He rubbed his eyes, as if exhausted from the memory.

"What happened?"

"Nothing, really. I guess going home reminded her of what we would face there."

"Sometimes being away makes everything feel different—the power of a place." Margot thought of Bow Lake. Soon she would be there with Lacey.

"Yeah, but we're home now."

"Lacey loves her home. Don't forget that."

Alex cleared his throat. "Have you talked to Wink lately?"

Margot and Lacey had been exchanging e-mails recently instead of using the phone and Margot realized she had fallen out of touch with the girls.

He went on. "She's upset again about college. Doesn't want to go."

"I thought she was over that."

"She's tried to talk to Lacey. They both get too upset."

"What do you think?"

"What's wrong with taking a year off?"

"Alex, you know how I love the girls, but this is something you all need to figure out. I've already upset Lacey with my meddling."

"It's not like that." Alex hunched forward and raised the dessert menu the waiter had left on the table to examine it more closely. He looked worn down. "I've missed you, Margot." He tossed the menu down.

"You're all managing fine without me."

"Not true." He lifted his head and met her gaze. "I'm really glad to see you. You're the only one who hasn't changed." He reached across the table and took her hand.

For a moment, he was the young Alex, smelling of sunshine, youthful and lean, pulling her close to him in the dark long ago at Bow Lake. "Alex. No." She withdrew her hand and picked up the menu.

"Shit, I'm sorry. I don't know what I'm doing anymore."

"It's okay," she continued, her voice growing stronger. "You need to talk to Lacey, not me."

"It's not that simple."

"You should be celebrating this deal with her, too."

"She doesn't care. It's always the girls. It's weaving."

"Stop it. You love her, Alex. I saw you both at graduation. When the girls received their diplomas, I saw the way you looked at Lacey, the way you took her hand. I'll never forget that."

Alex lowered his head and closed his eyes. "It's just not working now. This goddamned illness has made life impossible."

"Hard," she said. "Not impossible."

"Dessert for you folks?" The waiter had appeared at their table. He looked sweaty and frazzled. Margot smiled briefly and shook her head, as did Alex. The waiter reached for the bottle of Prosecco and refilled their glasses.

"Will you be okay?" she asked when they were alone again.

Alex said nothing. His pressed his lips together and looked away.

"You have all those years between you," she said softly. "You've built a life together. That's a gift. You mustn't ruin it."

"Maybe I already have." Alex's face grew slack.

Margot shook her head, thinking how she might have ruined what she and Oliver had together. This time she reached across the table and held fast to Alex's arm. "You haven't ruined it. Alex, you love her. She loves you."

He stared at her hand. "I'm sorry about . . ."

"Don't be sorry about anything. Just go home to Lacey." Margot pulled her hand back and felt relieved. At one time she had wanted this man more than anything. Not this man, but the boy, Alex, from a different time and place. There had been that moment of attraction between them. It no longer mattered. She thought of the moon path, that twinkling light on a warm summer night, dazzling, ephemeral, then gone. What always remained was the lake—deep, mysterious, and enduring.

. . .

"Daddy, I love it here," Jenna said. She lowered her fork into the deep bowl of pasta. She had made pasta carbonara. Oliver was pleased that she'd remembered it was one of his favorite meals. Jenna's cooking tasted especially good after so many dinners out.

He twirled the strands of spaghetti against his fork. "I'll walk you down to the studio later." He had given Jenna the money for a ticket to San Francisco so she could have a short vacation from her restaurant. "Kitchen okay? It's fine for me, but I'm not a professional."

"Perfect. Pretty easy to cook for two compared to my regular shtick."

"Speaking of regular shtick, how's Leo?"

"He's the best. Don't look at me like that." She reached for the Parmesan, a pale brick of yellow on a turquoise plate, and ran it across the grater directly over her bowl. "I'll give you plenty of warning when we decide to tie the knot."

"So you're thinking about marriage?"

"One day. Come on. And speaking of . . ." She pushed the cheese his way. "What's going on with Margot?"

"You mean why isn't she here?"

"Man, you sound cranky."

"She didn't want to be away this summer. First there was Toni and Wink's graduation. Mostly, she's been upset about Lacey's illness. She wants to have the end of the summer up at the lake place with her."

"That makes sense."

"You think so?" he said wearily. He had gone over it a thousand times in his head. Had he pushed Margot too hard?

"Dad, she loves her sister. And they've gone to Bow Lake since they were little."

"Has she ever taken *me* there?"

"Have you ever wanted to go?"

Oliver had finished almost all of his pasta. He needed to slow down. "I get your point, but since Lacey's been sick, it's like Margot is in this whole other mode. It's always Lacey and her family, never us."

"Yeah, but Margot's parents are dead. She has no kids of her own. It's natural that she wants to be near them and part of their lives when she can."

"I guess." Oliver pushed his bowl away and took a swallow of wine. He knew Margot had had a sad childhood and a disastrous marriage. For a long time all she'd had was Lacey and the girls. And Alex. In the depth of his heart, Oliver could feel that snake of jealousy rearing its head. Oliver had been furious that Alex seemed to seek out Margot at every turn.

"Come on, Daddy. I can see how Margot would want to be with her sister, especially as time runs out. It's really sad."

He sighed. Jenna, so young, all of a sudden seemed wise.

"Don't brood, Daddy. I've seen that before. It's not cool." She stood. "Let's clear this away and then give me the tour of your studio. From what you've said, you've been making a ton of art."

Oliver picked up his bowl, balanced the plate of cheese on top, and followed his daughter to the kitchen. When they went out to the terrace, it was beginning to grow dark, but the air was soft and a full moon cast a path eastward over the vineyards.

Jenna took his arm as he led her down the path to the studio. "You'll be home again next month," she said. "I bet Margot is missing you as much as you're missing her."

Oliver looked up at the sky and wondered.

18

Boat shuttle: A shuttle resembling a boat.

$\mathcal{M}$argot turned onto Lake Road. The rain had stopped, but the asphalt threw off a sheen from the recent storm. Her flight from New York had been more than three hours late, but she had called Lacey to tell her not to wait up. It was close to midnight. Margot, watchful and alert, drove carefully in her rented car. Now, off the highway, she opened the front windows. She'd had a hard time regulating the air-conditioning; the dashboard dials and switches in the unfamiliar vehicle seemed to make no sense at all. She was chilled. Alex and the girls had left for home earlier in the day. Margot would have this final week of the summer alone with her sister.

The lake, out of view, lay just off to her left beyond the trees. The air had that after-rain freshness, but the night sky remained cloudy and dense. The moon was hidden. She slowed, watching intently for Fire Road 34, the dirt road that led to the cottage. At the next bend the sign appeared, nailed to the trunk of a tree. The tires crunched on the gravel, the reassuring indicator that she was almost there. The tall pines on either side of the drive glistened from the rain, the needles dripping silently into the woods. Lacey had left the back porch light on. The old cottage, welcoming and snug, nestled in the trees, never changed. Before stepping inside, Margot paused and breathed in the night air. Bow Lake, at last.

Early the next morning the sky remained gray and the day heavy. The cottage was silent. Margot pulled a sweatshirt over her nightgown and tiptoed downstairs. The living room, dark and shadowy, smelled of charred wood from the fireplace. In the kitchen, she filled the kettle and put it on the stove. While waiting for it to boil, she went to the back door and looked outside.

The light was dim; it could have been six in the morning or six in the evening. The upper leaves in the trees had begun to stir and she wondered if it might storm again today. The kettle whistled sharply. She made tea in the old cracked mug with the pinecone on it. None of the china here at the cottage matched. She and Lacey used to argue over who got the bluebird mug when their grandmother made hot chocolate. The tea bag was a generic brand from the local grocery store and Margot jiggled it up and down, waiting for the hot liquid to darken sufficiently before carrying it to the screened porch.

"Oh," she said, "you scared me." Lacey was sitting on the wicker settee at the far end of the porch. "I hope I didn't wake you last night." Margot moved to hug her sister, then glanced down. "My God." Her heart jumped in her chest. The floor was covered with strands of yarn—blue, green, and silver bits scattered everywhere. Lacey's portable loom lay on the floor, tipped sideways as if it had been tossed aside. It was empty.

"What's all this?" Margot set down her tea and began to gather the fibers. The pieces were of all sizes, as if they'd been yanked out randomly. She scooped up handfuls. They had been strewn all over. Whatever Lacey had been weaving was in ruins.

"Welcome to the lake, I guess."

Margot picked up the loom.

"I pulled it out," Lacey said. "It wasn't any good." Her legs were drawn up to her chest, her back against the wall. She was staring up at the ceiling. Her hair hung loose on her shoulders, not brushed back and clipped at her neck. She, too, was still in her nightgown. "Remember the game?" Lacey asked, as if oblivious of the mess around her.

"What game?" Margot sat down at the opposite end of the settee.

"Remember when we were little. How we found . . . the animals on the ceiling."

"The tar picture game?"

Lacey nodded. "I can see the cow." She pointed to a blotch on the far side of the porch roof where the old pine boards had been stained from the tar seeping through.

Margot turned her head. She recalled how Lacey had declared that stain to resemble a cow.

Lacey's words came clipped and slow. "Your favorite was the cat."

Margot swallowed, uneasy with Lacey's unexpected behavior. She looked up. "I don't see it." The random blotches looked like nothing to her now.

"Above the door," Lacey said quietly, her eyes riveted to a spot. "Near the corner. The right bit is the tail."

Margot searched. "Yes, it's there. Now I see it." A protruding nail looked like the cat's eye. "Just below is the one I used to call the armadillo. Remember how Granny said it couldn't be an armadillo because they don't live in these parts?" She glanced at Lacey, who was smiling at this memory.

"Lacey, why did you rip out your work? It makes me so sad."

Lacey's smile faded. She stretched her legs out on the settee and continued to gaze above her, though now her expression was somber. "S . . . spider. Remember the . . . black widow? It's there. The same."

Margot shook her head. Here was Lacey, trying to play some game, as if retreating to her childhood, when she was obviously upset about something else. Nothing was the same anymore, Margot thought. Yes, the old cottage held on to the shapes of the past, but in the light of day she noticed that the roof was sagging more, the porch boards creaked more loudly, and some of the windows needed to be replaced because of rot. They, too, were middle-aged women now, no longer girls caught up in what used to seem like perfect summer days.

Neither spoke. Margot felt as if the sky were pressing down on them. She shut her eyes, no longer wanting to see the mess on the floor. The mourning doves cooed in the woods near the shore, their soft throaty voices in a sweet rhythm that felt out of place.

"Alex and the girls left yesterday," Lacey said. Her voice was resigned and flat.

"I know. I'm here now," Margot said, opening her eyes. "You won't be alone."

"We talked . . . and I said it was . . . okay for Wink to stay home. At least for the fall."

"You don't have to worry, Lacey. You know she'll make good use of her time."

"You knew about this?"

"We talked about it last winter. She was having such a tough time."

"Alex," she said, staring directly at Margot, "said he saw you in New York."

Margot nodded, feeling suddenly on guard. "We met last week," she said. "He had just finished the deal. He was excited about that. Worried about Wink, too."

Lacey rolled her head from side to side and then sat up and put her feet on the floor as if she had made a decision. "I see the way." She pressed her lips together. "I see the way you sometimes look at him."

"What are you talking about?" Margot stiffened.

"I know . . . what's going on."

"Lacey. Wait. Nothing's going on. I met Alex for a quick drink. That's all."

"No, no. Not just that," she said. "I remember . . . when you were with us . . . in June." She paused and seemed to attempt to slow her breathing. "I saw you once. With him on the garden bench. Talking." Lacey's eyes seemed to focus inward, her brows lowered, her jaw tensed. "He took all those . . . all those trips. To New York."

Margot froze. She should have told Lacey. Not saying anything made it seem wrong.

Lacey continued. "You and he. Are so alike." Her voice grew very small as she struggled to speak. "Are you . . . having an affair?"

"No!" Margot said, getting to her feet. "You've got it all wrong." She turned to Lacey. "Look at me. Alex adores you. He always has." Margot felt a lump in her throat, as if she were swallowing a large pill that refused to go down.

"When he looks at you like . . ." Lacey lowered her head.

"He's confused." Margot sat and put her arm around her sister. "He's been looking to me for help. He knows how much I love you. He's afraid, that's all."

"And you? I remember when we were young. Here at the lake." Lacey stared into Margot's eyes.

"Sure, back then I probably had a crush on Alex. What teenage girl here at the lake didn't? But that was almost thirty years ago." Margot removed her arm and brought her hands to her lap. It had been more than a crush, more than an infatuation, but whatever it had been was over long ago. Yet the lump in her throat now seemed to grow larger.

"But there was . . . one summer."

Margot held her breath. Had Alex told Lacey? She crossed her arms in front of her chest, feeling suddenly cold, cold like the bottom of the lake. "What do you mean?" she asked quickly.

"The end of the summer . . . before Alex . . . moved to Boston." Lacey paused, and shook her head. "I always wondered if . . ." She stood and looked out over the water. The day was growing lighter.

"Listen to me," Margot said, surprised by her own vehemence.

"Alex has loved you since the very beginning. He loves you, only you." She stood. She had to make sure Lacey believed this. Nothing mattered more.

"You think that?"

"Trust me," she said, stepping closer to Lacey.

"I don't care . . . about . . . back then. Just now."

"Now and always," Margot said emphatically. Her heart raced.

"So why does he talk . . . to you, not me?" Lacey's lips pulled together tightly.

"Okay, he sought my advice a few times." Margot's voice sounded wobbly, less sure. "He didn't want to worry you. I guess he was afraid of upsetting you. He felt like you were shutting him out."

"I'm his wife." Her shoulders dropped.

Margot drew herself up taller. "I know that." The sky had a pinkish tinge. She thought of Granny Winkler. Was red sky in the morning a good or bad omen?

"Listen, Lace," she went on, "I've only wanted to help you, all of you. I'm afraid I got too involved." She swallowed, and cleared her throat. "I should have urged Alex to open up to you, not me."

"Why d . . . didn't you?" She faced Margot, her face crumpled in disappointment.

"I really don't know." Her throat closed with shame. What could she say? Had some selfish part of her relished Alex's attention? Had she imagined something reigniting between them? What would be more despicable? Her own sister . . .

"Don't you?"

Margot breathed in deeply. She thought of her last meeting with Alex. "I finally confronted Alex last week. I told him how you both had so much love between you. I told him not to waste it. Not to unravel all the years, all you share."

Lacey nodded, as if in agreement, but said nothing.

The imagined pill in Margot's throat began to ease. "You will find your way through this. You need Alex now. And he needs you."

"Margot," she said, and reached over, placing her hands on Margot's face. She said nothing more, but her expression softened. "You're right." Her lips trembled. "I didn't mean to . . . shut him out. I only wanted . . . to be strong."

Margot tried to speak lightly. "You don't always have to be strong. Let the rest of us be the strong ones now and then."

What else could she say? She looked down at the floor. "Let me help you pick this up." She gestured toward the broken bits of yarn. "What went wrong?"

"So much."

As they gathered up the scattered yarns, Lacey told Margot how she was trying something new, making a more free-form design. She had decided to move away from her previous work, and give up the more ordered patterns, the clean lines, and the balanced repetitions that she had always favored. Showing Margot a wad of green and blue threads, she explained how she wanted to do something to capture Bow Lake, and all that it meant. She wanted the tapestry to tell the story. Using the small loom had been a mistake. Or maybe she had been trying to say too much. Margot told Lacey about trying to paint the moon path and urged her to try again.

Margot stood on the dock, surveying the lake. Their first beautiful day. She sipped her coffee and waited for Lacey. Today was the perfect morning to paddle to the island. So far the lake was absolutely calm, not a trace of a ripple on the surface. The nights had been cool, as nights often were this late in August. Now the sun warmed Margot's shoulders. She wore old khaki shorts and a fleece vest over her T-shirt—her Bow Lake clothes, forgotten pants and shirts she kept at the cottage that smelled perpetually musty and were softened from years of use.

By noon it would be warm enough for a swim. Granny Winkler used to love having a "dip" just before lunch. Margot smiled, remembering her grandmother in a funny rubber bathing cap and a flowered cotton bathing suit. The skirt would billow up around her grandmother's pale legs while she stoically stepped deeper and deeper into the lake. After a few gentle breaststrokes with her chin thrust up and forward, she would return to shore, rub her body briskly with one of the thin towels retired from indoor use, and amble back to the cottage to dress for lunch.

Margot turned her back to the water and called toward the cottage, "Are you coming?"

"In a minute." Lacey's voice filtered through the trees. A pair of doves cooed in a branch close to shore. The cottage with its dark shingles blended into the trees and was barely visible from the dock. This morning not a leaf moved in the stillness. Margot had left Lacey on the porch, weaving. She had begun to work again on her small lap-sized loom. She was trying to make the piece inspired by Bow Lake, using the same fibers as before—the rich blues and greens, even strands of lavender, along with metallic threads that created a sheen. Within the nubby texture, Lacey seemed to be weaving a pattern that reminded Margot of the ripples that broke the lake's glassy surface when they were little girls skipping stones.

Margot set her mug down on the dock and kicked off her sandals. She stepped onto the beach adjacent to the dock and untied the canoe. The shale was cool and gritty under her feet. After a few heaves, she had the canoe floating in the shallows. Next, she lifted the paddles, placing one by each seat along with two red boat cushions.

Margot could see her feet clearly in the water. Only at the end of the dock did the shore drop off, making the lake appear dark and opaque. When she was little she worried about the bottom of the lake, the mystery of it, the nagging dread of what might be lurking in the deep. Granny Winkler would tell her not to think about it, saying there were some things we would never see, things impossible to know and that that was just how life was.

Lacey's footsteps on the dock startled her out of her reverie.

"All set?" Margot asked.

"Uh-huh," Lacey said, stepping down onto the beach. She looked toward Junior Island and silently picked up her paddle.

Margot got in first, settling herself into the bow. Lacey put one foot in the canoe and pushed off. As she had since their childhood, Lacey took the seat in the stern, her job to steer. Within minutes they moved in an easy rhythm. Reach, lower, pull. Drops of water fell from the paddles and hit the surface of the lake like showers of jewels. Being on the water always made Margot feel free. Leaving the shore made it possible to put aside the ordinary day-to-day world.

Lacey had taught Margot to paddle as soon as she was big enough to manage in the canoe. She had made it look easy. She had shown Margot how to lower the paddle into the water without splashing, with the greatest economy of movement. Now, Margot kept her paddle on the left side, as was their custom, and switched over to the right only when directed by Lacey. Lacey moved her own paddle from side to side as needed to propel the canoe forward and to guide them in the right direction. Like a couple of dancers who never forgot their steps, they skimmed across the lake toward Junior.

"I was thinking," Margot said, "how Bow Lake is a muse for both of us." She drew her paddle up and let it rest across the bow in front of her. The trees on Junior looked very dark green against the blue sky. A small breeze now ruffled the leaves just slightly. She lowered her hand into the water and spattered her face, loving the way it cooled her skin in the sun.

"I'm . . ." Lacey paused. "I'm doing . . . " A second pause. "All the work."

Margot plunged her paddle down, inadvertently splashing the surface. "Sorry." She worked to regain her rhythm and move them toward the beach where they would land. "Monet had his water lilies at Giverny," she called out, "Cézanne did Mount Saint-Victoire, and we have Bow Lake."

Lacey said nothing. Margot went on. "I mean, look at this day. Have you ever seen another like it? Everything is so clean and pure. This day is absolutely perfect." Her spirits were high. She lifted her chin, feeling the warmth of the sun on her cheeks. They had put the difficult discussion behind them and had fallen into an easy routine. Both of them took advantage of quiet and serenity for their work. The day after she had arrived Margot had turned her upstairs bedroom into a makeshift studio, while Lacey continued to weave on the porch.

For a while neither spoke. Gradually, the shore of Junior grew nearer, but Lacey seemed to be guiding the canoe too far to the left. That part of the island was rimmed with rocks above and below the surface, making it a difficult place to land. Margot called back, "I think your aim is off," hoping to make a joke. She lifted her paddle to await Lacey's command for a change in direction and was met with silence. The canoe continued to drift toward the rocky part of the shore. Margot turned. Lacey was not paddling. She had balanced her paddle across the thwarts, and was leaning forward with her hands covering her eyes. She was crying. Her body shook soundlessly.

"Oh, Lace." Margot's own voice got caught in her throat. The bow of the canoe banged into the rocks, jolting them to a stop. At that moment Lacey began to whimper, at first softly, then louder. Margot looked forward, and when she realized that trying to push out with a paddle would only make it worse, she decided to get out and walk the canoe through the water to the sandy beach. She moved her weight forward, gripping both sides before lowering one leg into the lake. It was difficult to maintain her balance. The water was deep and her shorts got wet immediately. She pulled the canoe across the rocks. The rocks were of different sizes, and her body pitched unevenly with each step.

Lacey didn't move. She sat with her shoulders hunched, her chin to her chest. Her crying tore at Margot's heart.

"It's okay, Lace. I'm taking us over to the beach." And she continued across the rough shoreline until eventually she hit the shale bottom and then the smooth stretch of sand. She dragged the canoe onto the shore as best she could, not an easy task with Lacey's inert body weighing down the stern.

"It's okay. Come on now." She took Lacey's arm, and guided her toward the beach. "Let's sit here for a bit. We'll warm up in the sun."

By now Margot's shorts were wet and cold, like the icy fear that had settled in her heart. Lacey followed Margot and sat beside her on the sand, pulling her legs in and resting her forehead on her knees. Her sobs grew quieter. Margot put her arm tightly around her sister and leaned her head against her shoulder, rocking her gently back and forth.

"Tell me what's wrong." Margot said. Lacey stiffened and seemed to resist the swaying motion. "Please, tell me."

Lacey shook her head.

"Come on. You can talk to me."

Lacey shot Margot a quick glance, almost fearful. "You don't . . ." Lacey said, still crying. "You don't get . . . it."

"What don't I get?"

"Oh, God. What . . . will happen next? What will happen . . . when I can't talk? When . . . when I can't . . . even understand?"

"That might be years from now."

"It's so hard." Lacey wiped at her eyes. "All of this"—she waved her arm in an expansive gesture—"all of this is over."

"But it's not. Let's think about today," Margot coaxed gently. "Look out at the water. It's perfect today."

Lacey lifted her head and stared into the distance. For a while she said nothing at all. Margot kept her arm around her. Suddenly she realized this was the first time Lacey had really cried. All this time she had spared them all the terrible sorrow that was ripping her apart.

Lacey cleared her throat. "Nothing is perfect now. We can't . . . come here and . . . hide."

"I'm not hiding." Margot pressed her arm more tightly around her sister.

"We need . . ." Lacey shook her head. "You need to move on. Oliver wanted you with him. But you . . . didn't."

"I wanted to be near you. It's more complicated than you think. Besides, this is our week together. I've waited all summer for this." In her heart, Margot knew she had wanted it to be like the summers when they were girls.

"It's not the same now," Lacey said, as if reading Margot's mind. Her voice was level, without emotion. She had stopped crying. "I worry about you."

"Me?" Margot's soggy wet shorts clung to her legs. The dock seemed to be miles across the water and the paddle home looked longer from this direction. "Why would you worry about me?"

"I think you are stuck . . . in the past. Teddy is over. Let it go. It's like you're . . . too afraid to move on."

"I'm not afraid."

"Oliver," Lacey began.

"You haven't always been such a fan of Oliver."

"He's a good man. He loves you."

"He wanted me to arrange my entire summer to suit him. It's always about his career. I didn't want to be far from you. And the girls."

"They love you but they have . . . their own lives."

"You're saying they don't need me."

"They will always need you," said Lacey. She stretched out her legs on the beach and seemed to be considering how to continue. "I think we've . . . made it . . . hard for you. By pulling you into our . . ."

"What?"

Lacey lifted her hand in a motion to stop Margot's question. "We made you so much a part of our . . . family . . . that you've never made your own."

"You know I can't have children." Margot's old wound opened. She began to cry. "I ruined things with Teddy. There was no one after that. I always pick the wrong men." She thought of Alex and how she had once longed for him, thinking he was the love of her life. Shame swelled in her throat. What a fool she had been.

"That's not what I mean." Lacey shook her head. "We are your family. Yes. But we will be okay. You must think . . . more about what you want. What do *you* need?"

"Me?"

Lacey reached over, putting her arm around Margot, comforting her this time.

Margot couldn't think. What did she want? Was her work at the gallery enough? She loved painting, but she knew she had years of work ahead if she meant to master it. Did she have the desire to truly work at it, the way Oliver did? She stared out at the water and shivered.

All summer Margot had been trying to convince herself that she'd made the right decision. She'd had the weeks to paint, her work at the gallery, her time at the lake. Oliver had been pushing her to make decisions about their future. Lacey was right. She had been hiding—retreating to her old apartment, coming to the lake. "We should go back to the cottage," she said. "I'm freezing."

Lacey got to her feet and walked over to the canoe. Margot followed, pulling her wet shorts away from her skin. They took their same places in the canoe, Lacey pushing off from shore the way she always did.

"I hope you can steer this time," Margot called back, trying to laugh.

Lacey took her paddle, reached out across the water, and gave Margot a splash. Margot turned back to see her sister smile.

. . .

It was impossible for Margot to close the cottage for the season without thinking of Granny Winkler. A no-nonsense, down-to-earth, practical person, Granny Winkler always had a plan, a system that made even the most daunting projects seem manageable. She divided the work into the outside chores and the inside chores. Even when Lacey and Margot were little, they would be assigned some task appropriate for their age. At seven or eight they were capable of bringing the life jackets from the storage bin by the lake and putting them on the pegs in the back hall. By the time they were twelve they would help hang the last loads of laundry on the line and fold and store the blankets in the cedar closet in Grandmother Winkler's bedroom.

On the last day of summer everyone at the cottage helped out. Margot remembered how she and Lacey would complain: "Oh, Gran, why does summer have to end? Why do we have to go home?" Their grandmother always responded in her clipped, upbeat voice, "Well, ladies, if you don't go home you can't come back."

As Margot launched into these final chores she also thought about Alex. She had been here alone with him all those years ago doing these very same tasks. Strangely, over this past year, in the midst of Lacey's awful diagnosis and slow decline, she had finally faced the past. Her first love was over, had been over for years. The idyllic days at the lake that had been a retreat for her as a child were no place to hide. Oliver, with his own imperfections, his own troubles, his marred history, was real. She was ready to go home, and at the moment she didn't care if she ever came back.

She kept remembering the paddle to Junior with Lacey. She thought she knew Lacey better than anyone, yet a whole side to her sister was a mystery to her. How ironic that Lacey, who was ill and facing an uncertain future, actually worried about her.

This morning, just lifting and draining the garden hoses seemed like an ordeal. Her body felt sluggish, as if the muddle in her brain was slowing her down. The hoses kept twisting and knotting as she tried to arrange them into neat coils to hang inside the garden shed. Next she tackled the flowerpots. The largest of these needed to be emptied into a wheelbarrow, since they were too cumbersome to move while filled with dirt.

From the open windows she heard Lacey vacuuming. Her jobs in the house weren't any easier. The porch cushions needed to be cleaned before they were stowed in closets and drawers. Once the living room furniture had been wiped down and covered with sheets, the wicker from the porch had to be moved inside for the winter. What was Lacey thinking while she went about her work?

The heavy gray sky had gradually lifted and a warm wind blew in from the south. The lake, usually smooth and blue, turned brown and choppy, churning in the hot air. The sheets and towels on the line dried quickly. Surprisingly, it never stormed.

At the end of the afternoon the wind died down. Margot went to her room to pack the few clothes she would take to New York. They were both leaving early in the morning. Lacey would drive home to New Castle and Margot would return her car at the Manchester airport and fly to New York. Lacey was right. It was time to figure out what to do with her life.

That night they ate a cold supper in the kitchen. Neither said much. Margot was tired from all the physical work in the heat, and she could see from Lacey's flushed face and the scrim of perspiration on her forehead that she was exhausted as well.

"This is everything," Lacey said. "The fridge is . . . empty." They ate the last of a roast chicken, some leftover potato salad, and a platter of fresh tomatoes.

"I've got everything off the dock," Margot said. She took a drink of lemonade. "There's just the canoe left," she said. "I'll bring it up first thing in the morning."

Lacey nodded. She was carrying the last load of sheets and towels home to wash there and bring back the following summer, though neither of them said anything about what might happen in the future.

It grew dark. Margot insisted on doing the dishes and Lacey said she'd walk down to the dock to check on the moon. When she had finished in the kitchen Margot went out to sit on the porch steps. The air was filled with the sound of crickets with their end of season song.

"Margot." Lacey's voice came from the shore. "Full moon."

"Coming," she called, and headed to the dock.

The night was warm. In the near dark she had no trouble finding her way to the lake. All the years of running to the shore, following the well-worn path, were ingrained in her. She could find her way there blindfolded. The wind had died down. The end of summer, and knowing this might be her last day here with Lacey, brought tears to Margot's eyes.

When Margot reached the dock, Lacey was standing at the very end, facing Junior. The moon was full, casting a brilliant path onto the water. A perfect moon path. How could she have forgotten? All those nights of working on her painting and here, finally, was the full moon she had been waiting for. Margot wiped her eyes and stood still. She'd never seen one quite so definite. The moon path led straight to Junior.

Suddenly, Lacey bent down and untied her sneakers. She kicked them off and unfastened her jeans, pulling them down.

Margot moved quickly to the end of the dock. "What are you doing?"

Lacey laughed. "What do you think?"

"Swimming the moon path?" Margot was amazed. "But our bathing suits are packed."

"So?" Lacey laughed, more a giggle this time. "No one . . . is here." She gestured toward the lake and pulled her T-shirt over her head, removed her bra, and slipped out of her underpants. She raised her arms straight over her head, then dove into the lake.

Margot began to cry and laugh at the same time. It was as if her sadness and joy were woven into one great emotion. She yanked off her own clothes, not wanting to waste a second, and jumped out into the darkness, aware of the delicious sensation of the cool air on her hot skin. When she hit the water, the initial sting of cold melted into pure pleasure. She surfaced and began to swim the moon path toward Lacey. Her arms felt strong. She kicked hard, propelling herself forward, feeling wild and reckless. After a few minutes she grew tired and switched to the breaststroke, keeping her head above water.

Lacey, well ahead of her, stopped swimming and began to tread water. She called back to Margot, "We're . . . almost to the end."

Margot paused. She wasn't afraid. The thrill of being naked, of swimming the moon path in the night was exhilarating, like nothing she'd ever felt. Her body tingled and for a moment she felt the water's chill. She stretched her arms out ahead and continued to swim, moving her arms in sync with her legs in an easy rhythm.

Lacey's voice, unhesitating, carried across the lake. "Follow me, Margot Winkler. Follow me."

19

Loose ends: A woven piece not properly tied off.

*A*n instant energy came into the city with the first wave of cooler air. It was as if the inhabitants were tired of the long, lazy summer days and glad to resume life at a faster pace. Now, in late October, New York grew chilly in the early evening. The leaves had turned color—the blue sky in brilliant contrast to the burnished oranges, reds, and bold yellows. They even looked beautiful clumped together in wet clusters on the sidewalks after a rain. Margot needed to wear more than a heavy sweater outdoors. Soon it would be the season of hats, woolen scarves, and boots.

She had come home to New York with a new resolve. Her final glimpse of Bow Lake had been in the rearview mirror of her rented car. How fitting, she had thought. For the first time in years she wasn't sad that the summer was over. Lacey was right. Margot knew it was time to decide what should come next in her life. Over the last months she had come to the conclusion that painting truly mattered to her. As though it was a foreign language that she hadn't spoken in many years, she discovered that much of what she once knew was still there. Her skills, along with tubes of paint, brushes, and a simple blank canvas, were helping her discover another voice, a voice she hadn't known she had.

Oliver was supposed to have returned in mid-September, but at the last moment he'd decided to stay on in Sonoma for another month to complete a commission for his new collector. When he'd called her with news of his delay, she hadn't fully concealed her disappointment and anger.

"You could have been here all this time," he had replied bluntly, his tone acid.

Planning their future wasn't the kind of discussion they could have on the phone. She could tell that he was distracted and thinking about his painting. How simple it had been when they first met—those early months together, when she was sure they were in love. She and Oliver had been swept up in the early energy of romance, a time of discovery, excitement, and pleasure. Later, as they blended their lives together, the relationship had become more complex. She thought of Lacey's weaving, combining the warp and weft to create a tapestry, a smooth whole. But she and Oliver brought past stories with them, like threads unraveled from a different cloth that were impossible to weave into a smooth, effortless new design. Or was it possible?

Margot stepped into Joe's, the new coffee place where Toni had suggested they meet. The rich aroma immediately carried her back to Oliver's elaborate coffee rituals—grinding the beans, pouring filtered water into a certain gold cone best suited for the perfect brew, the dark blue ceramic mug he preferred.

Despite her annoyance and hurt feelings over Oliver's delayed return, Margot missed him. The sound of an elevator door sliding open reminded her of his step in the hall coming home in the evening. The smell of paint or the sight of a blank canvas brought to mind his intense feelings about art—bemoaning the difficulty of creating tension between positive and negative space, or even his frustration in trying to mix the right shade of purple to create the shadow on a wall. Art wasn't his job, it was his passion. Late at night, Margot thought about the feel of his hands, warm and solid, reaching for her in the dark.

"Over here," Toni called out. She was sitting at a table along the wall. Her hair had grown longer and she wore it in a ponytail anchored on top of her head, flopping every which way like an elaborate bird plume. Margot pushed aside her momentary nostalgia and smiled at her niece, then motioned that she would get a drink at the bar before joining her.

Margot scanned the blackboard. When the man in front of her stepped aside, she ordered a mocha drink. She paid her $4.60 and wondered how so many young people could afford coffee habits at prices like these, though once the cup was in her hand the fragrant chocolate mixed with coffee made her think she should indulge herself more often.

She sat opposite Toni, who was just closing her phone.

"A text from Mom," she said.

"How's it going?"

"I'm almost afraid to say it, but she's better than she was this summer."

"Her speech?"

"That's pretty much the same. I guess that's a good thing." Toni paused as if to reflect. "I think it's like her attitude has changed."

"Her attitude?"

"Well, sort of her outlook. She seems calmer, more accepting of what she can and can't do. Being home seems more important to her than before."

"How do you mean?"

"Her weaving, for one thing. No more place mats, or those table runners. She's not even doing the juried craft shows. It's like she's making art. She has this giant project going on the floor loom. And"—Toni's eyes began to tear and her voice became more childlike—"some days it seems like she's almost normal again. Not her speech, but more like her old self."

"Really?" Margot said. Her heart lightened at this news. "What kind of project?" she asked.

"A huge tapestry. I saw some of it when I went home for a weekend. She's been spending hours in her studio. It's like she's putting herself into her weaving."

"She's always done that," Margot said.

"This is different. In the spring, it was like Mom was hiding up there, angry all the time. She was making some weird stuff."

Margot felt her own eyes begin to well up. She reached for Toni's hand. "That's so good. I mean, I'm happy she's found a way to express herself."

Toni nodded and sniffed. She wiped her eyes. "Yeah, it is good."

"I'm glad you're staying in close touch with your mom."

"We text all the time. And she's really okay about Wink being home."

Margot sipped her drink, the hit of caffeine and sugar going right to her veins.

"Have you heard?" Toni smiled fully, looking happier.

Margot shook her head.

"Wink's dating some guy. Mom says he's 'adorable.' Wink loves that he's interested in astronomy too. And wait till you hear this—he's a lepidop . . . something. He actually collects butterflies."

"Is it lepidopterist?"

"Yeah, that's it. Can't you just see Wink and her boyfriend holding nets and stalking around the woods?"

Margot laughed.

"She assures me he's totally cool, very cute, and not geeky at all."

"What about you? Any cool new guys in your life?"

"Funny you should ask." She grinned. "I've sort of been seeing this guy." She raised her eyebrows and shrugged. "We met the second week of classes. I didn't think I could ever feel anything after Ryan. It's so weird. Sometimes I can hardly picture him. Ryan, that is. Aunt Margot, I'm sure you figured out, he was . . ." She paused. "Well, you know, my first."

"I'm glad you've met someone new. I had a feeling you would," Margot said, not wanting to seem to lecture Toni on how she was so young, and that there would probably be many men in her life. Sitting in this coffee bar surrounded by all the students made Margot feel middle-aged and fading.

"Do you think I'll forget Ryan one day? Like totally? I didn't think that could ever happen." Toni took a sip of her latte. "Do you ever think about your first guy?"

Margot felt her breath catch in her throat. She stared into her cup. "Oh, I guess some part of you . . ."

"Did I tell you that Mom's running in this year's Turkey Trot?"

Margot glanced up, relieved that Toni hadn't waited for her answer. And why should Toni care about her own first love? She turned her attention to Toni's lively chatter and plans for Thanksgiving. Kate and Hugh were hosting the dinner this year. Their sons would be there, too. "I'm dying to meet Wink's butterfly dude. She invited him for dinner, so you'll get to meet him too. You are coming, aren't you?"

"Not this year."

"No? But you always come."

"It's good to mix things up for a change."

"Mom counts on you. Dad, too. Thanksgiving won't be the same without you, Aunt Margot."

"Toni, you're so sweet. I love you all dearly, but I may do something different this year. It sort of depends on Oliver."

Toni had finished her latte. She drew her teeth across her lower lip. "I was wondering what was going on. I know he's been out in California. Maybe I shouldn't ask."

"No, that's okay. I hope he'll be back soon. We need to sort some things out."

"What do you mean?"

"It's kind of complicated."

"I understand if you don't want to talk about it." She stared into her now empty latte cup.

"It's been a hard year in lots of ways."

"You don't have to explain. Still, he's a wonderful guy, Aunt Margot. Wink and I always loved it when he came home."

"Thanks for saying that."

"I hope things work out okay."

"I hope so too." She reached across and brushed her hand across Toni's upright ponytail.

"You like the hair?"

"Pretty funky," she said, and smiled.

After leaving Toni, Margot waited on the corner for the crosstown bus. She had decided to go over to her old apartment. It was too late in the day to paint, but she wanted to look over her recent work. It was the evening rush hour. The wind had picked up and she turned up the collar on her jacket. Two older ladies sat on the bench inside the bus shelter, both with shopping bags gathered around their feet. A cluster of teenagers huddled at the far end, several with backpacks, one on a cell phone, two more wearing earphones, their bodies moving slightly to their separate music.

She reached into her handbag for her MetroCard. Slipped into the side pocket next to it was Oliver's postcard. She had found it with the mail on her return from Bow Lake. Diebenkorn's portrait of a woman. On the reverse side he had written, "I love you, Mags. Like they say on postcards—wish you were here." He had signed it with his large letter "O." She knew the message by heart. She had carried the card with her ever since.

A few days later Margot sat at the edge of the living room sofa, tense and very aware of Oliver's presence. He had arrived home that afternoon from California and Carl had given her the rest of the day off. When she had come through the door they had hugged and kissed each other awkwardly, more like a couple at the early stages of a relationship, when you weren't quite ready to give in to the pleasure of it, uncertain of what your partner's response was going to be.

"Mags, we need to talk," he'd said.

He stood before her now, holding two glasses of white wine.

"It's the same Chardonnay we had that afternoon in Sonoma," he said.

She reached out, took the glass, and said, "That seems like years ago now."

"I wish you'd been with me this summer." He sat at the far end of the sofa, looking distant, a little removed. He was tanned, but Margot thought maybe the lines around his mouth had deepened. She wanted to push his lips upward into a smile.

She sipped the wine, remembering the feel of the California sun and the gentle landscape outside Grant's house. That had been a perfect afternoon. It had been later, back at the hotel, when they had quarreled and everything had begun to fall apart.

"I'm glad you're home," she said. She drew in her breath, trying to muster up all her courage. "Every time I walk in Central Park I think about our last argument. I'm sorry, Oliver." She lowered her head. "At the time I thought I was doing the right thing and—"

"Wait," he interrupted. "Let's not look backward. It's not a good idea."

"You're right," she said.

"Cheers," he said, raising his glass, but not looking cheerful at all. After taking a sip, he stared down into his glass. Now that they were together, he didn't seem to know what to say. Finally he spoke. "I was miserable without you, Mags."

"Oliver," she said, choking back the start of tears. "I've missed you too."

"You have?"

"I know I've made it hard for you."

He moved closer to her and placed his hand on her knee. "I don't want to go into all that." There was an edge to his voice.

"I'm painting a lot now," she said. The apartment seemed especially quiet to her. She was aware of the sound of her own breathing.

"You know I've wanted that for you." He took her hand. It felt warm and solid. "Have you thought about us? I mean the future?"

Margot felt the weight of his gaze upon her. "I kept wondering what you were thinking. You didn't call much."

"You know I hate the phone. And it was never the right time."

"I began to think you no longer cared. That I'd ruined what we had."

"Margot, I love you. I need you to know that." He stroked her face with his wide hands, and cradling her head, he gently kissed her hair. "Mags, we need to be together."

Margot nodded and allowed her body to relax against him.

"I want to make plans," he said.

She put her fingers on his lips. "Please, just hold me." After more than three months apart he felt immediately comforting, familiar to her. "Let's talk later."

He pulled her into his arms and it felt so right. Suddenly, loving Oliver seemed simple. He kissed her on the lips. "Okay?" he asked.

"More than okay."

Oliver smiled fully, looking like his old self. She followed him to the bedroom.

Later that evening he ordered Indian food, saying he'd missed all the great take-out meals available in New York. They had both showered and Margot's hair was still wet and slicked against her head. They sipped the rest of the Chardonnay while waiting for the food to arrive. Oliver rested his hand on Margot's thigh.

"I've got so much to tell you," he said.

Margot smiled. He looked younger now, his eyes brighter as he launched into his plans.

"I've been thinking of staying in California. That's what I need to talk to you about."

Margot stiffened.

"I've found another house in Sonoma, one I'd like to rent," he went on. "I love it out there, Mags."

Margot's throat tightened. "Wait," she said. "You just got home."

"You told me you're painting more now. You loved it when you came out last June."

"What are you saying?"

"California would be a great place for us to start over. I'm getting closer to sixty. I want to get married."

"Leave the East?"

"Not totally. I'd keep this place for a while. I can rent out my studio."

"So I'm supposed to quit my job."

"Is it all that important? You said you wished you had more time to paint."

"Just like that." She snapped her fingers. "I'm supposed to follow you across the country?"

"Mags, change is good. My work is evolving. I don't totally understand it. In many ways I'm not on solid ground. It's scary. But it's exciting, too. I want that for us."

"And move to California?"

"We could divide our time. Maybe part of the year there, part here. You could still spend time with Lacey. I know that's important to you, and to her, too."

"Oliver, I don't know. I . . ."

He took her hands and pressed them between his own. "What don't you know? We love each other, right?"

"Of course." The words came out jaggedly.

"Mags, are you with me on this? I've found this place. I need to let the guy know if I want to take the house."

"Wait just a minute. You've picked out a house. You expect me to immediately quit my job, pick up my paints and follow you?"

He dropped her hands. "I don't want to have the same argument all over again. It's time for us. Don't you see that?"

"This is different. You're asking me to move across the country. Not just take an extended vacation."

"I'm asking you to marry me."

"On your conditions." Her irritation grew. That smooth, mellow feeling that came from knowing she was loved began to twist and knot.

"What's that supposed to mean?"

Suddenly a loud buzzer came from the intercom. The deliveryman had arrived with their dinner. Oliver pressed the door release button, his face in a grimace. He fumbled in his pocket and pulled out his billfold, taking out two twenties.

"Oliver—" She started to explain.

"Wait a minute," he said, turning on the hall light. A moment later, after a soft knock and a mumbled thanks, he carried the bags to the dining table by the window, and set them down. He came over to her, ignoring the food.

"Oliver," she began, "I want to be with you. I just want some say in it."

"You said you wanted to be with me. I need to be in California. You want to paint, too. I don't see the problem."

"That's not fair."

"Why isn't it?"

"There's a lot to consider. It's almost Thanksgiving."

"Here we go. I can see it already." He lifted his arms and gestured dramatically. "We have to be with my poor sister. I need to be near her to help." He dropped his arms. "We've been down this road before."

His words stung. "I know I've made mistakes."

"Do you? You're so stuck in that family, you can't live your own life."

"That's not true."

"Every time old Alex calls, you jump into action. That's how it was all winter. I've always wondered if there's something between you two. Now wouldn't *that* be interesting? The poor older sister fades away while the beautiful young one is waiting in the wings."

Margot felt her face go hot. She stood, flooded with anger.

"You are so totally wrong. How could you ever say that?" Her legs felt weak, her knees like jelly. "I refuse to listen to such horrible things." She started toward the bedroom.

"Now what?"

"I'm going to get some things and go over to my apartment. I can't be with you when you're like this."

"You're leaving?"

"I need to think. Let's just say you're not too good at marriage proposals."

"So you're saying no?"

"That's not what I said."

"It damn well is."

Margot's pulse raced. "I hate it when you're like this, Oliver. Pushing me. Telling me what to do. I don't know what to think anymore." She gulped back tears. "I wanted things to work between us."

"Yeah, right. So go back to your precious little place. Your hideout."

"Stop it!" she shouted. Margot didn't think she'd ever been so angry. The walls of the room began to spin. She had to get out.

"Wait, Mags," Oliver said, his tone more placating. "You have to understand what it's been like for me."

"Me, me, me. Do you hear yourself?"

The Indian food sat cooling on the table. She was no longer hungry. The smell of it sickened her. "I'm leaving," she said.

Oliver sat hunched forward, his face buried in his hands. He didn't say a word. He didn't try to stop her.

Oliver felt someone pinching his elbow in the crowd.

"Mr. Famous doesn't have time for an old friend?"

"Hannah? Sorry. I didn't see you." The huge gallery space was packed with guests.

"How about a smile? You're looking like a tortured artist. Aren't you a little old for that?"

"You read people pretty well." He tried to say it jokingly.

They stood facing each other in the Kalvorian Gallery at a reception for a Norwegian artist whose name kept slipping out of Oliver's mind and whose sculpture was composed of twigs, grasses, and hay. The overheated space smelled remotely like a barn.

"Good thing no one's allowed to smoke." He nodded at the closest piece and grinned. "This place would ignite in a flash."

"You're a wicked boy, Oliver."

He shrugged. "I'm strictly a painter. I don't get a lot of this."

"I understand you made waves out in San Francisco."

"Yeah. It was a good summer."

"I heard you might not come back to New York."

Oliver's expression darkened. "Who knows?" All he thought about now was Margot—his anger, her fury, and how now, in the same city, they were further apart than ever. She hadn't answered her cell phone since their argument. When he'd tried to reach her at the Van Engen Gallery, she wouldn't take his call. He was too afraid to stop by the gallery. Yet he didn't want to imagine a future without her.

Hannah seemed to be studying him intently. "California's been good for my work," he said. "I may spend some more time there."

"I knew you'd get suckered in."

"Is June here?" he said, changing the subject.

"Over there, talking to Stanley. I've heard the grand master himself wants to show your work. Rumor has it your prices will be going up."

"We've had some conversations. These things take time."

"No Margot?"

"Not tonight," he said, glancing at the door. Why did he even hope? She didn't know he was here. It had been three days. Three long, painful days without her.

He felt something tickle the back of his neck. He turned. A strange mound of twigs and woven grasses loomed up behind him at nearly eight feet. Was this art? Did it even matter? He thought of his own work. So what if Stanley Kalvorian was finally interested in his paintings? After years of wishing for only that, Oliver didn't seem to care. Without Margot, everything felt purposeless and flat.

Suddenly, he couldn't take it a minute longer. He excused himself from Hannah and worked his way to the door. The cold night air hit him—a relief. He began the long walk north from Chelsea, block after block, stoplight after stoplight, the sidewalks busy, then less so, then busy again.

Why had he let his anger overtake him the other night? He had come home to New York with such hopes. So many plans. A new life with Margot. Had he already blown it? He was ten years older. He had one failed marriage behind him. But so did she. And her adored sister was failing before her eyes. Margot couldn't change that. Yet life went on. Family went on. Toni and Wink were great girls, women really. And Jenna. He smiled at the memory of her visit this summer. You had to find the bright spots. Like a speck of yellow on a canvas, or a shot of light. The small things were powerful.

Close to an hour later he reached his building. Hector was on duty.

"Good evening, Mr. Levin."

Oliver greeted him and hurried to the elevator, thankful that Hector didn't ask after Margot, though he probably knew that she'd left. The doormen in New York knew everything that went on—a human comedy played out before them every day, he thought darkly. He let himself in at his apartment and tossed the keys on the table. He crossed the living room and stared out at the Hudson River. The wide expanse looked black and cold. Soon it would be winter. He turned to go into the bedroom. The red light of the answering machine blinked, on and off, hidden by a carelessly tossed jacket.

20

Tapestry: A woven cloth, sometimes depicting a story.

*A*lex pushed the leaves into the black trash bag he had fitted around the rusty wire frame. Fall had come to New Castle, and along with the brilliant blue skies and crisp air came leaf season. The front yard of their property was not large and the few leaves that fell there tended to blow away, but he would be raking the back garden periodically until December. He collected the leaves in the backyard, and he and Lacey together would feed them into a shredder before adding them to the compost bins behind the garage.

The repetitive scraping noise of the rake against the hard ground reminded him of doing yard work with his mother. His dad often went to the office on Saturdays and he and Daniel would help her in the yard before being allowed to go off with their friends. When Daniel was away at college Alex continued to help his mother on fall weekends and while he never admitted it, he liked that time of working alongside her; it was the first time he remembered her talking to him as if he were another adult, their easy banter making the time pass quickly.

He glanced at the back door. Lacey had said she would be there soon to help. Thank God for the everyday rituals that seemed to hold their lives together. The family meals, the errands, the daily chores, and garden work gave them a structure to shape their days. Family life felt different. With Toni away it was bound to. But there were also moments when life at home seemed almost normal, as normal as it could with Lacey's illness.

At least Wink seemed happy to be living with them. She and Lacey had started running together in the morning, a new routine they both seemed to enjoy. Cornell had granted Wink a deferral until January or the following fall, if she chose to extend it. She was taking two courses at the University of New Hampshire, worked part-time at a coffeehouse in Portsmouth, and volunteered two afternoons a week at the after-school art room that Lacey had set up for the children at the homeless shelter.

The wind grew stronger. Alex continued to rake. He stopped to zip up his fleece jacket. He reached again for the rake just as Lacey came into the yard. She wore her oldest jeans, the baggy ones she kept for working in the garden, a flannel shirt, and a down vest, one of the ones their daughters had once worn but had cast aside. Even in these tired old clothes, Lacey looked youthful and energetic. How could the brain cells in this vigorous, active body be breaking down? He watched as she clipped back the dead stalks of the daylilies at the far end of the flower bed, her movements rhythmic and confident. Alex tried to convince himself that Lacey's speech hadn't gotten any worse since the summer. They seemed to be living in a kind of limbo together: Lacey accepting that Wink was home for a semester or two; he quietly on guard, not wanting to say anything that would trouble Lacey. She had been terribly upset when he had told her about seeing Margot in New York. The memory of that argument was still painful. Seeking out Margot had been a dreadful mistake. He knew that now. Of course Lacey had imagined the very worst. He had denied it, but that simple truth had been wrought with shame.

What had come over him this past winter and spring? It troubled him to know he'd let himself think of Margot in the way he once had when they were both very young. He sensed that she had been remembering that time too, with all of her paintings of Bow Lake. More frightening than anything was how he could have put them all in jeopardy. Could he possibly have given up on Lacey? Like a man who had survived a near-fatal crash, he was now determined to live and to love Lacey more than ever.

He continued to rake. There was nothing controversial in the simple task of raking leaves. Working in sections, he bagged small pile after small pile, leaving behind the bright green grass. The lawn usually didn't turn brown and lifeless until December.

"Oh," Lacey called out and stood. She had put down her clippers and held a hand over one eye.

Alex stopped raking. "What's wrong?"

"It . . . hurts." She seemed to be trying to extract some piece of debris that had blown into her eye.

"Let me look," he said, coming to her side.

"No," she said, blinking. "I can . . . do it." She used one hand to protect her eye from the wind and with the other she tried to wipe away whatever had blown in.

Alex reached for Lacey's cheek. "Let me help." He pushed the hair off her face. Lacey flinched. She lowered her head and continued to try to extract what was in her eye.

"Damn it, Lacey."

"What?" She stared up at him, her right eye watery and red.

"Don't you see? It's like everything else. I just want to help you."

Lacey clenched her jaw and stepped back.

Alex went on. "Wink wanted to make the spaghetti last night. You wouldn't let her." The leaves at his feet swirled up in a sudden gust of wind and Alex kicked what was left of the pile. "We want to help you when we can. Please don't resist every time."

"But I wanted to cook," Lacey said. "Wink didn't mind. She had . . . homework." She wiped at her eye and blinked repeatedly. "Do you want me . . ." She paused. "To act sick? Will that make . . . make . . . you happy?"

"You know it's not like that."

"Do I?"

"Wink wants to feel useful. It's her way of dealing with the situation."

"You let her stay home. You won." Now both of Lacey's eyes glistened with tears.

"Is that what you think?" Alex let the rake fall to the ground. "For Christ's sake, we love you, Lacey." He felt like a balloon deflating. "We're just trying to love you the only way we can."

His words seemed to reach her this time. Tears ran down her cheeks and she doubled over slightly, as if to protect herself from the wind. She shook her head from side to side and didn't attempt to wipe away the tears. Her voice came out a whisper. "Some days it's so hard. I want to do everything . . . myself . . . as long as I can."

Alex pulled her into his arms. "I know, Chief. I know." He rubbed her back. "Please don't shut me out. I need you, too. Okay?"

Lacey nodded. "Just . . . remember what it's . . . like for me."

"I'm doing my best. Please, believe me."

She nodded. Her mouth softened. He took her face in his hands, raising her chin in his palm. "How's the eye?"

She blinked and brought one hand to her eye, touching it tentatively with her finger. "Fine." She blinked once again. "Fine. I cried it out."

Alex took her hand and held it briefly. "Sometimes tears are a good thing." He bent down and picked up his rake. "When I finish this bag, will you help me with the shredder?"

Lacey nodded. "Yes," she said softly. "I'll help."

Margot looked up at Oliver. He stood by the door of her apartment, holding a dripping umbrella in one hand. Something in the humility of his stance moved her.

"I got your message." He shifted his weight from one foot to another, his head lowered like a repentant schoolboy.

"Come in," she said, stepping aside. She had called Oliver yesterday, asking him to come see her this evening. She still felt traces of anger toward him, but in the course of the last few days her anger had somehow shrunk, and that allowed room for other feelings.

"I've got to explain," he said.

"Wait," she said, taking his umbrella and leaving it on the floor. She hung his trench coat, wet and rumpled, over the door to the tiny bedroom. He followed her to the living room. "First, I want to show you what I've been doing." She pointed to the dozen or so small canvases that she had hung together on the largest wall. "They're all small landscapes. They vary. I've tried everything from a realistic approach to more abstract. On these"—she pointed to the last row—"I've tried to vary the view, moving in and out, sort of like the lens of a camera."

"Did you work from photographs?"

"Does it show?" Her old anxiety was still there. Would she ever be able to snuff that out?

"They're beautiful, Mags," he said softly.

"I know they're small. Nothing like what you do."

"It's what *you* do that matters. We all portray the world differently. Like you just said, different lenses."

"Did I say that?" she said, growing nervous, but pleased that he had listened to her. "It's a start anyway." She pointed to the little couch. "Why don't you sit? There's hardly any room to move in here."

Having Oliver come to her place seemed best. This time she was going to lead the discussion. As if he understood her wishes, he sat carefully with his long legs to one side of the coffee table and waited for her to speak. She went to the small bamboo chair opposite him and perched on its edge.

"I want to study painting again," she said. "Full-time. I couldn't afford it when I first got to New York."

"You mean with a private teacher?"

"No. What I'd really like is to go to art school and work toward a graduate degree." She settled back into the chair, calmer and in control.

"I see." He leaned forward. "You know I'd love to help you. I could teach you."

"You can't teach me. I need different teachers, unbiased critique." She kept her voice firm. "It would always be personal. You can't help that."

"I understand." He looked up at her, as the little sofa was low to the ground.

"It means I'm going to give up my job. I love the gallery—Carl's been a great boss."

"So you'd quit?"

"Wait." She drew in a breath and went on. "I met with a Realtor yesterday."

"What?"

"Please hear me out." Oliver leaned back. She continued. "This place is worth a lot. With the money from its sale, I can pay for school and support myself for a while."

Oliver stared at her, moving his head from side to side, seemingly amazed. When she had come to this decision she had felt strangely lighter, as if she'd taken off a coat that weighed too heavily on her shoulders. With the inheritance from her grandmother, Margot had been given a place to live, and by selling it, she could gain the freedom to live as she liked. She was confident Granny Winkler would approve.

"The Realtor I spoke to thinks the apartment will sell quickly."

"Mags, I'm happy about all of that. But what about . . ."

"Us?" she said.

"I was way out of line. I was a jerk, really. Once I calmed down I realized that." He brought his hands together, then let them fall to his lap. "I guess I was jealous of Lacey and her family. They were taking you away from me. Alex too."

Margot flinched. "Oliver, we've both made mistakes. I've been too involved with Lacey." She paused, almost afraid to go further. "And with Alex."

Oliver's head snapped up. Margot looked back at him, her gaze unwavering. "I shouldn't have let him pull me into his troubles, their troubles. If anything, I may have made things worse. I think he understands that now." There. She had said it. She stood. "By selling this place I can manage on my own. I can do this by myself."

Oliver said nothing. Margot went over to the door leading to the terrace. She opened it slightly. The air cooled her face. Oliver ran his hands through his hair and remained seated, as if depleted. She turned back to him and said, "We've got to figure out where to go from here."

He stood.

"Wait. Please let me finish. I want to be with you, Oliver, but you can't be the one to decide everything. I'm willing to move. Maybe California will work. But I have to be near someplace where I can study." Margot could feel her voice giving out. She brought her hand to the doorframe and tried to steady herself. "When Teddy ran my life, I was miserable. The real problem, what's most upsetting to me, is that I let him."

"I understand, Mags," he said, stepping toward her.

"Lacey too. I was letting everyone run my life. The difference was Lacey wanted what was best for me."

"You've got an amazing sister."

"The awful thing is, I can't save her."

He shook his head and wrapped his arms around her. He felt solid and safe. "I'm sorry, Mags."

Gently, she pushed him back. "So, if we stay together, it's got to be different." She took his hand. "We're going to have to work at this. I've always loved you," she whispered. "That's never changed."

"So the answer is yes?"

"Do you understand what I'm saying? What I'm asking of you?"

He nodded and seemed unable to speak.

"Wait. I have something for you." She went to the kitchen and picked up the one painting she had kept out of view. Before handing it to him, she took one last look. "The moon path. Bow Lake," she said. She had ended up framing the view of the moon path through the trees—the light in the distance beckoning, full of promise.

Oliver held it in his hands.

"It's not perfect," she said, "but it's the best I can do for now. I want you to have it."

"It's a fine painting." His eyes teared up. "Terrific composition and"—he brought the picture closer to him—"the light. You've really got the light. How can I ever thank you?" Putting the picture down, he wrapped his arms tightly around her.

He smelled of the rain. She reached up and touched his face. The lines seemed etched more deeply, but his lips curved into a smile. His eyes, deep and familiar, looked into hers. "I think you know how," she said.

Alex rapped on the door to Lacey's studio. It was the day before Thanksgiving and the house already smelled of cooking. That morning Wink had made two pies to take to Kate and Hugh's dinner. Toni was in the kitchen working on the sweet potato casserole. Syrup from the sweet potatoes had oozed into the bottom of the oven, smoking up the kitchen. Wink had averted the bleating smoke alarm by opening all the windows just in time. When Alex had left them the culinary adventure seemed to be under control.

"Uh-huh," Lacey said.

"May I come in?" He hadn't been in the studio for several weeks, not wanting to interrupt her work. Lacey had been spending more time there, and seemed happy when she emerged at the end of the day.

She opened the door and took his hand. "I want you to see," she said, guiding him to the loom. Alex stared. He swallowed, opened his mouth, but he couldn't speak. He moved closer. Draped across the loom was an intense dark blue weaving. He reached out to touch it. It was thick, but soft. He realized it wasn't just blue, but many shades of blue, as well as gray, turquoise, emerald green and even black. The overall effect was riveting. Within the depths of blue he saw slender silver threads glistening in the light. These strands grew together into a wide, wavy line in the middle, looking like a road, or a path. Lacey had woven the many slender threads of silver into one strong band. The piece was so large that he could almost lose himself in it.

"You know where . . ."

He nodded and pulled her into his arms and kissed the top of her head. "It's the best thing you've ever done."

Lacey stepped closer to the loom. She ran her hands over the work, stopping at the silver threads. "Yes," she said. "Yes."

The swath of sun falling on the tapestry reminded him that the afternoon was on the wane. He wanted to take Lacey out and show her his surprise before it got dark. "Can you take a break?" he asked.

She hesitated but he urged her to come with him to the garage.

"The garage?" She looked dubious.

"Wait. You'll see."

They went downstairs and passed through the kitchen. Toni had the mixer roaring. Empty eggshells were strewn across the counter. A box of brown sugar lay on its side, the lid gaping, the waxed paper interior open to the air. Lacey paused momentarily as if considering whether she should put it away.

"Don't worry, Mom. It's under control. I promise to clean up." Toni nodded in Wink's direction. "Guess who she's talking to again."

Wink gave a small wave from the kitchen table, the phone pressed against her ear. She covered the receiver briefly and said, "You're going to like this, Mom."

Alex took Lacey's hand and led her down the three steps. Be-

yond the old Volvo, leaning against the shelves of garden pots, bags
of fertilizer, and assorted tools was a new blue bicycle with a silver
helmet hanging from the handlebars.

"Here it is," he said.

"For me?"

"What do you think?"

"I always . . . thought of the biking . . . as, as your . . ."

"I thought we could start taking rides together. I know you
love running. I just thought, well, why not?"

"Why not?" Lacey picked up the helmet and ran her hand
across the seat.

"It's a touring bicycle. I think you'll find the saddle's pretty
comfortable. You can see how you like it. We can always have upright handlebars put on if you think you'd like that better."

"It's like yours."

"It's good on the back roads." He studied Lacey's face. Her initial surprise had turned to interest. She put her hands on the handlebars, moving the bike into the center of the garage.

"You want to try it?" It was crazy that he hadn't thought of
riding with her before. When the girls were little, neither of them
had had much time to themselves. He had always thought his own
bike riding was an indulgence, a way to exercise but also a time to
be alone and away from his family. Lacey liked to spend her free
time learning to weave and he would take the twins off on some
expedition to give her time alone in her studio. It had seemed a fair
exchange back then.

"Just swing your leg over," he said. "I think the seat's the right
height."

Lacey nodded. "I hope I can do it."

"Sure you can. Take it out front. I'll go get our jackets."

A few minutes later Lacey was pedaling beside him through
the village. In the beginning she swayed a bit, and seemed nervous
about going too fast. Her helmet listed a little to the left. He would
adjust the strap when they stopped. Gradually, as they pedaled

away from the village, she became more confident. "Let's go out Hawley's Road toward the seawall," he called back to her. When he turned again, she lifted her hand and gave a quick but confident wave. He pedaled harder into the slight incline. Lacey was with him. The wind whipped at his face and entered his lungs, filling them with clean ocean air. He looked up at the sky, thankful for this day, this time with Lacey. It was just a simple bike ride on a country road. And it was everything.

"Who's ready for seconds?" Jenna emerged from the kitchen carrying a large platter of turkey.

"Count me in. I'll have the dark meat this time," Oliver said. "Best turkey I've ever eaten."

"Daddy, you're biased. You say that about everything I cook."

"I agree, though I'm biased too," said Leo, his cheeks rosy with wine, and his head a halo of curls. Margot thought he looked like a grown-up cherub. Leo and Jenna had arrived the day before. Margot and Jenna had spent a harrowing afternoon at Fairway Market, where seemingly half the population of Manhattan was hell-bent on raking the shelves for their Thanksgiving feast.

Margot had awakened this morning excited but slightly on edge. She and Oliver were back together. Home, she had thought. Yet she sensed they were both tentative and slightly afraid, as if neither wanted to tip the balance and unravel their newfound happiness. The early-morning rumble had begun. Heavy trucks roared into the city even on Thanksgiving. It might be nice to live with less noise after all these years.

Oliver had rolled over and whispered that he would go make her tea, and indeed he had pulled on his tattered plaid robe and tiptoed out past Jenna and Leo, who were sprawled on the living room sleep sofa. The refrigerator was packed with more food than it had ever contained, though they would be only four for dinner. Mario and his now fiancée, Julie, had promised to come by later in the evening for dessert.

While Margot had sipped her tea, Oliver had showered and gone off to get bagels and the paper. The apartment, usually so spacious, had become cluttered and crowded with Jenna and Leo in their midst. But it was a good clutter. Jenna's running shoes by the door, the extra towels on the hooks in the bathroom, Leo's laptop left casually in Oliver's favorite chair, a duffel bag bursting with clothes next to the sofa, and Jenna's notebook of favorite recipes on the kitchen counter—all signs of visiting family. Why hadn't she and Oliver invited them before?

"Awesome stuffing," Leo said.

"Jenna's a great teacher." Margot smiled over at Leo, thinking he and Jenna were a good match. They had been together for over two years. A computer software designer who played the flute in a community orchestra, he was the poet-scientist type who didn't pretend to know his way around the kitchen. He had spent Wednesday afternoon investigating wine shops and had returned with two bottles of Burgundy as his contribution, allowing that Jenna had advised him on his selection.

The four of them sat at the table by the window overlooking the Hudson. The candles and the glittering lights across the river added to the festive feel. Margot had purchased new linen napkins and place mats for the occasion and Oliver had come home yesterday with an enormous bouquet of flowers that towered over them from the middle of the table.

Margot took more brussels sprouts. Jenna had shown her how to cut them into fine ribbons before sautéeing them in olive oil and butter. Margot had been astonished at how simple and delicious this vegetable could be. Maybe she could learn to cook after all.

Jenna told them that she and Leo would be in Florida with his family for Christmas. Oliver raised his eyebrows in Margot's direction, as if to send a signal that this might mean something important.

"What are you guys doing for the holidays, Daddy?"

Oliver leaned back in his chair. "Mags and I are going to San Francisco for a week." He turned to her now as if in need of confirmation.

"I'm looking into art schools there. We may drive down the coast and explore. We're both ready for adventure." She met his gaze and smiled.

"Sounds great," Jenna said. "That's if you like school." She laughed.

"I still have to apply. So far my portfolio's pretty slim," Margot explained.

"She'll get in," Oliver said.

"More wine?" Leo asked.

Margot shook her head. Oliver had taken her hand and clutched it right there on the table. His grip was firm and warm. Her heart seemed to grow large in her chest. The flurry of questions she tossed around in her head just before sleep hadn't lessened. She didn't expect they would. But she was thankful—thankful for this dinner, this day, and this family.

"Are we ready for pie?" Jenna asked.

Margot glanced at her watch. "Mario and Julie won't be here for another hour."

"How about we go out for a walk before dessert?" Oliver suggested. He released Margot's hand and gestured toward the window. "It's a beautiful night. Margot's sister and her family always take a walk to the ocean before dessert. A Thanksgiving tradition, I've been told." He met her gaze, his eyebrows lifting hopefully. She smiled back.

Within a few minutes, they'd carried the dishes and platters to the kitchen. Oliver handed out their coats. Margot went to the window and looked at the river. The water glistened in silver light. The moon was full.

"Mags, I want you with me," Oliver called, heading into the hall to call the elevator.

She put on her coat and reached for her scarf hanging on the chair by the door. It was the blue one Lacey had woven in multiple shades. All the colors in Margot's eyes, she had told her. Margot ran her fingers over the soft threads and brought it to her face. The night was mild, she thought, putting the scarf down. She would be fine without it. She caught up with Oliver and took his arm.

About the Author

Katharine Davis is also the author of *Capturing Paris* and *East Hope*. She grew up in Europe, taught French for many years, and worked as a docent at the National Gallery of Art. She lives in New York City and York Harbor, Maine. She can be reached at www.katharinedavis.com.

A Slender Thread

KATHARINE DAVIS

*This Conversation Guide is intended to enrich the
individual reading experience, as well as encourage us
to explore these topics together—because books,
and life, are meant for sharing.*

A CONVERSATION
WITH KATHARINE DAVIS

Q. A Slender Thread *is your first novel since* East Hope, *published in February 2009. What idea first inspired you, and how did the book come together after that?*

A. While I was completing *East Hope* a good friend invited me to a luncheon and tour of a photography exhibit at the Corcoran Gallery of Art in Washington, D.C. Included in our group was a dear college friend of hers who was suffering from a degenerative brain disease. This woman, in her early fifties, walked around the museum, smiled and seemed to enjoy what she was seeing, but she had lost the ability to speak. I was greatly moved by her courage in the face of such a tragedy. I couldn't stop thinking about her and wondered how her condition affected her husband, her children, and her friends. I did not want to invade this woman's privacy in any way, nor did I want to tell her particular story. Instead, I began to contemplate a fictional character. What if that character suffered from a similar plight? How would those around her be affected? Suddenly, a story began to grow in my mind, and before I knew it I was completely absorbed in writing a new novel.

Q. Lacey suffers from a rare disease—primary progressive aphasia. Did the woman you met in Washington suffer from this same disease?

A. I researched this kind of degenerative illness, and the woman I met may have had this or a similar disorder. Primary progressive aphasia alters speech first; later the small muscle skills deteriorate, making it difficult to communicate by writing. Eventually, one loses the ability to read or understand. The symptoms and progression vary widely. I have learned since that the woman I met in the museum needs full-time care now and is unable to manage life on her own. In *A Slender Thread* I decided to focus not on the illness itself but on the effect that such a diagnosis might have on a family. The idea of communication began to permeate all aspects of the story I was writing. How do we communicate? What do we choose to communicate and why? We communicate by what we say or don't say, and by our actions. In my research I learned that people suffering from this illness are capable of activities not requiring language and often excel in the areas of art or music—both of which are forms of communication.

Q. In your novel Lacey weaves and Margot and Oliver paint. Describe your particular interest in people who pursue art professionally and personally.

A. I've been drawn to the art world all my life from visiting museums, taking classes in art history, and my work as a docent at the National Gallery of Art. Some of my friends are artists and I particularly love to hear their thoughts on the creative process. Artists sometimes have a hard time putting into words what they are trying to say in their work. They communicate visually, just as musicians communicate through sound. I've also had the pleasure of going on studio visits with my sister, who is the curator of an art gallery in Maine. I'm fascinated by the creative energy that artists bring to their work. The variety of talent and the diversity of the work are inspiring. In the beginning of *A Slender Thread* Oliver experiences the fear of losing his creative edge, in a sense his own way of communication, while Margot, who hasn't painted for years, seems to have lost her artistic energy entirely.

Q. So, you have a sister. The relationship between two sisters lies at the heart of A Slender Thread. *Did your relationship with your sister inspire the novel? In your mind, what makes Lacey and Margot's relationship so close and meaningful?*

A. I am fortunate to have two sisters and I am close to both of them. I decided to tell Lacey's story from a separate point of view. At no time do we go inside Lacey's mind. Instead, I wanted the events to be told from those extremely close to her—her husband, Alex, and her sister, Margot. I think the fact that Lacey and Margot's mother was an alcoholic and mostly absent from their lives made the two sisters especially close. Margot, as the younger, turned to Lacey for love and guidance, and Lacey in many ways took on a maternal role. Lacey and Margot's family is fictional, nothing like my own, but the loving bond between sisters has been an important part of my life too.

Q. You have a knack for capturing believable male characters who are flawed but sympathetic. Why did you want to include Oliver's point of view along with Alex's?

A. Alex, probably most of all, is affected by Lacey's illness. I wanted to show the repercussions of this diagnosis within a marriage. Alex's "voice" helps to reveal Lacey, as well as what is at stake for a man and wife when faced with a devastating change. *A Slender Thread* is also Margot's story. Her reaction to Lacey's illness has an impact on her life with Oliver—in a sense a ripple effect. I felt it necessary to the story to explore Oliver's point of view. At moments he seems understanding and forgiving when Margot is pulled away, but as a normal human being, he also experiences resentment, even jealousy. When tragedy befalls a family, everyone involved feels a difference in their lives.

Q. Bow Lake, where Margot and Lacey have gone every summer since they were children, plays an important role in their lives. Is there a Bow Lake in your life?

A. I think we all have a "Bow Lake" in our lives—whether it's a far-off vacation place or your grandmother's back porch where you went to escape now and then as a child. Bow Lake is one of those nostalgic places from our childhood when everything seemed simple and perfect. For Margot, Bow Lake was an escape. Often when we do return to a place we loved long ago, we find that it is no longer the same at all. Bow Lake represents the longing one might have for an idealized time or place. Also, when the future seems threatening, one has the tendency to look back and seek solace in what seemed like easier times. All of the characters in *A Slender Thread* feel the pull of the past—Lacey clinging to her girls and not wanting them to know the truth; Alex thinking about his childhood with Lacey and Margot; Oliver longing for his early years of artistic productivity and success; and, of course, Margot dwelling on memories of Bow Lake and the first time she fell in love.

Q. How were you able to make the art scene in New York seem so believable?

A. I visited galleries in New York City and spoke to artists about their painting and their lives in the city. One of the great pleasures of doing any research is that you quickly learn that everyone has a story to tell. Artists are like the rest of us in that they want to pursue their dreams and do the work they love. Becoming a successful artist is difficult in today's world. Not only is the creative work challenging, but the monetary rewards are scant for most.

Q. Why did you decide to make Lacey a weaver?

A. Lacey has a strong practical side to her character. Originally she chose weaving since she loved making things she could use—shawls, place mats, cloth for garments. Later, she finds joy in weaving not just for its uses but for the sheer beauty of the colors and textures. When I researched weaving, so many myths and stories fell into my lap. Weaving is one of the earliest art forms and it was dominated by women from the beginning. A woman could fit weaving in around her household chores and tending children. From ancient days people needed cloth for clothing. Eventually women wove more complex designs and depicted stories right in the cloth. The early textiles revealed myths and symbols. Think of the Bayeux Tapestry from the eleventh century, cloth that told a story to an illiterate audience. Textiles were language. For Lacey the imminent loss of language is terrifying and weaving becomes a powerful metaphor in the novel.

Q. Do you have a personal interest in weaving or textiles?

A. I've always loved beautiful fabrics and textiles. Over the years I've enjoyed home sewing, knitting, and needlepoint, but I have never learned to weave. While writing *A Slender Thread* I came to know Sarah Haskell, an artist in Maine. Sarah is an extraordinary weaver. In 2007 she began a project called Woven Voices; she collects positive messages from all over the world, cuts them into strips, and weaves them into Tibetan prayer flags. The flags are sent back into the world to fly and release universal words of hope. I spent an afternoon with Sarah and helped weave some of the flags. I loved learning about this project and taking part in a very small way.

Q. This is your third novel. Has the writing process evolved for you?

A. I think every novel comes out of a question. I am drawn to characters at midlife and find myself asking what if . . . ? The story grows from there. *A Slender Thread* was the most challenging novel I've worked on so far. The questions were difficult and I had to delve deeply into the characters in search of, if not answers, at least some greater understanding. The writing itself is always hard work—requiring time and attention. With this book I found the "thinking about the story" more difficult than ever before.

Q. Is there anything in particular that you hope readers will take away from A Slender Thread*?*

A. I always hope readers come away from reading my novels with a greater understanding of what it is like to be human. We are all faced with difficulty at different times in our lives—illness, failure, disappointment. The characters in *A Slender Thread* face problems they have never encountered before. How they cope, how they move forward, and how they eventually find their way is what the book is about. In the face of difficulty we all discover inner resources we never knew we had. I read for the experience of entering other lives and other worlds, and for the pleasure of a compelling story. I hope to give that same experience to my readers.

Q. What writing projects do you want to tackle next?

A. One of the hardest parts of finishing a novel is wondering what I'm going to do next. It's a little like having a child grow up and leave home. Fortunately, I've already felt the pull of a new story. So much for having an empty nest!

QUESTIONS FOR DISCUSSION

1. What's your overall reaction to the novel? Do you connect strongly with the characters and their situation?

2. Have you known anyone with a degenerative, debilitating illness? How were their lives, and the lives of those around them, changed by the prognosis? In addition to big, obvious changes associated with their care, were there also subtle shifts in the interconnected relationships?

3. Margot suffered a disastrous first marriage, which has made her reluctant to marry again. Have you known people who rushed into marriage and then regretted it? Were there danger signs that Margot might have recognized, or does marriage always require a blind leap of faith?

4. Why do you think it matters to Lacey to have Margot make a commitment to Oliver? If children are not involved, do you think a marriage ceremony is necessary for a long-term loving relationship between two people?

5. Do you have a place like Bow Lake, which you associate with idealized times from your childhood? Has it continued to be

part of your life? Have you known people in retirement who have decided to live in a vacation place where they spent time growing up?

6. Was your first love anything like Margot's few days with Alex at Bow Lake?

7. Do you think Lacey secretly knows that her husband was Margot's first love? Would it make a difference in how she feels about Margot all these many years later?

8. Are there points in the novel when the characters behave in ways that made you dislike them? Who and when? Are there times when you especially liked them?

9. What do you think of Margot's decision to return several times to Lacey's home to help out? Is Margot right or wrong to step in? Have you ever been torn between duty to your extended family and to those closer to home, including yourself?

10. Is *A Slender Thread* more a story about Lacey or is it more about Margot? Why? Lacey lives on a small island off the coast of New Hampshire and Margot lives on the island of Manhattan. Is there a significance to these locations? Does where the sisters live have anything to do with the way they choose to live their lives?

11. Discuss the importance of weaving in *A Slender Thread*, in other literature, and in the lives of women over the centuries. Remember Sleeping Beauty, who falls under an enchantment when she pricks her finger on a spinning wheel? Remember Pe-

nelope in Homer's *Odyssey*, who weaves by day and then secretly pulls apart her work at night while waiting faithfully for her husband, Odysseus, to return from his long absence?

13. The popularity of knitting and crafts suggests that women enjoy making beautiful things they can wear or use in their homes. Has our current reliance on electronic technology created a yearning in us for objects of beauty that we can touch, make, and admire? If you are drawn to handwork of any kind, how does it make you feel when you are doing it? Do you find it relaxing or meditative, or do you find pleasure in accomplishing something in your free time?